Dead World
Resurrection
The Collected Zombie Short Stories
Of
Joe McKinney

By
Joe McKinney

JournalStone
San Francisco

JOURNALSTONE
YOUR LINK TO ARTISTIC TALENT

This is a work of fiction. All of the characters, names, incidents, organizations, and dialogue in this novel are either the products of the author's imagination or are used fictitiously.

JournalStone books may be ordered through booksellers or by contacting:

JournalStone
www.journalstone.com

The views expressed in this work are solely those of the authors and do not necessarily reflect the views of the publisher, and the publisher hereby disclaims any responsibility for them.

ISBN: 978-1-940161-72-3   (sc)
ISBN: 978-1-940161-73-0   (ebook)
ISBN: 978-1-940161-74-7   (hc)
ISBN: 978-1-940161-75-4   (hc—limited edition—leather binding)

JournalStone rev. date: November 14, 2014
Library of Congress Control Number: 2014953320

Printed in the United States of America

Cover Design: Rob Grom
Cover Photograph © Shutterstock.com
Edited by: Dr. Michael R. Collings

This collection of stories is dedicated to my wife, Tina,
for giving me the best years of my life,
and to my daughters,
Elena and Brenna,
for making me believe in magic.

Acknowledgments

Works like this don't come together without the help, guidance and support of many generous people, and I have many to thank.

To Sanford Allen, Beckie Ugolini, Thomas McAuley, Brian Allen, David Liss, Robert Jackson Bennett, Rhodi Hawk, Hank Schwaeble, John Joseph Adams, Suzanne Robb, Kim Paffenroth, Bruce Boston, Marge Simon, Jeff Conner, Armand Rosamilia, Thomas Erb, Mitchel Whitington, RJ Sevin, Julia Rose Sevin, Peter Mark May, Michelle McCrary, Cathy Burburuz, Remy Porter, Jacob Kier, Joe and Jennifer McKinney, David Moody, Craig DiLouie, Rhiannon Frater, Scott McPherson, Jonathan Maberry, Michael R. Collings, Scott Shoyer, Ed Kurtz, Richard Dean Starr, Jim Donovan, Mitchel Whitington, Gary Goldstein, and a whole host of others,

I owe you guys, big time!

Endorsements

"Joe McKinney writes with heart and authenticity, and this collection is Joe at his finest and distinguishes him as one zombie fiction's first and foremost authors." -**Craig DiLouie**, author of *Suffer the Children*

"With vivid imagery and a knack for storytelling that puts on display all facets of the human condition, Joe McKinney takes the reader on a horror filled roller coaster ride through the zombie apocalypse. Like an upscale Vegas buffet, this collection of short stories has it all: from the incredibly technical, yet poignant, expose as to what Joe would do in the event of a zombie outbreak to a futuristic tale wrought with zombies and the telepathic humans and bots that hunt them. So run-don't trudge-and pick up this exquisite tome chock full of tales from the apocalypse."
-**Shawn Chesser**, Author of the best-selling Surviving the Zombie Apocalypse series.

Think zombie fiction is dead? Think again! With *Dead World: Resurrection*, Joe McKinney demonstrates how varied, complex, and yes, even literary zombie fiction can be. This collection further cements McKinney's reputation as one of the best writers of dark fiction working today. Don't miss it! – **Tim Waggoner,** author of *The Way of All Flesh*

"The publication of Joe McKinney's *Dead World: Resurrection* should be cause for celebration for zombie fans of all stripes. I cannot think of a stronger collection of zombie short fiction by a single author—or, for that matter, by multiple authors in anthology—available today. For whatever reason, we seem to be living in a 'golden age' of zombie fiction, here, in the early days of the twenty-first century. Anyone who reads *'Dead World: Resurrection'* will understand why Joe McKinney is responsible— in no small part—for a good degree of that gilding." -**Scott Kenemore,** author of *Zombie, Ohio*

"When Joe McKinney told me he was putting all of his zombie shorts in one collection, I was excited. When I read them and realized there wasn't a filler in the bunch, I was ecstatic. The diversity of the stories and brilliant writing makes me want to beg him to keep them coming!"
-**Armand Rosamilia**, author of the Dying Days zombie series

"Joe McKinney stands with Max Brooks, Robert Kirkman, and Jonathan Maberry in the pantheon of modern zombie authors, with *Dead World* holding its own with *World War Z*, *The Walking Dead*, and *Fall of Night*. The stories in *Dead World Resurrection* peek between the seams of the novels, and Joe's thoughts about each piece let us peek into the mind of the author. McKinney is a master of deeply personal, gut-wrenching storytelling. His every tale hits home, no matter how gruesome or mundane, and this collection is a master class on zombie fiction that matters." -**Patrick Freivald,** author of *Jade Sky* and *Blood List*

"McKinney writes zombies like he's been gunning them down all his life." -**Weston Ochse,** author of *Seal Team 666* and *Halfway House*

"Joe McKinney has been my favorite horror writer since he first broke on the scene. Here is the most original voice of modern horror." **-Jonathan Maberry,** New York Times-bestselling author

"Page-turning tension, sympathetic characters, and a unique setting – this is the real deal." -**David Liss,** New York Times-bestselling author of *The Day of Atonement* and *The Whiskey Rebels*

"Far too many writers of horror in general, and zombie stories in particular, think that the horror comes from the situation, and so they splash gore and foul language and viscera about with abandon, never understanding that horror only succeeds when it is happening TO someone that the readers care about. Joe McKinney never makes that mistake." -**Michaelbrent Collings,** author of *The Haunted* and *Darkbound*

"You'll want the shotgun seat for this wild ride. Bring a crash helmet." -**J.L. Comeau,** *Countgore.com*

"Welcome to Joe McKinney's Dead City universe, a relentless thrill ride where real characters do bloody things on nightmare streets. Break out the popcorn, you're in for a treat." -**Harry Shannon,** author of *The Hungry*

"A scary, fast-paced ride, full of hair-raising twists and turns that keep the reader spellbound. Do yourself a favor and snag a copy...thank me later." -**Gene O'Neill**, author of *Dance of the Blue Lady* and *The Burden of Indigo*

Table of Contents

Introduction
By
David Moody

I'm often asked what I think makes a good zombie story. I guess everyone has a different take on the answer to that particular question, but I know what I like. I have a kind of tick-list.

First off, I like a good set-up: an engaging scenario and something different, perhaps, from the usual 'evil/misguided/stupid scientist accidentally/intentionally releases a deadly virus into the atmosphere and all hell breaks loose' story clones which plague the genre. I also like that set-up to be imbued with an uneasy, unpredictable atmosphere so it's not immediately obvious from the first page who's going to live, who's going to die, and who's the one who'll get bitten, hide the wound, then "turn" and become a zombie at the least opportune moment.

We're dealing with flesh-eating ghouls here, so I like more than a liberal sprinkling of gore. And I like that to be inventive gore too. Well described, visceral, slimy... gross. Enough to put you off that sandwich you were thinking about having.

I like an element of realism. I know we're talking about reanimated corpses walking around and eating people—you'd be hard-pressed to think of a *less* plausible scenario—but I want to be unnerved and unsettled. I want the story to suck me in with its detail and leave me thinking *could this happen?* Or *if that was me, what would I do?*

I think good zombie stories should steer away from the overused clichés of the genre and take you by surprise. Most of all, I think the very best zombie stories are often not about the zombies at all. They're about the living: the people like you and me, trapped in the middle of an unimaginable nightmare and doing all they can to preserve what remains of their lives and loves from attack by the living dead.

Whenever I read a zombie story by Joe McKinney, I know I'm going to get exactly what I'm looking for. All those boxes on my list will be ticked.

Over the years, Joe's name has become synonymous with zombie fiction, and rightly so. He brings a unique approach to the table, a bi-product, I think, of the life he's led and, of course, the fact he's a damn good writer.

I'm sure you know this already, but Joe's a vastly experienced police officer. I'm willing to bet he's had to deal with worse things in his many years in uniform than a horror hack like me could ever come up with for a piece of fiction. I've always thought one of the most important skills a cop must have is the ability to understand people and to be able to communicate in even the most difficult and dangerous of circumstances. That skill shines through in Joe's writing. He really knows people! His characters are honest, genuine, and well-drawn, and their actions are always understandable. For me, that's key to the success of his stories. He sucks you in with people you quickly learn to care about, then throws them to the wolves (or, more often, to the dead).

It was an honor to be asked to write an introduction for this collection, and it was a joy to be able to dive into Joe's back catalogue of zombie shorts. You're in for a real treat here, reader! These stories cover the full gamut of the zombie sub-genre, from settings as diverse as futuristic wars between the last of the living and the all-conquering zombie hordes, to hitherto unknown outbreaks discovered by the earliest explorers of the Pacific Ocean. From present day San Antonio to the grime and poverty of the back streets of nineteenth century London. From huge battles involving armies of thousands to the smallest personal encounters between the living and the dead.

Reading this collection has reminded me why I love zombies so much. They're a unique creature—incredibly similar to us, but also immeasurably different. When we look at zombies, it can be like looking into a mirror. And when we imagine how we'd react when faced with the undead, it all too often shows how we treat (and mistreat) each other.

In this collection, by writing about the living dead, Joe has reminded us what's so great about being one of the living. I hope you enjoy reading (or re-reading) these stories as much as I have.

David Moody
Birmingham, UK
June 2012

Dead World Resurrection

The Collected Zombie Short Stories
Of
Joe McKinney

Resurrecting Mindy

The big Christmas tree in front of the Dayton Mall had fallen down sometime during the last year. Kevin's gaze drifted over the faded tinsel and mud-encrusted ornaments, and he wondered when that had happened. Probably during the rains back in early September. Those were bad. A lot of the area flooded, and the winds that came with the rains must have damaged the tree as well.

Of course, he really didn't know for sure. The only time he came here anymore was at Christmastime. The world had ended three years before, just before Christmas, and the inside of the Dayton Mall still had a lot of decorations hanging from the common areas and inside the shop windows. Every year around this time, he made the trek to the mall and scavenged whatever he could carry to decorate wherever he was living at the moment. These days, it had become a ritual, just like keeping up his calendar, and keeping his hair trimmed, and making sure his food stores were well-stocked. The rituals, in fact, were about the only things that kept his morale up.

And God knows there was enough to feel depressed about.

There was a sort of soul-sucking loneliness that came with being the last man left alive.

It made him wonder if there was any reason to keep going. After all, did it matter *when* he died? Tomorrow, or thirty years from now, the results would be the same. After he was finished, humanity was finished. Wasn't he just postponing the inevitable?

Could be. But he wasn't ready to throw in the towel just yet.

For now, he had a mission.

Kevin got down on his belly so he could squeeze between the front tandems of an eighteen-wheeler. From there, he watched the parking lot, figuring out a safe route to the doors.

It actually didn't look like it'd be difficult this year. The zombie hordes that had swarmed the area in years past had thinned quite a bit. He didn't know if the majority of them had moved on or decayed to the point they couldn't move anymore. Maybe they'd started to eat each other. Who the hell knew?

He supposed it didn't really matter.

Fewer zombies meant it was easier to stay alive, and that was all that mattered.

There were fewer than fifty of them out there walking the parking lot now, and it didn't take long for a wide gap to open in the crowd. Kevin tensed, ready to run. Another few seconds, and it would be wide enough for him to go.

And that's when he saw her.

Mindy Matheson.

Holy shit, he thought. He stared at her for a long moment, watching her curious, clumsy movements. That really was her. *That's Mindy Matheson.*

And she's faking it.

* * *

It had been a while since he'd seen a faker.

Most didn't last long. Right after the outbreak, Kevin and some other survivors he'd hung out with had seen one or two a week. The fakers tried to make themselves look like zombies. They smelled like zombies, moved like zombies, had flies swarming around their eyes and mouths like zombies. But they weren't zombies, and sooner or later, they messed up. They slipped out of character for just a second.

And that was all it took.

One tiny slip, one momentary distraction, and the zombies they moved with swarmed them.

Usually, at least as far as Kevin was concerned, it wasn't much of a loss.

The fakers only tried it because they had given up on their humanity. Surviving among the ruins of what the world had once been was hard. It sucked, in fact. In order to survive, in order to stay sane, you had to work at it. Every day was a fight. Every breath was bought with tears and sweat and loneliness. And sometimes, living free didn't seem much of a payback.

The fakers couldn't hack it. The world they'd lived in, believed in, trusted, had collapsed. Many had made weapons, built strongholds, fought bravely, but in the end, their spirit of resistance had collapsed. Everything had collapsed, leaving them alone, scared, miserably vacant of purpose. They looked at the world and saw ruins, they saw emptiness, they saw a pointless future without faith, without hope, without meaning. They accepted that this was the end, and that going on with this world didn't matter anymore.

But they didn't have the courage to end it all, either.

They were the real walking dead, not the zombies, and Kevin had never felt anything but disgust for them.

Until now, of course.

He and Mindy Matheson, they'd dated right after high school. She'd never said two words to him during school. Neither one of them had been all that popular, but it had been a big school, and she had her friends and he had his. But afterward, when they found they were working at the Home Depot together, neither one of them with the foggiest notion of what they were going to do with their lives, they sort of fell together.

For about eight months.

They didn't end on an obvious note. No cheating, no fighting, nothing like that. They just drifted apart. At the time he'd figured they just weren't right for each other. That explained why they hadn't noticed each other back in school. What happened while they were working together was just the natural gravity of two lonely people. And so, just as their orbits brought them together, those same orbits carried them apart. She grew distant, he grew irritable. She stopped calling, he stopped caring. Soon they were basically strangers again. The brief interlude was forgotten, and the two of them went back to their lives of uncertainty and quiet desperation.

He found it funny that the world had changed so much, and yet he and Mindy had changed so little. It made him laugh, the way the two of them were still living their half-lives, midway between life and death.

But he laughed louder than he wanted to, and she had heard him. He saw her cock her head to one side. She turned toward the truck where he was hiding, her shifting, searching gaze the only thing that separated her from the wandering corpses nearby.

Kevin whistled faintly, just loud enough for her to hear.

She staggered forward.

For a moment, he thought of running away from there. What did he think he was doing anyway? What could he do? It wasn't like they were going to run off together or anything. Not now. To fake it for any length of time at all, she would have had to go native in a mighty convincing kind of way.

And that she certainly had.

Kevin looked her up and down, from the stringy, matted mess that was her hair to her bare and blackened feet, and tried not to grimace at the stench that came off her. Her face was filthy, her lips cracked and flaking. Her clothes were so stained and ratty he couldn't even tell what color they had once been. Flies swarmed about her face.

But she was standing right in front of him now, watching him. She swayed drunkenly, her mouth hanging slightly open. He wanted to hate her, but her eyes were over-bright, pregnant with the suggestion of pain, and despite his loathing, he felt his heart breaking out of pity.

He could, after all, still see the girl under all that grime and slathered gore. She had gotten skinny in a ghastly kind of way, but the curves, at least the hint of them, were still in the right place. And she still had that cute little upturned nose that used to drive him wild when she smiled.

"Hi, Mindy," he said.

She just stared at him, no expression on her face.

"Hey, you know why they put fences around graveyards?" He waited a beat. "Because people are just dying to get in."

Again, he waited.

Her expression didn't change. She just stood there, swaying.

"You heard that one, huh?"

She might have nodded, but if so, it was faint, and he couldn't be sure.

"How about this one? A guy finds out he only has twelve hours to live. He goes home to his wife, determined to live it up for his last night on earth. So they have sex, and it's great. An hour later, they do it again, and it's even better. And then, a few hours after that, he tells her he thinks they can go at it a third time. 'Easy for you to say,' she tells him. 'You don't have to wake up in the morning.'"

He beat his index fingers on the truck tire in front of him like he was firing off a rim shot. *Ba dum bum.* He smiled at her, and then the smile faded. Why in the hell was he doing this? There was no reaching this girl.

And was he really so lonely that he was talking to a faker?

But then he saw a flicker at the corner of her mouth, the faintest trace of a smile, and that brought a huge grin to his face.

"Are you doing okay, Mindy?"

The smile disappeared. He saw what looked like a tear forming in her eyes.

He almost reached up for her hand then, and had one of the real zombies not let out a moan at that very moment, he might have thrown her over his shoulder and carried her away from there.

But a few more real zombies had spotted him. Several were moaning now, staggering toward him. He'd been careless, and now it was time to go.

"I'm staying in an apartment at Woodlawn and Spruce," he said.

A zombie dropped to the pavement and started crawling under the truck toward him.

"I gotta go," he said. "Remember, it's the Bent Tree Apartments. Woodlawn and Spruce, number 318."

More zombies had gotten under the truck now. The lead one held up a mangled, handless arm, the blackened, jagged tips of its ulna and radius extending from rotten flesh.

"Gotta go," he said.

* * *

Several days later, with Christmas right around the corner, Kevin was hanging ornaments on a fake tree. There was a Hallmark in the Dayton Mall, and he'd made good use of the Snoopy ornaments piled on the floor. When he was growing up, his mom had waited outside the local Hallmark in order to scoop up whatever was new that year. At the time, he'd thought it was stupid. But they're collector's items, she'd said. Or they will be. Which, to his way of looking at it, hadn't made it any less stupid.

But now, hanging the Snoopy with the little typewriter and Snoopy as a World War I ace ornaments on his tree, he sensed a surge of painful memories.

Christ, he thought. He didn't need this. Not now.

He heard moaning through an open window and jumped to his feet to look. There was no point in it really. The zombies keyed off what they saw and heard. Those were about the only two senses that seemed to work, and as long as he stayed out of sight and kept quiet, his little hiding spot in this third-floor apartment was as safe as any spot on Earth.

But he crossed to the window anyway because checking out the zombies was a way to stay busy, and staying busy kept him from his memories.

And that's when he saw Mindy Matheson for the second time.

Her group had wandered over from the mall, probably searching for the pack of wild dogs Kevin had heard baying the last few nights. This zombie group wasn't especially large. He counted about thirty, though there were almost certainly a few more out of sight. They wouldn't be much of a threat when he needed to go out, but even still, there were enough of them that they would probably be sticking around for a few days at least. They hunted collectively, he'd discovered, so the bigger groups tended to stay in one place longer.

Just as well, Kevin thought. It would give him a chance to talk with Mindy again.

He slid out the window and into the chilly evening air. It looked like it would probably rain later. There was a ledge just below his window that led to another building's roof. From there, he climbed onto a billboard that looked down on the intersection, where Mindy and the others were wandering around, moaning.

He kept a can of spray paint up here, just in case.

He gave it a shake and wrote:

HEY, MINDY! I'M IN 318 OVER TO YOUR RIGHT.
COME ON UP.

He'd gathered quite a crowd. At a glance, he noticed that he'd underestimated the size of the group by at least half, probably more.

Their mangled, upturned faces and ruined hands were all pointed at him, their moans taking on an urgent, pulsing quality that he had come to think of as their feeding call. He saw quite a few of them down there.

But Mindy wasn't with them. She was drifting away from the group, stepping back toward a screen of shrubs at the far side of the intersection while the others surged forward.

"Good girl," he muttered.

Moving quickly, he went back to his apartment. The zombies wouldn't be able to follow, and besides, he had some quick cleaning up to do.

* * *

She wouldn't sit down.

He offered her a place on his couch, at his table, on the floor. She just shook her head every time he offered.

Kevin tried small talk, but she wouldn't answer any of his questions, and after a while, he began to feel foolish and stupid, like he was wasting both their time. He jammed his hands into his pockets and looked around the room for some glimmer of inspiration.

Nothing.

"So," he said. "You know what they call a fast-moving zombie?" He waited a beat, hoping for another of her half smiles. "A zoombie."

She just stared at him, and the cold, lifeless emptiness chilled him.

"How about a hockey-playing zombie?" he said, forcing a grin. "A zombonie. What do you think, huh? I got a million of them. How about this? A zombie, an Irish priest, and a rabbi walk into a bar —"

"This was a mistake," she said. "Coming here. I'm sorry."

She spoke quietly, her voice cracked and hoarse, as though she'd almost forgotten how to use it.

"I'm going, Kevin."

"What? No."

He took a step toward her, but stopped when the smell hit him.

He tried not to let his surprise and his disgust show on his face, though it probably did anyway.

"Please, Mindy, don't. It's Christmas."

She didn't answer. But she didn't turn to leave either.

"I've got some food. Are you hungry?"

She nodded.

He went into the little kitchenette and slid a cube of Spam out of a can. He cut it into four big slices, then handed her the plate.

"I'm sorry I don't have—"

Mindy snatched it from his hands.

She ate with her fingers, jamming the meat into her mouth, barely chewing. Several times she nearly choked. Bits and pieces fell from the corners of her mouth.

She stopped eating only once, long enough to look at him over her plate.

"Don't look at me while I eat," she said, her words about as close to a snarl as any he'd ever heard a girl make. And then, more quietly, sounding damaged, "Please. Don't look at me."

He nodded. "Sure. Okay."

Kevin went to the cupboards and took down some more cans. He had Vienna sausages, some fruit cocktail, applesauce, a jar of sauerkraut. Better take this stuff out of the can, he thought, remembering the way she'd jammed her fingers into the pile of Spam. Last thing he wanted was for her to cut her fingers on the can's sharp edges.

He went to work putting the meal onto paper plates and then setting the plates onto the table.

When he turned around, she was standing right behind him, and it startled him. He jumped.

She was staring at his neck, and the look in her eyes, the way she wet her lips with every pulse of his carotid artery, disturbed him.

"Shit," he said, trying hard—and, he thought, uselessly—to hide his unease. "You scared me."

Her gaze drifted down to the food on the table.

"Go ahead," he said. "I have tea and water, whichever you'd prefer."

She fell on the food without answering, without bothering to sit in the chair he pulled over for her, so he got her a cup of water and set it down next to her plates.

She had asked him not to watch her eat, which was okay with

Kevin. The wet, slurping noises she made were enough for him to know he didn't want to watch. He went over to his couch and looked at some magazines he'd left there. A bunch of old *Playboys* he'd found at the used bookstore over by the mall. He gathered them up and stuffed them under the couch, but not before catching a glimpse of the sleepy-eyed plastic blonde on the cover of the top magazine. So much had changed, he thought sadly. So much had been lost. The good and the bad.

Eventually, Mindy's eating noises stopped.

Kevin walked over to the kitchen. Mindy was still at the table, looking around at the cupboards with a bovine vacuity.

"Are you still hungry?" he asked. "I have more. You can have anything I have."

She shook her head.

"More water, maybe? I can make you that tea I promised."

Again she shook her head.

A joke about Little Johnny, a bucket of nails and a zombie hooker came to mind, but for once his internal filter was working and he cut it off before it had a chance to get out.

Instead, he let the silence linger.

She had turned to face him, and now she was swaying drunkenly, the same way she'd done in the mall parking lot. It occurred to him that she had probably internalized so much zombie behavior that, even now, when she was completely safe, she was unable to turn it off.

But the silence was murder. He had never dealt well with uncomfortable silences. It was the main reason he told so many bad jokes. Better to fill up the void with inane nonsense than let a painful silence grow.

He said, "Listen, there's no need for you to go back out there. You're welcome to stay as long as you'd like. I've got some Sterno. We could heat up some water, let you take a hot bath maybe...."

All at once the tears started. One minute she was watching him, quietly and vacantly, and the next she was crying.

Big, muddy-colored tears ran down her cheeks.

"Ah shit," he said. "Mindy, I...I'm sorry. What did I say...I—"

"I shouldn't have come," she said. "This was a mistake."

She moved hurriedly to the door. Every impulse in him told him to go after her, hold the door closed, take her in his arms.

But he didn't do it.

He just watched her go without a word

* * *

Mindy shuffled through the rain, her mind a blank.

Or at least she tried to make it a blank.

Right now, that wasn't working out so well.

It was cold—windy and rainy and cold. Her clothes were little more than rags; they offered no protection whatsoever. For too long now she'd wandered, mindless, emotionless, denying all pain and shame, a true ascetic. The rain tore at her skin like icy razors and chilled her to the bone, but she did not tremble, nor did she cry. She let her arms swing limply by her side, her fingertips grazing the ice that formed on her clothes, as she kept pace with the horde of dead things brushing against her.

Thought was the enemy, not the dead. With thought came fear, and pain, and a memory of all that was gone. If she thought too long—if she thought at all—the dead would see it in her eyes, and she wouldn't last long after that.

But the mind was like a flood. It could be contained for a while, even a long while, but it could never be truly silenced. Sooner or later, the mind would turn to the low ground and dwell there.

And right now her mind was turning toward shame.

But it wasn't the shame of what had happened to her that bothered her so.

It was that damn Kevin O'Brien.

When she was by herself, she felt no shame for what she was doing. Why should she? She was surviving. And she was doing it in the face of a universe that didn't give a rat's ass for what happened to her. Or the rest of humanity, for that matter. She was surviving, damn it.

Then she thought of Kevin.

He too was surviving.

And he hadn't given up anything. He hadn't debased himself like this. He hadn't sacrificed every last scrap of his self-respect just to draw another breath.

She hated him. She hated him because he was still human. And because his charity reminded her that she was not.

Not any more.

So she turned off her mind and wandered. Damn him. Damn the world. Damn life. There was nothing of the world left for her any more. Nothing but emptiness and the slow, relentless crawl of time.

One foot in front of the other.

Forever after.

* * *

The billboard came as a surprise to her.

For a moment, just a fraction of a second, she stopped.

And she stared.

She hadn't realized where she was. But up there, up above the mindless crowd, was a message written just for her.

Hey, Mindy, it's cold. Come on up.
I've got a warm bed.

A memory floated into her mind, unbidden. The two of them, finishing their shift, her letting him walk her to the parking lot. He had a joint in his pocket, and she didn't have anywhere to go. They went around to the loading dock and passed the joint back and forth, talking about random shit, nothing either of them really cared about.

He was nice. A little dorky, but all right.

She could tell he was getting interested. It was in the way he cracked his lame jokes when he should have let the quiet grow, the way his fingers twitched when they touched whenever she took the joint from him.

She could have shut it down right then. He was the scared type. He'd back off, and nothing more would come of it.

But she didn't have anywhere else to go, and they both knew it.

She went back to his place.

Sitting on his couch, her hand on his thigh, he actually asked if he could kiss her. That had never happened to her before. Most guys went straight for the tits. Or put a hand on the back of her head and guided her down.

"You don't have to ask," she'd said and eased in close to him.

Before she knew it, they were some sort of couple.

But he wasn't wasting that kind of time now. The apocalypse, it seemed, had made him a little bolder.

Come on up. I've got a warm bed.

Yeah right, she thought, I bet you do.

But she'd been careless. She'd thought too long, dropped out of character.

One of the dead ones a few feet to her right had turned her way, and now his dead, vacant stare was locked on her. She tried to clear her mind, to stumble forward, but the zombie's gaze never wavered.

He raised his hands like he was trying to take something from her and staggered after her, a moan rising above the wind and the cutting rain.

She pushed his hands away and looked around.

This wasn't going to work. Every moment she lingered, more and more of them turned her way. She scanned the crowd, and in the dark, the only way out seemed to lead around the corner, where she had taken the stairwell once before to his apartment.

A limp hand fell on her shoulder and that was enough.

She ran for the stairs.

* * *

She stopped in front of 318.

Had she really sunk so low? Getting torn apart by the walking dead almost seemed a joy compared to coming to him like a penitent. She'd thought she was done with guilt, with shame. But it hurt now more than ever.

Utterly demoralized, she knocked.

* * *

He couldn't sleep.

In the dark, he rose and put on his boxers and went to the kitchen to light a candle.

Enough light filled the room that he could see her sleeping in his bed. The rain had washed away a good amount of dirt and grime from her body and hair, but her breath had still been enough to turn his stomach. And even in his sleep he couldn't quite hide his disgust. He had dreamt of a zombie forcing her face into the soft part of his neck, and when he awoke, he'd found her, pressing her cracked and ulcerous lips into the well beneath his chin.

Flinching awake, he'd recoiled from her, almost falling out of the bed before realizing that it was only a dream.

Now, fully awake, he watched her sleep and tried to hate her.

But he couldn't. He was feeling guilty.

Who in the hell was he to judge her, anyway? She was desperate. She was lonely. She was scared. Wasn't he all of that, and more?

In fact, the only thing he had on her was the appearance of normalcy.

But that was only appearances. The truth was he was drowning. His life was an act. His jokes, the Christmas decorations, his calendar keeping—all a terrible, useless, stupid joke. He drifted from one empty apartment to the next, from one false front to the next, like a ghost blown on the wind, and he called it a life.

Were they any different, he and Mindy?

He couldn't answer, not truthfully anyway; and eventually, he blew out the candle and crept back to bed and reluctantly put an arm around her as he drifted off to sleep.

When he awoke the next morning, he was alone, the only sign she had been there a muddy stain on the sheets.

He sat on the side of the bed, asking himself why he even bothered.

She had left him, again, and this time it was because she knew he was the one who was faking. He was the hypocrite. He was the disgusting one.

And she had found him out.

* * *

Mindy stopped in the doorway as she left Kevin's apartment building and scanned the street.

There were no dead in sight, but that didn't mean they weren't there. She'd seen it happen a few times over the last year. She'd be shuffling along with the others, absolutely nothing going on inside her head, and suddenly there'd be a scream. Another careless person had wandered into their midst, completely surprised by the sudden appearance of a zombie horde that, in reality, hadn't been trying to sneak up on anybody. Most of the group's kills were made that way, completely by accident, people caught by their own carelessness.

Without realizing it, she had assumed the awkward shuffle of the dead. Her bare feet, no longer sensitive to heat or ice or even broken glass, slid across the cracked and weedy pavement as though on autopilot.

She tried to turn off her mind as well, but she found that much harder.

She kept thinking of Kevin.

What, exactly, had happened last night?

Not *what*. Not really. She knew *what* had happened. That had actually been quite pleasant. Better than she remembered it, anyway.

No, what she really wanted to know was *why*. And why *now*? She'd seen others before him. She knew they weren't the only ones. She suspected—and she believed this without reservation—that there were more normal people out there than she'd seen. There had to be. The world couldn't simply be empty. That wasn't possible.

But none of the others had managed to arouse her pity. She'd watched them die, and in some cases rise again, and she'd felt nothing.

And then...Kevin.

He'd told her his stupid jokes. He'd offered her a place to stay, all the food he had, even a warm bath. In the few days since she'd first seen him, she hadn't been able to stop thinking about him. Before him, walking around being dead was no trouble at all. She could go days at a time without a single thought passing through her mind. The world was one unending parade of nothingness.

And then he came along, and she couldn't take three steps without falling out of character, without thinking of the life they'd once shared.

That's what it was, she told herself. He was a window to the world that used to be, a shipwreck from her past that had mysteriously surfaced to haunt her. There was nothing more to it than that. He was nothing but a ghost, and she was merely lonely.

But a voice at the back of her mind kept prodding, questioning.

What if this was more than just two people feeling lonely and desperate at the end of the world?

What if this was...love?

Maybe, she thought. It was Christmas day, after all. She'd seen the calendar on his wall—the days gone by dutifully crossed out with a big red X—right before she'd walked out of his apartment. Christmas had a way of warming even the coldest heart.

Wasn't that the secret to Scrooge's redemption? She'd never paid much attention to books in school, but she thought she remembered that much. For Scrooge, it hadn't been fear of the grave, but fear that the heart would no longer love again, that made it possible for him to accept the spirit of Christmas into his life.

She stopped then, a sudden alarm causing her pulse to quicken.

She had fallen out of character again. She'd stopped walking like the dead. Like her mind, her feet had started to wander. If she'd happened upon one of the dead while walking like that, they'd have torn her to ribbons.

But, for now, she was alone on the street.

Turning, she happened to see her reflection in a shop window. And at first, that one quick glance threatened to send her over the edge of reason. She looked horrible. In a word, she looked *dead*. And she played the part well. Her hair was stiff with mud and probably blood too. Her face, which hadn't been that bad back in the day, was discolored with God knows what; attractive, it seemed, only to flies. Her body was a bony jangle of sticks. She looked like a crack whore, though she imagined that even the crack whores of the world gone by had more self-respect than she did at that moment.

She had nothing.

But then her gaze shifted beyond her reflection in the window, to the Sexy Elf costume in the display. For a moment she experienced an odd sense of displacement. It was her face, her gaunt, exhausted face, but her body was draped in the red velvety finery of the elf costume. Her fingers reached for, and could almost feel, the cotton candy fringe at the edge of the playfully short skirt.

She smiled.

Kevin O'Brien, you wonderful bastard. I'm gonna blow your mind.

* * *

It was Christmas morning.

He had hoped to wake up late and spend the day with her, hopefully draw her out little by little. The two of them had been pretty good, he thought, back in the day. And they were certainly good last night. When they were good, it seemed, they were really good. He'd hoped it could be that way again.

But she'd left him sometime in the night.

His attempts to draw her into his world weren't fair, he supposed. Why would she want to join him anyway? Hadn't she found him out? She knew he was faking it. He knew he was faking it.

And he was tired of faking it.

The choice, once he'd given it voice, was surprisingly easy to make. The only hard part had been accepting *that* as an option. But once he opened his mind to it, it actually made a lot of sense.

He went to the billboard and spray painted a message for her.

Then he went down to the street and climbed on top of a brick wall and waited for one of the dead to come along.

He thought he'd be scared, but for the first time in a long time, he felt relaxed, at ease with himself and the world in which he lived. You can settle in quite comfortably to even the most horrific of circumstances, he thought, given enough exposure to it. All horrors lose their immediacy, their nastiness, sooner or later. The nerves can only be slashed and cut and shredded so many times before they deaden to the pain.

No, he was beyond horror now. What he was feeling now was far worse than that. In the time before he found her again, his world had been filled with zombies. The horror they represented was a shallow, fast-moving river that beat him down and cut him on its jagged rocks.

What he was feeling now, though, made horror seem small.

Here, in this world that suddenly included Mindy in it, the waters ran far slower, but they were deep, endlessly deep, and what lurked down there was something he could not fight.

For what lurked down there was love.

A zombie was at the base of the wall, its hands clumsily scratching at the bricks just below Kevin. Kevin stared into the thing's eyes and saw the emptiness he'd fought against for so long but had never truly understood. That would all change now. He had tried to get Mindy to live in his world, and that had failed. So now, he would live in hers.

And only love could allow him to do that.

He jammed his left hand down into the zombie's face. It shook its head, as though to shoo away an insect, and then realized what was in front of it.

The zombie grabbed Kevin's forearm and clamped its teeth onto his wrist.

"Mother fu—"

Kevin pulled his hand away, holding his wounded wrist in his right hand while blood oozed between his fingers. It hurt so badly he nearly rolled off the top of the wall. Already he could feel the virus creeping through his blood stream, racing for his heart. It felt like somebody was jamming a red-hot copper wire up his veins.

He didn't have much time. Maybe thirty minutes, but probably less.

Kevin rolled off the wall and trotted back to his apartment. Once inside, he washed the wound with hot water and wrapped it in a towel. It was already starting to smell like death. His head was soupy, and walking to the chair in the center of the room was hard.

But he made it.

He dropped down into the chair and turned it to face the door and waited for the pain to stop.

* * *

This felt absolutely glorious.

Mindy had spent the day cleaning herself up, scouring off the stain of more than a year of living among the dead. Now, her hair was washed and brushed. Her legs were shaved, her skin soft and fragrant from cocoa butter, still a little pink from her hot bath. The Sexy Elf costume showed a lot of leg, and a lot of bruises and cuts, but those would heal. If her heart could heal, her legs certainly would.

She felt better than she had felt in a very long time. She couldn't remember a time she'd felt this good, even before the world died. Mindy Matheson had come back from the dead, and love had done it for her.

And it was glorious.

Now, she picked her way carefully through the rubble-strewn

streets. The dead were out—the dead were always out—but there weren't many of them around at the moment.

Then she saw the sign, and she smiled.

It's all for you, Mindy Matheson.
I love you.
I want to be with you forever.

She couldn't hold herself back any longer. She sprinted up the stairs and down the hall to his door.

Slightly out of breath, she knocked on the door.

No response.

Maybe he was out getting stuff, she thought. More candles, maybe. Or, God help her, even a bottle of wine. Wouldn't that be great? And heaven help him if he got her drunk. She'd make his toes curl for sure.

With a huge grin on her face, she turned the knob and swung the door in slowly.

"Kevin?"

Dating in Dead World

Heather Ashcroft told me to come to the main entrance of her father's compound. She said the guards there would know my name; they'd be expecting me.

They were expecting me all right.

Four of them had their machine guns trained on me while a voice on a PA speaker barked orders.

"Turn off your motorcycle and dismount." The voice was clear, sharp, professional.

I did what I was told.

"Step forward. Stand on the red square."

I did that too.

"Stand still for the dogs."

Three big, black German shepherds were led out of the guard shack and began circling me, sniffing. Cadaver dogs, trained to sniff out necrotic tissue. No surprise there. Even the smaller compounds used them, and the one I was about to enter was no minor-league operation. John Ashcroft controls the largest baronage in South Texas, and his security is top notch.

"I'm Andrew Hudson," I said. "I'm here to see Heather Ashcroft. We're going out on—"

Somebody called off the dogs, and two guards came forward. One used the barrel of his weapon to point me toward a table next to the guard shack.

"Stand on that green square. Face the table."

"You fellas sure put a guy through a lot of trouble for a first date," I said. I gave him a winning grin. He wasn't impressed.

"Move," he said.

He asked me what weapons I was carrying, and I told him.

"Put them in there," he said, pointing to a red plastic box on the corner of the table.

"I'm gonna get those back, right?"

He ran a metal detector over my body, taking extra care to get inside the flaps of my denim jacket, under my hair, up into my crotch.

A guard fieldstripped my weapons.

"I *am* gonna get those back, right?"

"When you come out," he said. "Nobody's allowed to be armed around Mr. Ashcroft."

"But I'm not here to see Mr. Ashcroft," I said. "I'm taking his daughter out for a date."

He rattled a smaller box. "Ammunition, too."

I unloaded my pockets. There was no need to tell him about the extra magazines in my bike's saddlebags. They were already searching those.

He looked me over again, and I could tell by the contempt in his glare that he didn't see anything but a street urchin from the Zone. "Get in that Jeep over there," he said. "We'll drive you into the compound."

Several machine guns turned my way.

I shrugged and got in.

* * *

I hadn't been allowed within the inner perimeter fence on my earlier visits, so what I saw when I did finally get inside the Ashcroft compound took my breath away. Outside the compound's walls, downtown San Antonio was an endless sprawl of vacant, crumbling buildings, lath visible in the walls, no doors in the doorways, every window broken. Everywhere you turned, there were ruins and fire damage and rivers of garbage spilling into the streets. It's been twenty years since the Fall, and the streets are still full of zombies. But inside Ashcroft's compound, life looked like it was starting to make a comeback. He controlled most of the medicines, weapons, and fuel that South Texas needed, and it had made him rich enough to carve his own private paradise out of fifteen square blocks of hell.

Sitting in the back of the Jeep, I rode down what had once been Alamo Street and tried not to look like a barefoot barbarian gawking at the wonders of Rome. Ashcroft had preserved a few of the main roads from the old days, and he had left a few of the old buildings intact, but he had changed a lot more than he left alone.

Off to my left was what had once been Hemisphere Park. It was farmland now. Beyond that was a huge field where cattle grazed, their backs dappled with the golden copper hues of the setting sun. Men on horseback patrolled the edges of the fields, rifles resting on their shoulders.

Most of the housing was on the other side of the river, to my right— small cottages, comfortable and clean, a few children playing in a garden under an old woman's watchful eye.

But the crown jewel in Ashcroft's compound was the Fairmont Hotel. He'd turned the ancient four-story building into his private domain. It was flanked on one side by the ruins of the Spanish village of La Villita. The crumbling adobe buildings had once been stables for horses. Pre-Outbreak San Antonio had turned them into a tourist attraction, but Ashcroft had seen the wisdom of the original settlers and was once again using them for the horses. In front of the hotel was a Spanish-style garden fed by a large, circular stone fountain. A fork of the San Antonio River, blasted out of the streets that had once crisscrossed the area, curled around the rear of the hotel, supplying fresh water for the whole compound.

As we pulled to a stop in front of the hotel, I said, "Looks like you guys have got room for what, about five, six hundred people here?"

"Do yourself a favor," one of the guards told me. "Don't ask no questions. You ain't gonna be here long enough to worry about it. Now get out of the Jeep."

* * *

A few minutes later, I was standing in what had once been the hotel's lobby, waiting on Heather, checking the smell of my breath in my palm. I'd cleaned up as best I could, but that wasn't saying much. When you live in the Zone, in the rubble between the compounds, it shows. A lump of coal is still a lump of coal, no matter how hard you try to polish it.

I didn't even bother to make small talk with the guard in the corner, watching me.

Eventually, Heather came down the stairs. I watched her descend, my mouth agape. She was wearing a short denim skirt that showed about a mile of bare leg and a tight black camisole that got my Adam's apple pumping in my throat. Her eyes were gray as smoke, her dark hair pulled back into a ponytail that made her jaw and throat seem delicate as spun glass.

And she was wearing makeup. You never see that anymore. Her lips were so red they actually glistened. I couldn't look away.

She dismissed the guard with a wave.

"Hey," she said to me.

"Hi," I said. The word came out as a cracked, high-pitched sound. I coughed, lowered my voice, and tried to sound cool. "Hey," I said. I couldn't stop looking at her lips. They were so bright, so shiny, like wet candy. "You look great," I managed to say.

She blushed.

"They didn't give you any trouble at the gate, did they?"

"No," I said. "Well, maybe a little. No big deal."

"You sure?"

"Really," I said. "No big deal."

She smiled. "My dad wants to see you before we go. You don't mind, do you?"

Mano a Mano with Big John Ashcroft. Christ, I thought. "I guess I don't get to say no, do I?"

"Um, not really."

I watched golden light scatter from her hair and said, "Sure, why not?"

She led me back to her father's office.

"Daddy," she said, "this is the boy I told you about."

John Ashcroft wasn't the giant I was expecting to meet. You hear stories about these guys, the barons, when you grow up in the Zone, and they're like gods, reshaping the world in their own image. You expect them to be six and a half feet tall, neck like a beer keg, arms like a gorilla. But John Ashcroft, he was just a normal-looking guy in a white work shirt and khaki slacks, a crescent of gray hair around the back of his head.

He didn't offer to shake my hand. Without saying a word, he pointed me to a chair opposite his desk and ordered me to sit.

After an uncomfortably long silence, he spoke. "What kind of name is Andrew Hudson?"

"Uh, it's just a name, sir."

"Yeah, but I know it from somewhere."

"My dad, probably."

"Who was your dad?"

"Eddie Hudson. He was a San Antonio cop in the old days."

That got him interested. "You mean the one who wrote that book about the Fall?"

"That's right." I get that bit about my dad from some of the old timers. Dad wrote a book about the first night of the outbreak, about how he had to fight his way across the city to get to my mom and me. He left off a few weeks after that night, at a point when it looked like we were actually going to contain the zombie outbreak. Well, he was wrong, obviously, and sometimes the old timers who remember my dad's book look at me, and I think maybe they're remembering what it was like back then, back when it seemed we might win this thing. I think, at least for some of them, the memories make them angry, resentful, like they blame people like my dad for the naiveté that allowed the Second Wave to happen. But there are others who recognize my dad and they tune out, they become distant, like they've gotten over the anger and now they're dealing with something else.

Big John Ashcroft—he was one of the ones who just got distant.

"What happened to your dad?" His voice had grown quiet.

"He and Mom died in the Second Wave, sir."

"You would have been what, about six when that happened?"

"Yes, sir. Four, actually."

He nodded. "Did they turn?"

"Mom did. Dad got swarmed trying to stop a bunch of them from breaking into our house. Mom got bit, but she managed to stash me in a hall closet before she turned."

"And you've been on your own ever since, living off the streets?"

"That's right."

He said, "So what do you do now? How do you live?" But I could tell the question he meant to ask was, *How the hell did a Zoner like you meet my daughter?*

"Special deliveries. I take private packages all across the Zone. I've even done some work for you, sir. That's how I met your daughter."

He frowned.

"Where do you plan to take my daughter, Andrew?"

"Dinner, sir. And dancing. On the *Starliner*. On the lake."

He looked impressed, though I could tell he didn't want to be impressed.

"The *Starliner's* not cheap," he said. "Special deliveries must pay pretty good."

"Business is fine, sir." I paused, then said, "But that's not really what you're asking, is it?"

He raised an eyebrow and waited.

"Listen," I said. "Heather's a special girl. That's not something you have to convince me of. You want me to know how much she means to you, how special she is." I gestured at the old-world luxury around us, the books on his wall, the horse-and-rider bronze on his desk. "She means more that all of this. I get it, sir. I may be a Zoner, but I know a class act when I see one, and I intend to treat her accordingly."

I'd guessed right. That was exactly what he needed to hear. He knew as well as anybody the dangers waiting for his daughter outside his compound's walls, and he knew he wouldn't be able to keep her from them forever. Sooner or later, with or without his permission, she was going to brave that world. Maybe sending her out with me, somebody who had proven his ability to survive, was his way of hedging his bets.

But whatever his thoughts, he gave his consent. He called in his senior security officer, a slender, bowlegged man named Naylor, and Naylor drove us out to the main gate in an air-conditioned utility vehicle. He told the guards to give me back my gear and my motorcycle, and while they were doing that, he pulled Heather aside and gave her a little talk.

After that, Naylor said to me, "She has a portable radio equipped with a GPS tracker. My people will be monitoring it all night. We'll be close." Then he fixed me with a meaningful glare. "All she has to do is call."

The message came through loud and clear.

"I'll try to be on my best behavior," I said.

Heather jumped on the back of my bike and pressed her breasts into my back. I could feel the hard pebbles of her nipples through our clothes. "You better not be on your best behavior," she whispered into my ear. "Now drive fast, Andrew. Get me out of here."

* * *

In the days after the Fall, when the necrosis filovirus emerged from the hurricane-ravaged Texas Gulf Coast and turned the infected into flesh-eating, human train-wrecks, the old world collapsed, and men like John Ashcroft stepped up to fill the power vacuum. To protect their interests, they built compounds like the one Heather and I had just left, and everywhere outside their walls became a wasteland known as the Zone of Exclusion.

After my parents died, I became one of the fringe people, a Zoner, too young to be of any use to the bosses who were just consolidating their power and building their compounds, and no way of becoming anything else. But these days I know the Zone better than most, and what I know I learned the hard way, fighting every day with the infected in the ruins of San Antonio. I survived that way for ten years.

Then, right after I turned sixteen, I stole a motorcycle. And before long, I'd worked up a reputation as someone who could get packages delivered anywhere in the Zone.

That's how I met Heather. About two months before our first date, I brought her a package from a dying woman out in the Zone. How that woman got the money to pay me I don't know, because I don't come cheap, but she did pay me, in gold, and I made the delivery.

Heather opened the package in front of me and took out a badly worn pink blanket with her name stitched on it. There was a note attached, and she read it four times before she asked me about the woman who sent it.

"She's not doing so hot," I said, which was being charitable. The truth was, the effort it took her to tell me what she wanted nearly killed her.

Heather nodded quietly, and then the tears came.

She told me her parents divorced when she was little, before the Fall, and when the world turned upside down, her father took her away because he could protect her better than her mom.

She didn't have many memories of the woman, but from the looks of that blanket, I figured her mom had plenty of memories of her.

Heather gave me a long letter to take back to her mother, and though she could have paid my fee ten times over with what she carried in her pocket, I didn't charge her.

I took the letter to her mother, and because she couldn't see well enough to read, I read it for her. She died a few days later, but I think she was happy during those last few days. Happier than she'd been in years.

Heather and I got close after that, though we had to steal the moments we spent together.

At least we did before tonight.

Now, sitting on the back of my bike, she squeezed my waist and put her lips to my ear. "I love the wind on my face," she said. "Go faster."

*　*　*

Dinner was the best thing I'd ever tasted, roasted mutton with wasabi mashed potatoes and asparagus. To this day I have no idea what the hell wasabi is, or where you get it, but I sure loved the bite it gave those mashed potatoes.

And the scenery was fantastic. The stars dappled the surface of Canyon Lake. On the shore, the tops of the hills were silvered with moonlight. There was music, a few older couples dancing on the open air deck, glimpses of a world long gone.

The conversation, on the other hand, lagged. At least at first.

I'd never really talked to a girl. Not like you do on a date, anyway. I didn't know what I was supposed to say, how I was supposed to act. She knew little about weapons, or the Zone, and that pretty much exhausted what I knew. She was into growing vegetables and had plans for building schools.

But I told her dad I was going to treat her like a class act, and I did. The thing is, deep down inside, I am, and always will be, a Zoner. Life, as I had known it, was short and mean and cheap, and I spent a lot of time wondering if it was really worth the effort I put into it. When you think about it that way, when you've watched more lives than you care to remember come and go like they're nothing more than a crowd passing through a revolving door, it can be hard to look at a girl and think the two of you have a chance at romance.

She asked me if there was anything wrong.

"No," I said, trying to sound bright, happy, fun to be with. But then my smile wavered, and I said, "Yes. It's me. Sometimes, when I start feeling like I could be happy—like this—with you—I don't know. It's like I lose my nerve or something. I don't know. Maybe it's frustration with my life, with everything. Who knows? I just wonder what the point is sometimes."

She thought about that for a second.

And then she surprised me.

"There may not be a point," she said. "I don't know if there has to be. I mean, whether or not there's a point to all of this, we're here just the same. You and me. That should count for something, shouldn't it?"

"That's true," I said, marveling at her practicality. "I guess it does."

* * *

After dinner we danced on the open deck of the *Starliner*. A cool, late spring breeze was in the air, carrying with it the thick, marshy smell of lake water. I held her body close to mine, the first time I'd ever held a real girl, and lost myself in the warmth of her green eyes and the clean girl-smell of her skin.

That feeling, that comfort of absolute privacy, the romance of it, was why the *Starliner* cost so much. The infected were everywhere, and not even the strongest compound was completely safe from them, but when the *Starliner* was off her moorings and out on the lake, it was its own world, untouchable by the harsh realities of the Zone.

As the evening drew to a close, and the *Starliner* began her slow cruise back to the wet dock, Heather and I stood on the bow and talked about the future, about the stars, about anything and everything except the past. It was our night, and though our bonds had been forged in the heartaches of the past, we wanted our night together to be about the future. We wanted our own happy memories together.

There were no other boats on the lake. At least there hadn't been during most of our date. But as we rounded a final elbow of land and entered the cove, we saw a large cabin cruiser waiting for us, the vague shapes of men ringing the rails of the deck.

Heather broke off in the middle of a giggle and watched them.

"What is it?"

"Not good," she said. "I think that's Wayne Nessel. Daddy warned me he might try something. Daddy didn't think he'd do it out here though."

I knew of Wayne Nessel. I had delivered packages to his compound. He was Ashcroft's biggest rival, and a man with a lot of resources at his disposal. People in the Zone called him "The Bull."

"He couldn't know you're here."

"He knows," she said, and then she guided me to the far side of the *Starliner*.

"But how?"

"He's got spies everywhere, Andrew."

She crossed to the opposite side of the deck and climbed the railing.

"Wait a minute," I said. "Where are we going?"

She looked down at me. "Can you swim?"

"Yeah."

"Good." She waited until Nessel's boat lit up the *Starliner* with its spotlights, then she gave me a wink and dropped herself over the edge.

I went in after her.

I thought we'd cling to the side of the boat and wait it out, but that wasn't what Heather had in mind. She went under and kept swimming beneath the *Starliner's* Hull.

I followed.

Above us, through the green murky haze, I could see the glow of the spotlights and the shimmering outlines of men running on both decks. There were a lot of muffled popping sounds that I took to be gunfire, but none of that was directed down at us. It was all boat-to-boat.

We surfaced on the far side of Nessel's boat and swam to shore. Out of habit, I'd hidden my motorcycle in the brush next to the *Starliner's* docks, and now I was thankful for my instincts. As we swam, we decided it'd be best to come ashore a little ways from the dock, just in case Nessel had men covering his back on land.

We crawled ashore, and Heather pulled her black hair back with both hands, her camisole clinging to the curve of her breasts like wet paint.

There were voices nearby, just on the other side of the bushes.

"That'll be Nessel's men," I said.

She nodded.

We spotted them a moment later. Four men, all armed with AR-15s. They were lined up on the dock, looking out at the boats, pointing and laughing.

"Amateurs," I whispered. "Look at that. They're just watching the show."

"Can you get them all?"

"No," I said. "Not all of them. Maybe one or two, but not all of them."

"What do we do?"

The switchback road we'd taken to the docks led a short distance up a steep hill behind us before curving out of sight. Low, scraggly oaks and cedars lined the sides of it. I told Heather to go up around the curve and wait for me.

"What are you going to do?"

"Try not to get shot," I said.

She frowned at that, but she made her way to the road just the same, careful to stay in the shadows.

When she was safely out of the way, I made my move.

My bike was hidden in a clump of cedar behind an old rusted truck. I crossed behind the guards and made for the bike, praying they didn't turn around.

I got most of the way there before I heard one of them holler something. The next instant, they were firing at me. Little chunks of concrete exploded around my shoes as I made for the truck, but they didn't hit me, and if their lack of attention on the shoreline hadn't convinced me they were just hired goons, their shooting certainly did.

At that range, professionals would have killed me with ease.

I got down beneath the truck, pulled my Glock, and waited. They were running up the slope of the lot, straight for me. I steadied my sights on the lead guy and dropped him with my first shot. My next three shots weren't aimed. I just sprayed the crowd to make them duck for cover.

It worked. They dived behind an old boat trailer, giving me enough time to pull my motorcycle out of the bushes, start it, and race up the road. They fired after me, but they never got close.

I slowed long enough for Heather to jump on the back, and then we sped off into the night.

* * *

We were still wet from the swim, and it was cold on that bike. What had been a lovely cool breeze while we were dancing was now a fierce cold snap, biting through us to the bone. Heather wrapped her arms around my waist and squeezed, and I could feel her body trembling.

I slowed the bike down enough for her to hear me. "Are you okay?"

"Uh-huh."

"Why is he after you?"

"Anything to hurt Daddy," she said, her voice coming in quick, breathy stabs. "His people are always ambushing Daddy's shipments. Maybe he's upping the ante now to kidnapping. Or assassination."

"What do you want to do?" I asked.

"Warn Daddy," she said at once. "Daddy told me Nessel always attacks on two fronts at once. If he's coming after me here, he's probably trying to attack Daddy somewhere else too."

"The radio?"

She nodded. "I tried back at the lake. Nobody answered. We'll have to get closer into town and try for one of Daddy's safe houses."

"You got it," I said and laid into the throttle.

* * *

When we got closer into town, I pulled off the highway and parked in a lot on the top of a small hill so Heather could call Naylor on the radio.

"Are you sure it's Nessel's people?" he asked.

"I'm sure," she said.

He told us not to use the radio any more than we had to. Besides a good share of the gasoline market, Nessel controlled the sale of most of the electronic equipment in the area. The radio Heather was using was probably stolen from one of his shipments, and there wasn't much doubt he'd be able to overhear her transmission.

"Can you get to the pickup point?" he asked.

Heather gave me a sidelong glance and a smile. "I'm pretty sure we can."

We moved out, and as we rode, I thought about this old timer I used to know who told me what life was like before the outbreak. He said people were pretty much the same then as they are now, and that turning into zombies hadn't changed them much. What was different, he said, was the noise. It was noisy back then. There were cars and planes and trains everywhere, not to mention all the crowds. He said you couldn't escape it.

But these days, there are so few cars left you can drive around all day and never see another driver. Heather and I hadn't seen any all night. I couldn't remember the last time I'd heard a plane fly overhead. I'd never seen a moving train. Life in the Zone was quiet, even though it was rarely peaceful.

That's how I knew something was wrong. Heather and I got on the highway again and started driving, but we hadn't made it very far before I heard the high-pitched whine of a pack of racing bikes.

We glanced around, looking for them. They were behind us, coming down from an overpass and getting onto the freeway at top speed. I didn't need to ask if they were Nessel's men. All of them had machine guns slung over their backs, and the way they were riding, they clearly knew who we were.

I got my bike up to top speed, but they were faster. My bike was just a beat up Harley Sportster, but they were riding Honda CXRs—top-of-the-line racing bikes. I didn't have a snowball's chance of outrunning them in a dead sprint, so when they got close enough to take their shots, I did the only thing I could think of and veered over to the far left lane, let them come up on us, then downshifted and banked the bike hard to the right, taking the connector ramp to the Connelly Loop at almost a hundred miles an hour.

Heather yelled out in surprise. Nessel's men overshot us. I saw them lock up their brakes and slide, but none of them reacted fast enough to take the ramp with us.

Their mistake bought us a few valuable seconds. The Connelly

Loop led right into the heart of the Zone. There was nothing in there but crumbling buildings and legions of the infected. That made it low priority for the bosses who made it their business to keep the roads clear, so it was still choked with long lines of abandoned cars.

My old timer friend told me that rush-hour traffic used to be so bad the freeways would turn into parking lots, and when it was really bad, you could sit in your car for half an hour or more and never make it more than a couple of miles. Looking out over the abandoned cars ahead of us I felt like I knew what he meant. It was a three-lane, bumper-to-bumper junkyard as far as I could see.

As I slowed down to thread the gap between the cars Heather yelled in my ear, "What are you doing? You're going the wrong way."

I looked behind us and saw Nessel's men coming for us. They looked like a squadron of mad hornets buzzing down the ramp, shooting the gaps between wrecks at fantastic speeds.

"Hold on," I said.

One of the infected was stumbling along between two rows of cars about a hundred and fifty yards ahead of us. I dug into the throttle and went straight for him, darting through the narrow gap, feeling the *thump thump thump* of the air as we passed all the cars.

The infected are predictable. When they see you, they stumble after you. They don't care if you're on foot or driving a truck, they stumble after you just the same, which is exactly what the zombie ahead of us was doing.

About ten yards ahead of the zombie was a gap in the cars. It looked like a driver in the middle lane had tried to turn into the lane to his right and had hit another car in the process. The car was stuck at a forty-five degree angle, with just enough room for me to slip alongside it and cross over to the gap between the middle and right lanes. But I had to time it right. I had to get there just a fraction of a second before the zombie if I was going to make it work.

It was close.

When I got to the gap I hit the brakes, rocked the bike hard to the right, then hard to the left, feeling Heather gasping as she squeezed me. We threaded into the opening and took off at full speed.

I looked back just as one of Nessel's goons hit that zombie. He must have been doing at least ninety miles per hour when he realized what was happening and hit his brakes. But at that speed, not even the Honda's oversized racing brakes could help him. He hit the zombie, and both bodies went tumbling over the wrecked cars. The bike went sideways, hit the trunk of a car, and shot twenty feet up in the air, turning end over end the whole way back to the ground.

That slowed the other three down, but not by much, and I knew I couldn't play those games forever. I took us up another hundred yards or so until we came to a small box van. There I slowed, turned the bike around, and headed back the way we'd come.

"What are you doing?" Heather said.

But I didn't have time to answer. I ducked my head and charged.

One of the remaining three riders was in our gap, and even though he was wearing a full helmet and shield that kept his face hidden, I could tell by the way his body stiffened that his eyes were going wide.

I pulled my Glock and fired. I'm not sure if I hit him or not, but the bike shimmied beneath him, he lost his balance, glanced off a car, and crashed out.

I saw his head smack a bumper as he fell.

I stopped the bike and told Heather to get off. She looked panicked, but she did like I asked.

"What are you going to do?"

I pulled out my other Glock. "Just stay down, okay? I got this."

Those huge green eyes of hers melted me.

"We're going to be okay," I said.

She nodded, and I moved out on foot. The other two riders were going slow now, practically walking their bikes through the cars, looking for us. I crouched below the top of the cars and jogged into position. When the rider I was targeting got close enough, I stood and fired both Glocks into his chest, knocking him backward off the bike.

The other rider tried to react, but he was stuck between two pickups. I threw a lot of ammunition at him with both guns and managed to catch a lucky shot. He spun around, hit in the shoulder, and went down.

I ran over to where he fell and saw him rolling on the pavement, wounded. He pushed off his helmet and let it tumble away. He looked up at me, his eyes pleading with me. Most of the time my moral compass swings closer to the good than the bad, but some people just aren't worth the effort.

So I shot him in the head.

* * *

When I got back to Heather, she was holding that portable radio in her hands and crying.

"What's wrong?" I asked.

"Daddy was right about Nessel," she said. "The bastard used me as a decoy."

"What do you mean?"

"Daddy sent a squad of his best men to the safe house where we were supposed to go." She looked up at me and choked back tears. "Nessel was waiting for them. They're all dead. Now he's attacking Daddy's compound."

"Oh, Jesus."

"He said for us to stay away." She looked deep into my eyes. "But my God, Andrew. It sounded so bad. I heard explosions. And Daddy was screaming at people while he was talking with me."

I had no idea what to say. She told me while we were dancing that she had begged her father for a week to let her go out on a date with me, and now his empire was in serious risk of crumbling, and it was all because of our date.

It's a lousy feeling, knowing you're to blame for something that big.

But Heather, she was full of surprises. "Andrew," she said, "you were telling me the truth about my mom, weren't you? You really did read her my letter?"

I nodded.

"You worked a miracle bringing her back into my life."

I shook my head.

"You did," she said. "I believe that. And I believe you can do it again. I believe you can give me my father back."

It was my turn to look deep into her eyes. I felt confused. "What are you asking me to do?"

"Help me save Daddy, Andrew. Please."

She turned those big green eyes up at me, and in that moment, I knew I was powerless to refuse. I'd have handed her my soul for the asking.

"Let's go get your dad," I said.

* * *

I started toward the main gate because that was the only way into Ashcroft's compound that I knew of, but when Heather saw where I was going she pointed me in a different direction.

She had me go to the west side of the compound and drive into a crumbling building that looked like it had been a bakery before the outbreak. It was the corner shop in a block-long strip mall. She told me to stop. Then she got off the bike, opened a door that had been made to look like it was rusted shut, and ushered me into a freshly painted white corridor.

"This leads right into the compound," she said.

I nodded, impressed. Concealed doors and hidden tunnels were the kind of thing you'd expect from a powerful boss like Ashcroft, but it was still weird to actually see them in real life. That kind of engineering was way beyond what most bosses were capable of.

We took the motorcycle all the way to the end of the corridor, where we were met by guards who took us to see Ashcroft.

Ashcroft and Naylor were watching the battle from the third floor of the Fairmount. Nessel had focused his troops around the main gate, but they were hitting the compound's wall in a couple of different places, forcing Ashcroft's troops to divide their strength.

Heather and I stood back, listening as Naylor relayed to Ashcroft updates he was receiving over the radio.

The outer perimeter of Ashcroft's compound was made up of smashed and stacked cars. Nessel's men had used rocket-propelled grenades against that wall and it had partially collapsed in two places. A large group of Ashcroft's men were boxed in near the gate, fighting a close-quarter's battle in the rubble from the explosions, and Nessel's superior numbers were starting to wear them down.

Ashcroft surveyed the scene with night-vision goggles. "Pull them back, Naylor," he said. "Tell them to regroup around the courtyard."

Ashcroft's troops began falling back. Heather reached over and touched my hand as the soldiers ran toward the hotel. I looked over at her and saw she was holding her breath.

Just then another blast from a rocket grenade lit up the night, and when the smoke settled, we saw there was a huge hole in the wall.

Naylor was watching the space beyond the wall. "Something's happening," he said. "They're bringing up buses."

"Buses?" Ashcroft said. He focused his binoculars on the hole. "My God," he gasped.

Two yellow school buses broke through the burning debris that had once been the wall of flattened cars and rolled to a stop not far from Ashcroft's retreating troops. Some of the men stopped to fire at the bodies getting off the buses but took off running again when they realized they were the infected.

"That is fucking brilliant," Ashcroft said, impressed despite himself. "Using the infected like that. I didn't think Nessel had it in him."

"Problem, sir," Naylor said.

Ashcroft smirked. "What now?"

"There, sir. To the right of the main gate. See him?"

I followed Naylor's finger to a high point on the wall. There was a man crawling to the top of it, but he was too far away for me to see what he was doing.

"Sniper," Ashcroft said. And then, one at a time, Ashcroft's retreating troops started to fall. The only clue why were the bright muzzle flashes of the sniper's rifle.

In the confusion, Ashcroft's men didn't know which way to run.

"They're getting slaughtered out there," Ashcroft said. "Get some of your men back up to the front and take that sniper out."

Naylor said, "I don't have anybody, sir. Prescott is the only officer I have left, and he's coordinating the retreat."

Ashcroft said nothing. He gripped the railing and stared down at the battlefield.

"Mr. Ashcroft," I said.

"What?" he growled.

"I can get him, sir."

"Just stand still and shut up," he said.

For the second time that night I met his gaze and didn't look away.

It looked like his first instinct was to throw me over the railing, but then he stopped himself and nodded. "Okay," he said. "You want to do it, go ahead."

I turned to go.

Heather followed me.

"Andrew, wait." She said, "You're not serious? You can't go."

I nodded in her father's direction. "Heather, do you really think he'd ever let us be together if I don't do this? He'll always have it in the back of his mind that this happened because of me. But I can change that if I do this."

"Don't be stupid, Andrew. He's got people to deal with this."

"I'll be all right," I said. "I promise."

"You better be," she said.

I grabbed her roughly around the waist and pulled her close, planting a kiss on her lips right there in front of her dad.

"I'm coming back," I said. "Count on it."

* * *

The battle had reached the courtyard right in front of the hotel. Ashcroft's men were in defensive positions behind the fountain and the rows of small garden walls leading up to the front doors. Nessel's men were still getting into position, using the infected as a moving barrier.

That sniper on the wall was the key to the battle. From his position, he was picking off Ashcroft's men, no matter how well hidden they were, and it was only a matter of time before he got so many of them that there wouldn't be enough left to put up a fight.

I moved across the right flank of the battle and headed for a ditch that ran through the cow pasture. I figured that as long as I stayed inside it I'd be able to make it all the way to the wall of cars. I had no idea what I was going to do from there, though.

I got most of the way across the yard before I saw a small group of the infected wandering on the fringes of the battle. I was so intent on reaching the wall that I didn't even notice them until I was right on top of them, and by then it was too late. I jumped out of the ditch and ran for it.

The infected followed me.

I veered right and ran along the inside of the wall until I got to a section where rocket grenades had blown it apart. I jumped over the debris and landed outside the wall—right in front of a military-style Humvee where Nessel and two of his lieutenants were watching the battle unfold.

I wasn't wearing one of Ashcroft's uniforms, so they didn't know what to make of me for a second. I might have been a civilian, or even one of their own hired goons. That hesitation saved me. With the infected hot on my heels, I drew both Glocks and ran straight for Nessel, firing the whole way.

I wasn't aiming, just spraying and praying, but I got one lucky shot and hit Nessel's driver in the head. He went down onto the hood of the Humvee. The other lieutenant tried to break and run but got caught by the infected and went down screaming.

That left Nessel.

He fell over the back of the Humvee and landed face-first in the grass. Before he had a chance to get up, I shot him three times, once in the neck and twice in the chest. With Nessel dead, I turned to face the infected. There were eight of them, and with the Humvee for cover, I used up the last of my ammunition on them. That left me with nothing but my machete to fight the sniper.

I started to climb up the wall of flattened cars as quietly as I could. I heard him up there, popping off shots every few seconds with a bolt-action rifle. Maybe, if I'm lucky, I thought, he'd be so into his shooting rhythm that he wouldn't hear me coming.

But it wasn't to be. I made it most of the way to the top when I heard something moving below me. It was one of the infected, and he was coming after me. He made a gurgling, moaning sound as he bumped and clanged his way up the side, and I knew he was making enough noise that the sniper would be able to hear him even over the sound of his rifle.

I was stuck.

I couldn't go up because I would lose the element of surprise and probably get killed, and I couldn't go down, either. But there was a little gap between two of the cars on the top row, and I ducked into that, facing outward. I waited to see who would get to me first, the sniper or the zombie.

It was the sniper. He poked his head over the side, his face barely a foot above my waiting hands. I reached up, grabbed him by the back of the head, and yanked down as hard as I could. He came down the side of the wall like a snowball going downhill, picking up loose car parts as he hit the sides, trying to hold on, only to keep tumbling downward, right into the waiting arms of the zombie below us. The two of them hit hard, and both ended up on the ground.

I didn't waste any time. I jumped over the top and picked up the sniper's rifle. The sniper was fighting the zombie barehanded, and doing pretty well, until I shot them both.

Then I took up the post I'd just stolen from him. I looked through the scope and watched the battle taking place around the fountain. Ashcroft's men, who had a reputation as the best private army in the Zone, were earning their stripes. I saw at least fifty of Nessel's soldiers dead in the courtyard, and it looked like their advance was starting to break apart. Despite their numerical superiority, they just weren't as well-disciplined, or as well-trained, as Ashcroft's troops.

Ashcroft himself was leading the fight. I saw him waving a machine gun over his head, yelling at his men to hold their positions.

I went to work on Nessel's men, and as I started putting them down, one by one, I swept the scope across Ashcroft's position. He stopped yelling long enough to look my way. All at once he realized it was me doing the firing now, and he gave me an exaggerated overhand salute.

The tide of the battle turned, and soon, Nessel's men broke ranks and ran. Ashcroft followed up their retreat, and his men carved the retreating enemy up into pockets, showing no mercy.

Gradually, the steady, thunderous roll of the battle faded, and all that was left was the occasional sporadic popping of small arms fire. Ashcroft's men were still dealing with the infected, but those too were getting mopped up.

I could see the mood among Ashcroft's men changing. They had won big, and now they knew it.

With nothing left to shoot at, I got down from the wall and went over to where I'd left Nessel to die. I tossed his body onto the hood of the Humvee and drove straight through the gates to the hotel.

I parked in front of the fountain.

Ashcroft's men stopped their celebrations to watch me, and Ashcroft himself came over to see what was going on. He took one look at Nessel's body and whistled. Then he looked at me and smiled.

Behind him, coming out of the hotel at a run, was Heather. She ran right past her father and straight into my arms, pressing her lips into mine with an eagerness that I think surprised us both.

Then I felt a strong hand clamp down on my shoulder, pulling me back. It was Ashcroft. "You did real good," he said and offered me his hand.

"Thank you, sir." But I noticed he had planted himself squarely between me and his daughter.

"I owe you big, Andrew."

I shrugged.

In the background I heard Naylor giving orders to the men to start damage control. After he got the men moving, he came back to Ashcroft and gave a report. Ashcroft listened in silence, nodding his head, and when Naylor was finished, he gave him some more orders to relay to the troops.

Then he turned to me and said, "Andrew, it looks like we've got a lot of rebuilding to do." He glanced down at Nessel. "And I seem to have inherited several new businesses. I'm going to need some good men to help me run them. You interested in a job?"

Heather was smiling.

"Uh, a job would be great," I said.

His smile wavered. "I heard a 'but' in there."

"Well sir," I said, "a job would be great, but to tell you the truth, what I really want is a second date with your daughter."

Dating in Dead World: Coda
Joe McKinney Interviewed by John Joseph Adams on *Dating in Dead World*

I've done many interviews over the years, but the one that I did with John Joseph Adams as part of the promotional drive for his anthology *The Living Dead* 2 was my first devoted entirely to one of my short stories. Here's part of that interview, originally published at his website:

John Joseph Adams: Tell us a bit about your story. What's it about?

Joe McKinney: It's been almost twenty years since Hurricane Mardell swept through Houston, flooding the city and giving birth to a virus that turns the living into the walking dead. The world has been overrun by zombies and left in ruin. But there are still groups of people left alive, and they are carving out an existence in the wasteland. Some of the survivors have moved into protective compounds, but Andrew Hudson wasn't lucky enough to grow up in one of those. He was raised as a street urchin in the ruins of San Antonio, where he makes a living as a special courier between the strongholds of the dead world's warlords. During one of those runs, he had the good fortune to meet the daughter of the area's most powerful warlord, and he won her heart.

Now, they're going on their first date. How hard could that be, right? Kids have been dating forever. Well, when taking your date out involves high-speed pursuits through zombie-infested ruins and being used as pawns in an underhanded power-grab scheme, nothing is as easy as it seems.

JJA: What was the genesis of the story–what was the inspiration for it, or what prompted you to write it?

JM: "Dating in the Dead World" was written right about the same time that Kensington Publishing came asking me to do another zombie book. I had made a few readers mad with the ending to *Dead City*, and I wanted to address the criticism before I went on with the rest of the series.

The first person narrator of *Dead City* is a police officer named Eddie Hudson. The thing to remember about Eddie Hudson is that he is not a reliable reporter. Most people get that wrong about him. He's deeply fractured by the events he recounts in the novel, and the optimism he expresses at the end of the story is... well, let's just say he's not telling you everything. He's telling you about the world he wants to believe in, not the world as it really is. "Dating in the Dead World" came from that issue. And because "Dating in the Dead World" was written to refute Eddie Hudson's optimism, the logical lead for the story was Eddie's son, Andrew Hudson. So this story really becomes as much a conversation between father and son as it does a commentary on the Dead City series itself.

JJA: Was this story a particularly challenging one to write? If so, how?

JM: "Dating in the Dead World" came surprisingly easy. After I finish a novel, I'm usually struck by a sort of separation anxiety. So much mental effort is put into world building and getting to know the characters that it seems a shame to simply cut and run. I personally have a hard time leaving it all behind. So what I usually do is write a few short stories set in the world of the novel I've just finished. They don't always involve the same characters, or even take place at exactly the same time, but they all help me, in their own way, go on to the next book. "Dating in the Dead World" was a part of that process, and because I knew the world of the story already, the story developed without a lot of birthing pains.

JJA: Most authors say all their stories are personal. If that's true for you, in what way was this story personal to you?

JM: Personal accountability is a big deal for me. I don't respect a person who can't accept responsibility for their actions. That's something I learned from my dad, and something I'll always be thankful for.

But he also gave me a related piece of advice. Right before I left for my first date, he gave me the only bit of parental sex education I ever received. "Remember this," he said. "You will be held personally accountable for everything that happens to that girl from the moment she leaves her front door to the moment she walks back in it. Conduct yourself accordingly."

It wasn't until after I'd written "Dating in the Dead World" that I realized I was channeling that advice. I guess it took.

JJA: What kind of research did you have to do for the story?

JM: Well, the "world" of this story was one I already knew quite well, but I did do research on the use of cadaver dogs, and on building protective compounds. Believe it or not, there's a lot of material out there on how to create your own fortress to guard against the end of the world. To me, that's almost as scary as the end of the world itself, you know?

Bug Out or Hunker Down

This is an experiment. Part fiction, part speculative essay, this piece started with one simple question: If the zombie apocalypse came today, how would I handle it? Would I stay put or would I make a break for it? And what of my family? I'm a husband, and a father, and a cop who took an oath to protect the community that has paid me so well over the last two decades. What do I do with all that obligation, all that responsibility? What would I really do, given conditions exactly as they are now? Would I bug out or hunker down?

My goal is to answer this scenario as truthfully as I can, allowing myself only those options I really possess and given only the resources currently at my disposal. No wishful thinking, no cheating. I can't tell you that I would turn my Nissan Altima into an armored zombie killdozer because, well, I don't have anything to armor plate my Nissan with, and, truthfully, wouldn't know how to go about installing that armor even if I did. As I said, no cheating. This is basically a reality check. What could I do—what would I do—if Z-Day came today? Let's find out.

But first, a few ground rules.

What Kind of Outbreak Are We Dealing With?

Everybody's idea of what the zombie apocalypse will look like is different. For this scenario, here's what's happening:

1. The outbreak is viral in nature, and the virus is transmitted by a bite or some contact with the bodily fluids of an infected person.
2. Only the living and the very recently dead are affected by this virus. The buried dead play no part in this scenario.
3. The virus has a 100% mortality rate, meaning all persons infected with the virus die from it and, in turn, become zombies.
4. The virus begins in some part of the U.S. other than my home city of San Antonio. However, due to the fluid nature of our society, the outbreak spreads rapidly. Cities with major airports can expect to see incidents of infection within 36 hours. Cities that serve as major air-travel hubs and international ports of call will be in complete confusion for a period of perhaps four days, after which the outbreak will spread to the rest of the country and then, at an exponential rate, to the rest of the world.
5. Martial law will be instituted within the first week of the outbreak but will break down almost completely within the first three weeks of the outbreak.
6. Within a month of the first reported zombie incident, it will be every man for himself.

Given these conditions, I think this is how the outbreak would go for me and my family.

Right Now

It started on a Monday, just after lunch. I'd taken the week off work because I had some writing deadlines to meet before I left for the World Horror Convention in Salt Lake City that coming weekend.

My wife was home too. Ordinarily, she wouldn't be. She was a college professor at a local university, and though she was feeling a bit under the weather that day and had to cancel her classes, she was diligently grading papers on our home computer.

Our two kids, nine- and six-year-old girls, were at school a few miles away, near the entrance to our subdivision.

I usually wrote my rough drafts out long hand, which meant I was bent over my desk, scribbling on a yellow legal pad. My iPad was next to me, though, and I used that to check my email periodically throughout the day. The first indication I had that something was wrong was a rapid-fire series of notification chimes on my iPad. Curious, I opened it, and saw Facebook updates from several of the groups I belong to. Some included links to news stories out of Boston and Philadelphia.

The stories were confusing and contradictory. They mentioned rioting and people tearing each other apart. Local police departments were scrambling to deal with the situation, but so far, they weren't having much luck.

Homemade videos started popping up on Facebook, including footage from iPhones and video cameras. I watched a few of those, my mouth hanging open, and then I went to my wife's study, where I found her watching videos from a friend in Boston. A man covered in blood, part of his face missing, was pawing drunkenly at her front door. He spotted her filming him from the upstairs window and began groping the air, moaning frantically. I could hear our friend breathing in the background, panic-stricken. The choppy, bouncing video and off-camera panting reminded me of something out of *The Blair Witch Project*, but the growing dread in my gut was very real.

"What do you think is happening?" my wife asked. "Is this real?"

But we both knew the answer to that. It was very real.

Still, we'd never talked about what came next. I wrote this stuff, but it'd never been more than fun for me. My wife hated reading about zombies. What that amounted to was that we didn't have a plan for zombies. Natural disasters, which in San Antonio meant flash floods or possibly forest fires, sure, those we had covered. But not zombies.

"What about the kids?"

It was the only point that really mattered, and it stopped me. I was a cop. I was in decent shape...except for my high blood pressure, which I controlled with medication. I knew tactics. I knew how to handle guns, how to fight if I had to. But doing the zombie apocalypse with kids. Well, that was a different matter.

"It's just now 2 o'clock," I said. "They get out at 2:45. Let's figure out a plan right now. We'll go get them as soon as school lets out, bring them back here, and we'll make ready on whatever we decide to do."

That sounded reasonable to me. The part of my brain that had been trained to deal with critical situations liked that idea.

But my wife was looking at me like I'd just grown an extra head.

"Make ready? Are you serious? Joe, we're dealing with zombies here. *Zombies!* What in the hell are we going to do?"

That Night

We hadn't said a word to the kids, and we kept them away from the TV. We didn't want to scare them, but they wouldn't be going to school in the morning. Things were looking bad on the news, with outbreaks reported all over North America and a few in Japan and China and Europe. So far, the individual outbreaks had been contained, but if my own stories had shown anything, it's that a zombie scenario is always a war of attrition, and no matter how dedicated the military and the local responders may be, collapse was inevitable. It wouldn't be long now, I realized, before the first cases hit San Antonio, and I would have to meet this inevitability head-on.

"Okay," my wife said as she stepped down the stairs, "the kids are in bed. Let's talk about what we're going to do."

"I'm guessing my parents' place, right?"

She nodded.

My parents lived on fifty-three acres in the Texas Hill Country, about forty miles northeast of San Antonio. Their property was remote enough that the only way to get there is to want to get there, if you know what I mean, but it was close enough to civilization that getting supplies and medical aid wasn't impossible. Also, they had their own well, lots and lots of deer, a few chickens, and even a creek running through the lower twenty acres. My mom was also a pretty fair gardener, so we'd have food.

"Tomorrow morning we're gonna head out there. I want you and the kids to stay there."

"And my parents?"

"Your parents, my brother and his wife, your sister, and your brother, his wife, and their kids...all of them can go to my parents' house. There's room. Plus, for the kids, it'll feel like a big adventure."

"Your parents don't mind?"

"You know them. Family is first."

My wife nodded. She knew it was true. My parents are saints.

"You have the lists for everybody, right?"

"Yeah, I'm going to email them right now."

I had given her several long lists to email to the various members of our families. The idea was for everybody to buy the gear they would need and bring it with them to my parents' place. That way, we'd have far more than we needed.

At least at first.

"Okay," I said. "You email the lists. I'm going to pack up the cars."

Earlier that day, while my wife was picking the kids up from school, I went through our family disaster kits. About ten years ago I worked as a disaster mitigation specialist for the SAPD, and I learned the importance of having a good disaster-preparedness kit. I've made kits for the family, smaller ones for each member of the family, and one each for my car and my wife's. The family kit is of the homemade, 72-hour emergency shelter-in-place variety. It includes:

1. Flashlights (one for each member of the family and two large extra ones)
2. Extra batteries (for the flashlights, radio, and camera)
3. Canned food and MREs (the MREs take up a lot of space, but the idea of having a "kit" from which to make your own meal has a "Wow, this is neat!" factor that keeps the kids busy, which is critical for good morale)
4. Three 5-gallon water jugs
5. Water purifying tablets
6. A hand-crank powered emergency radio (ours is a Kaito KA500 Voyager 5-Way, but there are several other reliable brands just as good)
7. Manual can opener
8. Paper plates, plastic serving ware, cooking supplies, and a small, one-burner Coleman camp stove
9. A large first aid kit and a quick guide to first aid procedures
10. A pocket folder containing copies of our birth certificates, home owner's insurance and policy number, car insurance and titles, social security cards, passports, IDs, a lengthy phone roster of family, friends and other important numbers and addresses, photographs of the family, a list of medications and my older daughter's allergies
11. Rain gear for each member of the family

12. Heavy work gloves
13. Three disposable cameras and one waterproof digital camera
14. Unscented liquid bleach, eye dropper, and measuring spoons
15. Hand sanitizer and soap
16. Two large plastic sheets, duct tape, and a utility knife
17. A package of dust masks
18. A crowbar
19. Hammer and nails
20. Adjustable wrench
21. Bungee cords of several lengths
22. Two safety ropes, one 25 feet long, the other 50 feet
23. Four heavy wool blankets
24. Four sleeping bags
25. A 5-gallon bucket to use as a toilet, plus a box of heavy duty black trash bags to line the waste bucket
26. A large box of matches

Then there are four backpacks, one for each member of the family. The individual backpacks contain:

1. Two flashlights (one small and one large)
2. Batteries for the flashlights, camera and radio
3. A small AM/FM radio
4. A whistle
5. Dust masks
6. A Swiss Army knife
7. Roll of toilet paper
8. Envelopes containing cash
9. A local map and a state map
10. Three MREs and three 1-gallon water bottles
11. A Sharpie marker, notepads, pens, and duct tape
12. A pocket folder containing all important documents, phone numbers, maps with escape routes and meet-up locations, and family photos (my oldest daughter has a dog tag on her backpack with her allergy information)
13. Extra eyeglasses for my oldest daughter and my wife
14. Toothbrush and toothpaste
15. Extra keys to the house and to both grandparents' houses
16. A small waterproof box of matches

17. A small box of candles
18. Extra battery-powered chargers for our cell phones
19. A heavy wool blanket
20. A bedroll
21. A coil of safety rope, 25 feet long
22. A signaling mirror

My wife drives a Toyota 4Runner with 130,000 miles on it. It's in great shape, though, and still runs like a top. My Nissan Altima has 101,000 miles on it but isn't in as great a shape. Still, we have a store-bought emergency kit for each car. Ours are from Bridgestone and include:

1. A flashlight
2. Hood-mounted spotlight
3. Safety triangles
4. A heavy wool blanket
5. Jumper cables
6. A small air-compressor and pump
7. Duct tape
8. Heavy duty safety gloves
9. Latex gloves
10. Small Ziploc baggies
11. Black electrical tape
12. Batteries
13. A small first aid kit
14. A poncho
15. A tire gauge
16. Two screwdrivers, one of each kind
17. Heavy duty scissors
18. Zip ties

To this kit, I've added:

1. Fix-a-flat in a can
2. A 5-gallon bucket
3. Two 5-gallon water jugs
4. A signaling mirror
5. A box of heavy-duty trash bags

6. Another copy of our family's important documents and photos
7. A disposable camera

Earlier that afternoon I went through these kits and found a number of problems, such as:

1. The family kit and the individual kits were supposed to contain envelopes with a little cash in each. At some point during the last few years we'd used a good deal of that cash. I had to go to the bank to draw out our savings, which included the $8,400 dollars in our savings and the $3,200 in our checking account. I took out all but $50 of this in cash and refilled our emergency kit envelopes.
2. The feminine products in the family kit and my wife's personal kit were several years old. I had to buy new ones. Luckily, I knew which ones to buy. Incidentally, I used our credit card for this and all other purchases.
3. I gassed up my Nissan, my wife's Toyota, and the GMC Yukon we are currently borrowing from my parents. This behemoth has 220,000 miles on it, and has some problems, but still runs okay.
4. The pictures in our family's important documents binders were not current. I had to get up-to-date photos of our kids and put these into each kit. (These are invaluable in case members of the family get separated. Imagine a six-year-old, for example, trying to provide a physical description of a lost family member.)
5. The phone chargers I had in the kits were for the Android phones we used to own. We have iPhones now. I had to buy all new chargers, plus one for my iPad.
6. The water jugs had to be cleaned and filled. I did this, and bought fourteen more 5-gallon jugs from the local Bass Pro Shops. I filled these as well.
7. I went to the local Army Surplus store and bought as many of the MREs as I could find
8. I didn't trust the batteries in any of the kits, so I bought new ones.
9. The heavy work gloves I had for my kids were too small, so I bought new ones.
10. I hadn't packed clothes in the original kit because the kids grow out of these too fast and they can mildew if left in the kits too long. I packed extra clothes and warm gear and sturdy shoes for

each of us.

11. I take blood pressure medication. I had about twenty pills left in my current prescription, so I went to the pharmacist and asked for my next refill, which comes in 90-day packs. They told me the insurance wouldn't authorize a refill because I wasn't due to need it yet, so I had to purchase the next 90 days at the non-insurance price of $320.

12. I bought as much ammunition as I could find for my two Glock .40 caliber pistols, my 12-gauge shotgun, and my AR-15. There was surprisingly little .223 ammo to be found, though. I bought all four of the boxes I found for sale.

13 I bought extra over-the-counter medications for the whole family.

14 I bought more canned food, juice boxes, and cereal bars.

15 We have two cats, so I also bought four bags of pet food.

While my wife was emailing our family members and getting everybody's plan straight, I loaded up her 4Runner and my parents' Yukon. The Yukon had a lot of miles on it, but it was huge, and could carry everything we thought we might need. Plus, it still worked okay. In fact, we'd had fewer problems with the Yukon than with my Nissan, so that was a good sign.

We watched the news some more, the outbreak spreading faster than I had expected, and then my wife asked the question both of us had been too scared to bring up.

"What are you going to do?"

She meant about my job. Technically, I was on scheduled leave. The Department had emergency mobilization procedures for bringing all its officers back on duty, but so far, that hadn't been done. I figured it would only be a matter of time.

"I don't know."

"Well, you better figure it out!" she shot back. I blinked at her in surprise. "You have a family, Joe. You have a wife and kids. Your place is here with us."

She was right, of course. But even still, I did take an oath, and I wouldn't be the man I know myself to be if I didn't make good on that oath.

We fought about that the rest of the night.

The Next Morning

We drove out to my parents' place and unpacked. The mood was light. As we'd hoped, our kids were treating it like a big adventure, a day away from school to spend with Nana and Grandpa. By tacit agreement, none of us spoke of the crisis in front of the children. The longer they could live in ignorance, we figured, the better.

One by one the rest of the family showed up, and soon we had all fallen into a casual bustle reminiscent of Thanksgiving Day. The mood was friendly and everybody was cooperative; it was nice.

Then my cell phone started ringing. Because I hold the rank of an administrator, I get regular emails and text messages any time a news-worthy event occurs. I had received a few that morning, but all were of the common variety—a shooting here and there, an overturned eighteen-wheeler, a gas main ruptured by construction workers.

And then the airport reported its first case. Despite heightened security throughout the airport, a woman had collapsed near the baggage claim carousel and had gone unnoticed for almost thirty minutes. Then she stood up, waded into a crowd of people near the baggage carousel, and bit and clawed sixteen people before she was subdued. Airport police were eventually forced to shoot her in the head, but not before a general panic ensued. According to the reports I was getting on my phone, the airport still wasn't secure.

Then I checked my messages.

"What is it?" my wife asked. "Are they asking you to come in?"

I nodded.

"Don't go," she said flatly.

"Tina, we talked about this."

"Yeah, we did. And I told you not to go."

"I have to."

"No, you don't. What you have to do is stay here with us. With your family, Joe."

It was quite a dilemma, my sworn oath or my family. I couldn't believe how torn I was. And the funny thing about it is that I've made that dilemma the thematic focus of much of my zombie fiction, yet when it came time to decide for myself, for real, I found that it was so much harder than I'd ever portrayed it in my books.

Tina and I went off to the barn where we could talk without the kids hearing. Good thing, too, because we both started yelling. We both yelled a lot.

Actually, I think the yelling made it easier for me to make up my mind to go into work, because when I left, I was angry with her for not understanding. I don't know exactly what I wanted her to say, or do, or not do...I just knew that yelling at me was like driving a wedge between us. I got out of there, and I couldn't get gone fast enough.

The Next Few Days

I run the 911 Call Center for the City of San Antonio. I tell people this, and sometimes it confuses them. "So, you're like a dispatcher?"

"No," I tell them. "I run the place. That means I'm in charge of all 170 civilian and sworn dispatchers, call takers, and radio technicians—all of them report to me. I decide how those resources are deployed, and when the system gets overloaded, I'm the one making the tough decisions.

When I came into work, I found things pretty much as bad as they could get. We were unable to get in touch with about sixty percent of our personnel. Most had probably already left town or were simply afraid to come into work because they would be away from their families. We were down to a skeleton crew, and most of those were already eighteen hours into shifts that should have only lasted eight.

Then the reports started coming in.

The incident at the airport had gotten completely out of hand. Hundreds, if not thousands, were thought to be infected.

San Antonio has almost a hundred hospitals of one size or another, and already a few of them were claiming cases of zombie infection. Soon one hospital after another closed its doors, refusing new patients.

Officers in the field were reporting cases of zombie infection, too. In the first four hours I was at the center I heard about eighteen officer-involved shootings over the radio.

But for all that, that first night was not so bad. It wasn't anything like I portrayed in my book *Dead City*. Cell phones kept working. The radios kept working. Traffic flowed heavy but in an orderly fashion. Slowly but steadily, the city started to empty as people headed for rural areas outside of town.

And, perhaps most importantly, order was maintained. Our officers made their calls, handled the long hours and the uncertainty and their own fear in the face of mounting complications. The Fire Department did their part too. I was up until three that morning, monitoring incoming calls and feeding status updates to the Command Staff, and when I finally slipped off to my office to sleep on my couch, I thought we pretty much had things in hand.

I was wrong.

One of the civilian supervisors woke me just before daylight. Things, she said, had gotten much worse.

I got a bottle of water from the mini fridge beneath my desk and listened as she ran it down for me:

1. San Antonio is a military town with several large military bases, and we were being told that they were taking over. San Antonio, as of 0630 hours, was under martial law;
2. During the night, at least four officers had been killed by zombies. Fifty-seven more had been dispatched to incidents but were now unaccounted for;
3. A roll call of all sworn personnel in the department had been taken so that accurate numbers could be given to the military authorities. Our total strength was 2,290 officers of all ranks, but our roll call was only able to account for 643 of those officers. The others were either dead or AWOL;
4. Stage III of the Department's Emergency Action Protocol had been declared, which basically meant that the situation had exceeded the ability of the combined resources of the San Antonio Police Department and the Bexar County Sheriff's Office;
5. I had been a police officer for nearly twenty years at that point, and I had never heard of us declaring a Stage III situation. We were entering into unknown territory.

But declaring a Stage III situation gave me the authority to lock the doors to the Communications Center. At this point, no one was getting in...or out. The personnel still inside the center were stuck here, basically chained to their jobs, like it or not. And suddenly the gun on my hip took on an ominous new implication. I could see my dispatchers looking at it out of the corners of their eyes, wondering if I would really use it on them or not. I thought of Tina out at my parent's place, and of my two little girls, who I missed desperately, and I prayed that none of those dispatchers would call my bluff and dare me to shoot them for abandoning their post.

Thankfully, none did.

Six Days Later

A week passed, during which time those of us in the 911 Center saw the city, and in fact the rest of the world, fall apart.

I snuck away regularly to call Tina. She told me that things were quiet at my parent's place. Power was still on, they had lots of food and fresh water, and the kids were bored but okay.

Morale was still high, she said.

But for the rest of the world, the news was not good. Most of the news channels had gone to loops, playing the same clips over and over, trying to cover up the fact they had nothing new to report. In a way, it reminded me of the morning of 9-11, with the TV newscasters grasping at every new bit of rumor or official statement and deconstructing it until nothing made sense.

And for the officers on the street, the zombie apocalypse had turned into a rolling gunfight that raged from one street to the next. Martial law had never really taken on, and officers who thought that they'd be doing patrol alongside soldiers soon found themselves standing alone against hordes of the living dead, like rocks in the middle of a fast-moving river, slowly being worn down and consumed.

San Antonio, like the rest of the world, was dying.

I made a choice.

I called all my dispatchers, all my call takers, into a huddle in the middle of the communications floor. As a student of Texas history, and especially of San Antonio history, I knew the story of Colonel William Travis, commander of the Alamo during the famous battle with Mexican General Santa Anna. Travis, facing certain defeat during the final hours of the battle, received a note from Santa Anna demanding surrender. Travis, of course, knew his own mind on this issue. He would die rather than give up his command. And being the good commander that he was, he knew the value of having his men reaffirm their commitment to the cause. So he called the Alamo defenders together, drew his sword, and drew a line in the sand. He then asked the defenders to step across the line and join him in the final, and almost certainly fatal, hours of the battle. All but one, a man named Moses Rose, joined him. Travis then released Moses Rose and gave Santa Anna his formal answer in the form of canon fire. The rest, as they say, is history.

I was hoping for an equally strong show of support among my staff. Unfortunately, I didn't get it. I drew my line in the sand, and then told the assembled crowd that anyone who crossed it was welcome to leave the building. They could go wherever fate might take them, and God bless them on their way.

At first, no one crossed. Then one did. Another followed. Then three more. Nine more. I stood there in disbelief as one by one they filed past me. In the end, I was left with four dispatchers and one call taker. The other twenty-two hung their heads and hurried out the back door, bound for God knows where. I never saw them again.

But once they were gone, I turned to my hangers on and said, "Thank you, all of you. Bless you." I think I was crying. I'm not sure. I only know that one by one the remaining few huddled around me and put their hands on me and kept telling me, over and over, that they were behind me one-hundred percent.

I nodded, and together they went back to their stations.

28 Days Later

Even the faithful can eventually realize that all is lost.

Though the power remained on, and the cell phones still worked, and we did okay surviving on food from the break room and the vending machines, all radio traffic had ceased. If there were officers still alive out there, they weren't paying attention to their radios. It had been four days since we'd heard anything from anyone, and the time had come to decide.

During the worst days of the Black Death, back in the Middle Ages, the English developed the Twenty-eight Days of Confinement Law. The basic import was this, if a member of your family came down with symptoms of the plague, your entire family was quarantined in your home for twenty-eight days, the length of one lunar cycle. At the end of the time, your front door was opened. If any persons were still alive, and symptom-free, they were allowed to rejoin society. I don't know it for a fact, but I suspect this was in the mind of the makers of the popular film franchise which takes its name from the Twenty-eight Days of Confinement Law.

Anyway, we had reached the end mark. There seemed no point in maintaining our post. There were no officers to dispatch, no news to relay to the Command Staff. Everyone was dead.

But still walking around.

I told my personnel that we had gone down with the ship. We had fought the good fight all the way to the end. There was no point in going on because there was no point left to make. We had done our duty.

The only thing left to do was to survive.

"I release you," I said. "By the authority vested in me by the City of San Antonio, I declare your duty faithfully fulfilled. God bless you as you go forth. You are dismissed, and honorably so."

Thankfully, no one made any stupid speeches. They simply nodded, and we filtered out into the white-hot brilliance of a San Antonio afternoon in late March.

I went to my vehicle and started it, thankful now that I had taken the time to fill it up and that I had made periodic trips out here over the last month to start it and keep the battery charged.

I looked at my cell phone, fully charged, and wanted to cry. It had been days since I'd been able to reach Tina on the phone. The closest I'd come was a voice mail, telling me that they'd decided to go to Montana, but the message had been punctuated by a scream and cut short.

There had been nothing else.

Desperate, I called Tina's number and outlined my plan. I was going to go by my parent's place first. If they were there, wonderful; if not, I'd gather what information I could and track them down.

But I thought I knew where they might be, where they would go if they could. Paradise Valley in Montana, the place where my dad and brother and I had gone on the vacation of our lives. It was a secluded paradise, a bulwark against the undead.

I had a wonderful memory of that place, looking down on an abandoned apple orchard from the sun deck of some friend of my dad's. The bears would come down and eat the apples on the ground, most of which had fermented, and by the time dusk rolled around they were drunk on rotten fruit. More than once I had watched as the wasted animals staggered off into the dark of Yosemite's forests.

And as I put my Nissan in gear and drove out, I had visions of watching those same bears with my daughters, laughing as they teetered off drunkenly into the darkness.

Please God, that's my only wish, my only prayer. Let them, and me, live to see that day.

Bury My Heart at Marvin Gardens

For Jon Michael Freiger
1978-2011

Jon rolls double fours. He lifts his marker, the old shoe, his favorite, from GO and drops it onto...

* * *

...Vermont Avenue, where the zombies are drifting thick as fog through the cracked and weedy streets, picking their way through the rusting hulks of abandoned cars, searching, always searching, for food. The mother catches sight of one in particular, broken arms swinging limply at his side, ribs showing through tatters of decomposing flesh, flies swarming about its head, and she's worried. She's seen these before, the wounded ones. The ones that can get around more or less on their own power are predictable. They come straight for you, attack without strategy. But the wounded ones, like this one, are far more dangerous. They hide. They wait. They become part of this desiccated world, one of its hidden dangers. She knows if she loses sight of him, he will surface again when she least expects it.

She sets the wheelbarrow down quietly and finds her daughter's hand. She squeezes the girl's hand, just to let her know everything is going to be okay. She doesn't believe this, but she knows she has to be strong for the child's sake, and so she squeezes encouragement.

The little girl meets her mother's gaze and smiles. It's a pretty smile, lots of healthy teeth. She's a pretty girl, too good for this world.

The mother surveys their surroundings and shudders. Everywhere she looks she sees a world in ruins. So many buildings have been reduced to rubble. But where the walls still stand, she sees exposed lath and standing garbage and doorways without doors. Not a window has gone unbroken. A sign that reads PEDESTRIAN CROSSING has been bent over and nearly flattened by an out-of-control vehicle that still rests in the ruins of a dress shop, busted glass all around it catching the oranges and scarlets of morning light like an explosion frozen in time. Inside the car is a corpse, motionless and decomposed, but probably only dormant. Given a reason, it could walk again.

In the wheelbarrow is the body of the woman's dead husband. The woman, on the night the man died, went to great trouble jamming an ice pick up the dead man's nose to make sure he wouldn't come back as one of them. It was an agreement between them, something she never wanted to think about, let alone do, but did anyway when the time came because she loved the man with a love so deep it made her ache inside. She still aches. She aches all the time. Even when she's numb, she aches. She's told the daughter none of this and has no intention of doing so. She's told the girl only of the dead man's enigmatic wish to have his heart buried at Marvin Gardens; though now, as she looks around at the wasted landscape that is Atlantic City, and watches as the dead man with the broken arms and the flies swarming about his head wanders off, she wonders why.

Why this place?

* * *

Jon buys Vermont Avenue. At $100, it's a no-brainer. The cheap properties on the first leg of the square are good buys. Purchase cheap, build hotels, gouge your opponent later. They are investments in the future. It is the strategy of a man who thinks long thoughts, who goes deep into the future of things.

That's Jon, the studied approach. The logical approach.

I am different. I am the wild-scramble opponent, the one who buys, buys, buys, and worries about building hotels later, once I see what I've got to work with.

We have never decided who is right, Jon and I.

He rolls a puny two-one combo, but it is enough to skip over Jail and land him at...

* * *

....St. Charles Place, where the weeds grow up through the sidewalks and the streets have buckled and blistered in the endless cycle of seasons since the world gave way to zombies.

There are no apartments here, no casinos, no hotels. This is an urban wasteland of vacant lots and mounds of trash and the occasional dog sniffing out a rat among the piles of lumber and brick dotting the landscape.

Nothing of any substance grows here.

Only grass and weeds.

And the woman carrying the wheelbarrow and the mysteries of good men dead and the little girl with her hand clasped tightly around her belt can only stare around in wonder and confusion and bootless anger at the injustice of it all.

Why here? she asks the corpse in front of her.

Why, for the love of God, here?

* * *

The game is just part of the reason I've asked Jon over here. I'm a little worried about my kids. They fight with each other constantly. Jon, he's a wizard at things like this. The man has a way of getting to the heart of things. He's made it his life's work, understanding people, and especially kids.

It's nothing serious, I tell him, nothing bad. They don't do drugs. They don't try to hurt themselves. Nothing like that.

"They're just little kids," I say. "I know that. But damn it, they fight like two little beta fish. Put 'em next to each other and the next thing you know, they're trying to claw each other's eyes out."

"Exactly," Jon says, and meets my questioning gaze and won't look away.

"Huh?"

"Exactly," he repeats. "It's nothing like that."

I shake my head. I know he's parroting what I've just said, like any good psychologist, but I don't understand.

"It's nothing like that," he repeats. "Not at all. They're good girls. They're your girls, part of you. They love you, and you love them."

"Yes...?" I hope he'll explain more.

"Remember that. Even when you're mad. Even when you feel like you're not getting through. They are part of you and you are part of them. You may not think you're getting through, but you're imprinting yourself on them. Years from now they won't remember why they fought, or even that they fought at all, but they will remember you. It's pretty simple, when you boil it down to what really matters."

I don't have an immediate response. It's true, every word. Everything he's said is right on the money. But it's a hard thing to remember when you're mad.

"It's your turn," I say.

* * *

On Illinois Avenue, the mother has to move quickly.

Screams, the sounds of fighting, fill the air.

She pushes the wheelbarrow between two ruined cars and pulls her child underneath the lead vehicle. From their hiding spot, they can see the street, smell the tinge of death on the morning breeze.

Soon the screams of rage and desperation turn to panic.

Whoever they are about to meet is close.

Very close.

A young woman, her left arm limp at her side and blood streaming down her body, runs into the street. Three men, zombies, stagger from an alley behind her. Fresh blood stains their mouths, and the mother knows they have just fed. They'll be strong. But they'll also be focused on the young woman.

The mother's heart is a good one, and it's telling her to go help the woman.

But she's smart, and her head is telling her to stay down, stay quiet, keep the child quiet. She has responsibilities, and they extend far beyond this moment.

The child whimpers as the zombies fall upon the woman.

The young woman's screams seem louder than any human could possibly make, and they go on and on and on. The mother can only put her face in the dust and hold her baby and tell herself that there must be a reason, there has to be a reason.

Or else nothing in life makes sense.

And it has to make sense.

It has to.

* * *

Jon buys Illinois Avenue for $240, looks at me, and smiles.

"You bastard," I say. He has just secured two-thirds of the board.

He raises his eyebrow, like Spock, only it's not a casual sign of surprise that the universe is not as logical as it should be, but a smug, self-satisfied gesture denoting imminent victory.

He knows he has me.

"You bastard," I say.

"Your turn," he says.

* * *

Jon has me over a barrel. He has both Boardwalk and Park Place, and I have surprisingly little. Not for the first time I wonder about the fickleness of luck.

"Damn it," I say. "I surrender."

He nods. He's not above enjoying a victory.

"A pity, though," he says.

"What?"

He nods at the board. "Nobody got Marvin Gardens. I've always wondered about that place."

* * *

The mother has studied this place, she knows the history of Illinois Avenue, because this isn't the first time she's wondered about her husband's fascination with Atlantic City. She knows how the city started as a dream, a conversation among wealthy investors and railroad tycoons on a lonely, wind-swept beach, and how it ended as a nightmare.

Like the rest of the world.

Like her own life.

She knows that the city died long before the rest of the world fell beneath the relentless tread of the walking dead. The zombies are really only an afterthought to this place. They are the symbols of a world that has moved on, but they are redundant here. This place needs no reminder of the glory of the past, or of the wasteland that is the modern age.

She looks down at the body in the wheelbarrow, the man whose eyes had shown such surprise, such fear, such unknowable depth, at the time of his passing, and who were now closed against all time, and she wondered what was in his mind when he asked to be buried at Marvin Gardens.

Did he see the old world splendor that R. B. Osborne saw back in 1852 when he glibly described his vision to his investors, his pen scribbling out the names of the city to be—Oriental Avenue, States Avenue, Tennessee Avenue, New York Avenue, Pennsylvania Avenue? Or did he see the world of Charles B. Darrow, who stole the game of Monopoly from Lizzie Magie, daughter of the prophet of the single tax theory?

It is hard to tell, for her husband, who was so kind, so intelligent, so impossibly giving, was also—sometimes frustratingly so—an enigma to her.

She looks at the only map of the city she has, an old Monopoly game board, and doesn't understand. She wonders if she ever will.

Why this place?

Why would he want his heart buried at Marvin Gardens?

*   *   *

The crowd of zombies seems to materialize out of nowhere. One moment, the mother is putting on her brave face for her daughter, telling her how they are going to bury Daddy in his favorite place, and the next she is ducking for cover, pulling her daughter close to her breast.

She'd been forced to leave the wheelbarrow out in the open, and that made her mad. It seemed like a failure somehow, like leaving him was a weakness on her part, something she didn't do right. But the zombies don't like dead flesh. They rarely touch a corpse, even a fresh one, and so it's a chance she feels she can take.

The zombies pass the wheelbarrow. They hardly seem to notice it. One by one, they shuffle by, dragging their feet, pulling their weight endlessly through a world without meaning, without purpose, without even the hint of redemption. Even the grave is an empty promise for these dead ones.

Then one of the zombies stumbles—and howls in pain.

Mother and daughter raise their heads above the tall weeds where they've taken shelter, searching for the injured one.

Zombies don't make noises like that.

They damage themselves all the time, tearing hands and arms reaching through shattered windows, shredding bare feet on busted glass, and then they get up and walk away. Soundlessly. No emotion, no pain, no nothing.

But this one...he is standing up, holding his bleeding wrist in his other hand.

One by one, the dead turn their heads slowly in his direction.

Faker, the mother thought, and pushed her daughter's head back down into the tall weeds. She has seen fakers before. They live by pretending they are one of the dead, by walking among the dead. They live, if it can be called living, by abandoning all sense of self, by surrendering completely to the emptiness and pointlessness that is death in life, death on two feet. They live by giving up.

Her husband hated these people.

She looks down at his corpse, the runner of dried blood from his left nostril where she drove in the ice pick to keep him from coming back as a zombie, and she sees a man who lived his life like every moment mattered, who understood the importance of his life, even if he didn't fully grasp its meaning. His life stood for something, and his death was painful, and too soon, for the truly good are always gone too soon.

She looks again to the street. Already the zombies are closing in around the faker, moaning, clutching at the air in anticipation of the kill, and she feels nothing but disgust. Her husband never would have given up like that. Never.

She watches the man sink to his knees. She watches him drop his head to his chest rather than lash out with the last breath he has. The mother cradles the child's head in her hands, covering her eyes. But she herself does not look away, because what's going on out there reminds her so much of how strong her husband was, and how much is gone from the world.

She doesn't like it, doesn't want to admit it, but the faker's silent acceptance of death makes her feel a powerful sense of pride in her husband.

He had been a man worth having.

* * *

Our second game has gone down smoothly, like a fine whisky.

As usual, Jon has picked up a lot properties through his slow and studied method. But it has cost him. He has property, but little development, and he has next to no cash in reserve.

I, on the other hand, am sitting pretty. Fat on cash.

I have three houses on Pacific Avenue, and when he lands there and counts his cash, he has no choice but to concede.

"Too bad I didn't land on Marvin Gardens," he says.

I look up as I clear the board.

"I like Marvin Gardens," he says, catching the look in my eye. "It's special."

I wait for more, but it doesn't come.

After a pause, I finish clearing the board.

* * *

The mother knows what's coming, even before she passes the jail. She can hear the zombies banging their fists against the chain-link fence. She can hear the musical clanging it makes, even over the awful moaning of the dead.

She doesn't look at them as she passes down the alleyway. They are sticking their shredded fingers through the diamond-patterned wire, surging against it, pressing against it with the combined weight of their dead bodies, but she ignores them. All she does is move her daughter to her other side, putting herself between the little girl and the hungry dead.

The little girl is brave. She doesn't shrink or break down, the way some adults the mother has seen have done. This makes her proud.

But the thing that really strokes her pride is the way the little girl hitches her backpack up onto her shoulders, looks up, and smiles.

So young, and so brave.

It's then that the zombies break through the fence. It had seemed so secure just seconds ago, but now it's leaning into the alley like a drawbridge caught on the way down, and the dead are pouring over it, filling the alley behind her.

And now, in front of her.

The mother has no choice. She gently lowers the wheelbarrow. Even in death she can't imagine dropping him. Then, before the child can speak a word, she scoops her into her arms and runs, leaving the body of the man she loves in the middle of the alley.

He'll be safe.

The dead don't attack the dead.

The mother finds a bakery with a large oven and puts her daughter in it. Deer hide their yearlings in the tall grass, she remembers from the years she lived in the Texas Hill Country. Perhaps it will work now.

And some atavistic impulse seems present in the daughter as well, for she understands without words. She doesn't ask questions, but instead sinks into the darkness at the back of the oven. From the depths, her brown eyes seem to shine like jewels under halogen vapor lights. She is so vulnerable, so beautiful, so incredibly trusting.

The mother hopes she knows what she's doing.

"I'll be right back," she says. "I'm going to get Daddy."

She slips off her own backpack and removes a collapsible police baton she got from a friend during the early days of the outbreak. She snaps it open and circles back around the City Jail so she can re-enter from the other side.

When she steps back into the alley, she sees a small group of zombies gathered around her husband's corpse.

They seem uncertain, but interested, as though they just might fall upon the body. When one of them lifts her husband's hand and tries to put it in his mouth, the woman rushes in like a fury and swings at every face and hand that tries to close upon her. It's a fast job, a messy job, and she hardly registers the dull crack of flesh-covered bone, the give of skulls caving beneath the baton.

And when it's done, she jams the baton down on the pavement and collapses it with a sharp smack.

She looks around. Nothing else moves.

Then she picks up the wheelbarrow that holds her husband's body and carts him out of the alley.

* * *

We're thirty minutes into our third game and I have Jon handily by the throat. Pacific, North Carolina and Pennsylvania are dull properties, never seeming to gather much action, but they are the only properties I have left without hotels and so I start to develop them.

Jon, realizing he's beat, concedes.

* * *

The woman is looking down North Carolina Avenue, into the heart of the city. It is a vast ruin of empty buildings and darkened windows. This could be a war zone, abandoned to the scavengers. It looks that bad. Roofs have fallen. Bricks are strewn about as though thrown by an explosion. But this isn't some military scar. This city, this collection of empty buildings, is the product of decay, a complex rune speaking of all things past.

Dark clouds are rolling in off the sea, turning the sky to a washed-out gray. The wind carries sand down the cracked and buckled street, lifting it like curtains dancing on the wind, and the city seems so lonely, almost sublime in its desolation. Again she wonders why his last wish has brought her here. What could he have possibly seen in this world?

He was a kind man, a caring man, who knew that there is a presence moving in the background of our lives. That presence is hard to fathom, especially now, especially since her husband's death, but it is there. She can feel it. Her husband never doubted it. And because of that conviction, she knows there must be a reason.

"Momma, you're all gross."

The woman looks down at her daughter, her voice surprising her out of her thoughts.

"What?"

The girl points at the spattered gore on the woman's jeans, the clumps of blood and brain left from when she fought the zombies off her husband's corpse.

She wipes her palm across her shirt, clearing away the dirt and sweat and grime before taking her daughter's hand and giving it another reassuring squeeze. "We're gonna be okay," she says, and in her soul she tries to believe it, because she has to. She needs this one truth to be real.

She takes out the game board she's been using as a map, her gaze darting back and forth between the cartoon board and the sea of ruin before her, and she's confused. Marvin Gardens must be here somewhere. According to the board, it should be right here.

* * *

We've started our fourth game. Most people think Monopoly takes forever to play, but with just two players, and a deep understanding of its finer points, you can finish off a game in less than twenty minutes and still stay soundly within the rules.

This one is going fast, and Jon's luck is getting on my nerves. He takes Boardwalk and Park Place. He looks at me, sees me scowling, and laughs.

To lighten my mood, he asks about my writing. "More zombies?"

"Yep. And death cults too."

"Cool."

I like discussing horror with Jon. He gets it. After reading a rough draft of my first novel, he told me zombies were the perfect means to reinvent the world and all its problems. They're entirely metaphorical, more so than any other monster in fiction, and because of that, they can represent any societal issue or any personal crisis. They turn the real horrors into a fictional plaything we can around which we can wrap our minds.

As I said, he gets it.

But meanwhile there is still a game to be played, and I've just landed on Ventnor Avenue, where he has four houses.

"Stop smiling," I say, and concede.

* * *

Game five is our tie-breaker. We race around the board, and I get Ventnor and Atlantic Avenues, and then Water Works. Only Marvin Gardens remains unclaimed.

Jon looks worried.

* * *

The woman stands in the shadows of a movie-theater entrance, watching a death cult make its way down the street. These people she understands even less than the fakers. At least the fakers are a known quantity. Their motivation is simple. Death terrifies them so much that they're willing to embrace it in order to hold it at bay. She can understand fear. And she can understand—even though it disgusts her—why some people are willing to give up on their lives in order to keep them.

But these people, these death cults, they are a mystery.

She has heard of them in other cities. They believe that the zombies are a means to set the soul free. The zombies are prophets, they claim, and they welcome the act of getting slaughtered as though it were communion.

This cult is made up of a dozen people, walking two abreast down the street. They seem eerily content and unworried. They are happy to die.

Zombies stagger out of doorways, peel themselves away from the insides of abandoned cars, and close in on the cult.

Screams come with the killing, but they are not screams of pain. When the woman realizes this, she is truly and utterly horrified. These people are in love with their own slaughter, and for them it is some kind of grotesque joy. It is spiritual. It seems vile to her, obscene somehow.

"Come on," the woman says to her daughter. She takes up the wheelbarrow again and slips away.

* * *

Jon takes his fourth railroad, but looks disappointed.

"What's wrong?" I ask. He's pulling ahead, and the tie breaker that

I thought was mine seems to be tilting in his direction.

"I want Marvin Gardens," he says. "I keep missing it."

"You said that before. What's so special about it?"

"It's the only place on the board that isn't a real location in Atlantic City."

"Really?" I look at the board. I didn't know this. I've loved this game since I was a little boy, and I never knew. I wonder why they'd put it there if it isn't really there."

"Well, it's a mystery, isn't it?"

* * *

The woman and child have made it to the Boardwalk. The long pier extends far into the Atlantic, which has grown irritable from the weather.

"Momma?" the girl says. "Where do we go now?"

The woman has no idea. None of this makes sense. Why would he make this request of her, and why can't she find Marvin Gardens?

Acting almost on autopilot, she pushes the wheelbarrow out to the end of the pier, and stops before a bronze plaque featuring a raised relief of Charles B. Darrow, inventor of the game of Monopoly. Briefly she considers asking Darrow where she might find Marvin Gardens, but doesn't want to scare the little girl. No need to make her think Momma's lost her mind.

A strong wind gusts off the water and shoves her roughly to one side. She staggers, and the wheelbarrow topples over, spilling its precious cargo onto the pier.

The woman looks at her husband sprawled there, and she finally breaks down. She sits beside him. She's tired. She has no way of lifting him back into the wheelbarrow. Not now. Not like this. She doesn't know what to do.

She hears footsteps on the planks behind her.

The woman jumps to her feet and wheels to face the intruder, pulling her daughter behind her.

But it's an old man, not a zombie. She relaxes, but only a little. There are other dangers in the world besides the walking dead. But the man makes no move to attack. He actually looks kind. He's dressed in a full-length black coat, the collar pulled up tightly against a scarred cheek. The brim of a floppy old hat shields gray, weathered eyes.

"Let me help you," he says.

Together, they right the wheelbarrow.

There is another gust of wind and then the rain starts to fall. "We need to get under shelter," he says. He's holding his hat down on his head as he nods toward a nearby arcade. The inside is dark, but dry. "In there," he says.

She reaches for the wheelbarrow, but he puts a hand on her wrist.

"No," he says, "leave him here."

She wants to object. At first it seems like a gross disrespect of the man she loved—and still loves—with all her being. But as the rain turns to silvery sheets curling on the wind, it suddenly seems right to her, and the three of them run for the cover of the arcade.

The little girl knows the routine. They won't be going anywhere for a while, so she removes her backpack and sits on the ground and busies herself with the few belongings they've been able to carry with them.

"Thank you," the woman says to the man.

He nods, says nothing. The man removes his coat and hat and shakes the water from them.

"Can you help us?" the woman says. "We're trying to find Marvin Gardens."

The man looks up from his clothes and a strange smile tugs at the corners of his mouth. "There is no Marvin Gardens," he says. "Not here, anyway. Not in Atlantic City."

The woman is floored by this. Her first instinct is to get angry. She's been lied to, made a fool of. Why would her husband do this to her? Why would he send her on an errand like this, wandering a blasted land with only a stupid board game for a map? It doesn't make sense.

"Bubbles!"

The woman shakes her head, clearing her thoughts. Dozens of tiny bubbles are rising from the floor, filling the air around her head. She looks down and sees her daughter clapping her hands and giggling wildly as her little bubble-making machine whirs.

One bubble in particular drifts past the woman's nose. She focuses on it, and she's startled by its beauty. The way it shimmers and catches the light like a diamond. It is geometric perfection. It is a delicate thing, like a flower, or a life; and it is, she realizes, the most perfect, the most beautiful thing she's ever seen.

It explodes suddenly—even over the pounding rain she swears she hears a faint, muffled pop. It's gone.

She stares at the empty air where it once floated, but she isn't seeing the air. She's actually looking inward, and backward, across the years. Images of her husband crowd her mind, and though she doesn't realize she's doing it, she's smiling, for he lives there, whole and perfect, a part of her soul that will never die.

But what of this crazy quest he's sent her on? What of that?

He knew there was no Marvin Gardens here. He had to have known. Her husband was crazy smart that way. This was deliberate. Not a cruel trick. He wasn't that kind of man.

There is a lesson here. Something she is meant to understand.

But what?

And then she thinks of the bubble, how it was beautiful, and then gone. And she thinks of this world, how it too was once a thing of beauty.

It dawns on her all at once, understanding swelling inside her chest like a balloon until she can barely breathe, barely contain it. He gave her an impossible quest, not because he expected her to fail, but because he knew she would succeed. She would come to this point. The old world is gone, and though the new world, the world without him, is a little emptier, it is still a place for beauty, and a place to raise the little girl who is so much like her daddy.

She looks out across the rain-swept pier, to where her husband's body faces the open ocean, unknowable in its vastness, and she thinks again of bubbles.

And smiles.

Zombies and Their Haunts

For as long as I can remember, I've thrilled at the sight of abandoned buildings. Something about those dark, empty windows, the vacant doorways, the sepulchral quiet of an empty train station or hotel lobby, spoke of discontinuity and of the slow, relentless violence of passing time. There was a vacancy in those wrecks that evoked loss and heartache and the memory of dreams that have fallen by the wayside. They were a sort of negative space in the landscape, symbols of our world's mortality.

And then zombies came along, and I fell in love with them for many of the same reasons.

But here's the thing.

It took me a while—as a writer I mean—to figure out that abandoned buildings, and even abandoned cities, don't just appear because a horde of zombies happen to show up. Sure, most everybody gets eaten, and so you end up with a lot of buildings and very few people, but it goes a little deeper than that. Zombies and abandoned buildings, it seems to me, are actually two sides of the same coin. Aside from the obvious similarity—that they are both miserable wrecks somehow still on their feet—both are symbols of a world that is at odds with itself and looking for new direction. And in that way, zombies merge symbolically with the abandoned buildings they haunt in ways that other monsters never really achieve with the settings of their stories.

But just because the zombie and the abandoned building are intimately related symbols doesn't mean that they function in exactly the same way.

Consider the abandoned building first.

When a building dies, it becomes an empty hull, and yet it does not fall. At least not right away. Its hollow rooms become as silent as the grave, but when you enter it, its desolate inner spaces somehow still hum with the collected sediment of the life that once thrived there.

When we look at graffiti scrawled across fine Italian marble tiles, or a filthy doll face-up in a crumbling warehouse parking lot, or weeds growing up between the desks in a ruined schoolhouse, we're not just seeing destruction. We're also seeing what once was, and what could be again. In other words, we're seeing past, present, and future all at the same time.

The operative force at work here is memory. Within the mind, memory bridges the gulf between past, present, and future. But in our post-apocalyptic landscapes, our minds need a mnemonic aid...and that aid is the abandoned building. The moldering wreck forces us to consciously engage in the process of temporal continuity rather than simply stumble through it blindly.

Put another way, we become an awful lot like Wordsworth daydreaming over the ruins of Tintern Abbey. Like Wordsworth, we're witnessing destruction, but pondering renovation, because we are by nature a creative species that needs to reshape the world in order to live in it. That is our biological imperative.

And so, in the end, the abandoned building becomes a symbol of creative courage.

But now consider the abandoned building's corollary, the zombie.

Zombies are, really, single-serving versions of the apocalypse. Apocalyptic stories deal with the end of the world. Generally speaking, they give us a glimpse of the world before catastrophe, which becomes an imperfect Eden of sorts. They then spin off into terrifying scenarios for the end of the world. And finally, we see the survivors living on, existing solely on the strength of their own wills. There are variations within the formula, of course, but those are the nuts and bolts of it.

When we look at the zombie, we get the same thing—but in

microcosm. We see the living person prior to death, and this equates to the world before the apocalypse (or the ghost of what the abandoned building used to be). We see the living person's death, and this equates to the cataclysmic event that precipitates the apocalypse (or the moldering wreck of an abandoned building). And finally, we see the shambling corpse wandering the wasteland in search of prey, and this equates to the post-apocalyptic world that is feeding off its own death.

It is in this final note that the symbolic functions of the abandoned building and the zombie diverge. As I've mentioned, the abandoned building, so long as it stands, calls to our creative instincts to rebuild. But the zombie, so long as it stands, speaks only to our ultimate mortality.

And so, the ruined hotel or office park becomes our mind's cathedral, the spiritual and creative sanctuary of our memory, while the zombie becomes the devil that drives us out of it.

I see a satisfying sense of symmetry there.

The Day the Music Died

"But this changes everything," Isaac Glassman said. "You see that, right? I mean, you gotta see that. We can't... I mean, Steve, you can't... I mean, shit, he's dead. Tommy Grind is dead! How can you say nothing's changed?"

"Isaac," I said, "calm down. This isn't that big of a deal."

He huffed into the phone. "Great. You're making fun of me now. I'm talking about the death of the biggest rock star since The Beatles, and you're cracking jokes. I'm telling you, Steve, this is fucking tragic."

I let out a tired sigh. I should have known that Isaac was going to be a problem. Lawyers are always a problem. He'd been with us since Tommy's first heroin-possession charge back in 2002. That little imbroglio kept us in the LA courts for the better part of a year, but we got *The Cells of Los Angeles* album out of it, which went double platinum, so at least it hadn't been a total disaster. And Tommy was so happy with Isaac Glassman that he added him to the payroll. I objected. I looked at Isaac and I saw a short, unkempt, Quasimodo-looking guy in a cheap suit in the midst of a school-girl's crush. He's in love with you, I told Tommy. And I mean in the creepy way. But Tommy laughed it off. He said Isaac was just star-struck. It'd wear off after a few months.

I knew he was wrong about Isaac even then.

Just like I knew Isaac was going to be trouble now.

Behind me, behind the Plexiglas screen I installed across the entrance to Tommy's private bedroom after he'd overdosed and died from whatever the hell kind of mushroom it was he took, Tommy was finishing up on the arm of a groupie I'd brought him. The girl was a seventeen-year-old nobody, a runaway. I'd met her outside a club on Austin's 6th Street two nights earlier.

"Hey," I asked her, "you wanna go get high with Tommy Grind?" The girl nearly beat me to my car. And now, after two days of eating on the old, long pig, Tommy was almost done with her. There'd be some cleanup, femurs, a skull, a mandible, stuff like that, but nothing a couple of trash bags and some cleaning products wouldn't be able to handle. Long as the paparazzi didn't go through the garbage, things'd be fine.

I turned my attention back to the phone call with Isaac.

"Look," I said. "This isn't a tragedy, okay? Stop being such a drama queen. And secondly, The Beatles weren't *a* rock star. They were *four* rock stars. A group, you know? It's a totally different thing."

"Jesus, this really is a joke to you, isn't it?" Now he sounded genuinely hurt.

"No, it's not a joke." I looked over my shoulder at Tommy. He was at the barrier, looking at me, bloody hands smearing the Plexiglas, a rope of red muscle—what was left of the girl's triceps—hanging from the corner of his mouth. I said, "I'm deathly serious about this, Isaac."

"Yeah, well, that's comforting."

"It should be. Look, I'm telling you, I got this under control."

"He's a zombie, Steve. How can you possibly have that under control?"

Tommy was banging on the Plexiglas now. One hand slapping on the barrier. I could hear him groaning.

"He's a rock star, Isaac. Nothing's changed. He's a zombie now, so what? Hell, I bet Kid Rock's been a zombie since 2007."

"So what? *So what?* Steve, I saw him last night, eating that girl. He looked horrible. People are gonna know he isn't right when they see him."

For the last three years or so, Tommy Grind and Tom Petty had been in a running contest to see who could be the grungiest middle-aged rock star in America. Up until Tommy died and then came back as one of the living dead, I would have said Tom Petty had him beat. Now, I don't know. They were probably tied.

"Nobody's gonna know anything," I said into the phone. "Look, I've been his manager for twenty years now, ever since he was a renegade cowboy singing the beer joints in South Houston. I sign all the checks. I make all the booking arrangements and the recording deals and handle the press and get him his groupie girls for him to work out his sexual frustrations on. I got this covered. The show'll go on, just like it always has."

"Yeah, except now he's eating the groupies, Steve." I thought I heard a wounded tone in his voice. He hadn't liked to hear about Tommy's other playthings, even before he'd started eating them.

"True," I said.

"How're you gonna cover that up? I mean, there's gonna be bones and shit left over."

"We'll be careful," I said.

"Careful?"

"Get him nobodies, like this girl he's got now. Girls nobody'll miss. The streets are loaded with 'em."

I turned and watched Tommy picking the girl's hair out of his teeth with a hand that wouldn't quite work right. No more guitar work, that's for sure. But then, that was no big deal. He had a cameo in *Guitar Hero XXI*. Tommy Grind's reputation was secure, even if he never played another note.

Finally, Isaac said, "Did he finish that girl yet?"

Good boy, Isaac, I thought.

"Yeah," I said. "Just a little while ago."

"Oh." He hesitated, then said, "And you're sure we can do this? We can just go on like nothing's happened?"

"Absolutely," I said.

Tommy was always prolific. He wasn't much for turning out a polished product—that part we left to the session musicians and Autotuner people to clean up—but the man had had the music in him. He'd spent fifteen hours a day playing songs and singing and just banging around in the studio we built for him in the west wing of the mansion. Just from what I'd heard walking through the house recently, I figured we had enough for three more full-length albums.

It'd just be a matter of having the studio people clean it up. They were used to that. Business as usual when you work for Tommy Grind.

Isaac said, "Steve?"

"Yeah?"

"Can I...can I come over and see him?"

"You're not gonna screw this up, are you? No whistle blowing, right?"

"Right," he said. "I promise. I just want to see him."

"Sure, Isaac. Come on over any time."

* * *

"And this is how he's gonna live? I mean, I know he's not alive, but this is how it's gonna be?"

"For now," I said.

Isaac didn't look too happy about that. He was watching Tommy Grind through the Plexiglas, bottom lip quivering like he was about to cry. He put his fingers on the barrier and sniffled as Tommy worked on another groupie.

"He looks kind of...dirty."

"He's a rock star, Isaac. That's part of the uniform."

"But shouldn't we keep him clean or something? I mean, he's been in those same clothes since he died. I can smell him out here."

He had a point there, actually. Tommy was starting to reek. His skin had gone sallow and hung loose on his face. There were open sores on his hands and arms. The truth was I was too scared to change his clothes for him. I didn't want to catch whatever that mushroom had done to him.

"How many girls are in there with him?" Isaac asked.

"Two."

"Just two?" Isaac said, shaking his head in disbelief. "But there's so many, uh, body parts."

"His appetite's getting stronger," I agreed. "He regularly takes two girls at a time now, sometimes three. So, when you think about it, he's actually back to where he was before he died."

"That's not funny, Steve."

I didn't like the milquetoast look he was giving me. I said, "Don't you dare flake out on me, you hear? Between the record sales and the movie deals and video-game endorsements and all the rest of it, Tommy Grind is a one–hundred-and-forty-million-dollar-a-year corporation. I'm not about to let that fall apart because of this."

"Is that what this is about to you, the money? That's all you care about? What about Tommy? What about what he stood for?"

I laughed.

"Tommy stood for sex, drugs, and rock and roll. That was the world to him."

"His music was the soundtrack for my life, Steve. It means something."

"Bullshit," I said. "It means he liked his women horny, his drugs psychotropic, and his music loud. That was all Tommy Grind ever wanted. Now, all he wants is food. The way I see it, we're good."

"We should let him out. Let him get some sunshine."

"Yeah, right," I said. "Isaac, the paparazzi hide in the bushes across the street just praying for a chance to shoot Tommy Grind while he's smoking a joint on the lawn. You have any idea how bad that would be to take him out for a stroll? No, if we're gonna bring him out into the world, we need to do it under controlled circumstances."

He nodded, then leaned his forehead against the barrier and watched the love of his life pop a finger into his mouth. Smaller parts like that he could eat whole.

"Listen," I said, "you want a drink?"

"No, thank you. You go ahead. I'm just gonna sit here for a while and watch him."

I shrugged. "Whatever. I'll be out in the hot tub."

I made myself a whiskey over shaved ice and dropped in an orange slice for garnish. Then I stripped and climbed into the hot tub and let the jets massage my back. The hot tub was outside, but the little courtyard where it was located was covered with ivy to prevent helicopters from peaking in on Tommy's private parties, which were the stuff of legend. One of last year's parties had included half a dozen A-list porn stars and a pile of cocaine the size of an old lady's hat.

I took a couple of phone calls and arranged for a cover of Eddie Money's "I Think I'm In Love," that Tommy had done in his studio a month before he died, to appear on *That's What I Call Music, Volume 153*.

As was I finishing, I heard screams from the front lawn. I told the guy from Capitol I had to go, hung up, jumped out of the hot tub.

Fucking Isaac, I thought. *You better not have....*

But he had. The little idiot had gone and let Tommy out of his bedroom and taken him for a walk down on the front lawn.

When I got there, clothes soaked through and my feet squishing in my shoes, Tommy was staggering around in the middle of the street, a team of terrified paparazzi gathered around him, snapping pictures. The flashes were making Tommy disoriented, and he was swiping the air in a futile attempt to grab the photographers.

I waded into the crowd and grabbed Tommy by the back of his black T-shirt and guided him toward the lawn. I looked around and saw Isaac standing on the curb, a drooping question mark in a cheap blue suit.

"You get him inside," I growled at Isaac.

"I'm sorry," he said. "I just wanted to—"

"Go!" I said. "Now."

He led a reluctant Tommy back to the house. I watched him get most of the way to the front door, my mind scrambling for a way to explain all this, then I turned to the crowd and said, "Okay, people, listen up. Come on, gather around."

Thirty photographers just looked at me.

"What the hell, people? You don't recognize a press conference when you see one? Gather around."

That did it. Soon I was standing in the middle of a tight ring of bodies, cameras rolling.

"All right," I said, "we were hoping to save this announcement for the Grammy's, but clearly Tommy Grind wanted to give you guys a sneak peak. Tommy has just completed his first screenplay. It's called *The Zombie King*, and I just got word from our people in Hollywood that it's a go for next fall. We'll be shooting here in Austin starting around the end of September."

"A horror film?" one of the paparazzi said.

"That's right. And it's gonna be Tommy's directorial debut, too."

"So, that was... what? A costume?"

"Look," I said, and sighed for effect, "what do you think is gonna happen when you give a rock star access to a stable full of professional makeup artists? I mean, we've all seen Lady Gaga, right?"

That got a few laughs. I passed out business cards to everybody and told them to send me an email so I'd have their addresses for future press releases.

They scattered after that to email their photos to their contacts, and I went inside to kick Isaac's ass.

* * *

A few weeks later, in early February, I was back in the hot tub, helping another untraceable young lady out of her bikini for a little warm up before she went in to see Tommy. I was sitting on the edge of the tub, and the girl came over and positioned herself between my legs and put her cheek down on my thigh. The drugs in her drink were already starting to take effect, and I had to nudge her a little to get her to pay attention to what she was supposed to be doing.

She had just gotten to it when Isaac Glassman walked through the sliding glass door.

"Jesus, Isaac," I said, covering up my junk. "What the hell, man?"

"Sorry," he said. "But we have to talk."

The girl had pulled away from me and sunk down to her chin in the water. She wouldn't look at either one of us, even though it was a day late and a dollar short for any pretense at modesty at that point.

"Do you mind?" Isaac said, and pointed at the girl with his chin.

The girl's eyelids were drooping shut. I jumped in, caught her just as her face slid under the water, and pulled her out.

"Help me get her out of here," I said to Isaac.

He reached in and took one arm, and I took the other. We pulled her onto her back on the side of the tub. She had great tits, I thought absently. A pity.

I climbed out and slid into my trunks.

"This better be good," I said.

"What are you gonna do with her?"

"What do you think? You're gonna help me drag her into Tommy's room. Then he's gonna eat her."

"But you were gonna have her first?"

"I think Tommy's past the point of jealousy."

He was uncomfortable, stared at his shoelaces, then at the ivy-covered walls behind me. Then, finally, at me. "That's what I want to talk to you about," he said.

"Oh?"

"Yeah. I don't... I don't like the direction you're taking Tommy's career. The Eddie Money cover—"

"Has been number one on the Billboard charts for two weeks in a row. What are you trying to say?"

"That's not the point," he said.

Not the point? *Not the point!* I couldn't believe it. The little geek had the gall to stand there and tell me he didn't like my decisions. Christ, what did he know? The song was doing great. The critics were calling its stripped-down acoustic arrangement and gravelly-voiced lyrics a masterstroke from one of rock's greatest performers. Industry experts were already anticipating Tommy Grind's fourteenth Grammy, which I would accept on his behalf in just a few weeks.

"Tell me, Isaac. What is the point? I gotta hear this."

"It's a cover song, Steve."

"Yeah, a fucking successful one, too."

"But it's a cover song. Tommy Grind never did cover songs. It was always *his* music, *his* vision. That's what made him so special. That's why people loved him."

"Oh Jesus," I said.

"Seriously, Steve."

"You're so full of shit, you know that? You don't live in the house with him, Isaac. You never heard him playing in there, in his studio. The guy would sit in there and play cover tunes all day long. He loved 'em."

"That's because he loved the music, Steve. He played what made him feel good. But when he put his music out there for the world, it was always his own stuff. Don't you see?"

No, you little dweeb, I don't see.

I had managed to get together a lot more original songs off of Tommy's studio tapes than I first thought. We had enough for another eight, maybe nine albums. More if I included the cover tunes he loved so much. And it was good stuff, too. Plus, he had tons of live recordings from the heavy touring he did from 2003 to early 2008. I was thinking of putting together a double live album to go along with a DVD release of his Hollywood Bowl concert last August, maybe a viral marketing campaign on the web. Michael Jackson had been a bigger hit dead than alive, and it was looking Tommy Grind was going to be even bigger.

"What is it you're accusing me of?" I said. "You think I'm selling him out? Is that it?"

It took him a moment to work up the courage, but finally he squared his shoulders at me and said, "Well, yeah, I do. I guess that's exactly what I'm saying."

It took all the self-control I had to keep from killing him right there where he stood. I felt my face flush with anger.

Maybe he saw it too, because he took a step back.

"You listen to me," I said. "Nobody accuses me of selling Tommy Grind out. Nobody. You don't have that right. You jumped on this gravy train after it had already worked itself up to full speed. But me? I've been with him since the beginning. I was with him in Houston when he was working two daytime jobs and playing all night long in the clubs. I'm the one who got him his first radio time. I'm the one who made the club owners pay up. And when he got drunk and wanted to fight the cowboys who threw beer bottles at him in the middle of his sets, I was the one who stood back to back with him and got my knuckles bloody. So don't you stand there and think you know more about Tommy Grind's vision than I do. I'm the one who told him what his fucking vision was."

That cowed him. He stood there with his eyes fixed on his shoes, and it looked like he was about to cry. For a second there I thought he was going to run from the room like a scalded hound. But he suddenly showed more backbone than I knew he possessed. He raised his almost non-existent chin and looked me square in the eyes.

"What?" I said.

"You're the one telling Tommy what his vision is?"

"That's right."

"Well, good. Because I just talked Jessica Carlton's attorney over lunch. She heard your bit about *The Zombie King*, and she wants in."

"*The Zombie King...*"

"Yeah. The movie you told the press Tommy had just written. Remember that?"

"Yeah," I said, and looked down at the naked girl at my feet. I had almost forgotten she was there.

Jessica Carlton, damn. The bubble-headed blonde who broke onto the scene a few years back claiming to be as virginally pure as Amy Grant but had no qualms whatsoever shaking her ass for every camera from LA to Hamburg. The claims to virginal purity passed away unnoticed right about the time her first movie came out and she rose to the status of tabloid-cover starlet, which if you ask me was a brilliant piece of marketing. Now she was on the cover of just about every magazine in the grocery-store checkout line. The last I heard she was dating an NFL quarterback, was doing a new album, and even had another movie deal on the table. She had the goods, definitely. And if she said she wanted to be in Tommy's movie, well, there was no easy way to refuse that. People would ask questions. *People Magazine* would ask questions.

"That's a problem, right?"

"Yeah," I said. "That's a problem."

* * *

And a week later, I still didn't have a solution. The Eddie Money cover had slipped down to number fourteen on the countdown, but we were prepping a new single—a Tommy Grind original—and that would be out in another three weeks, so at least his name would stay out there.

But the Jessica Carlton thing was bothering me. She had come to Texas to see her jock boyfriend, and her people had been calling to set up a meeting. No surprise there. I just didn't know what to tell them.

I started smoking again. Cigarettes, I mean. I never quit weed. That was almost impossible when you hung around Tommy Grind. I had quit cigarettes back in 1998 and never felt better. But the stress of dealing with Tommy's unique needs—he was up to four girls a week now, and it was getting increasingly difficult to dispose of the garbage in a way that didn't attract dogs of both the canine and human variety— and the Jessica Carlton situation conspired against me. In a weak moment, I bummed a smoke off of Isaac and within a week was back up to a pack a day.

It made me feel ashamed every time I lit up. Like I was some kind of pansy or something, but to quote Tommy, a need is a need and it has to feed, like it or not.

The situation reached a head on the night of February 14th— Valentine's Day.

I was in Tommy's fully restored 1972 Triumph TR-6, headed back to the mansion from the store where I'd gone to buy another carton of smokes. It was a cool, crisp night, full of stars, and I had the top down and Tommy's 2003 album *Desert Nights* cranked up on the CD player. The night was cool and clear, and the little Triumph handled the Hill Country roads like a dream. Any other night, I would have been in heaven.

But, like I said, I was troubled.

The feeling got worse when I pulled into the driveway and saw the lights on upstairs.

I had turned them off when I left. Tommy was usually calmest when the lights were off.

"Fuck," I said, and in my mind I was already throttling Isaac.

I parked and went inside, just to make sure. But I wasn't surprised to find Tommy gone. Isaac hadn't even done a half-assed job of cleaning up Tommy's latest meal. Nice enough girl. Said she was from Kentucky, I think.

I went to the security room and replayed the tape. There was Isaac, talking to Tommy through the Plexiglas, opening the door, coaxing him outside. Tommy staggering toward Isaac, hands raised in a gesture that almost looked like supplication.

And then they were off camera until they got downstairs and out the front door.

I turned on the GPS tracker—basically a glorified version of what veterinarians use to track the family pet—that I had injected into Tommy's ass after the last time Isaac walked him outside. Then I called the signal up on my iPad and got a good fix on him.

He was heading down to the west point of Lake Travis. There was a secluded little pocket of vacation homes down there for the über wealthy. Sandra Bullock and Matthew McConaughey both had houses there not too far from Tommy's. It was his private little retreat from the world. Tommy didn't often like to disconnect, but when he did, that was where he went.

And then, a terrible thought.

Please dear God. Tell me he's not taking him to meet Jessica Carlton. He can't be that stupid.

I called Isaac's cell, and to my surprise, he answered.

"What the hell are you doing?" I said.

"Can't talk," he answered. I could hear Tommy moaning in the background. Car noises. Isaac struggling to keep Tommy off him.

"Isaac. Isaac, don't you dare hang up on me!"

But he did.

Damn it.

I got into my Suburban—the one I'd specially modified with a police prisoner barrier in the back so I could transport Tommy if I needed to—and headed after them.

Thirty minutes later, I was looking up at an eight-thousand-square-foot mansion done up like a Mediterranean villa—red-tile roof, white adobe walls, fountains and hibiscus everywhere. I had parked off the main road in a small gap in a cedar thicket that concealed the Suburban perfectly, and tried to figure what Isaac was doing. What possible reason could he have for bringing Tommy here? If Jessica Carlton saw him, we were done for. Despite the constant upkeep, Tommy was looking pretty rough these days. Worse than Willie Nelson after a three-day whiskey binge. Which I've seen, by the way. It ain't pretty.

And then it hit me. Valentine's Day. Today was Valentine's Day. Isaac Glassman had no chance of ever becoming Tommy Grind's lover. Not anymore anyway. The pathetic bastard's heart was probably breaking. He couldn't give Tommy flowers, or candy, or stuffed animals, or any of that worthless shit people give each other on Valentine's Day. But he could give him something pretty. Something that Tommy *did* still care about.

I heard shouting from the house. It was muffled, but definitely shouting.

Then gunfire. Three pistol shots, one after another.

That lit a fire under me.

I reached behind the driver's seat of the Suburban and took out a badly scuffed Louisville Slugger, the one with nicks in the business end that went back to the Houston beer joint days.

Old School persuader in hand, I advanced up the driveway and tried the doors and windows until I found an unlocked servant's door off the kitchen.

I looked up and saw a camera in the corner, pointed right at me.

Same system as at Tommy's. I could deal with that.

I looked around and noticed the stove. A huge Viking gas range with a dozen burners.

I cranked them all up to full and walked into the living room, where I could hear a man whimpering.

I didn't recognize him, which probably meant he was part of the legal community. Maybe one of Isaac's lawyer friends. He wore a light gray double-breasted suit with a canary yellow silk shirt and no tie, both of which were torn and splashed with blood. He was clean-shaven and fit-looking, but his eyes were crazed.

Had to be Jessica Carlton's lawyer. He must have brought her here so the talent could play while the lawyers talked contracts.

He turned his insane eyes on me, and that's when I saw the pistol in his hand, the slide locked back in the empty position.

"Help me," he pleaded.

I grabbed him by the shoulders. "Who else is in the house?"

"To-Tommy Grind. Oh Jesus. He... Something's wrong. He attacked Jessica. He bit her leg off. I... I think she's... I think she's hurt real bad."

Then he held the gun up in front of his face like he had never seen it before.

"I shot him. I emptied the whole magazine into his chest. He just... he just kept coming. He's... oh, Jesus."

"I see. Listen, what's your name?"

"Leslie Gant," he said. He was in deep shock, functioning on autopilot.

"Great. Listen, Leslie... you mind if I call you Leslie?"

"Huh?"

"Leslie, I want you to kneel down right here, okay?" He let me guide him to his knees. "That's right," I said. "Just like that. Now put your arms down at your side. Look over there."

"What? Why?"

I pointed his face toward the sliding glass doors that led out to a beautifully dappled swimming pool.

"Perfect," I said. "Now I'm gonna tee off on your head with this bat."

"Wha—"

I swung for the fence. Laid him out like a sack of rocks.

Then I went to find Isaac and Tommy.

* * *

Isaac was standing in a hallway outside the master suite. He turned when he heard me approach, and his eyes went wide as the bat came up.

"No!" he said, showing me his palms. "It's okay. Stop, Steve."

"Like hell it's okay. I ain't gonna let you ruin us, Isaac."

"No," he pleaded. "You don't understand."

I was close enough now to see into the master suite. Jessica Carlton, blouse torn off, exposing her absolutely amazing tits, skirt hiked up high enough to give a peek of a white, lacy thong, was pulling herself across the deep pile, honey-colored carpet. There was blood on her face and a huge big bite mark on her right leg. From her expression, I could tell she'd been drugged.

Tommy was staggering toward her, moaning like I'd never heard him do before. There was fresh blood on his face and hands and chest, but if I didn't know better, I'd have sworn he was aroused.

"What the hell?" I said. I turned to Isaac. "Did you drug her?"

"Yeah. GHB."

"How much did you give her?"

"The usual."

"The whole dropper full?"

"Yeah."

"And she's still moving around?"

He shrugged.

"Damn," I said, and whistled. "The girl must be in pretty good shape."

"Yeah."

Tommy caught up with her, fell on her, started to feed. She let out a weak scream, but there was nothing behind it. In less than a minute, she had stopped thrashing.

Feeling stunned, I said, "Isaac, I'm not sure if I'm gonna be able to unfuck this situation."

"I was...," he said, and drifted off feebly. "It's Valentine's Day."

I didn't even bother to respond.

"I wanted to give him something, you know? We just take and take and take from his talent. Nobody ever gives back to him. I wanted to give him something special."

"So you gave him Jessica Carlton? Jesus, Isaac, how did you expect to pull that off? This isn't some two-bit groupie chick. People are gonna notice she's gone."

"She wanted to meet Tommy. Leslie Gant called me. He said she was going to be in town. He asked me if we could set up a private meeting between them. You know, a little romantic Valentine's Day dinner the paparazzi wouldn't know about. She's still with that football player."

I took a moment to absorb all that. Then, "So no one knows she's here. Is that what you're saying?"

"Leslie Gant knows too."

"I'm not too worried about him," I said.

But I was worried about Isaac. In his mind, he must have felt he was making the supreme lover's sacrifice. He must have felt almost like a martyr, giving someone else to Tommy Grind so that they could satisfy him the way Isaac only wished he could.

"This must have been really hard for you," I said.

He looked at me, a suspicious note of caution in his eye.

"I mean that," I said. "I know you've been in love with him for a long time."

Isaac started to object, then hung his head and nodded.

"Listen, come with me. Let's go have a drink and let him eat. What the hell, right? There's nothing more you can do here."

I put my arm over his shoulder and led him back to the living room. He balked at Leslie Gant on the living room floor, but I guided him away from the body.

"Don't worry about him," I said. "Here, we got time for one drink. Then, we got to think about how we're gonna clean all this up. Can't afford any loose ends."

He looked back at Leslie Gant and grunted.

I handed him his drink. "To Tommy Grind," I said. We clanked glasses. I downed mine in one gulp. He sipped his, but managed to get most of it down just the same.

"Hang tight here, okay? I'm gonna go get Tommy and put him in the car."

About five minutes later, I was done with Tommy and back in the living room. Isaac was nearly passed out on the couch.

I slapped his cheeks to rouse him. "Come on," I said. "Don't fade on me yet."

He stirred.

"Okay," I said, "here's what we're gonna do. You got your lighter on you?"

He reached into his pocket and held up a pink Bic.

"Pink?" I said. "Seriously?"

A corner of his mouth twitched. As close as he was going to get to a smile at this point.

"Well, it'll work. Start lighting those drapes on fire, okay?"

He nodded.

I took the whiskey and a couple of other bottles back to the master suite and lit the bodies on fire. Once I had it going, I came back to the living room and grabbed Isaac by the shoulder.

"Come on," I told him. "Gotta stay on your feet until we get to the car."

We passed his car in the driveway, and though the drugs I had slipped into his drink had made him so groggy he could barely walk, he was still able to point at his car and groan.

"Don't worry about it," I said.

At that very moment—and I mean it was cued like something out of a movie—the house behind us blew up.

And I'm not just talking a part of the house, either.

The whole fucking thing exploded.

The shockwave nearly knocked me down.

Isaac stared at me, stupidly. His mouth was hanging open, a thick rope of drool hanging from the corner of his lips. Some people don't handle the GHB well at all.

"What did you do?" he managed to say, though it came out all as one slurred syllable.

"This is your big chance," I said. I leaned him up against the front fender of the Suburban, reached into the driver's side window, and turned up Janis Joplin's "Take Another Little Piece of My Heart."

One of Tommy's favorite songs.

Then I helped Isaac to the back and balanced him on my hip as I opened the door.

Tommy was waiting inside, watching, his dead eyes locked on Isaac.

Isaac groaned and slapped at my hand in a futile show of resistance. Poor guy, he knew it was coming.

Janis was singing never, never, never hear me when I cry.

"She's playing your song," I said. "Happy Valentine's Day, Isaac."

Then I chucked him inside, closed the door, and drove out of there before the first sirens sounded in the distance.

I listened to the sounds of weak screams and tearing meat coming from the back seat, but I didn't look back.

Instead, I turned up the radio.

It ain't easy being the manager for the biggest rock star on the planet. Sometimes you gotta get your hands dirty. But what the hell? I mean, the show must go on, right?

Survivors

The ramp dropped open and Canavan's squad un-assed from the LAAV fighting vehicle to take up their positions amid the rubble. They'd been fighting for weeks, street by street, building by building, trying to retake San Antonio from the zombie hordes that had overrun it, and now the city lay in smoking ruin all around them. Everywhere he looked, Canavan saw dead bodies, and most of them were still moving.

They were facing south down Broadway, right into the heart of downtown. Echo Sector. Their mission was simple. The lieutenant had located some survivors, but now he was surrounded and taking shelter in a fire station off Bonham Street. Canavan and his squad were to extract the lieutenant and the survivors and fall back.

Quick and easy.

A pair of helicopters sprinted overhead, flying so low Canavan could feel the thropping of their blades echoing inside his helmet.

One of the pilots spoke to him over his headset. "Squad Two, you got incoming ahead and to your left. Clear behind and to the east."

"Roger that," Canavan answered.

He turned and motioned to PFC Bill Travis to position his M249 machine gun forward. Noise from the fighting was bringing more and more zombies into the area, which is what they wanted. It would ease some of the pressure on the lieutenant and at the same time put the infected into the meat grinder they'd set up with the LAAVs.

Clouds of smoke and powdered concrete floated across the street ahead of them, blanketing everything in a depthless, churning gray fog. In the haze, Canavan saw zombies staggering toward them. He scanned the rest of his squad. Their eyes were bloodshot and hollow, exhausted, but they knew their jobs. They'd been through this plenty of times before. They were steady, and Canavan was proud of them.

Above them, one of the helicopters banked hard and came in low, the downwash from its props momentarily pushing the screen of dust from the street.

It was enough for Canavan to see how deep the shit really was.

Thousands of zombies choked the street. They poured through the gaps made by the abandoned cars and crumbling buildings, and their moaning was audible even over the rumble of the LAAVs and the ear-splitting shriek of rockets overhead.

The gunners in the LAAVs opened up and Canavan gave Travis the signal to do the same. Before the fighting had really gotten bad, back when clearing the infected from the overrun cities was still a matter of bullpen strategy, some of the pundits on TV had said it wouldn't work to unleash bombs and machine guns against the zombies—that only carefully directed sniper fire would work. That was the only effective way to ensure the headshots that would stop the zombies, they had said.

Well, whoever said that had clearly never fought on the ground with a seasoned urban-combat group, Canavan thought.

White lines appeared in the creases at the corners of his mouth as he smiled.

They were kicking ass.

For nearly two minutes, the LAAVs churned up the advancing hordes with a steady stream of fire. Swollen, rotten bodies were perforated by large caliber shells and oozed gore upon the ground like oatmeal bursting from a bag. The roar of gunfire echoed off the sides of the buildings. The sky was laced with the smoky trails of rockets. Canavan took it all in, his eyes moving from side to side as he scanned for gaps in the fire pattern.

But there were no gaps. They were thinning the zombies out in huge swaths. The operation was going smoothly, and he was already planning their route through the rubble when the LAAV to their left went silent.

Canavan turned back, but all he could see of the LAAV in the dense screen of dust was a dim, dark outline.

A moment later, the LAAV one block east of them fell silent too.

Above them, the helicopters banked again and sprinted over the rooftops to the east. Canavan waited, maintaining radio discipline.

Then one of the pilots came on. "Squad Two, you got a whole bunch of bogies to the east. Ya'll need to hump it out there. Head for Delta Sector."

"What about the LAAVs?" Canavan asked.

A pause.

"Negative," the pilot finally said. "Your fire support's been compromised. Ya'll need to hustle yourselves back to Delta Sector."

"Roger that," Canavan answered. He could almost picture an out-of-work rodeo bull-rider in that helicopter. "Travis, take right. We got hostiles on the way."

All at once the radio erupted with the sounds of men shouting in panic. Canavan recognized the voice of Carlton Weir, the gunner from their LAAV, screaming about zombies entering the gunner's hatch of his LAAV. They heard three pistol shots and a whole crowd moaning as one, and then Weir screaming with sounds that didn't seem like they could come from a man before somebody got smart and cut the feed to Weir's headset.

Images of a flooded street in Houston a year before crowded his mind, a young girl being pulled under a sheet of brown water by the living dead, and he had to labor against the confines of his MOLLE gear to breathe.

He raised his right hand to deliver orders to his men and realized his fingers were shaking. Canavan closed his fist and his eyes and forced himself to focus. When he had mastered the fear and trembling in his extremities, he ordered his squad to move out, putting Travis's heavy gun in the lead. He guided them back toward Delta Sector, keeping them tight. To the north the street was awash in smoke and dust. The air was an ink wash of gray shot through with black roiling clouds of oily soot so dense that in places it seemed to have no depth at all and left him with a terrifying sense of vertigo.

And then, through the swirling dust, he saw a flash of red.

It stopped him in his tracks.

It was a woman. Her red dress was vividly bright against the haze, and he rose subconsciously from his crouch to watch her.

She wasn't a zombie. He could see that plainly enough, even from fifty meters out. She was looking to the east, toward the silenced LAAVs, her body tensed and uncertain, as though she couldn't figure out which direction to run. Canavan called to her, but she didn't look his way.

A screen of dust passed between them, and when it cleared, the woman was gone.

Canavan stood confused.

"Corporal!"

Canavan spun around. Travis was pointing into the haze, at a figure coming their way. Canavan squinted into the swirling dust and saw their lieutenant. He had his right arm bent in front of his chest, his palm showing, waving his arm around in a large horizontal circle.

The signal to assemble.

Travis and the others moved forward obediently, but Canavan stood his ground. Something was wrong. The order made no sense. Not when they needed to un-ass the area as fast as possible.

Only then did he see the blank, dead look in the lieutenant's eyes, the blood staining the hips of his trousers.

He yelled for Travis to halt, but the words didn't come in time. The lieutenant fell on the machine gunner and both men went down, the gun sprawling off to one side, the gunner's arms flailing awkwardly at the air as the lieutenant tore into him with his fingers and his teeth.

Stunned, it took Canavan a long moment to look away.

When he did, he saw dark forms staggering closer through the haze. He turned, looking for a way out, and realized he was surrounded.

His team was gone.

He raised his rifle and fired into the crowd, burning through three magazines as he hunted for a way out.

But there were too many of them.

He screamed into his radio for air support, reloaded, and went on firing.

He was still firing when he heard the whistle of artillery above him. He dropped to his belly, covered his ears and opened his mouth to equalize the pressure. But the explosions were too close, and the blast bounced him violently off the pavement.

For a moment, he was too stunned to think. He was bleeding from his nose and his mouth, and he couldn't breathe.

He had just staggered to his feet, driven by a desperate, instinctive urge to get the hell out of there, when the second wave of artillery rolled in. A concussion blast knocked him off his feet, but he was unconscious before his back hit the ground.

* * *

When he came to, Canavan was on fire.

He could smell his hair burning beneath his helmet, and even beneath forty pounds of gear and ammo, his skin felt like it had been splashed with hot grease.

Canavan tore at his clothes frantically, pulling off his helmet, protective mask, body armor, and even his tunic. Right down to his T-shirt. He rose to his feet, swatting at his body as though he were covered in bees, his head reeling.

The air was full of dancing sparks that slanted across his field of vision like snowflakes in a light breeze. He thought his optic nerves had been damaged by the concussion blast. His inner ears, too. He couldn't walk straight. The ground felt like it was rolling beneath his feet, and there was a throbbing pain in his head that made his eyeballs shake.

He staggered drunkenly and dropped to one knee.

He heard moaning and looked up. A zombie was limping toward him, carrying the stench of burned flesh and decaying meat with it. Most of its clothes had melted into its skin, leaving it encased in a slick, black slime. Only then did Canavan understand that the sparks he saw were actually burning bits of airborne dust. This zombie had no doubt been at the edge of the blast area, for Canavan could see dust mote lances of light passing through the holes in his chest.

Canavan reached down to his right thigh and pulled his pistol from its holster.

The front sight was swimming before his eyes. Canavan fired and missed four times. He teetered backward and took aim again and with his next shot managed to hit the zombie in the left shoulder, blasting off a piece of charred flesh and spinning the zombie around.

But the zombie didn't drop.

The thing moaned and raised the stumps of its arms as though it were seeking absolution and came at him again.

Canavan stepped back. He raised the pistol and fired through the entire magazine before landing a lucky head shot and dropping the wrecked corpse to the ground. It lay there in a heap, and Canavan, moving backward uncertainly, could only gape at it.

Some vital connection between Canavan's mind and muscles and bone had short-circuited. Walking was a painful, doubtful process. He felt like he was moving through water, and in his confusion, his mind tumbled back across the last year to the flooded streets of Houston in the wild days following Hurricane Mardell, the city whelmed beneath the oil-streaked waters of the Gulf of Mexico. Once again the air was unnaturally green and cool and wet, like it was made of damp cloth. He was up to his hips in water the color of melted caramel. It stank like raw sewage and shone with an unnatural, chemical luster. The living dead were in the water with them, survivors waving their arms over their heads frantically as they screamed for help from the helicopters racing overhead.

For two days, he and his twelve-year-old daughter, Sarah, had wandered the wreckage in a numb stupor, chased ever onward in a blind frenzy of helplessness by the living dead and the looters and the flood waters. Shots rang out constantly. The bodies of deer and dogs and humans festooned the limbs of fallen trees. And worst of all, they were unable to tell the difference between those bloated, lifeless corpses bobbing in the water and the infected zombies that could seem part of the trash but were in fact only waiting for someone to come too close. All the hospitals had become necropolises, and they learned quickly to avoid those. The flooded houses, too—for the moans coming from the attics were not all made by the living, and they could never be sure when a submerged section of a roof had been punched through by the limbs of a live oak or a snapped telephone pole, allowing the zombies an easy place to hide.

On the morning of the third day, they saw a bass boat appear from behind the leafy top of an upturned pecan tree. A National Guardsman with a rifle was waving them on.

Turning to Sarah, Canavan stuck out his hand. She was holding a pink backpack by the straps, splashing frantically as she struggled to keep up. "Come on," he shouted at her. "They're right there."

The girl was exhausted, and every word out of her mouth took the form of a plaintive whining that at first had touched the atavistic protectiveness all fathers possess for their daughters but now met only an impatient hardness and more shouting.

"Daddy, help me."

"Come on, move!"

A zombie sprang out from beneath the canopy of an immature live oak next to Canavan, and in a moment of pure, base fear, Canavan leapt onto the roof of a nearby car. He spun around only to see his daughter bent forward at the waist, her hands reaching for him, her eyes flashing with fear as the dead man wrapped his arms across her middle and pulled her down.

She sank beneath the debris-strewn water yelling, "Dad-dy! Dad-dy!" He reached for her, but she was already gone.

"No!" he shouted. "No."

He scanned the water, unable to believe what had just happened, when more of the living dead emerged from the water.

Another wave of burning ash hit his skin, and he swatted at his face.

The memory of Houston vanished, and he was back in the dusty ruins of downtown San Antonio, disoriented at first because the memory had seemed so vivid and so very horrible. A small crowd of zombies, about a dozen or so, were closing on him. There were more behind them, picking their way through the rubble of a collapsed building.

With his mind still numb with guilt and loss for Sarah, he raised his pistol and tried to fire.

Nothing happened.

Confused, he looked at the weapon. It took him a moment to figure out it was empty.

He had two more magazines on his thigh, next to his holster, and muscle memory took over as he ejected the spent magazine, slapped a fresh one into the receiver, and released the slide.

Canavan fired through his second magazine and reloaded the third.

Moaning behind him.

He turned and saw another badly burned zombie coming toward him, trailing a shredded leg. Canavan pointed the gun at the zombie's head and fired until it fell. Then he dropped his hands to his side and staggered into the swirling clouds of ash and dust, the moans of the dead trailing away behind him.

* * *

He walked on until he heard a woman sobbing.

It was coming from a white stone building with all the windows on the first six stories blasted out. The lobby on the ground floor was littered with plaster and garbage, lath visible through the walls. There was an acrid, dusty taste of aerosolized concrete and ash in the air that collected in Canavan's mouth, leaving his tongue dry, like it was wearing a sock.

Looking through one of the openings, he saw the woman in the red dress, the vivid splash of color he had seen earlier muted now with a fine powdering of dust. She was sitting on the floor, her legs spread out in front of her like a little child, her hands on the floor between them. Her hands were wet with blood.

He stepped inside the lobby, and the crumbled plaster and broken glass on the floor crunched beneath his boots.

The woman in red spun around and screamed. Her sudden movements scattered photographs across the floor. Canavan watched the pictures skid toward his boots, then turned his attention on the woman. Her chest was heaving, her eyes wild. She held her injured hands out in front of her, as though to push him away, the gore dripping from them a stark contrast to the bloodless pallor of her face.

"Don't hurt me," she whimpered. "Please."

She thinks I'm one of them, he realized. Without his gear, and with the blood leaking from his nose and mouth, and the punch-drunk stagger in his walk, he must have looked just like a zombie.

"I won't hurt you," he said.

A long pause.

She lowered her hands and made a low, huffing noise that came from the somewhere deep in her throat.

Canavan reached down and picked up one of the photographs. It showed the woman in front of him, younger, smiling, nestled in the arms of an overweight, dark-haired man in a Hawaiian shirt and sunglasses. They were on a small boat, a heavily wooded shoreline in the distance behind them.

He held the photograph out to her. "Your husband?"

"My brother, Paul."

He nodded. When she didn't take the photograph from him he dropped it in front of her. "What's your name?"

"Jessica Shepard."

"I'm James Canavan."

There was a beat. The muscles at the corners of her mouth twitched, as though she might smile. "Are you a James or a Jim?"

"Either. Jim to my friends."

"Well, Jim, pull up a chair. The place is kind of dead tonight."

He couldn't really laugh, but he liked the easy way she used his name, the gallows humor, the way it gave him a glimpse into her personality.

She was staring up at him, her eyes yellow and bloodshot and almost lifeless, rimmed with red. Her face was lost in shadow, and her hair clung to her damp forehead and cheeks like wet thread. When she breathed, she made a labored, painful sound, as though she had fluid pooling in her lungs.

"Can you get me out of here, Jim?"

He shook his head. "You've been infected."

She closed her eyes and let her chin sink to her chest. She was silent for so long he thought she hadn't intended to answer. But when she lifted her head again there were tears cutting rivulets down the dust on her cheeks and a knot was working itself up and down furiously at the base of her throat.

The look in her eyes made him turn away.

"I'm sorry," he said.

"You're sorry? You fucking bastard. You God-damned fucking pig-headed bastard." She wiped a forearm across her eyes, her bloody fingers trembling. "I'm dying," she said. "I don't want to die. I don't want to be one of those things."

The air seemed to go out of her lungs.

Then, so faintly he barely heard her, she said, "I've been one of them for too long as it is."

Canavan had no idea what to say, and it shamed him. She was pleading for some sign of human compassion, and it was just her lousy luck to meet with a man who could no more give it to her than he could cure the riot raging in her bloodstream.

"Will you do it?" she asked.

"Will I...?"

"Please. I don't want to be one of those things."

He followed her gaze to his right hand and was dumbfounded to see his pistol still there, the slide locked back in the empty position.

"I don't," he said, and trailed off. "It's empty. I'm sorry."

"Stop saying that." Her voice was muted in resignation. "Stop saying you're sorry. It only makes it worse."

He nodded.

A helicopter passed overhead, its blades a padded staccato rhythm. Soon they would start hearing more gunfire, he realized. He'd need to be ready to signal the rescue squads before they gunned him down like one of the dead.

She started to cough, and to Canavan it sounded like her insides were being shredded by knives. The coughing went on for a long time, and when it subsided and she could once again lift her head to look at him, the deep valley between her breasts was flecked with black, clotted blood.

"Can't you do it? Please, Jim. I don't want to be one of them. I can't...."

Canavan forced himself to swallow, as though there were an almond stuck in his throat. His chest hurt when he breathed. The shame of his own impotence in the face of this woman's pathos at first left him speechless, but gradually, his feelings of sympathy gave way to a vague, unfocused anger. He resented her for making him remember how lost and helpless he could feel.

He turned to leave.

"Wait!" she said. "Please, don't go. Please. God, it hurts so bad."

He knew it did, and he wasn't without pity. During their training,

Canavan and his fellow Marines had been given the skinny on the necrosis filovirus and how it worked its way through the body, how it waged war in the bloodstream and gradually took complete control of the host body, leaving only a staggering train wreck of a virus bomb.

This woman was pretty far along. Infection had probably happened as much as an hour ago. Her temperature was spiking, leaving her face flushed in sweat. Already the blood in her veins was coagulating. A blueberry stain of cyanosis was forming around her mouth as her cells starved for want of oxygen. Her eyes were milking over. The coughing and the fluid in her lungs had affected her ability to speak, her voice taking on a whiskey-edged roughness that was becoming less and less human with each passing moment.

He wanted very much to leave her.

She began to cough again, the hacking shaking her like a rag doll in a dog's mouth. She seemed unable to control her movements. A sudden sour odor of defecation reached him, and he knew she voided her bowels. She didn't have long to go. Complete depersonalization would no doubt happen within the next ten minutes, probably less.

"Please, I need you to do this," she said, barely able to lift her head now. "One bullet. Don't you even have one bullet? That's all it would take. Please, I hurt so bad. I can feel it inside me."

He shifted uneasily and the glass crunching beneath his boots sounded loud in the sepulchral stillness of that ruined lobby.

She watched his feet. She lifted her milky eyes and webs of wrinkles spread from the corners of her mouth. Within the few minutes he'd been with her, she seemed to age horribly, as though she were a peach left on the sidewalk, puckering in the sun.

And then her face cracked with rage as she screamed at him.

"Why won't you fucking help me? You bastard. All I want is a bullet."

Canavan had to force himself not to look away. The look on her face, the baffled anger and desperation, brought images of his daughter into his head. Once again he saw her slipping under the waves. Heard her screaming, "Daddy! Dad-dy!"

He realized he was crying and swiped the tears away angrily. But the dying woman didn't notice. She had started to cough again. When it subsided, she seemed detached and blunted, as though her mind had been scrambled and left her little more than a babbling idiot.

But he would not have told her about the depth of his self-loathing and shame, even if she had been capable of comprehending it. Perhaps she had her own issues, her own regrets, and perhaps she too had failed someone who had depended on her for their very life, but there were some things that cut so deeply into a man's conscience that they could not be mentioned to anyone.

"One bullet," she said.

"I'm sorry."

She groaned once, and his gaze fastened on her. Her breathing slowed, her mouth working like a fish left on the shore by a wave. She tried to speak and couldn't. He watched her struggle through two final breaths. There was a phlegmy rattle in her throat and her shoulders sagged, as though at rest after carrying a great weight.

Stillness descended on the lobby.

And then, slowly, laboriously, she climbed to her feet. Her head drooped to one side, her mouth hanging open. A fine patina of dust coated her lips. She reached for him, but he did not move until she began to moan, and when that happened, he slid the collapsible baton from its holster at the small of his back and snapped it open.

She never acknowledged the danger. He sidestepped the woman and slapped her in the back of the head with the baton, knocking her forward onto her face. But he was still dizzy from the concussion bombing and was uncertain on his feet, and the force of his swing also knocked him onto his hands and knees.

In the stillness that followed, he heard something small and metallic drop to the floor.

He looked into the puddle of broken glass below him and saw a single, perfectly clean bullet glittering amongst the dusty rubble. At first he didn't know what to make of it, but gradually it came to him, the loose round he'd accidentally ejected while clearing a malfunction in his pistol during the fighting the evening before. He'd forgotten it was there.

That one bullet.

He stared at it for a long time. He could have helped her if he'd only had his wits about him. It was like Sarah all over again.

The thought curled around his heart like a cold, wet vapor.

He heard the echo of automatic rifle fire in the near distance, like people clapping in the next room.

"Marines, stand and identify."

"In here," Canavan shouted.

Another Marine appeared in the doorway, his rifle at low ready. "Identify," he said. "Are you wounded?"

It was a question Canavan didn't quite know how to answer.

* * *

Fourteen months later, Canavan made his way up the front walk of a one-story, white wooden house in a Nashville suburb and rang the doorbell. It had been raining all that evening and the air was thick with the damp scent of mown grass and pulsing with the sound of frogs. He had researched a lot of dead leads, but now his hunt was at an end. This was the house.

Paul Shepard was the spitting image of the smiling fat man Canavan had seen in Jessica's photograph, though he had begun to gray at the temples and the bright smile had been replaced by nests of wrinkles around his eyes. He invited Canavan into the entryway but no farther, and the two men stood in a web of soft white light and shadow cast by three glass chandeliers in the hallway that led to the rest of the house.

"My twelve-year-old has the flu," he said in a whisper. "She just got to sleep about twenty minutes ago."

Canavan nodded, though images of Sarah rose in his mind like corks that won't stay submerged.

Then Canavan told him about San Antonio, and about his sister's final minutes. Shepard listened to it all without interrupting, the expression on his face never wavering.

A woman poked her head around the far corner of the hallway and said, "Paul?"

"It's okay. This is Mr. Canavan. He was with Jessica when she died."

The woman looked at Canavan without expression. "I have Cokes and Dr. Pepper in the icebox," she said. She waited a beat. "Scotch, if you'd like something stronger?"

"No, thank you, ma'am."

She nodded and slipped back into the quiet darkness at the back of the house.

Shepard said, "You've come a long ways, Mr. Canavan. Are you sure I can't offer you something?"

"I'm fine, really. I ought to be going."

But before Canavan could leave, Shepard put a hand on his arm. "A moment, Mr. Canavan."

"Yes?"

"Fourteen months is a long time to spend looking for somebody."

"Your sister wasn't completely lucid there at the end," Canavan said by way of apology. "She never told me anything about you. Besides your name, I mean. It took a while to find you."

"I don't mean that. I want to know why you didn't stop looking. You didn't have to come tell me this. We all figured my sister was dead. Deep down we knew it. You must have realized that too."

"I guess I figured I owed it to... I don't know. To her." Canavan's eyes slid off of Shepard's face. "Maybe to myself."

Shepard's brown eyes seemed to soften, and the knots of veins that stitched his temples slackened.

He said, "Mr. Canavan, when my sister left for San Antonio, she did so to escape our mother. The woman was dying of cancer of the small intestine. Have you ever known anyone with that particular condition? She was in terrible pain. There at the end, she was living with Jessica because we couldn't afford a hospice nurse, and sometimes when I'd visit, I'd see Jessica sitting on the curb in front of her house, crying her eyes out. You could hear our mother moaning all the way out in the driveway. I've sometimes asked myself if Jessica didn't go down to San Antonio knowing what she'd find there. I think maybe she found what she was looking for."

Canavan just stared at him.

"Did you know, Mr. Canavan, that the Japanese have a word for the people who survived Hiroshima and Nagasaki? Those people with the thousand-yard stares. Those people who cannot hold down a steady job or stand in a crowd without wanting to cower into a ball, or even carry on a conversation that goes beyond a few inane pleasantries. They called them *Hibakusha*. It means 'sufferers.' Our word for it is *survivors*. But I think their word seems much more fitting, don't you?"

Canavan said, "Are you trying to tell me something, Mr. Shepard?"

"I think I just did, sir. I think all survivors carry hell around with them like a turtle does his shell."

Canavan thought about those words several hours later as he washed his face in the sink of a gas station bathroom south of Nashville.

He went into one of the stalls and locked the door and sat on the toilet without pulling down his pants.

In his hand he held the bullet that had dropped from his pocket back in San Antonio. He turned it around and around in his fingers, feeling its gun-oil smoothness, as slick as bacon grease against his skin. It was raining outside, really coming down, too. Out the windows that lined the wall near the ceiling to his left, he could see the wind gusting across the station's roof, feathering the rain off the corner flashing. His mind was crowded with images of the living and the dead, and those in between. His mind echoed with the screams of the innocents.

He looked down into his lap and studied the single bullet and the pistol that rested there, and he wondered if he was strong enough to go on being a survivor.

Suburbia of the Dead

There are others—I am not the only one—who believe that houses too can become zombies. Urban spelunkers and ghost hunters have built legends out of such places. On Callaghan Hill, for example, on the east side of San Antonio, stands a regal, plantation-style mansion built by Frank Betancourt, whose company brought the first air-conditioning to San Antonio back in the 1920s. During the Crash, Betancourt lost everything, and as the Depression raged, his mansion was abandoned and turned tumbledown. Gutters rusted against the wooden exterior, streaking the fading brilliance of its exterior like runners of blood. Children and birds broke its windows so that it stood, sightless and not sane, over an empty street. There's a very reasonable, a very economic, explanation for the spread of diseased houses that grew up around the Betancourt House in the following decades. A neighborhood becomes unfashionable. The rich move away. The poor, the gangs, the prostitutes and junkies, move in. But the house, dead and vacant, festers like a polluted wound, and everything around it dies, yet remains upright.

On the Monopoly game board, you can buy Pennsylvania Avenue for $320, but when I last visited Atlantic City, in 2002, Pennsylvania Avenue was hardly worth that price. The Hotel Astoria, once so gay, so vibrant, so like a ship at sea with bright pennants flying, stood boarded up with nothing but an unpainted scrap of plywood for a door. It now commands a view of Mediterranean and Baltic, where packs of dogs thread their way through piles of debris in vacant, overgrown lots. The paint on the walls of the Faith Temple Church of God in Christ just down the street is peeling down to the curb, one corner of the roof drooping like the brim of an old hat. Pigeons alight on the eaves of the buildings, picking at termites in the wood.

In a way, you don't have to stretch the imagination too far to see these hulking urban wrecks as zombies. They are created for people, and though not meant for permanence like the pyramids or ancient temples, we expect them to outlive us. We root them solidly in the ground, like mighty trees, like dreams made real, and like our dreams, they have a life all their own. They faithfully shield us, comfort us, sustain us, and in return we fill them with life. They don't know it, these forsaken buildings, but they too live. Through us, they live. Perhaps that is why they stand for so long after the life inside them fades. Perhaps they feel, though blindly, that loss so intensely, that when it's gone, they reach for their neighbors, hoping once again to be filled with the rattle and hum of life.

A few months after I learned you'd cheated on me, and after we tore our marriage apart and let the lawyers sort out the pieces, I went driving up and down our street. It was a cold March night, the streets still wet from the rain that afternoon, but I had the windows down. I didn't notice the cold. I paid more attention to the houses, to our neighbors' houses. I reached the dead end down by the greenbelt and turned around, came back, still driving slow, still watching the crumbling bricks, the weedpatch yards, the gray, ugly, disturbingly sick-looking houses, and I realized they were dying, corrupted by the dark, dead thing that used to be our home.

The Crossing

A cold February wind fingered its way through the gaps in the walls. The shack where we'd taken shelter had been cobbled together from cinder blocks and castoff lumber, the roof a rusting sheet of corrugated tin held down by baling wire. Rotting sheets of plywood covered the windows. It was thin protection from the zombies massing outside. The place smelled of stale beer and sweat, mildew and rot, and the dim morning light revealed a lot of ice-encrusted trash on the floor—broken beer bottles, tin cans, a scattering of cigarette butts, an occasional spent shell casing—sad markers of others, like Jessica and me, who had taken refuge here.

Jessica hunkered down in the corner to get out of the seething wind. She had a tattered bath towel wrapped around her shoulders, but it was too threadbare to warm even her, withered as she was from starvation. She scanned the garbage, her breath pluming from the cold. I figured she was looking for something she could use. Depravation had made her keen that way. She never missed anything.

"Looks like we're not the first to hide out here," she said.

I looked around. It was hard to believe this was luck, but she was right. We were lucky to find the shack when we did. The surrounding countryside was empty grassland, nothing but an occasional mesquite thicket to break up the soul-sucking emptiness of it. There were few places to hide from the zombies. I tried to imagine all the others who had come this way before us, how every bit of garbage on the floor was a marker representing anxious days and nights waiting for the zombies to move on down the road. There was a faded blood stain on the wall above Jessica's head, spattered, as though from a gunshot, and as I stared at it, I felt overwhelmed by the emotional sediment of desperation and exhaustion that permeated the small space. I never really believed, even as a little girl, that a place could be haunted. But if ever a place had a right to be, it was that shack.

Jessica went to the wall and stared through a crack. I joined her, noticing as I did that the gap in the lumber was smeared with dried blood left behind by fingers trying to claw their way inside.

There were two other shacks that we could see, both about the size of ours, and both surrounded by thick knots of the infected. From one of the shacks, we heard a man screaming. He was one of the people we'd been traveling with when the zombies found us. Jessica had said she didn't trust him, that he seemed unstable, and from the way he was shrieking, I believed it. But crazy or not, his screaming was driving the infected mad. He'd yell and they'd beat on the walls with renewed fervor, answering his fear with an ululating chorus of moans.

We didn't know who was in the other shack, but every once in a while, someone jabbed a sharpened stick through the walls at the crowd.

"They're idiots," Jessica said in a whisper.

They were idiots. She was right about that. But I was too scared to talk. As disgusting as the shack was, we were safe. I didn't want to say anything or do anything that would change that. I didn't want those things out there to hear us talking. I just wanted to shrivel up into a little ball and wait for the horrors to pass us by.

Be the reporter, I told myself. Watch, observe, soak it all in. Don't get involved. That was why I was here, after all, to report on living conditions in the Zone.

I almost laughed at that.

Like it or not, I was involved. I was involved up to my ears.

Just outside the door, a young female zombie had her face buried in the abdomen of a corpse. One of the men we'd been traveling with who hadn't made it inside quickly enough. A lot of meat had been torn from his bones, and what was left of the body jerked and twitched as the zombie tore bits of the remaining flesh away. We probably could have slipped by her, but she would have sent up a moan to bring the rest of the zombies after us.

"Why in the world would they bring attention to themselves like that?" Jessica said, still whispering. "They should know better."

I shrugged, silently praying that she'd stop talking.

"It's okay," she said, like she could read my mind. "Just whisper. They won't hear us."

"How do you know?"

I looked through the crack in the wall again. Most of the zombies were too intent on beating against the other two shacks, and those few that weren't with the main group were busy feeding off our dead companions. But still, scared as I was, I didn't want to chance it.

"They don't hear so well," she said. "They'll pick up on our movement, though, so try not to make any sudden moves."

She was right, of course. Moving would cause the light coming through the walls to flicker on our clothes, and that would be as good as jumping up and down and waving a flag. Though I'd known Jessica for only three days, I found myself amazed yet again at her common-sense grasp of tactics. She was like a soldier or some hardcore beat cop. Living in the Quarantine Zone had sharpened her survival instincts far beyond my own.

"I bet you're sorry you came, aren't you?" she asked.

I was scared like I'd never been in my life, but I wasn't sorry. Not a bit. I would have been dead without her, and when you get to the point that you can say that about another person, can you really be sorry about it? Doesn't that create a sense of loyalty that's worth a world of hardships?

Before I could answer, she put a hand on my shoulder.

"Look there," she said.

I put my face up to the crack again. Something was happening over at one of the shacks. The building trembled. As we watched, a section of the wall caved in, and the zombies poured through the breach, tearing the two men inside to pieces.

"Oh my God," Jessica said. There was no shock in her voice, just sadness.

"They were brothers, weren't they?" I asked.

"Yes."

The commotion caused even the female zombie in front of our door to join the swarm. My pulse quickened. Looking off to the right of the shack where the crazy man shrieked, I saw that the field beyond was absolutely empty. If we were quiet, we just might be able to get enough of a head start to leave this crowd of zombies behind us.

Before I could say anything to Jessica, the crazy man burst out of his shack and tried to make a break for it. Several of the zombies lunged for him, causing him to swerve. But he was too scared to control his footing on the muddy ground and fell face-first into a puddle of water. He was up and running, still screaming, before any of the zombies could get to him. Jessica and I watched him go, shocked to see most of the zombies shambling after him.

"Wow," she said.

I agreed. I was impressed, despite the man's lunacy. "Lucky for us."

"Yeah."

We waited about two minutes, neither of us speaking. Only a few zombies remained near the shacks, and those were busy feeding on the fresh corpses of the two brothers. It looked clear to me, and I reached for the brace on the door.

Jessica grabbed my wrist.

I started to speak, but the look on her face stopped me.

With a glance, she gestured toward the gaps in the wall. A moment later, a male zombie stepped into view. It stopped and slowly turned its head toward us. The thing's hair was a stringy mess, matted with dried blood. Its beard was filthy. Its mouth swarmed with flies. What clothes it had left were little more than soiled rags hanging from its emaciated frame. The wind shifted. It was cold enough to cut us to the bone, and though it carried the zombie's stench with it, I didn't dare shiver or gag. Reacting would get us killed.

After a bit, it went on its way, leaving us alone again.

I let out the breath I'd been holding. "That was close," I said. "Thanks."

"Tell me about it." Jessica pointed to the door. "It should be clear now."

* * *

My first night in the Zone I got caught in a sudden, hard rain that left me cold and miserable. I wandered into an abandoned bus depot, looking for someplace warm to sleep. Jessica and the rest of her group huddled in the back, barely visible in the darkness.

They watched me, alarmed because they didn't know me but intrigued because I didn't look like they did. My clothes were still fresh. My skin wasn't sun-burnt. I wasn't starving. For a long, uncomfortable moment, we stared at one another, nobody speaking, nobody moving.

Then a woman separated from the crowd and walked toward me. She almost looked like a zombie herself, emaciated, filthy, face sunken and haunted-looking.

Only her eyes were different. They were bright, full of life.

And, when she got closer, I could see they were curious, even friendly. The warmth there that reassured me.

"What in the world were you doing out in the rain?" she asked.

"I...." It was hard to speak, I was trembling so badly.

"Didn't you see the clouds forming?"

I shook my head.

"You couldn't smell the storm coming?"

"I'm cold," I said. My tone demanded mercy, not questions.

"I wouldn't doubt it. A storm like that, even the zombies have enough sense to get indoors."

"Can I stay here?" I asked. "Just for the night?"

"That depends." She looked me up and down. "Are you hurt? You bit anywhere?"

"No. Just cold."

She paused for a long moment, studying me. Her face was honest, and I felt like I could actually see her in silent discussion with her conscience.

Then, abruptly: "I'm Jessica."

"Samantha."

"Samantha, or Sam?"

I tried to smile, but my lips were turning blue from the cold. "Sam," I said.

"Sam it is. Come on, let's try to get you warmed up."

Jessica led me to a corner away from the door and showed me where I could sleep.

And that was how I spent my first night in the Zone.

* * *

When I woke the next morning, she was nudging my shoulder. I looked around, disoriented, and it took me a second to realize we were the only two people left in the depot. The others were outside on the road, set to leave.

"If you want to come with us, we have to leave now."

"Where are you going?"

"East of here. We're gonna cross the wall into Free America."

I think my mouth must have fallen open. "Are you serious?"

"Of course, I'm serious. You want to come or not? We have to leave now."

I couldn't believe my luck. My publisher had commissioned me to sneak into the Quarantine Zone, make a circuit of South Texas, and get back out again. I was to report on the conditions of the people there and come up with something to challenge the government's claims that the necrosis filovirus was so widespread as to make reclaiming the Zone a suicide mission. I knew going in that it'd be a dangerous assignment, but I figured it'd be no less dangerous than being an embedded reporter in Afghanistan or Iraq. It wasn't a necessary risk by any means, but it was a risk I was willing to take, especially when the whispers of a Pulitzer started to reach my ears.

My publisher hired one of their other authors, an ex-Navy SEAL, to sneak me through the Coast Guard blockade of the Texas coast. He got me onto a weed-choked beach near Port Lavaca in the middle of the night. I still remember the sour look on his face when the wind carried the sounds of moaning in our direction.

"You sure you want to do this?" he said. "I can get you out right now."

"No," I said. "I want to do this. I'll be okay."

"Where's your weapon?"

I hooked a thumb toward my backpack. I had a .40 Glock in my bag, plus three loaded magazines, for a total of forty-six rounds—forty-six more than I figured I'd need. "I have it in there where I can get it."

The wind carried more moans our way.

"If I were you, I'd have it out and ready."

"I'll be okay. I know what I'm doing."

I don't think he believed that for a second. All he was supposed to do was drop me off on the beach, and yet he had our Zodiac boat loaded down with night-vision goggles and machine guns and a box of something that looked a lot like grenades to me. He kept asking me if I was sure I wanted to do this, and it was starting to get old.

"I'll be fine," I said. Our plan was for me to meet him on the same beach three weeks later. I had a cell phone to signal him. It was my first experience as an embedded reporter, but I had done my homework. I knew the lay of the land. I had studied up on the infected. I knew how to evade them and how to deal with them when I couldn't evade them. In my mind, it was all going to be quite simple. "I'll call you," I said.

He shrugged and quietly slipped back out to sea.

But then came that night in the rain, and my unforeseen meeting with Jessica. When she asked me to join them, I jumped at the chance. Busting the wall—something the government assured us was impossible but that pretty much everybody believed was happening regularly—was just too much of a story to pass up.

In my eagerness, I got up too fast and upset my backpack, spilling the contents on the floor between us.

Jessica reached down to help me pick up my stuff, but paused when she saw what I was carrying. She moved my pens and notebooks out of the way, uncovering the iPhone and a battery-powered charger. I saw her mind racing.

Dark clouds of suspicion gathered in her face.

"Who are you?" she asked, her brow furrowed.

I'd been advised to keep my identity a secret for my own protection, but something told me I could trust Jessica. She had been the first to extend any sort of welcome, and she had come back for me while the others were ready to leave me sleeping in that bus depot.

"I'm a writer," I admitted. "I'm down her to write a story on life inside the Zone."

She stared at me for a long moment in frank, slack-jawed amazement. She must have thought I was out of my mind. And then she laughed.

"Hey, Jessica," one of the men called from the road. "You coming or what?"

She waved to the man, then turned back to me. She studied me, my clothes, my shoes, shaking her head the whole time. "Well," she finally said, "we're leaving. You want to see life in the Zone, I guess now's your chance."

So I left with them.

We walked a long while, and the whole time I was thinking of the quarantine wall, and what it would mean for these people to get into Free America.

The idea of a wall to protect one society from another is an old one. Ancient China tried it. The Communists tried it. The U.S. tried it along the Mexican border. But none of those historical precedents were entirely effective. They all came with a great cost in human life and a lot of insane politics. Political borders, after all, rarely coincide with societal borders. To think otherwise is just plain stupid. Fences may make good neighbors, but walls do not keep countries safe.

That is, until the zombies rose from the flooded ruins of Houston. The military was able to contain the outbreak by constructing a wall from Gulfport, Mississippi to Brownsville, Texas. Imagine the scope of that project. That's 1,100 miles of cement, chain-link fencing, and endless spools of concertina wire, constructed in a month and a half. Many have claimed it is one of the modern wonders of the world, while the critics maintain it's a wonder it doesn't have more holes in it than a fish net. But according to the government and several independent quality-control groups and news outlets, it doesn't. The wall is sound. It's the truth Free America entrusts its safety to, and its impermeability is, to most Americans anyway, a lock-step guarantee.

But Jessica and her group didn't accept that. Lots of people break through every month, she assured me. And I could tell she honestly believed it.

Yet when I pressed her, she didn't seem to have much of a plan.

"We want to get across somewhere between Flatonia and Weimar," she said.

I waited for more. But after a moment, I realized there wasn't more.

"That's it? You don't know where? I mean, exactly? That seems like an important detail to me."

"How can I know something like that? That's up to the coyotes, isn't it?"

"I guess so," I said doubtfully. It seemed like an awful lot to take on faith, though. After all, to trust your life like that to a total stranger seemed crazy. But I answered myself with the same mental breath: Wasn't that exactly what I was doing here with Jessica?

"How much do they charge?" I asked.

She shrugged. "Nobody in the Zone has any money."

"Well, how then?"

She glanced around to make sure no one was looking, then showed me a handful of jewelry. They were nice, but nothing special, a few necklaces and charm bracelets, probably worth a couple hundred dollars at most.

"Is that how most people pay, with jewelry?"

"Mostly, yeah. It's the easiest way. But I've heard people paying with all kinds of stuff. Gas they've siphoned off old cars. Drugs they found in pharmacies. Liquor. Anything people want, you can usually trade with."

This was insane, I thought. I guess it showed on my face.

"What?" she said. She was amused by my distress. She was almost laughing.

"I just don't see how you can be so blasé about it. Where exactly you're gonna cross, how much it's gonna cost, those things seem like a big deal to me. I mean, right? You see that? They're important. It scares me you're not more worried about it."

The bemused smile left her face, replaced by a bitter seriousness. "There's always a way for a woman to pay her way," she said.

"Jessica, I...."

She didn't flinch. "I won't go on living this way. Not in the Zone like this." She gestured at the soiled rags that passed for her clothes, at her emaciated body that barely hinted at a woman's natural curves.

"Tell me, what would you do?"

"I don't know."

When I went on with my questions, I was more subdued. I'd been humbled.

"What do you plan to do when you get to Free America?"

"I taught Fourth and Fifth Grade before the wall went up. I thought maybe I could do that again."

"What about friends, family? They could help you get back on your feet."

"Maybe. I hope so. I had a boyfriend, you know. His name was Robert. He did IT stuff for an oil company. Made pretty good money. He was smart. We were living in an apartment together down in Corpus, but he left for a job in Oklahoma about a month before Mardell hit." She ran her left hand down the length of her right arm, fingers touching the cuts and scars and fresh bruises there. "I guess there probably isn't much chance of picking that up again."

"You never know," I said in what I hoped was an encouraging tone.

She gave me a weak smile. "I won't kid myself. That old life is gone. It'd be like that Tom Hanks movie. Remember the one, he's on that island...."

"*Joe vs. the Volcano?*"

She grinned. "The other one. The deserted island. Remember? His plane crashes?"

"*Castaway.*"

"That's the one. I was thinking of the end, after he gets rescued. Remember that? He goes home and his wife... What's her name?"

"Helen Hunt."

"Helen Hunt, that's it. Remember what happens when he tries to go home? Helen Hunt's character has remarried, and they have that awkward moment on the doorstep. Life has passed him by, and there's nothing he can do about it."

I nodded. "You can't go home again."

"I remember hearing that. Was that from the movie?"

"No," I said. "Thomas Wolfe."

"Ah."

We talked about the movies. We liked a lot of the same ones—*French Kiss, Sleepless in Seattle, While You Were Sleeping,* anything starring Molly Ringwald—and that was nice. But it didn't last. It couldn't last. Movies are movies, and real life is something else entirely. Jessica had changed too much. This world, this awful place, had changed her, and we both knew it. Soon she grew sullen and morose.

I couldn't blame her.

*   *   *

When we left the shack, we left the bodies of Jessica's friends where they lay. Nobody buries the dead in the Zone.

We walked the rest of the day, and around dusk we came upon a group of people headed toward a place off the main road. They said there was sort of a compound, an old ranch house, and that we could get some fresh water there and probably something to eat, too.

But it was dark by the time we arrived, and they were out of food. They didn't have any room left inside the house, either, so we couldn't even sleep where it was warm. It's easy to forget, while you're walking all day in the Texas sun, how cold the desert gets at night. The best we could do was to huddle beneath a vent that carried some of the hot air from inside. We spent the rest of the night in each other's arms, trying to stay warm.

The next morning we woke to gunshots.

"What was that?" I asked.

We had both flinched awake. We stared around in panic. Jessica said nothing. Then we heard some men talking. Jessica and I traded a look. The men didn't seem excited at all, just talking.

"What's going on?" I whispered. Guns weren't all that common in the Zone. There were still a few around, of course, but not many. That seemed odd to me, at first. This used to be Texas, after all. I had expected there to be guns everywhere. When I asked Jessica about this, she said most had been confiscated by homegrown militias in the early days of the Outbreak. Where those guns had gone to she didn't know.

"Jessica, what do we do?"

"Let's go see what they're doing."

"Let's go...?" I didn't get a chance to finish. She was already moving.

I followed her to the front of the house and got my first look at the place in daylight. It was dilapidated, of course, but still large and impressive, and I could see that it must have been something rather special before the wall went up. There were several fenced-off areas that looked like they had once been horse pastures but were now being used for crops. Enormous Spanish Oaks, rising like green skyscrapers over the flat, grassy landscape, dotted the countryside. Until the shooting started again, it was quite beautiful.

The men we'd heard talking were standing in the middle of a wide circular drive. Beyond that was a long, straight driveway that led to the county road. A large hurricane fence, topped with razor wire, surrounded the property, and a wrought-iron gate that I didn't remember from the night before stood boldly at the entrance.

The shooting came from a pair of men in camouflage hunting outfits in a deer blind near the gate. Their target was a knot of zombies that had gathered outside the fence. The men didn't seem to be in a hurry to do much killing though, taking a shot when it suited them, and one of the men standing nearby remarked on that.

"Don't matter," one of the other men said. "They got three good ones."

"No fast ones, though." The man sounded sullen, like a pouting kid.

"They're good enough for the likes of Barry."

The men turned away from the drive and walked to the east side of the house.

"What was that all about?" I asked.

"No idea."

A crowd had gathered to the east, so we went that way.

One of the horse pastures had been sectioned off with hurricane fencing. In the middle of the small enclosure was a man chained to a metal pole. He was sitting, his back against the pole, knees pulled up to his chest, refusing to look at the people gathered around the fence. A few people were chatting, but most seemed to be milling around, waiting.

We weren't there long when the two men in camouflage who had been shooting from the deer blind trotted over to a horse trailer attached to the fence. One of them got up on top of the trailer and used a broom handle to pry open the door latch. Nothing happened. The door stayed close.

"Hit it," somebody yelled.

"Yeah, yeah," the man on top of the trailer said. He slapped the door with the broom handle, and the door swung open. Three zombies piled out, lurching into the sunlight. They looked confused and lost. Then they saw the man chained to the pole, and as soon as that happened, they staggered toward him, hands raised and clutching at the air.

"They're gonna kill him."

Jessica gestured for me to be quiet.

I watched the man chained to the pole, and I thought for sure I was going to throw up.

The man climbed to his feet, backing away to the length the chain clasped to his neck would allow. He watched the zombies advancing on him, his eyes bulged in panic, lips trembling. He looked pathetic, tugging on the chain.

But he didn't lose all self-control. When the lead zombie closed in, he made his move. Holding the chain in front of him, he sprinted to one side, catching the zombie under the knees and sweeping it off its feet. The zombie pitched over, landing face-first in the dirt, then slowly climbed to its feet.

I waited for a bunch of redneck hooting and hollering from the crowd, but hardly anybody spoke, much less yelled. One man, drunk though the day had hardly started, made a feeble attempt to stoke the crowd by yelling at the condemned man, but everybody ignored him and eventually he too fell into a sort of sullen, bored silence.

It was ennui, I realized then, that was the root cause of misery in the Zone. There were no prospects, no way to improve one's life, save through savagery and the debasement of others. Whatever the man had done wasn't enough to overcome the feelings of emptiness and bootless rage that afflicted these people. They watched him scramble around that enclosure, and even when he made a narrow escape, it wasn't enough to change the exhausted listlessness in their expressions. It was like all the life had been bled from them.

Then he got lucky. One of the zombies was a man in the remnants of an orange T-shirt and jeans. The zombie slipped and went down to one knee. The chained man got behind him, looped the chain around its neck, pushed it face down in the dirt, and stood on its neck. I saw the zombie's expression change as he struggled against the weight holding him down. I don't know if it was muscle memory or some atavistic terror surfacing in its ruined mind, but I swear, for a moment, I thought I saw fear in its eyes.

The crowd grew interested, too. They murmured. One man chuckled. Most just leaned forward, hoping for something to break the boredom.

Meanwhile, the chained man was pivoting around, making sure to keep the other two in sight. They were closing on him, but he didn't seem willing to quit with the zombie in the orange shirt until it was dead.

One of the zombies reached for him, but the chained man was faster and kicked the zombie's legs out from under it. More people were getting interested now. The man who chuckled just a few moments before was nodding. He shucked his shoulders from side to side, the way my dad used to when he watched the fights on TV.

The zombie in the orange shirt and jeans stopped fighting. It looked dead to me. It wasn't even twitching. The chained man tugged on the chain, pulling the zombie away from the other two, and then started unraveling the chain from the dead man's neck.

He'd almost freed himself when the zombie reached out and grabbed the hem of his pants. The chained flinched. He kicked the zombie in the face, but he wouldn't let go. Unable to pull himself free, the man lost his footing, and the other two fell on him. The man screamed horribly, but those were choked off soon enough, and just like that it was over.

The zombies began to feed, and people wandered off in groups of two or three, nobody speaking, their expressions inscrutable.

As we walked away, one of the men in charge asked us if we were hungry, and we told him we were. He said we could have a can of pork and beans to split if we were willing to clean some clothes first. We said that'd be all right. He showed us where we'd be working, and we got busy on three big piles of laundry, chatting about nothing in particular as we cleaned.

We were finished by midday and collected our food, then went out back to cook it over a fire pit there.

I took a few bites of my pork and beans and gave the rest to Jessica.

"You don't have to do that," she said.

"I know."

She pushed it back at me. "No, I mean you really don't have to do that. I've been hungry before. I don't need charity."

I felt a flush of embarrassment rise in my cheeks. "It's not charity," I said. "I can't eat. Not after what we just saw. Please take it."

She nodded and took it.

"Why would they do that to that man?"

"Who knows?" she said through a mouthful of beans. "He probably stole something. That's about the only thing that gets people upset enough to put a man to death that way."

Most of the work had stopped for the midday meal, and people milled about in the grass with paper plates topped with whatever they could scrounge. If it weren't for the rags they wore and their unkempt hair and the sour smell of unwashed bodies, you could almost make yourself believe it was a good old-fashioned backyard barbeque. Almost.

I found it hard to marry the sight of so many people enjoying such a commonplace thing with the realization that we'd all just watched a man die.

"I guess a lot of people stay in places like these," I said, nodding toward a group of men lounging in the grass.

"They won't be staying here," she said. "This is just a quick meal. Most of them will probably be trying to get to Free America sometime tomorrow."

"Are we that close to the wall? I didn't realize."

She nodded. "Twenty or thirty miles."

"And these men"—for they were almost entirely men—"they all want to cross."

She nodded again. "See the way they're dressed? The extra shirts, multiple pairs of pants? They don't dress that way because it's cold. That's everything they own."

She was right, of course. These men were hard-looking fellows, weathered faces, starvation in their eyes. A few had improvised sacks with them, but most had nothing but the clothes on their backs and heavy sticks to use against any zombies they happened to encounter.

"This worries me, Jessica. With all these men trying to cross, aren't we drawing a lot of unwanted attention to ourselves?"

"I doubt it. There's a lot of land out here. There are many places to—"

She broke off mid-sentence as a large man in a red Coca-Cola T-shirt sat next to us. He leered at us, exposing a mouth full of black teeth and a tongue that wouldn't stop moving, like he was chewing on it.

"Where are you ladies headed?" he asked, and when he spoke, I could smell booze on his breath.

"Nowhere," Jessica said.

He turned my way and looked me up and down, eye-fucking me like I was some whore he'd already bought and paid for.

"Well," he said, "if you're gonna be hanging around here for a couple of days, let me know if you meet anyone interested in getting across to Free America. Me and my buddies know how to get them there. It's what we do."

My pulse quickened. Jessica had told me that it would probably happen like this, a quick, unexpected encounter, and while I wanted to catch every nuance of this exchange, I still found it hard to believe that this man was a coyote. In my mind I had formed a picture of what such a man was supposed to look like. He'd be shifty, mean-looking, the kind of man men fear. But above all, the man I pictured in my imagination would actually look like he could do the job. This man, this boozy, greasy, black-toothed redneck, looked like a caricature of himself.

Jessica didn't shrink away like I did, but I did see her gaze sink to the grass. I didn't know it at the time, but Jessica was trying to save us both from looking too eager. This man was a coyote, true, and he seemed sure enough of himself that he could get us into Free America, but there was a certain etiquette to these things of which I was wholly unaware. Men like our thoroughly stewed companion in the red Coca-Cola shirt were, above all else, dangerous. They were opportunists. No doubt they provided the service they claimed, but appearing too eager, jumping right into the conversation, meant that you had something valuable to barter, and for that you were practically begging to get robbed. Or worse.

"I know a good place to cross. Quiet. The patrols pass through there, but they don't hardly ever stop."

"Why not?" I asked. Despite my better instincts, this guy had me curious. He was so sure of himself, like he knew the Quarantine Authority's business better than they did.

"Nothing around there. No towns, no nothing. Just open countryside."

"Well, they have helicopters, right? Robot drones and stuff, too?"

His smile faded then, and I got the feeling that he was reevaluating his first opinion of me. He looked suspicious now, the wheels turning behind his eyes as he took in my clothes, which were dirty, but still holding together, my sturdy shoes, my skin, sun-burnt, but still healthy looking. I was different, and that was making him uncomfortable.

I happened to catch a sharp, warning look from Jessica just then. *Careful*, it said.

"Where are you from?" he asked.

I lowered my gaze. I'd just done a very dumb thing and put us in a bad spot by doing so.

"All over," I said.

I could feel him staring at me, but I kept looking at my hands in my lap. When I didn't offer anything more, he went on.

"The Quarantine Authority is no trouble. How much money do you have?"

"I don't have anything," Jessica said.

"Gold? Any diamonds? A wedding ring, maybe?"

Jessica shook her head.

He looked at me. "How about you? I know you've got something."

I shook my head.

The man went silent again. After a long moment, he got up to leave. "My friends and I are gonna be here till tomorrow. Let me know if you find something you can pay me with." Then he walked away without waiting for us to say good-bye.

"I hope we never see that man again," I said.

Jessica watched him go, frowning, but said nothing. I should have wondered then if she knew something I didn't.

* * *

After lunch, we walked away from the main house so we could talk.

"We should get moving," she said. "It's not smart to stay in places like this longer than you have to."

"Okay," I said. "Where?"

"We should keep going east, toward Weimar."

"We can find somebody there to help us cross?"

She nodded.

"You're sure?"

"Pretty sure, yeah."

"Jessica, look. I gotta say, this is scaring the hell out of me."

"Me too."

"No," I said. I was fumbling for my words. I swept my hand in a vague arc, trying to make a point about everything we'd been through together. "I don't mean all this other stuff we've been dealing with."

"What then?"

I was frustrated with her, angry in fact, and it crept into my tone. "We don't have a plan," I said. "Doesn't that bother you? Even a little bit?"

"If you want to change your mind," she said, "I won't be offended. I can make it from here on my own."

"Jesus, Jessica." I threw up my hands.

"Why are you so upset?"

"Why am I so...?" I stopped there and huffed at her. "Jessica, don't you see? We could die doing this. This isn't some kind of game. The Quarantine Authority, those guys are for real."

"I'm very much aware of what's real," she said. She sounded injured, not haughty. "And for people like me, this was never a game. I hope you remember that when you write your story."

He words floored me.

"Jessica, no. I didn't mean it like that."

"It's okay."

"No, it's not. That was cruel of me."

"No, really," she said. "It's okay. You're sweet. I know you mean well, but we're living in different worlds, you and I."

I felt ashamed. I didn't want to look at her.

But the shame made it easy to make up my mind, and when she got up to go, I did too.

"You're sure?"

I nodded. No words.

We set out on a county road, with a little water but no food. Luckily there was no wind, and though it was cold, the sky was a bright cobalt blue and the sunlight felt good.

After a few hours we came to one of those little towns that used to dot the Texas landscape, a mill or a cotton-processing plant surrounded by a couple of rundown buildings. This town was little more than a stop sign and a handful of moldering doublewides, but it was enough to put us on guard.

"I lost a friend in a place like this," Jessica said.

I hadn't heard her talk about people she'd lost before, and so this caught my attention. "Someone you knew before the wall was built?"

She shook her head. "Just a girl I traveled with. We stopped in a little place like this to try to find water. We were standing behind a counter, and a crawler came up behind her and bit her on the leg before either of us knew it was there."

"I guess you have to be prepared all the time, don't you?"

"Yep." She scanned the town, taking it in with one slow stare. "See! Look right there!" she said, pointing toward a dilapidated gas station. "See it?"

I did. Stumbling through the waist-high weeds that had grown up around the gas pumps was a female zombie. Its hands hung limply by its sides, its hair a stringy, blood-encrusted curtain hanging over its face.

"The place looks deserted, but there are probably more," Jessica said. "Usually they can't survive if it's just one of them."

I watched the zombie for a moment, and was about to look away, when a shot suddenly rang out.

The female zombie collapsed.

Startled, Jessica and I spun around. We hadn't heard the truck coming up behind us, and for a moment, I couldn't believe what I was seeing. I knew there were a few vehicles still working in the zone, like the truck that had pulled that horse trailer full of zombies back at the ranch, but I hadn't seen any actually driving around.

And then it hit me. Oh shit, the truck from the ranch!

"Run!" Jessica said, grabbing my shoulder and pulling me toward one of the trailers.

As I ran I pulled off my backpack and struggled to get the zipper open. I started to fall behind. Jessica turned and yelled at me to hurry up, but I was too busy trying to get my Glock out of the special compartment I'd stitched into the interior.

I slowed down even more. It wasn't there.

Jessica looked back over her shoulder. "What are doing? Come on."

I was frantic now. With the flaps open, my stuff was spilling out of the backpack, going everywhere. I lost my iPhone, my charger, my notebooks, a change of clothes.

But no pistol. Where was it?

"Hurry!" Jessica yelled.

But it was too late. The truck overtook us, swung around wide, and skidded to a stop, kicking up a wave of dust that covered us. I dropped down to one knee and groped for the knife I'd stashed there.

Again, I was too slow.

Two men in camouflage jumped out, and I recognized them immediately as the two men who had been shooting zombies from the deer blind at the ranch.

A third man got out of the truck's back seat.

Our friend, the booze-soaked coyote with the black teeth and the dancing tongue.

His eyes narrowed. It was a sinister gesture, full of menace. "That one right there," he said. "In the black top." He motioned to one of the other two men, who promptly searched me, confiscated my knife, and then pulled my shirt up to my chin.

"Holy shit!" he yelled. "Hey, Jake, you were right. This one ain't no Zoner. Look at this; she's got a brand-new bra on."

* * *

They put us in the backseat and drove east. The two guys in the camouflage hunting outfits looked enough alike that they could have been brothers. They sure acted like it, both of them stinking of beer and sweat and singing along with an Iron Maiden CD they'd plugged into the truck's stereo. The older man, they called him Jake, sat in back with us, a pistol across his lap. Jessica seemed to have slipped into a morose silence. She didn't react to anything the men said, just stared silently out the window at the empty countryside. Riding between them, listening to the two idiots in the front seat, all I wanted to do was be invisible.

Eventually I saw a sign for a town called Harmony Springs,

population 1,405. Harmony Springs was bigger than the little town where we'd been abducted, and it had obviously been hit hard since the Outbreak. Most of the buildings were burned or so thoroughly looted that they looked like little more than empty shells. But there were zombies here. A crowd of them heard our truck coming and stopped, turning their heads to follow our progress.

We pulled into a small motel. From the parking lot, I could see zombies on the road, shambling toward us.

"Why did we stop?" I asked.

The man in the driver's seat found me in the rearview mirror. "Girl, if you gotta ask, this is gonna be more fun than I thought."

His brother guffawed and slapped him on the arm. "Hey, that was a good one."

Jake kicked the back of the passenger seat. "Shut up, Tommy. Go get the collars out of the back."

The laugh died in Tommy's throat. "Sure thing, Jake," he said, and climbed out.

I heard him rummaging around in the bed of the pickup. He came back to Jessica's side and pulled her door open.

"Get out," he said. He glanced over his shoulder at the zombies. They were still a few hundred feet away, but close enough to worry about. "Come on. Hurry up, girl."

Jessica climbed out.

"You too," Jake said and nudged me in the back with his pistol.

I climbed out and stood next to Jessica, my eyes squinting against the sudden brightness of the sun. The man named Tommy had two blood-stained leather collars in one hand and two dog leashes in the other. My heart sank. These men were clearly no strangers to this kind of thing. Whatever sick abuse they had planned for us, they knew how to go about it.

Jake and the other man climbed out of the truck.

"Do it," Jake said. "Hurry up, so we can get inside."

"Yeah," the third man said. "Oh, yeah." Only then, when I saw the way his hands were shaking and the wild look in his eyes, did I realize he was amped up on something, probably meth.

I was crying when Tommy put the collar around my neck. His breath smelled foul, and when he ran his dirty fingertips across the outside of my bra, pausing long enough to give me a hard squeeze, I began to shake. Tommy handed the leash to his brother and a terrible sort of acceptance washed over me. I was going to die, and worse, I was powerless to stop it.

Then he went for Jessica.

I was only half watching what happened. He put his hands on her. She flinched, backed away, swatted at his hands. He closed his arms around her, laughing, despite the zombies who were getting closer every second.

"Hey," he said, "what you got there?"

I saw him take a step back. He looked amused as he reached for her belt buckle. She pushed his hands away. Her clothes were so loose, she had no trouble sticking her hand down the front of her pants, from which she produced a small pistol.

My pistol! The one missing from my pack!

Jessica's face looked utterly blank.

Tommy stood less than an arm's length away, and he took the bullet in the left side of his chest, just under his arm. He didn't fall, though. He staggered away, his hands hanging limply at his side, and bounced off the side of the pickup, leaving a smear of blood. His face was deathly white. He stared, confused by pain and the sudden crazy turn of events, and eventually found his way to one of the concrete curbs at the edge of the parking lot, where he collapsed.

Jessica didn't stop shooting. As soon as Tommy stepped out of her way, she turned her pistol on his brother and shot him once in the chest. The man fell back onto the pavement, rolled onto his side with a sickening groan, and died.

That left only Jake, the coyote.

He was reaching for his own holstered pistol when Jessica stepped right in front of him and deliberately lowered her pistol to his groin before firing.

The man collapsed to his knees, his face stricken, mouth open in a scream that never quite left his throat.

It took me a moment to recover. Jessica stood over Jake, watching him writhe in agony. The two brothers were dead or dying. And the zombies were closing in.

"Jessica," I said, snapping back into the moment. "Get in the truck."

She didn't answer me. She looked back over her shoulder to where the zombies were already entering the parking lot. They were seconds away now.

"You bastard," she muttered to Jake.

I watched as she scooped up the dog collar from the pavement and clamped it around Jake's neck. He tried to push her away, but he was in too much pain to do anything beyond a few feeble gestures. Next she took one of the leashes and clipped it onto Jake's collar, pulled the free end to a light pole, and tied it off.

Jake groaned, trying to regain his feet. The zombies were close. Jessica turned away from him without another word and motioned me to get in the truck.

"Will you drive?" she said. "I don't know if I remember how."

I didn't need to be told twice. I jumped behind the wheel, slammed my door, and rolled up the window.

Jessica got in beside me.

I turned the ignition, and the sounds of a big block V8 roared to life just as Jake let out a terrified scream. I looked in the rearview mirror and saw him wrestling with the collar around his neck, his fingers shaking too badly to work the clasp. The next moment, half a dozen zombies fell upon him and his screams choked off.

"Go!"

"Where?" I asked. "They're all around us."

"Run them down. Hurry!"

I dropped the truck into reverse and punched it. We took off with a lurch. Tires barked on pavement. Several zombies were right behind us, and the truck shuddered as we ran them down. I kept my foot on the gas as we bounced over the curb and spun out in the middle of the road.

We paused there for a moment. The zombies in the parking lot were confused. Some were getting up from the three dead bodies of our abductors and starting after us.

I looked from them to Jessica.

"When did you take my gun?" I asked.

She kept her gaze forward, eyes hard flints of rage. "I've been raped before," she said. "I made myself a promise no one would ever rape me again."

I wasn't mad. Maybe I should have been, but I wasn't.

She took a deep breath, then put the Glock on the seat between us. "I'm sorry," she said. "Stealing from someone is the most serious crime we've got out here."

I left the gun where it was. "I'm lucky you were there."

"Thanks," she said. She pointed east. "Weimar's that way."

* * *

Before the Outbreak, Weimar was a town of some 2000 people. It had a Wal-Mart, a movie theater, a couple of motels, and a string of fast-food restaurants and gas stations clustered around an exit ramp off IH-10. Its survival depended on the traffic flowing between San Antonio and Houston, so the town had grown up in pretty much equal measure on both sides of the highway.

"You don't think it's strange, crossing here?"

"No. Why?"

"Well, I'd kind of thought we'd cross somewhere...I don't know...a little less developed. Why do you suppose this is the place?"

"I don't know."

"I've asked you that already, haven't I?"

"Yeah."

I looked around, trying to see what made this place such a favorite crossing spot. But I still didn't get it. I didn't see anything that popped out at me. We'd made the trip to Weimar in no time in our newly acquired pickup, and we'd even managed to find a good campsite that afforded a view of the town and the wall. I saw a blasted war zone on our side, with at least a hundred zombies wandering the streets, and on the other side of the wall, a gently decaying, abandoned ghost town. The difference between the two parts of the town was striking.

"You done eating?" Jessica asked.

She sat by our camp fire, picking the meat off a rabbit's leg bone.

We'd figured out how to use the assault rifle our former abductors had been kind enough to leave us, and a small, but quite delicious spit-roasted rabbit was the result. I stood there, watching her eat the first good meal we'd had in days, examining the town, and for a second it was easy to trust her. She had gotten me this far, after all.

But the feeling we were in way over our heads just wouldn't go away. "You can have it," I said, and went back to examining the town.

In the few hours since we'd made camp, I'd seen dozens of Quarantine Authority trucks racing up and down the length of the wall. I even saw a few helicopters wheeling overhead. Now, with dusk settling around us, the trucks were playing zombie moans over loudspeakers, and it was driving the zombies crazy.

"Why do they keep playing those sounds?" I asked.

"Augment their numbers, I guess."

"What do you mean?"

"What's the term, a force-multiplier? With the zombies wandering around, it's a lot harder for people to cross."

I thought about that. "So that means they must know about this place? Do you think that's true?"

"How should I know?"

"I can't believe I haven't heard anything about this. I mean, I researched the Quarantine Authority for months before coming on this trip."

"I'm sure they don't want to make it public knowledge."

"I should think not."

Jessica went back to her rabbit. She wasn't letting any of it go to waste. I watched her work the meat from the bone with a thoroughness that only someone well acquainted with hunger could manage. By contrast, my own small pile of bones on the flat rock by my feet contained a fortune of meat. Not for the first time I realized that I was a long way from walking a mile in her shoes.

"Hey, I've got to pee," I said.

"There's a good place over there by the fence." She pointed to the remnants of a white split-rail fence along the ridgeline where we'd camped. "Better take the pistol, though. Rattlesnakes are apt to come out at night."

"Oh," I said. "Okay."

I didn't see any rattlesnakes, which is good, because I don't do well with snakes. Even still, I took my time doing my business, my butt down in the tall grass, my head full of at least a million reasons why crossing the wall in this place was a bad idea. But despite all my studying and all my knowledge of the technology the Quarantine Authority had at its disposal, something about Jessica's simple faith in crossing at Weimar kept quieting my fears. She seemed so sure of herself. Maybe this was doable, I thought. Maybe all the people Jessica had heard of actually did find a way to the other side, and maybe all the rumors back in Free America were true. Maybe we really could do this.

By the time I was ready to start back, I'd made up my mind to follow her the whole way.

I rounded the old live oak that sheltered our campsite and was about to step into the circle of fading firelight when I heard voices. Jessica's and someone else's. A man's voice.

I froze, my hand dropping to the pistol tucked into the front of my jeans.

I could only make out snippets of their conversation, but from the little I could hear I realized that I'd made a mistake. That wasn't a man's voice. It was a boy's. A teenager. He sounded like he was fifteen or sixteen, a kid, but still close enough to a man to be dangerous. I had my hand on the pistol when I heard something behind me.

I spun around to see an older man and a dog staring at me.

"There's no need for your gun, miss," the man said. "I'm sure you ladies have seen your fair share, but my grandson and I are harmless. We're not armed."

"That doesn't seem very smart."

"Why in the world would I need a gun?"

The question caught me by surprise. I didn't quite know what to say. I looked from him to the dog and back to the old man. I had nothing.

"What's your dog's name?" I finally said.

"Guthrie," he said.

"Named for Arlo or Woodie?" It was the first thing that came to mind, but evidently, it was the right thing, for his smile grew wide.

"Both, actually. Nice to meet somebody who remembers the joys of good music."

"My dad," I said. "He was kind of an old hippie."

"Sounds like someone I would have liked," the man said. "My name is Frank. That's my grandson over there talking to your friend. His name is Will."

I nodded. I was starting to like this man, though my hand hadn't gone far from the pistol tucked into my pants. It didn't matter how nice his smile was. And certainly not after what had happened earlier.

"You mind if we go over to the campfire there?" he asked. "I'm a bit chilly."

"Sure," I said, turning to allow him a path to the fire. "Lead the way."

We entered the campsite and I took up a position next to Jessica. I could tell from her body language that this was a good thing, that she wasn't afraid of these men. It wasn't like before, when she spent long stretches of silence trying to shrink into herself, contemplating whatever lay beyond her death. This was different. There actually seemed to be mirth in her eyes as she listened to the old man tell of what had led them here.

They were coyotes. That they admitted from the start. In fact, they told us they had just come from a successful trip across the wall, for they knew of a good spot to cross.

Frank liked to talk, and as he was the first coyote I'd met who wasn't a drunken rapist with bad teeth, I started asking him questions. I was worried he'd be offended, but I think he was actually kind of amused by the whole interview process.

"Wasn't much of a stretch for us," he said. "Will here was living with me on my ranch about twenty miles from here. I've had a flag flying off my doorstep since I came back from Vietnam, and when the government started building the wall, Will and I, we did our part. We even helped those sons a bitches put up some of it. The way I saw it, it was my patriotic duty.

"Course then everything went to hell. I figured even an officer coulda told we wasn't infected, but they locked us up anyway. I couldn't believe it. I stood there on the Zone side of the wall and carried on a twenty-minute conversation with a major, and all I got was fucked."

He looked at us then and actually blushed.

"Er, I'm sorry about my language, ladies. I don't usually talk that way in front of women. But it gets a fella awful mad thinking about it."

After what Jessica and I had just been through, I wanted to laugh.

But instead I said, "So you two became coyotes. How many people have you helped across?"

"I don't know." He looked at his grandson, as if he might know, but the boy just shrugged. "I guess we've taken, what, a couple hundred?"

"A couple hundred?" I said. "No."

"About that," Frank agreed. "We don't work cheap, though." He said it almost as an afterthought. "We're in this for the greater good and all, but we still gotta live, you know?"

"How about a truck?" Jessica said.

The directness of her offer surprised me. I gave her a questioning look, but she didn't acknowledge it. She was looking right at Frank.

"We have a Ford pickup, with a quarter tank of gas. Get us across and it's yours."

Frank seemed as stunned as I was. "I don't know," he said slowly. He looked to his grandson, then back to Jessica. "Where is this pickup of yours?"

"About a hundred yards down the rise there, behind a clump of hackberry."

Frank smiled. He didn't believe us. "That might be okay. You mind if we see it?"

* * *

Frank's expression changed as we pulled the vegetation away from the truck. He recognized it. That much was obvious right from the start.

"Where did you get this?" he said. The good-natured friendliness was gone from his voice now. He was suddenly alert, scanning the dark landscape all around us for signs of trouble.

"They won't come looking for it," Jessica said. She reached inside the cab and pulled out one of the assault rifles Tommy and Jake had left behind. "I can guarantee you that."

"You took this from them?" Frank asked.

"Like I said, they won't come looking for it," Jessica said.

She let that one sit for a moment. The two looked uncertain, maybe even a little frightened. Clearly the men Jessica had dealt with so handily had had reputations. But eventually, their uncertainty was replaced by a grudgingly offered respect and renewed curiosity. We had changed in their eyes.

"You'll give us this?"

"You'll get us across?" Jessica countered.

Frank paused for a long moment, then smiled. "We can do that."

"Then the truck is yours."

"Okay then." He nodded at his grandson. "I guess we have a deal."

* * *

I got frightened by how quickly things happened after that.

I've always been the kind who plans ahead. When I go on trips, I have a schedule laid out. I've done my research. I know what to see and how to get there and how much I'm supposed to pay.

But now, as Will explained to us how this was going to work, I felt panicky. My heart raced. Where were the details? I had tons of questions, and none of them were getting answered.

Jessica, meanwhile, seemed to take it all in stride. She listened to Will with a detached air I found unnerving. I couldn't believe she was so calm about it, like we were discussing plans for dinner or something.

I finally found my voice when he started putting bells on the dog.

"Why are you doing that?"

"This?" he asked. He had taken a harness, a lot like the kind they put on service animals for blind people, and strung bells down its length. He slid the harness into place and scratched Guthrie behind the ears. The dog seemed to love the attention. He wagged his tail eagerly, sending a wave of music through the bells lining his flanks. "Guthrie here runs diversion for us."

A few minutes later I saw what he meant.

Weimar had a greenbelt that ran north to south through town, underneath the highway. Judging from the old-growth vegetation around its banks, I figured it must have doubled as some sort of drainage system. It was the kind of thing a small town that relied on through-traffic for its livelihood would have kept hidden behind a screen of tall trees.

This was apparently Will and Frank's secret, for Will led us to a cross street close to the greenbelt. It was dark, and the streets were lit only by starlight. I could see very little, but I could hear the zombies moaning, and they were getting closer every minute.

Will leaned down and whispered into Guthrie's ear.

For the dog this was clearly some kind of game. It began to bark and spin around in a circle, like it was chasing its own tail, sending the music of bells into the night.

The bells were answered by a chorus of moans that seemed to come from all around us at once.

"What in the world are you—?"

But I didn't get to finish my objection. Will put up a hand and motioned at the dog. Guthrie sprinted forty yards or so down the street, right into the face of a growing crowd of zombies, and began to bark.

"What's he—?"

"Shhh," Will said. "Don't make a sound."

Zombies poured out of the buildings, so many that for a moment I lost sight of Guthrie. But he reappeared, still barking furiously, the bells on his harness like Christmas music in the cold night air, and he sprinted away.

My pulse quickened. The zombies were actually following him. This just might work.

But then he stopped. He turned and watched the zombies, almost like he was waiting for them to catch up.

"Go," I whispered. "Come on you stupid dog. Run!"

"No," Will said. He turned his palm toward me without moving his arms. "No sudden movements. They key on movement and noise. Just wait. Guthrie knows what to do."

And he was right.

The dog was good at what he did, and I began to see how Weimar had earned its reputation. Within a few minutes, Guthrie had managed to lead all the zombies away from our position with an air of practiced efficiency that would have been the envy of any Border collie. I heard him barking in the distance, apparently happy as a clam.

"He'll be okay?" I asked.

"He's a dog," Will said. "Why wouldn't he be?"

I couldn't deny the sense in that.

When the zombies were gone, Will led us to the bottom of the greenbelt and began pulling away vegetation. I looked at Jessica, hoping to catch a glimpse of what was going through her mind. She had grown quiet since we left the campsite, and that bothered me. But she neither returned my glance nor gave any indication that she was anxious about Will's next move. She just stood there, patient as a saint, a strange, almost vacant acceptance on her face. She seemed to have gone robotic, much as she had been in the truck with Jake and the two brothers.

"This is it." Will stepped back to reveal an open standpipe, a gigantic maw, like the entrance to a cave. "Go through here. When you come up on the other side, you'll be in Free America."

"Just like that?" I asked.

"Yep. Pretty much."

Again I looked at Jessica. I wanted some indication that she was okay with this, but all I got was a blank stare. She turned away from me, ducked her head, and slipped into the standpipe.

"Jessica, wait," I said.

Only then did she turn to look at me.

"What?"

"You're okay with this?"

She shrugged. I'll never forget that. There was no expression, just a vacant shrug. She turned into the darkness of the tunnel and started walking. Will gave me an encouraging nod, and the next instant I entered the tunnel, trying to catch Jessica.

The crossing itself was anticlimactic.

We entered a pipe about five feet in diameter, so I had to duck slightly to move through it, and began to feel our way forward.

There was about an inch of standing water, and every step made a splash that echoed through the tube. It was dark, too. Even though Jessica was only an arm's length ahead of me, I couldn't see her.

It would have been the perfect setting for something scary, for every sound sent reverberations in both directions, but the truth is, I felt completely safe the whole way.

The crossing was a piece of cake.

I don't know how long we walked. A couple of minutes, maybe. Eventually we came up on the other side. I saw some shrubs, a patch of starlit sky, and then we were out, standing on the grass.

We had arrived in Free America.

But it was not the joyful homecoming I'd expected. I looked around. Something was wrong. The hairs on the back of my neck were standing up. But what was the problem? What was wrong?

There was a street to our left and abandoned buildings, shop fronts mostly, on the other side. A cold breeze blew dust across the pavement. I heard moans in the distance, and even though all else seemed quiet, my gut told me we were in real trouble.

Jessica stepped into the street, looking back toward the wall.

A Quarantine Authority truck rolled slowly down IH-10.

It stopped.

"Oh, no," Jessica said.

"What's going on?" The truck was maybe a hundred yards away, which was close, but in the dark, I thought there was a chance they hadn't seen us.

The truck started to pull away, and I thought, Good! Yes. Keep going.

"Jessica," I said, "they're leaving!"

She turned to me and shook her head. "We have to get out of here."

"But they're driving off."

It was true. The truck was accelerating away. It went down the highway a few hundred yards, and then suddenly its brake lights came on and it veered off the main lanes and back toward our position.

I couldn't believe what I was seeing.

The truck bounced over the median, crossed a parking lot, and then accelerated down a surface street that would carry it behind us.

"How did they...?" I asked.

"Hurry," Jessica said. "Across the street."

"Where?"

"Those buildings." She pointed to the shop fronts across the street. "Hurry."

I ran.

I made it all the way across before I realized Jessica was still standing in the middle of the street.

"Jessica?"

"You need to go," she said. "Get out of sight."

"What are you doing?"

"I can't go with you."

The truck was getting closer. I could hear its engine pulling hard. And something else. Voices, the sound of boots on the pavement. Men running. Someone shouted orders.

"Like hell. Come on, Jessica."

"No, I can't."

"What do you mean you can't?"

She looked utterly deflated, miserable. "I can't go with you."

I could make out individual voices now, and the clatter of equipment and guns. The soldiers were seconds away.

"But Jessica...?"

"That world doesn't exist for me anymore. It's all changed. I've changed. You can't go home again. Isn't that what you said?"

"Jessica, I—"

"Don't," she said. "There isn't time. I can't go with you, and I can't go back. But you need to hide. Now!"

Halfway down the block, the truck came roaring around a corner. I was out of time. I had to act. There was a narrow alleyway between two buildings a few steps away. I backed into it, into the shadows.

Out in the street, Jessica stood her ground.

From my research on the Quarantine Authority, I knew they'd have helicopters over the area in just a few minutes. They'd have heat-sensing cameras and all sorts of sophisticated people-hunting equipment to bring into play, which meant I had only seconds to escape.

But I couldn't look away from Jessica. Quarantine Authority troopers bore down on her, yelling for her to get down on her knees, while the truck skidded to a stop on the other side of her and hit her with a super-intensity floodlight.

I anticipated the gunshot, but when it came, I flinched just the same.

I turned and ran, tears streaming down my face, and as I slipped away into the night I realized that the woman had given her life for me, and I never even knew her last name.

Paradise of the Living Dead

After the wreck, Andres de Vega stood waist deep on a sandbar, shivering miserably against the cold Pacific waves, unable to catch his breath. A quick glance around made it plain they were worse off than he'd first thought. Only a handful of the *Santa Dominga's* crew had survived the desperate swim for safety after abandoning her to the deep. Those who hadn't been so lucky floated face-down in the water with the wreckage and the dead horses, their bodies slowly rolling on the swells of the dark sea.

The survivors were spread out in a long, disorganized line along the sandbar, the water at their waists oily and burning with a reflected orange light from the setting sun. Most of the men had stripped down to their breeches and linen undershirts to keep from drowning under the weight of their armor, though some still wore their doublets and jerkins, and an improbable few still had their weapons.

Somebody called his name and he turned. The Governor Don Miguel de Luna Cavazos, a man hardly older than himself, barely in his thirties, was supporting de Vega's fellow captain of the infantry, Esteban Caval, with one hand and waving his sword in the air like a battle flag with the other.

"Help me with him," Cavazos yelled out to him.

De Vega waded over to him and put Caval's arm over his shoulder. Caval's beard was black with blood from a gash on the side of his head, and he moaned and muttered something in protest as de Vega took his weight.

"Easy," de Vega said.

"Have you got him?" Cavazos said.

"Yes, sir."

"Good." He pointed to the shore with his sword. "Keep moving."

He didn't wait for an answer. He splashed off toward the others, calling the men by name and shouting orders.

De Vega watched him go, then began to move. The shore, a thin strip of white sand in front of a low wall of dark trees, was still far away, and de Vega was exhausted. He put his head down and trudged onward.

A nearby soldier screamed, a high, unnatural sound that stopped de Vega in his tracks. The man was ahead of him, slightly to his right, and de Vega watched in horror as the man went down, waving one arm wildly as he fell.

De Vega thought, *Oh dear God, a shark!*

But it wasn't a shark. The man sank to one knee and stayed there as others moved in to help him.

When they pulled him from the water, he had his hand out in front of him, showing it to them like it was a gift, the arm covered in blood up to the elbow.

Another soldier only a few feet from de Vega stepped on something and fell over screaming, the sound cutting off as the man went face deep into the water.

De Vega splashed forward to help, but stopped when he saw what the man had fallen in.

Cavazos came up behind him. "What are you doing? Help him."

"No, sir," de Vega said. "Stop."

With his free hand, he pointed at the water.

"Look there, at your feet."

Cavazos squinted at the water, cloudy with the man's blood, and said, "What are those?"

Large black rocks dotted the sea floor. Clinging to the rocks were hundreds of thousands of coin-sized clams, their shells a dusky white, the seam where the shells split open oozing some sort of mucousy growth that was as red and poisonous-looking as the eyes of the jungle frogs from the Peruvian rain forests up the coast. Everywhere they turned, they saw more of the clam clusters, thousands of them.

"Can you move?" Cavazos asked the injured man.

"It sliced through my boot," he said. "They're like knives."

"But can you move?"

The man trembled in the freezing water, but nodded.

"Good man," Cavazos said. "Keep going. But be careful. All of you."

To their right, they heard the Franciscan, Fray Juan Lacayo, moaning theatrically. The man was grossly fat and habitually drunk and complained more than an old washer woman, and now he was hollering at one of the Negro slaves to carry him through the clam beds.

Cavazos hissed under his breath. Lacayo was a menace to morale. The Governor started that way to silence him but suddenly veered off to help yet another man who had gone under.

He grabbed the man by the back of his shirt and hoisted him up, but the man had cut himself badly on the clams and was panicking in his pain. He grabbed for the Governor and pulled him down on top of him, and when Cavazos finally managed to regain his feet and pull the man's head out of the water, de Vega could see he had a deep gash on his arm.

"Your Excellency!" de Vega said, reaching out for him.

"No!" Cavazos said. "Stay back."

"Let me help you."

"No. Keep going." Cavazos waved him on. "I'll be fine," he said. "You go."

De Vega nodded, and then, very slowly, began picking his way through the clam beds, Esteban Caval in tow.

* * *

It took de Vega the better part of two hours to carry his fellow captain ashore. He put his friend down on a flat black rock the size of a table and tended to his friend's injuries as the others slowly lumbered out of the water. More than half of them had ghastly wounds from their trek through the clam beds, and all were exhausted. De Vega had never seen battle himself, but looking at these men, at their wounds and their haunted expressions, he thought of weary, wounded soldiers dragging themselves from the field of a terrible fight.

He and Caval had both cut themselves on the clams as well, but their wounds were minor, Caval's a scratch as long as a man's finger just above the top of his right boot, and de Vega's a small but deep cut on the heel of his left hand. The wound hurt a lot. It was a hot, steady pulse of pain that seemed to keep time with the *thump, thump, thump* of his heartbeat, but he could tell he was suffering less than some of the others.

"So much for honor, eh?" Caval said.

"Honor?" de Vega said. He looked down at the man and thought that he had never looked so weak, so demoralized, as at that moment. The young man he'd sailed with from Spain had been a loud, reckless joker, his eyes bright with expectation and the thrill of adventure and a touch of mischief. But not now. Now he looked half-dead, utterly demoralized.

"It's amazing how fast it all goes to the devil, isn't it?" Caval said.

De Vega nodded. For a moment, he almost tried to bolster Caval's morale by reminding him of Cabeza de Vaca, whose story of shipwreck, extreme privation, and desperate survival had so recently excited the Court in Castile and had even prompted Hernando de Soto to leave Peru and brave the wild interior of Florida, but he knew that now was not the time. Whatever he might say would just come out sounding pathetically naive, and he was too tired for that kind of nonsense.

The sky above them was turning to gold, the horizon on fire. All that remained of the storm that had wrecked the *Santa Dominga* was a few long, smoke-colored clouds reaching like fingers across the sky. De Vega breathed deeply, smelling the sea and feeling the chill of the approaching night in his throat. *Under different circumstances,* he thought, *this place must seem a paradise, like Eden.*

He turned and watched the last of the survivors coming ashore. The Negro carrying Fray Lacayo on his back staggered out of the waves, his legs glistening with blood from cuts so deep the white of the fat beneath his muscles showed, yet still he carried the fat Franciscan.

The Negro tried to put him down, but tripped over himself and let Lacayo fall onto his face in the sand.

"Idiot!" Lacayo growled, spitting sand. The Franciscan always carried an olive-wood walking stick with a stamped brass ball at one end, and after he wiped the sand from his lips, he began to beat the Negro with it, lashing him across his bare back. The Negro did not resist. Rather, he pitched over and landed on his side. He lay there wheezing, his tongue fat between his teeth, like a horse that's been run too hard.

"Get up," Lacayo shouted.

The man didn't move. Furious, Lacayo struck him again.

"Stop that!"

Lacayo wheeled angrily, ready to shout down anyone who would deny him his right to beat the slave, but his hard expression melted when he saw it was Cavazos yelling at him, the Governor now coming ashore with an injured soldier in his arms. Cavazos handed the man off to another soldier and said, "Put that damn thing away and start tending to the wounded."

"But, Your Excellency," Lacayo said, "this slave—"

"I don't care to hear it," Cavazos said, and as he stood there, the gash on his right arm oozed with fresh blood. Large, red raindrops fell in the sand at his feet and turned brown. "You're not injured. Find some cloth and start dressing the wounds of the men who are."

Lacayo seemed like he wanted to argue, but he looked at the blood dripping from Cavazos' arm and evidently thought the better of it. He ducked his head and went off, making a terrific show of looking busy.

Seemingly oblivious to his own hurts, Cavazos began organizing the men, giving them orders to prepare a camp.

De Vega had a great deal of respect for Cavazos. Like de Vega and Caval, Cavazos had missed his chance for glory with Pizarro and de Soto against the Incan king, Atahualpa, and the seizing of the Incan capital city of Cajamarca. They were all three products of an aimless generation, inheritors of a Spain gutted by the long and debilitating civil war their fathers had fought, a war that had left the country bankrupt of everything but a standing army, no glory left to claim.

But if glory and honor had passed him by, Cavazos gave no indication of it. He called de Vega over and told him they needed to find food and fresh water for the men.

"Gather a small party together and scout the area. The men need to eat and rest before we start moving again. We'll need firewood too. It'll be dark in a few minutes, and I want a fire to chase away their misery."

But before de Vega could answer, the Negro Lacayo had beaten let out a horrible groan. Cavazos gave the man a curious glance. Others near the man gathered round him. The Negro rolled over onto his back and stared up at nothing. His eyes were mapped with cracked veins as bright as red thread, and his mouth was warped with pain.

The Negro tried to speak, but couldn't. He opened his lips and gulped twice for air, the breath finally leaving him with a throaty rattle.

And then he was dead, his eyes still open, sightless to this world.

Cavazos walked over to the dead man and looked for a moment at his face. Lacayo tried to speak, but Cavazos silenced him with a hard stare.

"Captain de Vega," Cavazos said.

"Your Excellency?"

Cavazos lowered his voice so only de Vega could hear. "Find some men to take the body away from camp."

"Yes, sir."

"And, Captain...."

"Yes, sir?"

"Take it a good distance away. In case there are animals around."

"Yes, sir."

De Vega got four uninjured men to carry the body. They gathered around it, and each took a foot or a shoulder. There was a quiet moment, an odd, silent moment, when things were almost routine, the men putting their hands on the corpse, looking at each other to time their lift.

And then, abruptly, things were no longer routine. Everything changed.

The Negro—de Vega did not know his name, or even think to ask it—rolled his head to one side and sat up. His mouth fell open and his yellow, bloodshot eyes fell on the man holding his left shoulder. Those who saw what was happening froze, not in fear, but in confusion.

A gravely snarl came out of the dead man's throat, and he lunged for the soldier at his shoulder. The man was too stunned to pull his hands away, and before he could shake himself out of his confusion, the Negro had his mouth on him, his teeth tearing into the thick wad of muscle at the bicep, ripping it away.

The others stood by in shock, unable to believe that this man— this *slave*, for God's sake—was doing this, was attacking one of their own. De Vega watched the moment spin out in unreal time, each second seeming to go on indefinitely as a thick rope of gore fell from the Negro's mouth.

He thought, *Do something! For God's sake, do something!* But his feet were stuck in place, his hands grasping reflexively at the empty air at his side. A soldier named Rivera stepped in front of de Vega, his shoulder blocking de Vega's view of the attack, and in one smooth motion plucked the Negro off the man and threw him to the ground.

The Negro's shoulder struck the rock at Caval's feet, and Caval stumbled to one side, away from the gore-stained mess the man had become.

The man who'd been bitten was screaming, long and hollow-sounding, like a wounded animal. The sound was unearthly, seemingly too big for one man to make, but it acted like a gunshot in de Vega's mind. A sudden, violent chill ran over his skin. He began to swallow convulsively, uncontrollably. He felt like a swarm of bees were buzzing angrily inside his ears. But somehow, through his fear, he found himself and moved. He grabbed Caval and pulled him back. The Negro, meanwhile, had regained his feet and was staggering into the middle of the other injured men, who did their best to get away from him. He pivoted on his shredded leg, swiping the air with his fingers, his mouth open in a continuous groan.

Cavazos stepped through the panicked crowd and ran his sword through the Negro's chest, right through the heart, the tip of the steel erupting from the man's back.

Cavazos stopped, waiting for the man to fall, for him to sink to his knees and his weight to slide down the blade, but the slave gave no indication that he even noticed the steel through his heart. His expression never changed. He didn't even blink.

"What in the name of—?" Cavazos started to pull away, panicking now himself as the Negro grabbed him by the arm and tried to bite him.

Cavazos kicked the man in his injured leg, knocking him off balance enough to pull the blade free. The Negro staggered forward, his ruined leg barely able to hold his weight. Cavazos side-stepped him, and the Negro fell face-down in the sand. With the grace of a man raised with a sword in his hands, Cavazos spun the blade a half turn in the air, so that the tip of it was pointed at the flailing man, and ran it through the back of his head.

The Negro's body went instantly still.

And with that stillness came a silence as all the men stared from the dead man to each other, looking for answers to questions too strange, too wild to put into words.

"That man was dead," one of the soldiers said.

Rivera scoffed. "Impossible."

"He was I tell you. I saw his eyes." The soldier looked at the others around him. "You all saw him."

"I saw," said another man.

"And I," answered still another.

Rivera sounded angry now. "Impossible. You don't move when you're dead."

"A devil," said Lacayo, the Franciscan.

That made everyone pause. A few men muttered nervously, while here and there others crossed themselves.

Lacayo held his olive-wood walking stick up, the stamped brass ball catching what was left of the daylight and glinting with a lurid russet light. "I knew it when I beat him. A devil."

The men were silent, even the wounded.

"I knew the man was possessed."

"Be quiet," Cavazos said.

"You cannot possibly ignore what you have seen with your own eyes. Your eye is the lamp of your body, and when—"

"I said be quiet!"

Cavazos reached for his sword and yanked it out of the dead man's skull with a great show of one-handed strength. He turned on the friar and was about to order him to make himself busy when de Vega moved close to Cavazos and whispered.

"Sir, over there. In the tree line."

Cavazos looked de Vega in the eye, then scanned the wall of vegetation that marked the beginning of the jungle.

A face peered back at him—a young boy, terrified, wide-eyed, his brown, almost round face streaked with ochre paint. The boy knew he'd been spotted. He jumped up and ran into the jungle at a full sprint.

"Get him!" Cavazos said. "Hurry!"

De Vega took off into the jungle with a few others close behind. He could see the boy slipping through the heavy, damp vegetation, moving with incredible speed, like an animal. De Vega was clumsy. He slapped at leaves as big as a man's shirt, falling farther and farther behind in the pursuit, tripping over tangled vines at his feet.

Then he unexpectedly burst through the vegetation and teetered at the edge of a ravine, swinging his arms for balance with his toes over a sheer face of rock some forty feet down.

Rivera appeared beside him and nearly went over the edge, and would have, had de Vega not caught him and pulled him back.

"Careful," de Vega said.

Rivera's eyes went wide, staring down at the fall he could have had. "Yes, sir."

Two more soldiers dragged up noisily behind them. De Vega heard them coming before he saw them, and he realized that they weren't going to catch any jungle Indian boy who had spent his life hunting and playing in this place. They made too much noise. He turned and looked at them as they stepped out of the leaves. One was hurt badly from their trek across the clam beds. His right leg was shredded from mid-thigh to below the knee, and his boot was glistening with his blood. The man's face was awash in sweat, and his eyes had turned piss yellow. He was coughing, gagging.

"Where did he go?" the other soldier said.

"We lost him somewhere back there," de Vega said, pointing toward the jungle behind them.

"Captain," the man said, "he was just a boy. There are probably others. A village, maybe."

De Vega didn't give it his full attention. The wounded soldier was swaying on his feet, still coughing, his pupils rolling up into his head. His tongue looked swollen and black.

De Vega was about to tell the man to sit down for God's sake when the soldier suddenly doubled over and vomited something that looked like fish guts onto the ground. De Vega wrinkled his nose at the smell, and then, before he could do or say anything, the wounded soldier teetered toward the ravine, lost his footing, and tumbled down the rocks.

They watched him fall, saw him land on his back on the rocks below, heard his spine snap. The man was bent over backward and his body lay motionless, a wreck.

"What was wrong with him?" Rivera said.

De Vega thought, *The clams. That's what's wrong with him.* He looked down at his own palm and felt the pain anew, a sharp stabbing pain in time with the *thump, thump, thump* of his pulse. *Blessed Virgin,* he prayed, *keep me safe.*

They stared down at the soldier, the three of them silent.

When the body started to move, Rivera gasped.

De Vega didn't even blink.

The man pulled himself to his feet, his mangled, misshapen body moving unnaturally. He staggered to the edge of the ravine and clawed the air between himself and the men watching him from the edge of the ravine's wall.

"That can't be happening," Rivera said. "That man... Captain?"

"Let's go," de Vega said. "Come on."

He turned and trudged his way back to the beach, the others turning reluctantly from the edge of the ravine, the dead man still reaching for them, and followed de Vega in stunned silence.

De Vega told Cavazos that they lost the boy in the jungle and that another soldier had died in the ravine, but didn't tell him about what came after that. About two dozen men were injured to some degree by their walk across the clam beds, and they were starting to show signs of fatigue that worried de Vega. They were lethargic, absent-minded, their eyes turning yellow and bloodshot. Even Cavazos, ordinarily a man of limitless energy and drive, was breathing funny, and sweat had popped out all over his face.

De Vega looked the men over, at the injured and the healthy, then went to where Caval still sat on the flat black rock, nursing the cut on his leg. He looked better than most of the others, but he was pale, his eyes dull and out of focus.

"What's wrong?" Caval said.

"We have a problem," de Vega said.

* * *

De Vega was exhausted, but he couldn't sleep. With nightfall, the wind off the ocean picked up and whipped the hair around his face in a constant, bone-chilling roar. He shivered against it, all the while listening for... what? He wasn't sure, exactly. It was hard to think clearly. He only knew that something was inside of him, and whatever it was, it terrified him.

Caval whispered to him. De Vega rolled over and looked at him through the moonless dark. Glinting sparks of light danced at the edges of de Vega's vision.

"We're going to die out here, aren't we?"

"I don't think so," de Vega said.

"Don't lie."

"I won't."

There was a long, quiet moment.

"Are we going to die?"

"We're soldiers," de Vega said.

"Soldiers are supposed to fight for honor. There's no honor out here. Not like this."

De Vega closed his eyes.

"Andres?"

"Go to sleep," de Vega said.

* * *

De Vega woke several hours later to a pitiful moaning. He tried to push himself to a sitting position, but the pain in his hand had turned his blood to fire in his veins and he winced, biting his lip to keep from yelling out. He rolled over onto his side and used his good hand to sit up.

The Franciscan, Lacayo, was sitting on the sand, holding himself, rocking back and forth like a mother in mourning.

"Be quiet," Cavazos hissed at him.

"I'm cold."

"We're all cold. Be silent. Be a man."

Lacayo's eyes were those of a scolded child. "But I'm cold."

From where he knelt in the sand, de Vega could see Lacayo and

Cavazos in detail, but the sleeping shapes beyond them were only dark humps on the lighter shade of dark that was the beach.

Motion caught his eye, and de Vega saw one of those dark humps sit up.

Cavazos saw it too.

"Go back to sleep," he said to the man, his voice suddenly quiet, gentle, paternal.

But the man sat there, silently, his back straight, hands down at his side. Another man, three humps over, sat up, too.

As de Vega watched, two men to his left sat up also, and the hairs rose on the back of his neck. Something was wrong. The something that he'd been dreading was finally here.

He shook Caval by the shoulder. Caval murmured grumpily, and de Vega shook him again.

Caval's eyes fluttered open.

He stared up at de Vega, then turned and saw the others.

He moved slowly, reaching for one of the two heavy lengths of drift wood he and de Vega had secreted away before nightfall.

"Go back to sleep," Cavazos repeated.

De Vega grabbed the other stick.

What happened next happened very quickly. The dead men moved with amazing speed. They scrambled to their feet and fell on the uninjured men, most of whom were still sleeping.

Screams filled the night, drowning out the breaking surf. Cavazos leapt into the middle of a fight, where two dead men were tearing the windpipe out of a man's throat with their teeth, and tried to pull one of the dead men away. The dead man turned on him and wrapped him in his arms, and the next minute Cavazos was down.

Lacayo screamed, a high, feminine shriek, a strange sound coming from such a fat man. He pleaded to be left alone, for someone to save him, and as de Vega and Caval fought the dead, swinging their clubs wildly in the melee, one of the uninjured Negro slaves grabbed Lacayo by his armpits and dragged him to safety.

Cavazos threw off his attacker and rose to his feet. He was bleeding horribly from the side of his head, his ear torn off. He wasn't able to stand up straight and stayed bent over, swaying drunkenly, his arms swinging by his side. Lacayo cried out for Cavazos to save him, but Cavazos couldn't hear anything anymore. His eyes had turned to blanks, and though it took a great deal of effort for him to stay on his feet, no breath steamed from his mouth in the cold, sharp air.

"Run!" de Vega said to Lacayo. "You have to move!"

The friar stared about him in a panic. Cavazos' corpse lumbered forward, advancing on him. Lacayo shook his head back and forth violently, like that would make the whole thing go away, but Cavazos still advanced.

De Vega swung his improvised club at a soldier whose teeth were thick with red meat and blood and knocked him to the ground. He swung the club over his head and brought it down on the back of another man's head. It burst like wildflower in early spring.

"Do something," de Vega said to Lacayo, and Lacayo did. He staggered backward and nearly fell over the Negro who had pulled him to safety. The slave was fighting two dead men, keeping them at bay, but just barely. Lacayo caught himself on the man's shoulder, then threw him into Cavazos' path. He was left standing on his own, at the edge of the fight, and he didn't waste the chance. He turned and ran into the jungle.

De Vega watched him run, and knew that that was their only chance as well. Caval was next to him, clubbing a dead man into the sand. De Vega grabbed him and pointed at Lacayo slipping into the vegetation. "Follow him!" he said, and pushed him that way.

The jungle was dark, and once they fled into the cover of the underbrush, the noise of the ocean and the fight all but disappeared. They could hear Lacayo crashing through the vegetation, and it was easy to catch up with him.

He screamed when they stopped him.

"Shhh!" de Vega hissed.

"Stop! Don't touch me! Leave me alone," Lacayo said.

"Be quiet."

But Lacayo couldn't. He swatted their hands away and screamed.

De Vega hit him in the ear with his cupped palm, knocking the fat friar back onto his butt.

The friar looked up at him, his hand over his ear.

"Be quiet," de Vega said. "They'll hear us."

The three of them were silent then, listening to the sounds of dead men moaning as they entered the jungle.

"They're going to eat us," Lacayo said.

"Shhh!"

"What's wrong with them?"

"Shhh!" de Vega said.

They were silent again, listening.

"What are we going to do?" Caval whispered.

"Be still," de Vega said. "We'll wait here."

Lacayo settled in to a rhythm of whimpering noises while de Vega and Caval listened. They stayed there, still as reptiles in the sun, and listened. The dead were entering the jungle now, moaning like ghosts in the pale, false dawn.

"We need to go," Lacayo said. "Run while we still can."

"Shhh!" Caval said.

"I want to go. I want to go!"

"Be quiet."

But Lacayo couldn't. The man was worm-eaten with fear, he vibrated with it, and de Vega, staring at him, thought to himself, *He's going to run*, just as the Franciscan pushed himself up and ran.

"Damn!" de Vega said.

There was enough light that they could see a sort of unorganized skirmish line of the dead approaching through the tangle of twisted vines and leaves and strange black trees. Lacayo's blind fear had put them in a position where their only choice was to run, and de Vega and Caval tore after him.

The three ran till they came to the ravine, then turned parallel to it, away from the beach. Gradually, the ravine shallowed out, and then disappeared altogether, and they were left with nothing but dense underbrush. They slowed their pace, but didn't stop. They couldn't. The dead men were still back there, their moaning distant now, but not *that* distant.

Lacayo was in front, de Vega and Caval keeping a nervous eye behind them, when they unexpectedly broke through the wall of dank undergrowth into a clearing, the smell of wood smoke in their noses.

They all stopped.

"My God," de Vega whispered.

Before them was a village of tall, cylindrical huts with grass roofs, a curl of white smoke rising into the air from a communal fire, a bare-chested, dark-skinned woman nursing a baby, a sudden flurry of frightened murmurings from the villagers as they took cautious, uncertain steps forward to get a glimpse of the white men.

"Damn," de Vega said again.

"Let's go," Lacayo said. He stepped forward, wanting to run through the village.

De Vega grabbed him by the back of his robe, and started to pull him back into the jungle.

"What are you doing?" Lacayo said. "Let go of me."

"There are children here," de Vega said.

"Let go of me!" Lacayo said. "Stop. I don't want to go back."

They advanced into the jungle, the moaning of the living dead ahead of them and also to their right, coming closer, attracted by Lacayo's screams.

When the ravine appeared, they entered it, climbing over rocks, splashing through puddles of stagnant black water that stank of rotting vegetation, de Vega and Caval both in silent agreement about what they had to do. Lacayo fought them the whole way, screaming to be let go, and soon the dead men were at the edge of the ravine, tumbling down the rocky sides in an attempt to reach them.

"Please," Lacayo begged. "Please let me go."

Ahead of them, in the narrowing V of the ravine, was the broken-backed dead man who had fallen into the ravine at the end of their foot chase with the boy with the ochre-painted face. The broken-backed man moved in stop motion, like a series of pictures skipping from one moment to the next, and de Vega thought of a crab scurrying across the beach in slow motion.

"Oh my Lord," Lacayo said.

Caval stepped forward and swept the dead man's legs out from under him with his driftwood club. The dead man fell, and de Vega hit him with his own club, crushing his skull.

The whole exchange had only taken seconds, but it was enough time for Lacayo to break free and scramble up the slope of the ravine.

The dead lumbered closer, clawing their way toward the two captains through the funnel of the ravine. Above them, peering down at them through the walls of vegetation at the edges of the ravine, were ochre-faced warriors, armed with bows and arrows and spears.

The dead closed on them.

"Andres?"

De Vega stared at the faces above them, then at the moaning

dead, only a few feet from them now. His head was swimming, a roar like a waterfall gathering just behind his eyes, and he wondered how much longer he'd be able to stand. He certainly didn't have anything left for a fight.

"You wanted honor, my friend?" he said to Caval, and tossed his club to the ground. "This abomination has to stop here. That is our honor."

Caval, his eyes heavy and cloudy, tossed his own club down and waited. De Vega looked up at the gallery of dark, round faces, meeting their black eyes.

His gaze settled on one of the warriors.

The man nodded at him.

De Vega nodded back that he was ready, and then the ravine filled with the first volley of arrows.

Jimmy Finder

"Is that your experiment?" Captain Fisher asked.

The infantry captain gestured toward the boy on the other side of the one-way glass. From the look on Fisher's face, it was obvious he didn't think much of the kid. He certainly didn't see humanity's greatest hope in the war against the zombies. What he saw was a mop-haired runt, too skinny, too short, too awkward, about as far from a soldier as one could hope to find.

"His name is Jimmy Finder," Dr. David Knopf replied. "I try not to refer to him as my experiment."

"Finder? You're kidding. That can't be his real name, can it?"

Knopf smiled amiably enough, but inside, he was holding onto his patience with both hands. It was always the same with these military men, their smug condescending abuse and smirks of disdain whenever they were confronted with something that challenged the conventional wisdom of the battlefield.

"*James* is all we were able to learn from him," Knopf admitted. "We started calling him Finder after his abilities became apparent."

Fished shook his head. "Frankly, Doctor, I think this is all a load of crap. You should probably know that from the start."

Knopf's expression carefully masked his frustration. It wouldn't do any good to alienate the military now that they'd finally agreed to let him demonstrate Jimmy's talents in the field. It had only taken twelve long years.

"That's all right, Captain. I'm used to skepticism."

"It's a wonder you still bother trying."

You bastard, Knopf thought. Fisher was really trying to bait him. "I believe in what we're doing here, Captain. I wouldn't have put twelve years of my life into this project if I didn't. That boy in there is going to save lives and help us turn the corner on this war."

Knopf, afraid he was about to say something he'd regret, turned his attention on Jimmy, and a familiar mix of pity and pride rose up in him. Twelve years earlier, a contingent of Warbots discovered the boy wandering the hills above the nearby town of Mill Valley, Ohio. The provisional government gave him to Knopf's Weapons Research Team with orders that they find out how a two-year-old toddler had managed to survive an entire summer right under the noses of ten thousand zombies. It had taken Knopf three years to discover the answer. It took another nine before anybody in the military's High Command would take him seriously enough to let him prove it. But he did find the truth.

"You really believe that kid in there has psychic powers?"

"That's not exactly what he does," Knopf said. "He's not a psychic. He doesn't predict the future or read minds, none of that gypsy-fortune-teller stuff. Think of him as a sort of bloodhound that we've trained to sniff out zombies." Fisher was staring at him, his expression inscrutable. "Look," Knopf went on, "you're familiar with the morphic field theory, right? The idea that zombies move in large groups because their brains are linked by a neuro-electric field in the reptilian core of their brains. Jimmy can pick up on that morphic field."

"I've heard the theory, Doctor. I've also heard a lot of respectable scientists say that it's a bunch of rubbish."

"It's not rubbish, Captain. You've probably experienced it yourself. Ever felt somebody staring at you from across the room? Or have you have ever thought of somebody completely out of the blue, and then moments later they call you on the phone? Ever watched a large flock of birds change direction without running into each other? How about watched a school of fish? Same thing. It's not rubbish. It's a documented fact. And it's what allows Jimmy to do what he does. Think of how helpful that would be on the battlefield. Think of the tactical advantage you'd have if you knew where your enemy was all the time."

"Anybody can find a zombie, Doctor. Just go outside the walls and make a lot of noise. You'll find plenty in no time."

The military, Knopf thought. Such fools. They couldn't even come up with new jokes, much less open their minds to new possibilities. It was no wonder they were getting their butts handed to them on the battlefield. And if Captain Fisher was any indication of the kind of officer the High Command was turning out, the future looked bleak indeed.

"Yes," Knopf said, "but the trick, as I'm sure they taught you in your officer training school, is to find the enemy before they find you. Wouldn't you agree?"

"We already have sensors, doctor. The robots can detect zombies with an eighty-six percent accuracy rate. In my opinion, that's—"

"Hardly an acceptable margin of error," Knopf said, shaking his head. "Not when lives are on the line. And eighty-six percent is nothing compared to what Jimmy's capable of. Wait until we arrive in Mill Valley, Captain. Your robots claim to have cleared the town of every last zombie. What will happen if that boy in there is able to lead us to even one zombie? What will you say then?"

"It'll never happen."

"All I ask is for you to keep an open mind, Captain," Knopf said.

"You're asking me to believe in mumbo jumbo, Doctor. I prefer to put my faith in robots and bullets."

Knopf glanced over at Jimmy. The boy was tossing in his sleep. Nerves, probably. Or bad dreams. Poor kid. Sleep was usually the only time his mind got any rest, the only time he could turn off his gift.

"Just you wait, Captain. Tomorrow, that boy's going to make a believer out of you."

* * *

"All stop!" Fisher shouted.

The expedition ground to a halt. They'd been walking for hours, and the clattering and clanking and whirring of a full company of robots had made a tremendous racket that even now, in the sudden silence that followed the captain's command, continued to ring in Jimmy Finder's ears.

But the ringing only lasted a moment. Once the racket faded, the pulsing images of the dead flooded back into his brain. The town was definitely not clear. He could sense hundreds of pulses going off all around him, like he was standing in the middle of a huge orchestra made of nothing but big bass drums, all of them pounding out a violent and relentless and tuneless rhythm.

He groaned in misery, wanting only to curl up in his hammock and fall asleep. Going outside like this, with nothing to shield him from all those morphic pulses, was crippling. Dr. Knopf had tried to teach him a few tricks to get rid of the pain, like focusing on a single thought-presence and letting everything else fall away, but most of the tricks were too hard to do outside of the lab. And right now, he could barely open his eyes his head hurt so badly.

I can't do this, he thought.

James.

Jimmy stiffened in alarm. He looked around, uncertain who was talking to him. He was surrounded by Troopbots. They had no faces, only curved, featureless metal plates that they turned toward their human masters whenever they needed to speak or were spoken to, but none of them were looking at him now. They stood like statues, tall and mute in the settling dust and gloom of evening.

And there were no humans anywhere around him. Dr. Knopf and the soldiers had moved to the shade of the portico of a deserted gas station, talking in hushed tones. Knopf wasn't even looking in his direction.

It is you, isn't it? My God, how long I've waited!

That time the voice was so strong it caused his eyes to fly open. The hairs on the back of his were standing on end, as though from static electricity. He could feel the blood rush to his head. He was dizzy, his cheeks flushed with an uncomfortable heat. It wasn't just a voice, he realized, but a thought. A thought with weight, with force behind it.

The sensation didn't last long, though. The dizziness faded. A cold sweat replaced the heat on his cheeks. He had a real, almost tangible sense of the contact fading. The next instant, all trace of the link—yes, that was it; it had been a link he felt, like another mind wrapping its grip around his mind—echoed away, leaving him confused and somehow vulnerable.

Again he looked around.

No one was paying him any attention.

He cocked his head to one side, trying to make sense of what he had just felt. Dr. Knopf had always said his power was of a class known as remote viewing. He could sense zombies, locate them with a degree of precision the machines couldn't even begin to approach, but only that. He had never heard voices before. Thought-speech was out of the range of his abilities, much as people were unable to hear the high-pitched tones of a dog whistle. And for that Jimmy was supposed to be thankful. Dr. Knopf had told him so, and his own short excursions outside the lab had backed that up. It was hard enough holding on to his sanity while sensing the morphic fields that emanated from the dead. If he could hear the thoughts of the living as well...

But then, what was happening to him? Was this something new?

The expedition had stopped on a hill above the little town of Mill Valley. Jimmy walked through the perfectly ordered rows of Troopbots and continued on until he was well in front of the expedition. From here, he could look overlook the expanse of the ruined town. The mind-voice was coming from somewhere down there, under the rubble.

Cautiously, one small bit at a time, he opened his mind and searched the ruins. This always hurt, even in the controlled circumstances of the laboratory, but he was curious.

Gritting his teeth, he sent out a thought.

Who are you? How do you know my name?

Jimmy waited, his mind open and unguarded.

Who are you?

But there was nothing. Not even the morphic pulsing of a zombie's brain. The evening gloom settling over the town was like a burial shroud, silent and unfathomably deep. Was it any wonder it frightened him so?

* * *

Why won't you answer me!

The mind-voice slashed like a knife through Jimmy's sleep. He flinched awake, eyes shooting open in panic. His breaths were coming in fast, shallow gulps, his body soaked with sweat.

Please stop! Oh God, please stop. You're hurting me!

He sent the thought out in desperation. His head felt like it was about to split open, like there was a crazy little man inside there going to town with a hatchet on his brain.

I need help. I need help now!

Jimmy gasped. The pain was coming in waves now. He gritted his teeth against it, tensing the muscles in his temples, and surprisingly, that helped a little. The pain started to ebb away.

Who are you?

But there was no need to ask the question, for now that the pain was no longer tearing him apart, Jimmy knew.

The mind-voice belonged to his father.

Yes, James! It's me! Oh, thank God you've come!

They told me you were dead.

Jimmy dropped out of the hammock he'd slung between the gas pumps of the abandoned gas station and staggered numbly toward the moonlit road, where the robots stood in silent, perfectly ordered rows.

They told me you were dead.

Do I sound dead to you? James, come to me. I need help.

Nodding slowly, transfixed by the mind-voice pulling him toward the town, Jimmy began to walk.

* * *

The silence hanging over the town was massive. Jimmy could feel it like a presence, vast and powerful, full of menace.

Many people had died here. In the four days since the army retook the town the birds and the rats had descended on the corpses heaped in the gutters and had begun to feast. The carrion feeders watched him silently as he passed, their eyes gleaming yellow and full of hate, their bodies wet with gore. *So many dead,* Jimmy thought. *Such a terrible waste.* Instinctively, he found himself emptying his mind, measuring his breathing, the way Dr. Knopf had taught him, so that he could stay calm when facing the horror of a badly decomposed zombie.

But not even Dr. Knopf's calming lessons prepared him for the horror of this place. The fighting here must have been intense. Besides the bodies and the carrion feeders, hardly a wall was free of bullet holes. A few of the buildings had been reduced to rubble. Many more were burned to blackened skeletons.

And no matter where he looked, no matter what road he took, the silence was everywhere.

Daddy, which way?

Daddy.

That word stopped him, and he couldn't help but smile. It sounded funny to him. He'd spent his entire life an orphan, the subject of countless stupid tests, trying to justify what he did for people who seemed only interested in mocking him and treating him like a freak—and now here he was calling for his daddy.

The military men already thought of him as a runt; he knew that. What would they think of him now? They'd call him pathetic. Or worse. But what did they know? They weren't orphans. They hadn't walked in his shoes, cried his tears, felt the kind of heartsick loneliness that carried him off to sleep each night. Screw them. So what if he walked around the world calling for his daddy? What did they know about it?

Feeling mean, feeling bitter, Jimmy wandered the ruins, searching for a way under the town. He sent out his mind-voice constantly, trying to get his father to answer. But he never felt anything more than a curious tickling sensation at the base of his skull. Even as out of desperation, he opened up more and more, there was nothing but the town's foreboding silence.

And then, he found it. A way down.

He had turned into an alleyway because he sensed it was the right way to go, and that same feeling had led him to a half-hidden flight of stairs. They terminated in a rusted metal doorway marked:

MILL VALLEY WATER AUTHORITY
AUTHORIZED PERSONNEL ONLY

This was it.

The hint of a smile appeared at the corner of his mouth. *Trust your instincts*, Knopf had told him. Well, he had trusted his instincts, and they led right where he wanted to go.

Jimmy wriggled the knob.

Locked, damn it.

He rammed it with his shoulder and only managed to hurt himself.

Out of frustration, he picked up a piece of rebar from the sidewalk and banged on the knob until it snapped off.

The hinges groaned as the door fell open.

Leaning forward, he peered into the darkness, gagging on the noisome stench of sewage coming up from the levels below. Jimmy opened his mind, intending to find his father's mind-voice, but instead was hit by something else.

Do not go down there.

"What?" Jimmy said. As before, he looked around, because this voice was different from his father's. It seemed to be someone talking to him. But he was alone. A sheet of newspaper, carried by a breeze, drifted down the empty street. Nothing else moved.

"Who's talking?" Jimmy asked.

If you go down there, you will die.

"Tell me who you are," Jimmy insisted.

This is Comm Six. State your designation.

"My designation? What the...? I'm Jimmy."

He shook his head, trying to understand the sensation the voice was causing in his ears. It wasn't a voice. Not exactly. It was a mind-voice, like his father's, but different. Where his father's voice was a spike trying to hammer its way into his brain, this voice was like insects buzzing in his head. And yet it was just as clear, just as insistent, as his father's. Only it was... soothing somehow. Not at all harsh.

What's a Comm Six?

I am Comm Six.

Yeah, but what does that mean? Who are you? How come you can talk to me?

I am a Combot. I directed the robots that fought to retake this town. I was damaged. I was left behind.

I've never heard of a Combot. And you don't sound like any robot I've ever heard of.

I am not like other robots. I am a Combot. I am sentient.

Sentient? What's that mean?

It means that I am aware of my own presence. I know there is a me and a you and that we are different from each other. I can think.

Can't other robots do that, like Warbots?

Not like I do. Warbots have adaptive programming. They have built in algorithms that allow them to interpret their environment within a narrow variety of preprogrammed ways. I do not have those limitations. My thinking is based on non-linear models, more like your own.

I've never heard of robots being able to do stuff like that.

I was an experiment.

Jimmy laughed. "Uh-huh. You and me both."

Why do you laugh? You are in danger. Do not go into the sewers. There are still many zombies down there.

I don't sense any. Usually I can sense the zombies. That's what I do.

Perhaps the lead residue is blocking you.

I don't get blocked. My sensors aren't like yours. And besides, my dad's down there.

A pause.

There are only zombies down below.

Yeah?

Yes.

Well, I guess we'll see about that, won't we?

* * *

The ground shook beneath the Warbot's weight. To Knopf it looked like some grossly deformed Tyrannosaurus Rex, a tank on two monstrously thick mechanical legs. It advanced down the rubble-strewn ruins of Oak Street and stopped in front of Fisher, bowing its enormous head down to eye-level with the captain in a whir of servos and pneumatic sighs.

"We have searched the town, sir. The sensors do not register the boy or his ankle monitor."

"Yeah, well, he didn't go somewhere else. He's here."

A pause.

"What are your orders, sir?"

"Find him."

"We have scanned everywhere, sir."

"You haven't scanned where he's at. Scan again. I'll tell you when to stop."

"Yes, sir."

The Warbot left to resume its search.

"Trouble?" Knopf asked to the young captain's back.

"It's all the lead dust," Fisher said, turning on him. The captain adjusted the surgical mask he wore, clearly frustrated with it. Mill Valley's smelting factory had been destroyed during the fight to retake the town, and it had scattered lead particulates and aerosolized bits of brick all over everything. The masks *were* uncomfortable, tending as they did to trap sweat at the corners of the mouth, making the wearer feel like they were constantly drooling, but they were necessary. No one wanted to breathe in that stuff. Especially because the robots kicked so much of it into the air. "It's playing havoc with the robots, everything from their sensors to their servos. It's no wonder we lost so many robots in the fight."

"Or that you misstated the presence of zombies here."

"You have no basis to support that comment, Doctor."

Fair enough, Knopf thought, and nodded.

They had already looked over a good part of the town, and now the Troopbots were sifting through buildings and overgrown lots. But even with the robots tirelessly performing their duties, Knopf couldn't help but feel frustrated. He'd grown used to Jimmy's precise directions, his ability to describe exactly where a zombie was hidden, and the waiting and the uncertainty of doing it the military's way was maddening.

Before Jimmy, everyone believed the zombies were nothing more than dead meat-husks. Beyond a few weak electrical impulses in the reptilian core of their brains, which generated the morphic fields that allowed them to find each other and to move around, searching for living brains, the zombies were thought to have no neurological function whatsoever. Certainly they retained no sense of self, no memories, no desires. They possessed only an insatiable need to feed on living tissue. Most scientists stopped short, however, of accepting Knopf's ideas of morphic fields. That was, until Jimmy came along.

Knopf remembered asking him once how he did it, what it felt like to sense a dead man's mind.

"It hurts," Jimmy had said. "Beyond that, it's hard to describe."

But then, several months later, on a foggy morning in early May, the two of them had taken a walk outside the lab, and through the dense screen of fog they'd seen sentries up on the walls, picking their way with flashlights, the beams muted but distinct in the sodden air.

Jimmy had stopped and stared.

Knopf continued walking for a few steps, then turned back to see what was wrong.

"That right there," Jimmy said, pointing at the flashlight beams bobbing on the wall. "That's what it looks like in my head."

"When you sense the zombies, you mean?"

"Yeah. It looks like that. Like flashlight beams in the fog. Only the light feels like a current, you know? Like the way you can feel water moving over your skin. Or how you can sense static electricity when it makes the hairs stand up on your arms."

The description had impressed Knopf. Little moments like that had brought them closer together, and if he wasn't exactly a father to Jimmy, he imagined he at least qualified as a benevolent uncle.

"If the boy's around here, we'll find him," Fisher said.

Knopf realized he'd been drifting. He glanced at Fisher, a vacant look on his face.

"Doctor? Did you hear me? I said we'll find him."

Knopf nodded.

"Why do you suppose he ran off?"

"I don't know," Knopf answered truthfully. "It hurts his head terribly to be out of the laboratory like this. There's so much mind-noise."

The captain rolled his eyes. "Well, if he can't handle the heat, sounds like he needs to get out of the kitchen."

Knopf looked at him in surprise. It was a cruel thing to say, even for Fisher. But what did Fisher know, anyway? He was too young to remember a world before the zombies. All his adult life had been spent in the Army. Fisher knew soldiering and little else. It may have made him an impressive man, commanding and resourceful beyond his years, but it hadn't taught him compassion.

Knopf, though, remembered the world as it had been. He remembered eating a meal without having to glance over his shoulder. He remembered not having to sleep in shifts, a weapon always at the ready. He remembered his wife and his little boy. Knopf remembered being human, something he doubted Fisher could lay any claim to.

But perhaps, more importantly, Fisher wasn't a father. He couldn't speak to the world of a child. Sure, he had been a child, but he hadn't also been a parent. What did he know of the pain, the fear, the joy that came with raising a child? As a soldier he claimed to be fighting the most important war humanity had ever fought, a war for the survival of the species. Yet he had no direct emotional stake in its survival. It was just an academic proposition for him. Human lives were simply numbers for him, pieces to be moved around a game board, little different from the robots under his command.

Knopf had essentially raised Jimmy. The boy had been handed off to him less than a month after Knopf's own son had died at the hands of the zombie horde, and Knopf, wounded to his core, had at first held the screaming toddler at a disdainful and resentful distance. He had looked at the scrawny, screaming brat, and all he'd been able to think about was himself, standing in the middle of a road at the crest of a hill, looking down on the base housing where he'd lived with his wife and child, zombies streaming out of the bungalow, blood covering their faces and chests like bibs, and the resentment had grown to an intense hatred.

But that hatred softened by degrees.

For several years, Jimmy had been unable to do anything but cower in a corner, screaming and yelling anytime anybody got close to him. Only gradually, through repeated effort and a thousand small acts of kindness, had Knopf managed to lure the boy out of the shadows. It was longer still before the boy would sleep anywhere but under the cot in Knopf's office. And across the gulf of those years, the two of them had healed each other. They'd learn to trust one another. Neither was emotionally seaworthy, not yet anyway, but together, they were getting close.

And now this. The boy missing....

* * *

Jimmy stopped at the top of a rickety metal staircase, waiting for his eyes to adjust to the darkness. Ahead he could see what looked like a glowing blue slime coating the handrails and parts of the walls. The glow was faint, but it provided enough light to give him a sense of the curved, tiled tunnel around him.

The stairs shook and groaned beneath his weight, moving with every step, and he was almost to the bottom when the metal suddenly snapped and gave way, dropping him into the muck on the bottom level.

He barely managed to roll out of the way as the structure crashed down around him.

Afterward, surrounded by tangled pieces of rusting metal, he sat there, blinking up at the ruined staircase, looking like the exoskeleton of some giant, malformed insect.

Grunting, he sat up.

The room in which he found himself was a horror. There were rotting bodies everywhere. Arms and legs and ropes of intestines hung from rusted piles of equipment, and the place smelled powerfully bad, worse even than the zombies Dr. Knopf occasionally brought into the lab for Jimmy to practice with.

Something moved beside him, and Jimmy turned, only to find himself nose to nose with a zombie. Its face was dripping with blood and sewage, eyes opaque, like cataracts, yet at the same time intensely alive with hunger and violence. The skin around its mouth was ripped and shredded, exposing its blood-blackened teeth so that it almost seemed to be grinning at him.

Jimmy screamed, backpedaling as fast as he could go.

The zombie stayed where it was. It sniffed the air. It opened its mouth, almost as though to taste what it smelled, but instead let out an aching moan.

The next instant it scuttled after him.

Still scrambling, Jimmy tripped and landed in a mass of arms and legs. He jumped to his feet, only to realize a moment later that the arms wrapping around him belonged to a Docbot; the cord tightening around his knees, the shoulder sling from the Docbot's medpac.

The zombie was closer, clawing its way over the wreckage of robots and dead bodies. Jimmy looked around for a way out, but there was none. He was at the apex of a curving tunnel, both directions extending into darkness that could hide anything.

But he did have the medpac. Those things were heavy. Jimmy had seen them used back at the lab. Carrying one was like lugging a bag of bricks, and it would make a good weapon.

He tugged at the shoulder strap until the pack came loose from the muck.

The zombie was almost on him. Jimmy stumbled backward, and at the same time swung the pack with both hands, smashing it against the zombie's jaw, hearing the satisfying crunch of broken bone.

The zombie went sprawling backward into the sewage and rotting bodies, landing in a twisted heap.

Jimmy didn't wait to see if it would get back up. He turned to run.

No!

Jimmy slowed, but didn't stop. That was Comm Six's voice.

I have to get out of here.

No! There is no time to run. Hide. Right now.

Where?

Under the robot. Now. Before the zombie gets up.

Jimmy dropped to the floor, crawling under the wrecked bodies and robots, and pulled the Docbot whose medpac he had just used on top of him.

Be very still.

It was good advice. During Dr. Knopf's many experiments, Jimmy had learned that the zombies' morphic-field acuity was imperfect at best. Certainly not as strong or as finely tuned as his. If he remained still and cleared his thoughts, a passing zombie would think him no different from a lamp post, or a mailbox, or any of the other inanimate objects that populated the world.

Through a hole in the Docbot's damaged skull, Jimmy watched the zombie scan the ruined figures at its feet. Flies swarmed around its head. Filthy water dripped from its beard. It turned its mangled face left, then right, then walked into the darkness of the receding tunnel.

Jimmy listened as its splashing grew faint, then he climbed from under the Docbot.

You must find a way out. There are many zombies down here. You must leave.

Jimmy shook his head.

I can't. My father's down here.

You will not leave?

I can't.

Your decision is unwise. But if you must stay, you should have a weapon.

Jimmy huffed at that one. *Thanks, that's great advice. I'll remember to bring one next time I'm crawling through a zombie-infested sewer.*

I can lead you to a weapon.

Jimmy stopped. *You can?*

One-hundred-and-sixteen feet to your left you will find a small room. One of the soldiers who died retaking this town is still there. He is a zombie now, but his corpse still carries a weapon. Go now. Move quickly.

He made his way to the room Comm Six had told him about, noticing as he went that the luminescent scum on the walls seemed thickest at the water line.

Where's this light coming from?

When the army realized they would have to fight down here, they seeded the sewer water with bioluminescent algae. It cleans the water and glows with the light you see. Eventually, the water in these sewers will be clean enough for human use.

Oh. That's kind of cool.

The room you need is on your left. Careful, now. The zombie will attack when he sees you.

Jimmy stepped into the room. There were several pieces of metal tubing at his feet, old, rusted pipes that had fallen from the ceiling. He picked one up, tested its heft, and decided it would work.

The zombie Comm Six had warned him about was on the far side of the room.

As Jimmy watched, it pawed at the wall, scratching uselessly at the mold-covered stone wall, its fingernails long since ripped from its fingertips.

Then Jimmy noticed that the thing had no legs.

From the waist down, there was nothing but ropes of viscera and blackened shards of bone protruding from the torso.

His stomach rose into his throat, and he coughed.

The sound got the zombie's attention. It turned its head sharply, and an urgent, hungry moan rose up from its rotting throat.

Move quickly. Do not let it make noise.

The zombie pulled itself toward Jimmy with its ruined fingers, its moaning growing more insistent, more desperate.

"Right," Jimmy muttered.

He stepped into the room with the metal pipe in both hands, raised high above his head. The zombie held its broken fingers up toward him, trying to grab him.

But Jimmy was quicker.

He sidestepped the zombie's hand and brought the pipe down as hard as he could.

Jimmy had never killed a zombie before, and he was surprised, and sickened, by how easy it was. Three quick strokes, and the back of the thing's head was a pulverized, ruined mess of blood, hair and bone.

It took a moment for his mind to break through the adrenaline rush.

I did it. Oh, God, I think I'm gonna puke.

The weapon is against the far wall.

"Huh?"

The weapon. Take it now.

Feeling dizzy, lightheaded, Jimmy scanned the far wall. The weapon was in a leather gun belt wrapped around the zombie's severed hips and legs.

You must move quickly. The zombies have heard you. They are approaching.

He had to peel the gun belt off the corpse's bloody hips. It made a sucking sound as he pulled it free.

This is so gross. I don't know if I can —

Hurry.

He worked the buckle open, then wrapped it around his own waist and pulled it as tight as it would go. Jimmy moved his hips back and forth. The belt was loose, but it didn't fall off, and that was something at least.

Okay, I've got the gun. Which way do I go now?

Nothing.

Jimmy opened his mind a little more.

Comm Six, you there? Which way do I go?

But the Combot's voice was gone. There was nothing but the echoes of water dripping from the ceiling somewhere down the tunnel. And from farther on, barely audible, came the distant moaning of the living dead.

Well, he thought, pulling the pistol, here goes nothing.

And he stepped out into the tunnel.

* * *

With only the faint blue light from the algae on the walls to guide him, Jimmy headed deeper into the sewers. The water was up to his knees, and every step made a splash that echoed a long way down the tunnels. He tried to reach out with his mind and sense the zombies that Comm Six had told him were down here, but in his mind, he saw nothing but a gray, depthless fog. For the first time in his life, he realized, his mind was quiet.

It might have felt good if he hadn't been so scared. And so unsure of himself. *What are you doing down here?* he asked himself. Dr. Knopf had told him bunches of times that his parents were dead. He'd accepted that a long time ago. And didn't he have his own memories from the night the dead overran this town? They were vague, cloudy memories, but they were there.

He remembered a room with dark-colored carpet and wood-paneled walls. He remembered a striped couch and a big chair that his infantile mind understood as DADDY'S CHAIR.

He remembered his mom, the source of kindness and nourishment and safety. She smelled like comfort, like goodness. At least that was the way she smelled in his memories. But the next instant, she'd gone wild with fear.

And he remembered his father, not his father's face, but the anger in the man's voice. Daddy, the protector, the violent one, driving his shoulder into the door, yelling at his mother to take the boy and *go, go, go!*

The room filled with smoke, seeping under the door, crawling in through the windows.

The memory broke apart with the first tinges of smoke. From there, all he remembered were broken images, crazy things. More screaming, and zombies reaching for him everywhere he turned. He remembered getting separated from his parents, his mother's cries echoing away into nothingness in the smoke that was filling their house.

And then, when he realized he was alone, that his parents were gone, a kind of light had turned on inside his head.

Through the smoke, through the screams, he could sort of see the bad people trying to hurt him. They glowed in the smoke, shimmering like flashlight beams, except that the light carried with it a bad... was it a smell? That was the only way his mind had been able to frame the sensation. Their minds smelled bad. The light that came from them was bad. They wanted to hurt him. He'd taken that knowledge and he had....

What?

He didn't know what he'd done from there.

He had gone walking, he supposed.

The next thing he could remember for sure was sleeping on the cot in Dr. Knopf's office, crying himself to sleep. Sometimes, Dr. Knopf would read from a book about a big rabbit and a little rabbit and the big rabbit saying this is how much I love you. He remembered sometimes Dr. Knopf would cry when he read the book, and how the man's tears and the choking sob in his voice had scared him for some reason he couldn't quite understand. And he remembered grabbing Dr. Knopf's leg in a stranglehold whenever the military men came by to ask questions and laugh at the answers they got.

Ah yes, Dr. Knopf.

There was the other problem of Jimmy's life.

For several years now he'd understood what he meant to the High Command. He was an experiment, an asset. They talked about him the same way they talked about programming groups for Warbots. Or pallets of ammunition. Or the shifting lines in the sand that divided the living from the dead.

Only Dr. Knopf thought of him as *Jimmy*.

And that was what made things so hard.

Dr. Knopf was as close to a parent as Jimmy had ever really known, but he wasn't the ideal parent that Jimmy always imagined his real parents would have been. He was distant. He could be cold. Sometimes, he could be harsh, even cruel when Jimmy failed to cooperate. Dr. Knopf was the one who made the rules, and Jimmy hated him for that. He had many memories of the two of them screaming at each other, Jimmy calling Knopf the meanest man he'd ever met, and Knopf, so angry his fists trembled with rage, making harsh, declarative statements that made Jimmy shrink into himself. Things like, "I don't care what you think. I just care that you do what I say." Or, "Nobody asked your opinion. Just do what I tell you. Why can't you get that through your head?" Or, "I'm sorry. I love... I just want you to be happy, Jimmy. Please, do this for me. This one last test. Finish this, and we can get some dinner. I'll do the macaroni and cheese you like so much...."

It was the occasional kindness that made things so confusing. There were times when Knopf actually felt like a father to him. And he was sure Knopf felt the same. Why then did they always pull away from each other? Why did the rare moments of closeness always end with the look of love fading from Knopf's face, and a terribly remote sadness invariably taking its place? The man was haunted by his memories. Jimmy knew that. But why did memory have to make things so hard?

There were so many questions, and so few answers.

But still you haven't asked the right question.

Jimmy stopped.

"Daddy?"

Yes, James.

What question? What did I forget to ask?

How, James. How come you can sense the dead? Didn't you ever think to ask? When the military men were laughing at you, didn't it seem strange that you knew you were right?

Yeah, I guess. Well, no, not really. I always felt like I was wrong.

Because they weren't inside your head. They didn't know what you knew. But I do, James. And you know how I know?

Jimmy shook his head, unable to articulate the thought aloud.

I know because I have the power too. Yours turned on the night the zombies came to Mill Valley, didn't it?

"Yes," Jimmy said, breathlessly. *Turned on* was exactly how he had come to think of that night, like somebody had just flipped a light switch inside his head.

The same thing happened for me, James. My power to sense the zombies, it flipped on that very night.

You mean, like a light switch.

Yes, exactly like that.

Daddy?

Yes?

Why isn't it working now? The sight, I mean. Usually I can sense the zombies. I could sense them before I came down here.

I don't know. It doesn't work down here for me, either. That's how I got trapped. Now hurry, James. I need help.

But Jimmy didn't move. Ahead of him was some sort of catwalk, another metal platform like the kind that had collapsed under his weight back at the entrance to the sewers.

What's wrong? Why aren't you coming to me?

Jimmy turned and looked behind him. The blue light from the algae didn't carry far. Twenty or thirty feet along, and his visibility was gone, swallowed by the darkness. But something was there. He could hear it splashing, and moaning.

James?

He could see silhouettes now, bunches of them, coming toward him.

Daddy, I think I'm trouble.

* * *

Jimmy pulled his pistol as the first zombie lumbered into view.

As she came closer, the faint blue glow from the algae lit her ghastly features. It was a woman, or had once been. Her shoulder-length hair was matted with blood and clods of mud. Her neck seemed unable to support the weight of her head, making her hair hang like a curtain of yarn in front of her face. The skin on her arms and neck was oozing with abscesses and open cuts that no longer bled. The clothes had been torn from her chest, and when she moved, black ribs showed where the flesh had been eaten away. She raised her gnarled hands and began to moan.

There were more behind her.

A lot more.

Jimmy raised the huge pistol, holding it with the two-handed grip all children inside the walls were taught. He squeezed off a round, and the blast clapped over his ears like an enormous pair of hands, leaving him momentarily deaf and stunned.

He didn't even realize the lead zombie had closed the distance between them until she put her filthy hands on him.

But that was enough to get him moving.

He ran for the platform he'd seen a few moments before, but stopped at the railing. The stairs leading to the aqueduct must have collapsed during the fighting, for they lay in a broken, rusted heap twenty feet below him.

Where more zombies had gathered, attracted by his gun shot.

The dead went into a frenzy when he appeared on the landing.

Oh God, oh God, oh God, Daddy, what do I do?

The woman with the black ribs was clutching the air between them. He could smell the rotten-meat stench she carried with her. Even over the open sewage he could smell her. Another three steps and she'd be on him.

"No," he said, kicking at her. His heart was pounding painfully in his chest. "Stay back!"

But zombies, of course, don't ever stay back, and Jimmy was forced to back up until he was pressed against the railing.

It was then he knew what he had to do.

He jumped.

* * *

Dr. Knopf stood in front of what was left of the Huntington Movie Theater, wiping the sweat from the back of his neck. Not even ten o'clock yet, and already the sun was punishing him. He had never handled field work well, and now that he was getting on into middle age, he had even less patience for it.

But he had to deal with it. At least this one last time. Jimmy was out here, somewhere, and he had to find him.

But which way?

To his left the street was piled high with the rubble of collapsed buildings. To his right, the street was a silent canyon between windowless buildings. It would be easier to go that way, but just because it was easy was no guarantee that Jimmy had gone that way. The boy had survived here as a toddler because of his gift, going not where the going was easiest, but where his senses told him it was safest. Avoid the zombies. That would have been his only concern.

So which way was that?

"Well, how about it, Dr. Knopf? Any ideas?"

Knopf shifted his attention from the crumbling buildings and looked at the young captain. Fisher's uniform was still crisp, his tie knot still regulation perfect. Despite all the walking they'd done in this God-awful heat, his gig line was straight as an arrow. The man didn't seem to know how to sweat.

"He could be anywhere," Knopf said. "I suggest doing another sensor sweep."

"We've done eight sensor sweeps already, Doctor. Are you sure the boy even went into town? Perhaps he ran back to the compound."

God save me from idiots in uniform, Knopf thought. Yes, they'd done their sensor sweeps, but Fisher himself had admitted that the high concentrations of lead in the ground were playing havoc with their equipment. It was probably doing the same thing to Jimmy, though to what degree there was no way of knowing. He'd have to do further research. The only remedy was to keep running the sensor sweeps, keep tracking over the same ground. Eventually they'd hit pay dirt.

"He's here, Captain. I'm sure of that."

"Hmm," Fisher said. "You have a special bond with the boy, I suppose."

Knopf looked at him sharply. He didn't like the way that sounded, the nasty implication in the Captain's tone. "What exactly is that supposed to mean, Captain?"

Fisher raised his eyebrows, as though to feign ignorance.

"Only that you raised him. It would be natural, I suppose, for you to learn how he thinks."

Knopf didn't answer that.

"You were given charge of the boy shortly after your own wife and son were killed. Isn't that right, Doctor? It would make sense that you'd invest extra effort to keep the boy close. Perhaps he filled some psychological hole in your head?"

"That's pretty damn bold of you, Captain."

"Perhaps. Perhaps not. You forget, Doctor, that I have an assignment as well. You are trying to get me to believe in magic. My job, if you'll pardon my French, is to make sure you aren't full of shit."

And then it hit Knopf what was really going on here, what the Captain was actually accusing him of.

"Captain, are you suggesting that I faked more than a decade's worth of research just so that child could take the place of my own son? Is that really what you're suggesting?"

Fisher shrugged. "You tell me."

"You're a bastard, Captain. A certifiable bastard."

"Maybe. But that still doesn't answer my question."

Knopf nearly hit him in the nose. He might have, too, if at that moment the street to his right hadn't erupted with yelling and gunfire.

Knopf ducked his head, backing away from the commotion.

"What the...?" Fisher said. He was standing with arms akimbo, peering into the clouds of dust pouring down the street.

The next instant two troopers hurried out of the fog. A steadily retreating line of Troopbots was right behind them, firing into the dust.

One of the troopers, a soldier named Collins, hurried toward Fisher. "Zombies, sir! A whole mess of 'em!"

"What the hell happened?"

"We were going building to building, searching the rubble. A couple of our Troopbots found a door down to the sewer system and when they opened it, they uncovered a whole nest of them things."

"How many?"

"Hard to tell, sir. Forty, maybe fifty. They overran our Troopbots."

They could hear moaning now. A few of the approaching zombies were visible through the screen of dust, but from the volume of the moans, it was obvious there were many more behind them.

"So much for the eighty-six percent accuracy of your sensors, Captain?" said Knopf. "Guess you can never trust a zombie to play fair."

"Don't start with me, Doctor."

The next instant he was on the radio, calling for the Warbots to converge on his location.

Knopf felt their approach before he heard them, the tread of their Tyrannosaurus-sized legs sending shudders through the pavement.

When the Warbots entered the intersection, they turned at once to the advancing horde of zombies. Their limited A.I. capability allowed them to process the scene and reach immediate conclusions about what had to be done. Without waiting for orders, they strode to the leading edge of the street, took side-by-side positions, and opened fire into the approaching horde, mowing down the zombies with a hail of automatic-weapons fire.

To Knopf, it seemed the shooting went on forever, and when the dust finally settled, the rattle of the guns still rang in his ears.

But the street was still. Nothing moved.

One of the Warbots turned to Captain Fisher. "What are your orders, sir?"

Fisher looked mad enough to spit. He glared at Knopf before turning back to his robots.

"Another sensor sweep," he growled. "Find that kid."

*   *   *

As he went over the edge, Jimmy saw a crowd of zombies lunging for him. Their ruined faces and bloody hands loomed large, and for a terrifying moment, he thought he was going to be shredded alive before he hit the water. But when he landed in the sewer channel, he kept his head under the water and started thrashing for the far side of the channel.

The water was black as ink, and he couldn't see where he was going. He pushed and pulled his way through a forest of legs even as hands groped at his back.

One of them managed to grip the collar of his shirt.

Jimmy twisted away, breaking the zombie's fingers, but still it held on. He swatted at the hands and kicked whenever he could, and somehow managed to reach the stone ledge on the far side of the channel.

They stayed on him, though.

He saw a rotten, wooden pallet leaning against the wall under the ledge and climbed on top of it. The ledge was another five feet or so above that, and he jumped for it, hooking his elbows over the edge so he had enough support to pull himself up. He kicked at the smooth cement wall below him, his toes sliding on the algae that grew there while hands groped at his shoes.

"Get away!" he yelled, pumping his legs with everything he had. "Get... away!"

And then he was up and over the edge, his full weight resting on the ledge. Jimmy rolled over onto his back and sobbed, his chest heaving.

What was he going to do? There was no place to go.

He rolled onto his side and stared down at the hungry crowd. Their hands were just a few inches below the ledge, their moans reaching a frenzied intensity. He knew he should keep moving, but the panic and adrenaline that had helped him climb had left him numb, and all he could do now was stare with glassy eyes at the clutching hands.

You must get up. You must leave.

Jimmy blinked. The Combot again.

How am I supposed to do that? There's nowhere to go.

Stand up. I will help.

What're you gonna do?

Stand up.

With a strange, disconnected feeling, almost like he was dreaming, Jimmy rose to his feet. The ceiling was arched, and this close to the wall he had to bend slightly to keep from banging his head. It made him feel like a diver looking over the edge of a cliff. Staring straight down into the ravenous horde brought a wave of nausea over him, and he groaned.

What now?

You must move to your left. Eighty feet down that tunnel you will find a large platform. Go there.

That's your plan? What am I supposed to do when I get there?

There is a functioning Warbot there. It will protect you. Go now. You must move quickly.

The Combot wasn't kidding, Jimmy thought. One of the zombies in the front had fallen against the wall, pushed down by the weight of the horde behind it, and its fellows were ramping up its back. A zombie in some kind of uniform was pulling itself onto the ledge. The zombie's lower jaw was almost completely gone, like it had been torn off. Or shot off. Maggots swarmed in the rotting flesh where its chin and cheeks had been.

"No," Jimmy muttered, shaking his head.

You must move quickly.

Slowly, inching along the narrow concrete ledge, zombie hands grasping at his feet, Jimmy made his way to a corner up ahead. The zombies matched him step for step, their moans echoing horribly off the walls and quickening his pulse.

How am I supposed to get down from here? They're following me.

Round the corner. You will see.

And when he reached the corner, he did see. Immediately below him was a railing that went across the channel. It wasn't high enough to keep the zombies at bay forever, but it was high enough to give him a chance at escape.

Yes, he thought, that's how I'm gonna do it.

He jumped into the water.

The zombies stuck their hands through the railing, but he was already out of reach and running for the platform.

Right where you said it'd be.

They are coming. You must move quickly.

Jimmy looked back over his shoulder and saw, once again, that the Combot was correct. Already the zombies had tipped the railing forward and were scrambling over it. He had maybe a thirty-foot lead on them.

He closed the last few feet to the platform and rounded the corner. A sudden, intensely white light flooded his vision, momentarily blinding him.

"You are human," a robotic voice said.

It took a moment for the purple blotches to clear from Jimmy's sight. When they did, he saw a badly damaged Warbot trying to stand on its Tyrannosaurus legs—but something was wrong. One of its legs wouldn't work. Its status lights blinked and flickered. It stumbled forward, then sagged to the ground, the spotlight on its shoulder lighting up the carnage at its feet.

The ground was covered with rotting corpses.

Fear gripped him anew. He had gambled on the Combot's instructions, and this was where it had led him. To an abandoned sewer platform, and no way out.

"Zombies," the Warbot said, raising a .50 caliber machine gun. "Human, you must take cover at the rear of the platform. Move quickly."

Jimmy heard moaning behind him. That was all it took. He ran forward, scrambling over badly decomposed bodies, too frightened to allow the gore into which his fingers were sinking to slow him down.

The shooting started a moment later.

Jimmy reached the back wall, turned, and saw a zombie's head and shoulders atomized by a three-round burst from the Warbot's guns. But every zombie that was shot as it rounded the corner was replaced by more, and soon the Warbot's gun was blazing in a continuous stream.

It wasn't enough. The dead kept coming, pouring around the corner faster than the Warbot's gun could put them down. Jimmy, who was so exhausted he could barely move, pushed himself against the back wall of the platform. There was some kind of vehicle abandoned there, like a rail truck, only on rubber wheels. Its windshield had come loose and broken into two pieces. Jimmy pulled the bigger of the two over him and tried to shrink into the gore of ruined bodies below him.

But it was only a matter of time.

There were just too many of them.

Jimmy's eyes found one zombie staring straight at him as it climbed over the pile of torn-up corpses. Its gaze never wavered. It had zeroed in on him and meant to have him.

Jimmy braced himself for the attack.

The zombie fell on top of him, moaning, pawing at the glass with its bloody hands. Jimmy screamed at the thing, pushing back with everything he had.

And the zombie's head exploded. One moment it was pounding on the glass, smearing it with blood and sewage, and the next the glass was splashed with bits of bone and brain and clumps of bloody hair. The zombie's headless corpse sagged against the glass as Jimmy gaped in shocked silence.

The sound of gunfire was gone.

So too were the moans.

"Human," the Warbot said. "Human?"

Jimmy had to tilt the glass like a ramp to roll the corpse away, and once it was off him, he could see the gun smoke lingering in the foul sewer air.

"Human, they are gone. Please acknowledge."

"I hear you," Jimmy said.

He stood up and looked around. The far wall was dripping with fresh gore, and there were bodies piled high near the corner. How many? Forty? More than that?

Jimmy couldn't tell.

He turned to the Warbot.

"Thanks," he said, because it was the only thing that came close to how he was feeling at the moment.

"I cannot move. You must go. Gunfire will travel far in these tunnels. More zombies will come."

"How many?"

"Unknown. You must go."

He watched the Warbot as its status lights blinked and dimmed once again. The machine could not die, but if it had an equivalent, it was doing it now. Its lights were going out.

It was then that a thought occurred to Jimmy. Something he had overheard once in the weapons lab.

"Don't Warbots usually work in teams?" he asked. "Where's your partner?"

But the Warbot didn't answer. Its status lights continued to fade, and as Jimmy watched, they went dark permanently.

There was nothing else to do but leave.

* * *

Jimmy found the second Warbot a few minutes later.

He had returned to the main channel and was following it further into the sewer system. There were more platforms here, lots of them, and other channels leading off in other directions.

He had entered some kind of hub, he realized, the main part of the sewer system.

What did you do? The zombies are all gone.

For once, his father's mind-voice didn't knife into his head. It was almost pleasant, in fact. Jimmy wasn't sure if it was the tone of surprised gratitude that softened it, or if he was just getting used to their thoughts passing back and forth, but either way the pain was gone. Jimmy let his mind reach out to his father.

Daddy, where are you?

I'm close, Jimmy. Keep coming. Around the next corner to your left.

The fighting, Jimmy saw, must have been intense through here. He had seen plenty of rotting bodies along the way, and even more wrecked Troopbots, but the carnage was especially bad here. In some places he had to climb over the twisted, severed limbs of dead people and the faceless heads of downed robots rusting in the sewer water. And everywhere he turned there were bullet holes in the walls and the ceiling.

Then he rounded the corner, and the smell of rot nearly knocked him over.

What lay before him was a gallery of horrors. The room must have been a staging area for large equipment before the fighting, for there were oversized sleds loaded with machinery, and portable pumps and generators scattered around. But those were only the backdrop for the carnage Jimmy saw. Corpses were piled three and four deep. Most were so badly decomposed they were unrecognizable, their bodies swollen and discolored and swarming with flies and writhing worms. Others had been eaten, and what remained of their faces was twisted by pain frozen there like a picture. One man lay on his back atop a generator, his arms hanging limply off either side, his mouth open in an eternal scream, his torso ripped apart and emptied of its viscera so that he looked like the gaping belly of a canoe. Jimmy saw a dismembered foot here, an upturned hand there, the fingers curled up and inward like the legs of a dying crab.

And standing in the middle of it all, a grotesque king presiding over his court, was his father.

Jimmy's mouth fell open.

The man could barely stand. His right arm had been chewed off just below the elbow, stringy lengths of sinew and shredded flesh hanging from the blackened wound. His neck, too, was open. Worms fed on the ruins of his throat. The green T-shirt he wore was stained with dried blood, and all Jimmy could read was the word *Nationals* in what had once been white lettering. And his face! Bits of skull showed through the holes in his forehead. His lips were gone, revealing the full horror of his bloodstained teeth. He leered at Jimmy. Almost like he was grinning at him.

Jimmy turned his head, the bile rising in his throat.

Jimmy, look at me.

Slowly, uncertain for a moment that he would even be able to keep his feet, Jimmy straightened up. He faced the train wreck that had once been his father and, running the back of his hand across his face, wiped the spit from his lips.

You lied to me.

For a reason. I had to get you here.

But you lied to me.

You don't need to be frightened of me.

Jimmy backed away, shaking his head.

That was when Jimmy saw the other Warbot. At first it had blended in with the other machinery, one more piece of metal streaked with human gore.

Then it rose to its full height.

Eighteen feet of rusting metal on Tyrannosaurus legs.

It stood so tall it had to stoop to avoid scraping the ceiling. It had fully automatic machine gun cannons for arms, and it turned them in Jimmy's direction.

"I am human," Jimmy said, reciting the mantra that Dr. Knopf had taught him when dealing with robotic sentries. "Confirm my status as human."

The Warbot's status lights flickered wildly but it made no sound. The guns remained trained on Jimmy.

"Confirm!" Jimmy said.

It's not the robot it used to be. Watch, Jimmy. Let me show you.

The Warbot stooped forward then and swung one of its machine gun arms under his father. As Jimmy watched, his fear mounting, the robot raised the zombie version of his father into the air and placed him on its shoulders.

Jimmy took a step back.

Do you understand?

Yes. You control that robot.

Yes! That's exactly right. It has a limited intelligence. A.I., they call it. It isn't a smart machine, but it's smart enough to be used. Do you see?

No.

Jimmy, look at me.

Jimmy did. He stared up at his father, who rode the Warbot like some demented child playing horsey on his daddy's shoulders, and he was frightened.

This is bad. This is very bad.

No! That's wrong. Jimmy, this is right. Don't you see?

See what?

I control this robot. I can control zombies, too. Anything that has a mind, or had a mind, is like a pawn waiting to be moved. Don't you see the potential? All it takes is a mind that can move those pawns. A mind like mine. A mind like yours.

I want to go home.

You are home, damn it!

The robot took three long strides forward and knelt, bringing Jimmy's father closer to eye level. Jimmy tried to back away, but his heel caught on a Troopbot's severed arm and he pitched over backward, landing on his butt.

Don't back away from me!

But Jimmy wasn't moving anymore. For the first time, he could see the wall behind the Warbot. There was a flight of stairs there, and on the wall at the back of the first landing was a red EXIT sign.

A way out.

Don't you see what I'm offering you? Don't you understand what this means? I can make you a king, boy. I've seen into your memories. I've seen how they've used you. Do you want it to stop? Don't you want to give it all back to them? I can help you do that. As father and son, the way it was meant to be.

Slowly, Jimmy stood up.

Answer me.

Glancing across the floor between where he stood and the stairs began, Jimmy picked out the route he was going to take. Dr. Knopf had tried to teach him a trick once to hone his psychic-locator skills. Visualize each move, Knopf had told him, picture it in advance. See yourself making it. That way, when you make it for real—

Knopf is the man who raised you, the scientist?

Yes.

The one who experimented on—

Jimmy blocked the rest of it, slamming the door on his father's mind-voice. He heard his father grunt in surprise, and Jimmy ran. He darted around the Warbot's right side, ducking to miss the robot's heavy cannon arm as it rotated toward him, and then he was past it, running for the stairs.

But he didn't move so fast he missed his steps. He picked his way through bodies and machine parts carefully, planting his feet exactly as he had pictured them in his head. He couldn't afford to miss a step. Not now. Not with his father and that Warbot behind him. If he tripped, slipped, they'd be on him. The heavy cannon would knock him to the floor and hold him there. And he had no idea what his father would do after that.

Jimmy was still blocking him with his mind. He had his teeth clenched so tightly his jaw was trembling, his breaths coming fast and noisily through his nose, but he didn't dare let up. His father was no doubt screaming into his brain, and if one of those mind-voice screams got through, Jimmy knew it would be enough to cripple him with pain. He'd never be able to get up.

He hit the stairs at a full sprint and ran up them three at a time. When he reached the landing, he turned and saw his father astride the Warbot, the two of them crashing forward.

They were close, almost on him.

Jimmy kept running up the stairs. He had to scale three flights to reach the promised EXIT door. Once there, he grabbed the handle, and twisted.

It was locked.

"No," he said.

Below him, the Warbot was trying to climb the stairs, even though it was far too big to fit into the narrow confines. But it could force its way up, and it was doing that, banging its huge cannon arms against the railing, smashing through the floor with its enormous metal shoulders. The landing beneath Jimmy's feet was moving, trembling from the impacts.

He tried the door again, yanking on it with everything he had, and it still wouldn't budge.

"Please, no," he said, his voice almost a whimper.

He looked down. The Warbot was slowly crashing his way up through the floor, but that wasn't the worst of it. Through a gap in the split-level stairs Jimmy caught a glimpse of his father's zombified face. It was hideous, dead, yellowed with disease and dark with scabs and open, rotting wounds. The right side of his mouth had been damaged somehow, so that the corner of his lips hung slack in an ironic grin.

The eyes, though, those were most certainly not grinning. They were lit by mad, malignant hatred. The violence in those eyes frightened Jimmy down to his bones.

But he still had to get through the door. How?

The gun. Use the gun.

The Combot's voice.

The gun?

Jimmy looked down at his waistband. Sure enough, the pistol was still there, right where he'd stuck it after his narrow escape at the ledge.

How do I...?

Shoot the knob. Move quickly.

Jimmy took a step back. He drew the weapon and steadied its front sight on the knob. Below him, the Warbot was fast approaching.

It was on the next landing down. Jimmy had a few seconds, maybe less. He swallowed hard as he tried to center the front sight on the knob and pulled the trigger.

The gun nearly jumped out of his hands as he staggered backward, the sound of the shot deafening.

Shaking his head, he looked down at the lock. The knob was hanging at an odd angle from the plane of the door, a big gaping hole just to the left of it. He reached for it, and the knob came away in his hand.

The door fell open.

Run. You must run.

The Combot again.

Where?

I will guide you. Run now. Move as fast as you can.

He lunged through the doorway and into the lobby of a large, shabby building. This, he gathered, had been the home office of the Water Authority. There were desks everywhere, most of them pushed haphazardly out of the way. Trash lay thick on the floor. A few pieces of furniture had been jammed up against the front door of the building, which meant people must have made a final stand here.

But the furniture had been toppled, and the front door behind the pile was hanging from the bottom hinge.

Jimmy ran that way, scaling over the furniture. He was almost through the door when the ground shook and he lost his footing. He landed on top of a desk, facing the length of floor he'd just traversed.

A heaving mound formed in the middle of the floor, the cement popping and groaning from the Warbot's efforts to push itself upwards from the other side. There was a crash, and the mound cracked and popped. A second crash came immediately after, and the next thing Jimmy knew, the Warbot was busting through the floor, sending bits of tile and chairs and desks flying in every direction.

The Warbot climbed out of the hole, Jimmy's father still hanging on to its neck, still staring at him with those same hate-filled eyes.

"No," Jimmy said.

Run. Now.

But Jimmy didn't need to be told. He was already sprinting into the street.

* * *

A bullet skipped off the pavement at Dr. Knopf's feet, hitting the wall behind him. He ducked, and with his hands over his head, turned in every direction, trying to find someplace to run. The air was full of dust, the noise deafening. He felt disoriented, and in his confusion, stepped right into the middle of the fighting.

After their first successful skirmish in front of the movie theater, some of the Troopbots had surrounded another Water Authority access point to the sewers, their weapons at the ready, and opened the door. It had been like knocking the top off an ant pile. One minute they were expecting a simple mop-up operation, and the next, they were overrun, trampled underfoot, ripped to pieces. Knopf had been standing fewer than thirty feet from one of their Docbots when a wave of zombies knocked it to the ground and pulled it apart like a man being drawn and quartered. They'd been overrun so quickly there was hardly a chance for Knopf to question the strangeness of what he saw.

But Captain Fisher was a good soldier, a capable leader. He regrouped his forces, pulling his troops back in ordered rows while at the same time bringing his Warbots forward, where the bigger guns could do some damage. But the battle was decided almost from the beginning. Fisher's expeditionary force was small, intended more for light escort duty than a stand-up fight, and the best he could hope for at this point was to keep his escape route to the rear open. By keeping his lines moving, they at least stood a chance of escaping to a better defensive position.

That was how it looked to Knopf, anyway.

But there was something else, something disturbing. Knopf had spent years studying the zombies every possible way. Know thy enemy, as Sun Tzu had said. He'd used that knowledge to design and perfect the weapons systems his shop built for the military. But in all his studies, all his observations, he'd always worked under the philosophy that the zombie was a mindless, relentless opponent with no sense of strategy and no skills. Their only strengths were their numbers, a complete lack of fear, and the ability to fight without sleep, without pain, and without ever quitting. They advanced headlong, regardless of the odds, with no sense of winning or losing.

That didn't seem to be the case here, though. Knopf had accidentally wandered into the middle of the fighting, and while he was ducking and dodging bullets like some kind of fool, he watched a large number of zombies break away from the main horde and circle around the ruins of a hardware store, so that they could come up from behind their robot opponents in a well-executed flanking maneuver.

Knopf was shocked. Doing something like that took strategy, it took forethought, it took goal-oriented behavior. None of the game-theory equations he'd put into the robots' programming could deal with behavior like that. The zombies weren't playing by the rules. And yet the action was undeniable. It was a wide street, with a park off to his left. There had been plenty of room for all the zombies to continue their advance. By all rights, they should have massed into the open areas, where Fisher's strategy would have turned the street into a meat grinder.

But they had deliberately turned off. They had taken themselves out of the fight in a clearly premeditated way, almost as though...

Another bullet hit the pavement at his feet and glanced off with a loud, high-pitched whine. Knopf blinked at the little white cloud of dust that drifted from the impact point.

"What are you doing?" someone yelled. "Get out of the street!"

Knopf looked up. Zombies and robots were swarming around him. The ordered lines had broken, and everywhere he turned Troopbots were being ripped apart.

"Knopf, you idiot, get out of the street!"

Captain Fisher was running at him, a pistol in his hand. He looked angry, white flecks of spit flying from his lips, the white scar across his chin almost obscured by the dirt and mud and blood on his face.

"Get out of the street!"

The next instant Fisher was on him, grabbing him by the sleeve, pulling him toward the corner of a red-brick building. Then he slammed him against the wall.

"What the hell are you doing?" he demanded.

"Those zombies are using strategy, Captain. Something's guiding them—"

But Fisher wasn't listening. His attention was already back on the street, eyes darting from one corner of the battle to the other.

"We're pulling out," he yelled. "I'm ordering us out of this town. Get yourself ready to move out."

"Wait," Knopf said. "What? No, you can't."

"I can, Doctor, and I am. We are leaving!"

"But Jimmy... he's still out there somewhere. We have to find him."

"Like hell we do. He ran off. He's dead."

"You don't know that!"

"I know this experiment of yours has failed, Doctor," Fisher said. He emphasized his point by jamming a finger into Knopf's chest. "You're done. You and this whole ridiculous experiment—you're done! This is over. My only concern right now is to salvage what's left of my command. Now get yourself ready. We are leaving."

And with that he stormed off, yelling for his human soldiers to fall back.

* * *

Jimmy hit the street running.

Behind him, the front of the building he'd just escaped exploded, the force of it knocking him onto his hands and knees. He glanced back in time to see the Warbot erupting into the street, crouching like a bird, furniture and bits of rubble tumbling around its feet.

From atop the thing's shoulders, with the cold, hard light of insanity in his eyes, Jimmy's father leered at him.

"Oh, God," Jimmy said.

He pulled himself to his feet and started to run again.

But he only made it a few feet before he stopped. Ahead of him, zombies staggered out of alleyways and out of buildings. At first there were only five, then eight, then more. He turned to his left and saw the side street filling with more of the living dead.

It dawned on him then what was happening. The zombies closing in on him... the things his father had said down in the sewers... the fact that all the town's zombies had retreated into the sewers, as though waiting for something... his father was controlling them, steering them toward this spot. Jimmy could feel the force of his father's thoughts moving around him like the current in a river, but gaining in strength. Now that he was out of the sewers he was growing more powerful every second.

What am I supposed to do?

Jimmy stretched his thoughts, trying to connect with the Combot.

Help me, Comm Six. Where do I go?

There is a building to your right. Run through there. Hurry.

Jimmy turned. The building was made of red brick, the windows empty and dark. He sprinted toward it just as the Warbot reached for him, its enormous machine-gun arms missing him by inches. Jimmy jumped through one of the empty display windows and hurried through the shop toward the back.

Go out the back door. When you reach the alley, turn right. I will guide you.

Jimmy did as he was told. The shop was crowded with trash and bits of tile and insulation where the roof had collapsed, but he threaded his way through it and out the back door.

He found himself in a narrow alley between low buildings. Looking to his left he saw zombies turning the corner. To his right, the way looked clear.

Go. Hurry.

His father's Warbot had already started smashing its way through the shop, and Jimmy knew he only had a few precious seconds. He ran for the end of the alleyway, rounded the corner, and kept on running.

The next corner is Tanner Street. Turn left there. You will see a movie theater at the end of the street. But you must hurry. The humans are leaving.

Leaving? What? No. Stop them.

I cannot. But you can.

Me? How?

With your mind. Reach out. Find one of the humans and enter his mind. Hurry. The Warbot is coming. Do it as you run.

Jimmy rounded the corner onto Tanner Street. He could hear his father's Warbot back there, wrecking everything in sight.

Focusing his mind, he tried to picture Dr. Knopf, to remember the sound of his voice, the shape of his face.

Dr. Knopf.

Something clicked for Jimmy then. He could feel the connection when it happened, like toy blocks snapping together. Dr. Knopf was confused and frightened by the contact. Jimmy could sense his fear, and feel him trying to pull his mind back and break the contact. He could picture Knopf standing perfectly still, his back rigid, Adam's apple pumping up and down like a cylinder, much as Jimmy had done when his father first made contact with him.

Dr. Knopf, I need help.

Jimmy, you're alive! Where are you?

There was no time to explain. Instead, Jimmy pushed his thoughts into Dr. Knopf's mind, showing him everything he had seen and heard since coming to Mill Valley. He wasn't even sure if it would work, but he sensed it would, and so he pushed.

Doctor?

Silence.

Dr. Knopf, I need you!

Oh you poor boy. Jimmy, I'm so sorry. I had no idea.

Help me!

Zombies were moving through the smoke ahead of him. Now that he was free of the sewers, he could sense them.

They were facing away, and Jimmy sprinted right for them. With luck, he'd get past them before they knew he was there.

But then, all at once, the dead stopped their attack on the retreating Troopbots and turned to face Jimmy. Several of them lunged forward, reaching for him.

It happened so fast Jimmy barely had time to adjust.

He veered to his left, shooting through a gap between them just as his father's Warbot reached down to scoop him up. Instead of pinning Jimmy, it flattened one of the zombies.

Jimmy didn't slow. He ran into the thick of where the battle had been. He was in No Man's Land, midway between the retreating Troopbots on the one side and the zombies and his father's Warbot on the other.

Jimmy looked back as the Warbot crashed through the zombie horde, trampling some and throwing others out of the way. Still carrying his father atop its shoulders, the Warbot stepped slowly into the intersection. They were close now, less than twenty feet between them, the Warbot towering over Jimmy. His father's badly decomposed face was incapable of expression, but Jimmy could still sense the madness, the betrayal, the rage, emanating from the man's mind.

Jimmy met his stare without blinking, and at the same time realized he was feeling exactly the same thing, betrayal and rage. The thought scared him, and for a moment, Jimmy felt his resolve waver. This was his father, after all. The man had done nothing but hurt him. And yet, angry as Jimmy was, a part of him wanted to love the man... needed the man's approbation. But the scariest thought of all, the one Jimmy couldn't get around, was that maybe they weren't so very different, father and son. Maybe there was nothing but a fine line between them. Maybe Jimmy was just a gentle shove away from being exactly like him.

"No," Jimmy said suddenly. "I won't join you. I won't."

Maybe there was just a fine line between them, but the line was there. He looked up at the horror that his father had become and he was suddenly, absolutely, irrevocably sure. That zombie up there was not what he wanted to be. He was more than that.

"Go on and do it, if you can," he told his father.

The Warbot straightened. Jimmy could see it gathering itself for the final, crushing blow, like stomping a bug, and he tensed to leap out of the way. But as the Warbot's leg rose, Jimmy saw a flash of movement to his left. A second Warbot, bearing the insignia of Fisher's expeditionary force, smashed into his father's Warbot, and both robots went tumbling into the side of a building, knocking down the brick wall.

The expeditionary robot stood up first. It backed away from the collapsed store front, and right before it started firing, Jimmy caught a glimpse of his father's Warbot inside, its enormous Tyrannosaurus legs bent in front of it like a man who has fallen into a low, deep couch.

And then the shooting started.

The expeditionary Warbot fired both its .50 caliber machine guns, the bullets glancing off the other Warbot's armor plating, but doing little harm. His father's Warbot pulled itself loose from the wall and charged its opponent, and when they hit, it felt like the ground was splitting open beneath Jimmy's feet.

Their great weight tore up the pavement. Every step sent bits of rock and vast quantities of dust into the air, and within moments, Jimmy couldn't tell the difference between the two. He could only marvel at the destruction they caused. They threw each other into the air and into the sides of buildings. The zombies swarming around their legs were crushed like bugs. Both robots were firing their machine guns continuously now, and the noise grew so loud Jimmy fell behind a pile of rubble, his hands clapped over his ears.

Jimmy had no idea how long the fight went on, but gradually, the guns fell silent.

And when the sound stopped altogether, and Jimmy looked over the pile of rubble, he saw one of the Warbots tangled in a collapsed wall, wrapped in metal cables, one of its cannon arms missing. It tried to step out of the wall, but one of its legs wasn't working, and all it managed to do was fall face-first onto the pavement.

The other Warbot was in two large pieces, electrical cables and wires oozing from its severed parts like guts. Neither machine was going to be getting up again. Jimmy could see that plain enough. And when he searched them with his mind, he could tell the one was dead, and the other, the one face down on the street, was shutting down.

But there was something else.

Jimmy turned. A lone figure was limping toward him through the dust and smoke.

"Don't come any closer," Jimmy said. "I'm done with you."

His father's face was dark with blood and dust, except for the eyes, which were milky-white and vacant. He raised his one good hand to Jimmy, the fingers clutching, and inched his way forward.

You can't have me! Do you hear? I'm not yours.

Jimmy scooped up a heavy chunk of asphalt and threw it at his father. It hit him in the shoulder, but he showed no reaction.

He kept coming.

Just then Jimmy felt a hand on his back. He knew who it was without having to look around.

"Step away, Jimmy," said Dr. Knopf. "I've got this."

Dr. Knopf raised a pistol and pointed it at Jimmy's father. But before he could pull the trigger, Jimmy touched his arm, guiding the weapon to the low ready.

"No," Jimmy said. "It's for me to do."

Dr. Knopf looked at the pistol, and then at Jimmy.

"Let me have it."

Knopf handed it to him without saying another word. Jimmy looked down at the pistol, so many things weighing on his mind, and then pointed it at his father.

"I'm sorry," he said. "But we're not the same. Not at all."
And he pulled the trigger.

* * *

Later, after the last of the zombies had been put down and the dust and smoke had cleared, Jimmy walked into the middle of the street and looked around. There was a darkened movie theater just ahead of him. He felt drawn to it.

"Jimmy?" Knopf said, coming up beside him. "You okay?"

Jimmy nodded.

"You put a lot into my mind. I guess we have a lot to talk about, don't we?"

"Yeah, I guess so."

Both of them were silent for a time, watching the movie theater.

"There's something I have to do," Jimmy said.

"What's that?"

"The Combot." Jimmy pointed to the movie theater. "Comm Six... it's in there."

"You're sure?"

Jimmy nodded. He was sure.

Knopf looked around uncomfortably. He seemed uncertain, doubtful. "I don't...," he said. "Stand back for a second, okay? Let me send in a Troopbot first."

Jimmy looked at him but said nothing.

Knopf grabbed the first Troopbot he saw and pointed it toward the movie theater. After he'd explained what he wanted done the robot marched inside, weapon at the ready.

Jimmy and Knopf waited, listening.

Several human soldiers stood nearby, looking on curiously.

About a minute later, a single gunshot sounded from deep in the recesses of the theater.

"One female zombie neutralized," the Troopbot announced over the walkie-talkie.

Knopf motioned to one of the human soldiers, who nodded back and went inside the theater to check it out.

When he came back out, he was holding something in his right hand.

He walked to Knopf and handed it to him. A photograph. Black and white. Dirty with grime and creased where it had been crumpled and wrinkled over the years. It showed a little boy, about two, smiling, still a lot of the baby he once was in his chubby face, playing with a toy truck on a kitchen floor.

"That was pinned to the zombie's shirt," the soldier said, nodding at the photograph. "There was nothing else in there."

"Thank you," Knopf said.

He stared at the picture, lost in his memories of a boy he had once hated, but had grown to love as though he was his own son.

"What is it?" Jimmy asked.

Knopf handed him the photograph. "It's you," he said.

"Me?" Jimmy swallowed, his attention shifting from Knopf to the entrance to the movie theater. "But, Comm Six...."

"I'm afraid so," Knopf said. "I'm sorry, Jimmy."

Jimmy nodded, his mouth pressed into a thin, tight line. Then he slid the picture into his pocket.

"Dr. Knopf, I'm done. I want you to know that. I'm done. I don't want to do this anymore. No more experiments."

Knopf put his arm around Jimmy's shoulder. His touch was warm, kind, accepting.

"Come on," he said. "Let me take you home."

"I'm not going back to the lab."

"No," Knopf said. "I know that. I'm taking you home."

Bugging Out

Greg Sutton sat watching the news, a smile tugging at the corners his mouth. On the TV a rookie newswoman struggled to make sense of the jumbled and, in some cases, contradictory updates she'd just been handed. Her composure was fading fast. Behind her was a map of the United States, and on the map, overlapping red circles spread like bloodstains. Greg knew it wasn't right to be happy about this, but he couldn't help it. He watched the red circles grow bigger, listened to the fear and trembling in the pretty newscaster's voice, and all he could think was, *Hell yeah, baby!*

Because he had this.

He was ready for it.

Zombies. He shook his head. That was some crazy shit. He had expected some sort of pandemic. The flu, probably. Maybe some airborne variety of mad cow disease or something like that. Zombies hadn't even made his list of top-five most likely world-enders. But zombies would do.

On the couch beside him was a Glock. He had dozens of high-capacity magazines for the pistol, plus enough ammunition to turn his little hometown of Gatling, Ohio, into his own version of the Chinese New Year. And he had MREs and water and extra clothing and first-aid supplies and matches and camping gear and water-purification tablets and sturdy shoes.

Yeah, he had this.

Everything was gonna be just fine.

Hell yeah, baby!

* * *

Her mother wasn't screaming anymore, but that didn't make it any better. The things were still eating her. Rose Sherman flinched each time they tore away another piece of flesh; every time one of them snarled and snapped at another for getting in its way, or slipped in the pooling blood, or lifted her mother's corpse and then let it thud to the hardwood floor like a bag of rocks. All this taking place not ten feet from her. Rose could have seen it through the slats in the louvered closet door of her spare bedroom if she'd had the stomach for it. Instead, he kept her eyes closed and her hands clapped over her ears.

Rose had no idea how long she sat there, terror squeezing her chest, tears running down her cheeks, the sounds of the feeding frenzy tearing at her nerves, but eventually the noises stopped.

She opened her eyes—and wished she hadn't.

Mr. Masello, her across-the-street neighbor, had been mowing his lawn when the ghouls descended. With the roar of his mower, he hadn't heard the dead man stumbling up behind him, and Rose's cries and frantic arm-waving had gone unheeded. He still had little blades of grass stuck to his socks and shoes. The rest of him was black with her mother's blood and viscera.

He stood up from her mother's body and staggered off.

The others followed.

Rose heard them bumping through the hallway, the living room, then onto the front patio.

Her mother's dead eyes stared at her across a vast pool of blood. Rose stared back, angry at the woman. Her mother had had no reason to come over today except to bitch at her about the Fourth of July. Rose's brother's wife had gone into some kind of meltdown because the dinner was at Rose's house and not their new place over on Katy Street. Her brother and his bat-shit-crazy wife had skipped the party, which was fine by Rose because she'd never liked that woman anyway, but somehow, because Rose's mother was the craziest of them all, the whole thing had turned into Rose's fault. Here it was two weeks later, and her mother was still finding excuses to call or come over and start the argument all over again. She wouldn't let it go. She had to keep picking at it, refusing to let it go. The needless stupidity of all that drama made Rose furious, not only at her mother, who might still be alive if she'd just been able to leave well enough alone, but at herself because she was feeling angry when her mother was dead and what she should be feeling instead was sorrow and a great, soul-numbing emptiness. Rose nearly kicked the closet doors in her frustration. Even in death her mother made her crazy.

But she knew she couldn't stay in the closet forever. Already she was thirsty. Hunger would soon follow. And she would have to go to the bathroom eventually. The idea of doing that in here, being closed up with the smell, was the deciding factor. She stood up, listened carefully, and not hearing anything but the distant warble of a receding police siren, slowly and quietly pushed the door open.

An afghan pulled from the foot of the bed had soaked up a lot of her mother's blood, giving Rose a straight shot to the door. At least she wouldn't have to walk through it, even if she couldn't exactly help looking at it.

She turned her head and walked toward the door.

She was almost to the hallway when she caught movement out of the corner of her eye.

Mr. Harris, the creepy Gulf War vet who lived two doors down, was kneeling between her mother's knees, his face buried in a massive gash a few inches from her groin. He was tearing at the flesh there, ripping it away, when suddenly the leg separated and hit the floor with a dull, heavy thud.

Rose sucked on her teeth, a whimper escaping her throat.

Mr. Harris looked up. Half of his face was torn away, and what was left of the eye in the ruined socket twitched and jumped constantly like a moth caught in a jar. He climbed to his feet, and to Rose's horror picked up her mother's severed leg before stumbling after her.

Rose ran screaming from the room.

She tore through the hallway, the living room, and out the front door, tumbling down the front steps and landing face-first in the grass. When she looked back at the house, the front door yawned open. Mr. Harris stood there, holding her mother's leg by the ankle, letting it drag behind him.

It was getting dark. Gloom was pooling beneath the trees and in the spaces between the houses. But there was still enough light to see the dead gathering in the street, turning their heads as one in her direction. They began to moan and, one by one, started toward her.

Mr. Harris dragged the leg down the stairs. The next instant, he was standing over her, his damaged eye jumping madly in its socket.

Rose turned and ran. She had no plan, no idea where she was going. All around her huge columns of smoke climbed to the darkening sky. Dogs barked wildly. Here and there a gunshot. A siren. Screams.

And then, several streets over, she stumbled out from between two houses and found herself facing Greg Sutton's house.

She'd gone out with him a few times during her junior year but had told him, quite publicly in fact, to cram it when she found out he was telling the whole school they were fucking.

All that drama seemed like a million years ago. She'd forgotten he lived so close.

Looking past the lies that they'd been intimate (he hadn't even gotten under bra, the bastard), she remembered that he was a survival nut, always talking about what he was going to do when the big one hit. She didn't know if he was still into survivalist stuff, but the tall brick wall surrounding his yard certainly promised more than standing out here in the street.

She went to the wrought iron gate at the front and found it chained and locked.

"Damn it."

A low, stuttering moan behind her caused her to whirl around. Mr. Harris was there, still dragging her mother's leg.

She turned to the gate and rattled the bars, calling for Greg.

A moment later, Greg opened his front door. He stared at her, then his eyes widened with recognition.

He hustled down the front walk.

Greg Sutton had gained a little weight since high school, but it had only served to fill him out. In his flannel shirt with rolled-up sleeves and faded jeans, he actually looked better than Rose remembered.

"What are you doing out there?"

"Greg, open the door. Hurry, please!"

He looked over her shoulder to where Mr. Harris was staggering into the street, the severed leg leaving a gory trail across the pavement to mark his progress.

Greg nodded. "I got the key here somewhere," he said, and pulled a large carabineer key chain from his pocket and started flipping through the keys.

"Jesus, Greg, hurry!"

"This is it," he said.

The lock sprang open and Greg pulled the chain free from the bars. Rose pushed past him, into the yard. "Close it," she said. She was out of breath, blood pounding in her ears. "Hurry!"

She started babbling, telling him about the zombie that had attacked Mr. Masello while he was mowing the lawn and how they had gotten into her house and how her mother had pushed her into the closet and closed the door and tried to fight the dead men who had managed to get inside the house and how her mother had died and was eaten.

Greg grabbed her shoulders and shook her until she stopped.

She closed her eyes and breathed deeply, collecting herself.

"We have to get inside," she said.

"Uh," he said.

He looked terrified, though Rose hardly noticed. She thought it was because Mr. Harris had finally made it to the gate. He still held her mother's leg in his right hand, but now he was beating on the metal bars with his other hand.

And he was starting to draw a crowd.

"We have to get inside," Rose said again.

"Uh, yeah." He looked like a man steeling himself against bad news. "Come on. It's easier if we go in through the kitchen around back." He led her around to the back, where a short, covered walkway connected the back door to the garage.

"Watch your step," he said, and opened the door onto a mudroom. There were boxes stacked along the walls, most of them showing pictures of police and hiking boots. Coats piled high on the washer and dryer.

At first Rose thought that Greg had hastily attempted to barricade the door, but then she saw the kitchen and the living room beyond that, and she gasped. Everywhere she looked there were piles upon piles of boxes, stacks of clothes, plastic storage bins, clutter everywhere. But not just clutter, she saw. The clutter was made of tents, backpacks, portable camping stoves, sleeping bags, jackets, medical first-aid kits, plastic buckets marked 72-HOUR DISASTER KIT, jumper cables, more backpacks, machetes and knives and pistols and ammunition, nearly all of it still in the original boxes and stacked three- or four-feet deep in a jumbled mess that resembled a junkyard after a tornado. It was everywhere. There weren't even lanes through the clutter. It was simply one large amorphous mound of stuff. Greg Sutton, the guy she had once dated, was a hoarder.

"Greg," she said hesitantly. "What...is all this?"

"Watch your step," he said. "It gets a little tricky. Here, come on, there's a spot on the couch where I sit."

He held out his hand, but when she didn't take it he climbed onto a pile of boxes and crawled over the clutter toward the living room.

"Hey, Mom! Somebody's here!"

His sudden scream jolted her loose from her thoughts. She blinked at him as he climbed over the piles of survival gear, testing his footing before putting his weight down, one hand out to steady himself on a teetering stack of plastic storage bins.

She had seen this on TV, on those reality intervention shows, but seeing it now, like this... for the moment, the zombies were forgotten. Even her dead and mangled mother was forgotten.

Her nose crinkled in sudden disgust. There was a rotten-food smell that she was only now noticing. Greg didn't seem to notice, though. He had made it to the couch and was giving her a wounded, apologetic smile.

"You're the first person I've let in here in four years," he said.

She didn't know what to say. She tried to speak but couldn't find her voice.

"I'm sorry about your mother," he said. "I remember her. She was nice."

Rose guffawed. It was a crazy, hysterical sound.

Greg frowned.

He tried again. "I've got some water, if you're thirsty. Food, too. Some of those MREs, you know, the Meals Ready to Eat? They have like thirty-five hundred calories each. Enough for one meal to last all day."

Greg slid down the side of a stack of boxes and shifted some ponchos and rain-proof tarpaulins to one side. He lifted a cardboard box labeled ASSORTED MEALS—READY TO EAT and dropped it onto another stack of boxes. The bottom of the box was wet and split when it hit. A brown, sludgy goo ran down the side of the stack, giving off a vile, rotten smell.

Rose gagged and pushed the heel of her hand against her nostrils, trying in vain to block out the smell.

"Oh, man," Greg said.

He peeled away the side of the box, lifted a ruptured bag of something rotten between his index finger and thumb, and dropped it to one side.

Rose saw flies buzzing around his head.

"Some of this stuff is probably still good," Greg said. "Yeah, I can save some of this."

Rose gagged and nearly vomited.

"You can't eat that, Greg. Oh, God."

"No, no, it's okay. This is military stuff. It's made to keep the food inside safe. Really, it's okay."

She shook her head.

"We should leave here," she said. "It isn't safe."

"Yeah, those things out there," he said.

"Do you have a car?"

He nodded. "A '74 Bronco. Four-wheel drive."

"Has it got gas?"

"Yeah," he said, the word coming out as a part chuckle. "I got plenty of gas. I've got gas cans and spare tires and enough gear to rebuild that thing three times over if we need to."

"That's good. Maybe we could, uh, pack up some of this stuff in the Bronco and leave. I don't know, go into the country someplace, away from the big cities. I heard it was happening everywhere, but that it was really bad in the big cities."

She was nearly babbling again, but something about the look on his face made her pause. He was horror-stricken. He looked as frightened by what she was saying as she had been when Mr. Harris stood up from her mother's groin, blood running down his chin, strips of flesh hanging from his teeth.

"What?" she said.

He shook his head. "No, you don't understand."

"Huh?"

"I can't leave... here. I can't leave this stuff. It's my stuff. I need it."

"Your stuff? Greg, most of this is trash."

"Trash?" He laughed. It was a whiny, delirious sound. "No, it's my stuff. I have lots of stuff. I'm protected."

She didn't like the look on his face, the way he was looking at her. It was all wrong. She felt suddenly nauseous.

"I have stuff," he said. He tone was becoming defensive, angry. "Do you have stuff? You don't, do you? That's why you came here. You're not prepared, are you? But I am. I have all this stuff. You may think it's trash, but it's not. It makes me feel safe. I am safe. Are you safe?"

She stared at him, utterly dismayed. For the first time she noticed the TV was on, some news show, the same spreading red circles on the map she'd been seeing since earlier that morning. The light from the image cast half of his face in a flickering yellow glow. It made his skin look sallow in the dimness of the living room.

"Greg, what happened?" She gestured at the piles of crap all around them. "How did it get like this?"

"This is the way I like it."

"Yeah, but, what purpose does all this serve? How could you possibly expect to use all of this stuff?"

He seemed honestly perplexed by the question. He pointed toward the street. "You just came from out there. How can you not see that all of this stuff has value? Those zombies can swarm for years out there. I can hold out. I have all this stuff. And if things get really bad, I can bug out."

"But that's just the thing. You won't bug out. You so tied to this stuff you can't leave it behind, even when it's the right thing to do."

"Stop trying to get me to leave my stuff!"

The sudden fury of his words shocked her. He looked savage and cruel, like she had just threatened something he held sacred. It scared her. She wanted to leave. Or least not be around him.

"Greg, I... I need to use the bathroom."

Gradually, the heat left his eyes.

"Yeah," he said. "Yeah, ok. Um, it's through there. Down that hallway. Can you get through there?"

She climbed onto a pile of boxes and worked her way back to the hall that led to the rest of the house. Boxes were stacked floor-to-ceiling down the length of the hallway, though a narrow lane had been left to allow access. If she turned her shoulders sideways and shuffle-stepped, she could make it.

She came to the end of the hallway and looked around. The power was out or the lights didn't work, Rose wasn't sure which. Either way she was standing in the dark, wondering why in the hell she was doing this. It was ridiculous for her to be groping her way around this horrible house, but she was doing it just the same, going deeper and deeper into the outward manifestation of Greg's insanity. Anything to be out of his presence.

There were several doors back here and any one of them could have been the bathroom. Each one was nearly blocked by trash and for a moment she thought again of the hoarder shows she'd seen on the TV, the way some of those bathrooms looked. She didn't know if she could handle something that disgusting. Clothes and junk—that was one thing. Even the spoiled, oozing food she could sort of deal with. But to walk in on a bathroom spilling over with mold and human waste, that would put her over the edge.

She opened a door next to her and coughed. The smell of rotten food was even stronger. Rose was closing the door when she heard a faint rustling, like a chain-smoker breathing.

Something moved in the darkness.

"Hello?" she said. "Mrs. Sutton?"

She put a hand over her mouth and stepped as far into the room as the stacks of survival gear allowed.

"Mrs. Sutton?"

Again, something shifted in the darkness. The smell was awful. Rose turned her head to one side in a grimace and saw a flashlight poking out from beneath a pile of coats. She picked it up, turned it on, and pointed it through the stacks of the boxes.

A desiccated woman, long, long dead, nearly mummified, stared at her through a bird's-nest tangle of gray hair. She looked brittle, dusty, and when she moved, a swarm of flies moved with her. She opened her blackened mouth and a gravel-rough gurgle escaped her throat. A gnarled bony hand shot through a gap in the stacks, and Rose stumbled backward, tripping over something and landing on her butt in a box of medical supplies.

Mrs. Sutton was really struggling now, raging against the boxes that trapped her in the far corner. Rose stared at the woman's leathery arm, the sliver of her face visible through the crack, and then turned toward front of the house. This was Greg's mother, for God's sake. How long had she been back here, dead? Was this some weird *A Rose for Emily* thing, or did he even know she had died? Rose couldn't decide which alternative was worse.

The boxes toppled. They crashed at Rose's feet, and Mrs. Sutton stumbled forward, the gurgle in her throat rising an octave, becoming urgent.

Rose scrambled from the room, tripping over boxes, groping along the wall until she found the hallway in the dark. Mrs. Sutton was right behind her, the flies murmuring angrily around the gummy pits that had been her eyes and the blackness of her mouth. Rose pulled boxes down behind her, hoping they'd prove a barricade against the woman.

Then she was out in the living room and Greg Sutton was there, standing exactly where she'd left him in front of the TV, staring after her.

"Gonna head out on my own," she said to him. "Thanks for taking me in."

"You're gonna what...?"

He crawled onto the boxes and tried to go after her, but she was already dropping down into the kitchen.

"Rose, wait."

She didn't slow. She waved once over her shoulder without turning and headed for the mud room. She had her hand on the back door when she heard him say, "Mom, what are you—?"

His screams were cut off by the slamming of the door.

She crossed the yard to the driveway, not bothering with the front gate. She didn't have the key, after all; and besides, there were plenty of those things out there, hovering around the front of the house. Better to jump the side fence and slink into the darkness, unseen.

She was impressed by how calmly she decided this. All things considered, she had every right to behave like a stark-raving lunatic right about now. But she wasn't going to do that.

Rose reached the brick wall and climbed over it, taking her time to make sure she landed safely. There was no point in rushing this. Rushing would get her hurt, and a sprained ankle right about now would be as almost as deadly as a bite from one of the walking dead roaming the streets.

But being careful wasn't the same thing as being quiet, and she ended up making a lot of noise. She turned the flashlight, still clutched in her hand from when she'd taken it from Greg Sutton's back room, on the front of the house and was not surprised to see Mr. Harris rounding the corner, still dragging her mother's severed leg. It was the kind of day, after all, when mothers kept coming back for more.

Ethical Solutions

Ben Richardson saw his first zombie from the window of a registered charter bus on the Gibbs-Sprawl Road as they entered San Antonio. She was strangely sexless, not at all what he expected. Standing barefoot by the weeds that had grown up at the edge of the road since the city had been abandoned, her greasy, stringy hair hanging over her face, her body thin and rickety-looking in a bag-like, blood-stained hospital gown, she reminded Richardson of an emaciated meth junkie. It disturbed him. But the most bizarre part of it, the strangest thing, was that she never looked up, not even as the bus drove by. She stood there, hugging herself with her bone-skinny arms, oblivious to their presence. Richardson had the feeling she'd been there for hours, maybe even days, and that she might go on standing there until her body simply gave out, and she dropped.

She caused quite a stir on the bus, all the college kids rushing to the windows, gawking, saying, "Wow, look at that!" and "My God!"

A pretty blonde sitting in front of Richardson cupped her hand over her mouth and said, "She looks so sad."

Richardson glanced at the blonde, then back at the zombie, receding as the bus pulled away, leaving it in a veil of road dust.

Gradually, the kids went back to their seats, restless with excitement. They were the University of Texas at Austin's branch of People for an Ethical Solution, and they were finally here, in San Antonio, amongst the zombies.

A woman stood up at the front of the bus and clapped her hands. "Listen up, everybody."

The woman, an English professor in her late forties, a little older than Richardson, but quite attractive with her brown hair pouring over her shoulders and her snug green blouse and blue jeans showing off her small-breasted but still impressive curves, told them they were going farther in, to the downtown area. She wanted to get plenty of photographs of the zombies around the Alamo, she said, it being the most widely recognized symbol of San Antonio's past, and, she hoped, a symbol of its future. She wanted the world to see these zombies weren't monsters but living people, with a sickness. People who needed help.

Her name was Sylvia Carnes. Richardson had heard her bit back in Austin and thought it pure rant, nothing worth writing down. When he turned his notes into the finished article he was writing for the *Atlantic*, he planned to characterize her as a passionate college-campus liberal— sincere, and honestly devoted to making things better, but almost completely lacking in real-world common sense.

Carnes, talking to a young girl and her boyfriend standing near the front of the bus, said, "Christy, you and Michael need to take your seats now, okay?"

Richardson chuckled quietly at the scene. At times, Carnes could sound more like a grade-school teacher taking her fourth graders on a field trip to the museum than a hot-blooded political activist.

"Yes, ma'am," the girl said. Her name was Christy Carter, and her lip-smacking East Texas drawl was obvious in only a few words.

Her boyfriend, Michael something or other, was nothing special. A little under six feet tall, an uncombed mess of blond hair on his head, brown eyes sleepy and bloodshot from the joint he'd smoked behind the convenience store bathroom where they'd stopped to pee before crossing the roadblocks that led into San Antonio, Michael looked to Richardson like your run-of-the-mill frat boy. He was well-muscled and slow-thinking, a freshman beer belly starting to spread at his beltline.

But the girl was something else. She was a Lolita if he'd ever seen one. She bounded down the aisle between the seats with a playful skip. She wore a shear, tight-fitting, white camisole and a short, green, pleated skirt. The camisole was cut to show a lot of midriff, and every time she bounced, the skirt rose at the hem to show a few extra inches of well-tanned thigh.

Richardson didn't even notice when the boyfriend, Michael, sat down on the seat across the aisle from him.

Christy leaned against the seat in front of Richardson, swiveling her shoulders a little one way and then the other with the gentle rocking of the bus on the uneven road, her smile beaming at him with a curious mix of innocence and temptation.

"Hi," she said.

"Hi, yourself."

"You're that reporter, ain't ya?"

"Sure am. Ben Richardson. You're Christy, right?"

"Very good," she said, giving him a playful slap on the shoulder.

"Uh, Christy?" said Michael. There was an unpleasant look on his face, like he'd just tasted something sour.

Her smile slipped a little. "Yeah, yeah," she said to Michael. "In a minute."

Then the smile reappeared. She leaned closer to Richardson and said, "That witch Dr. Carnes wants me to change before we get to the Alamo."

She smelled very nice, Richardson noticed.

"I think this looks fine. Don't you?" Christy said, clasping her hands together behind her back and turning her shoulders this way and that, her pert little tits pointed right at him.

Richardson felt the heat spread all the way to the tops of his ears.

"I think you look nice," he said. "But you should probably wear something with a little more coverage. You don't want to risk getting scratched, or bit."

"I want to be a reporter too," she said.

He blinked at her. "You do?"

"Mm hmm. I'm the only freshman on the school paper. That's why I'm here. I'm writing an article on these people for the paper."

"You're a freshman, huh?"

"Mm hmm, but they call us First Years these days. I turned eighteen last month."

Oh Jesus, Richardson thought.

"Uh, Christy?" Michael said, tugging at her wrist now.

"What?"

He shrank back from the look she gave him. "Nothing," he said.

Richardson said, "How 'bout you, Michael? Why are you here?"

"I... well, I...."

"He's just here to protect me," said Christy. "You know how boys are."

Michael looked out the window, sullen-faced.

"So, you're a journalism major?"

Richardson winced inwardly. *Christ*, he thought, *did I really just ask her major?*

"Is that what you did, Mr. Richardson?"

He did a double-take at the mention of his name. The way she said it, she might as well have been calling Daddy.

"Communications," he said, wondering if anybody else but him had picked up on the hitch in his voice. Through the window on the other side of the bus, he could see a small crowd of zombies shambling toward the bus and he tried to get himself back in his mental zone. Enough with the Lolita.

"So tell me, Christy. What's your opinion of what these people are doing?"

"You mean Dr. Carnes?"

"And the rest of them."

"Well, my editor on the paper says we ain't supposed to write our opinions. He says he only wants objective reporting."

"He said that?"

"Mm hmm."

"Christy, I got news for you. Your editor's an idiot. There's no such thing as objectivity in journalism. Opinions are the only things that count, and if you don't have an opinion, you don't have a story."

"I think they ought to send in the Marines and blow 'em all away," Michael said.

Christy, annoyed, said, "Michael, shush, 'fore somebody hears you." To Richardson, she said, "What about you, Mr. Richardson? What do you think about what's going on here?"

Richardson smiled. *Turn the question back on the one asking it. The girl's got good instincts.*

"I think it's a really bad idea bringing a bunch of unarmed college kids into a city that's been overrun by zombies, abandoned by the survivors, and quarantined by the U.S. military."

"But Dr. Carnes has a court order allowing her to be here."

"True. But just because you have the right to do something doesn't mean you should."

"Are you saying this is a moral issue?"

"Not at all. I'm saying it's a common-sense issue."

"But you're here."

"I'm paid to be here, Christy."

The girl shrugged, and suddenly, she was a bouncy teeny-bopper again. It wasn't until she started speaking again that Richardson realized the ditzy school girl routine was an act. All she'd done was bat her eyelashes and stick out her tits, and she'd managed to make him put his cards on the table. She was good. With a few more years' experience under her belt, no man in the world would be able to tell she was intentionally putting them off their guard.

"Well, I think she's doing a good thing," Christy said. "After all, those zombies out there ain't dead. They're just sick, same as if they had AIDS or malaria or the flu."

"Apples to oranges," Richardson said. "The necrosis filovirus, what turns those people out there into zombies, is the worst form of viral hemorrhagic fever ever encountered. Researchers wear space suits to handle samples of it. Those zombies out there aren't dead, like you say, but they're pretty damn near untouchable."

"Dr. Carnes says she wants to show people their fear is in the wrong place. She says if people see that unarmed people can walk around safely with those zombies that maybe the government will finally agree to come down here and help 'em."

"I seriously doubt that's gonna happen."

"Uh, Christy?" Michael again. "Don't you think you ought to get dressed, sweetie?"

Christy gave him one of her hard stares, but softened quickly. "Oh, all right." To Richardson, she said, "Will you excuse me, please?" And then in a whisper, with a wink, "I need to go change."

"Of course."

Her eyes sparkled, big and brown. "It was nice talkin' with you, Mr. Richardson."

"You too, Christy."

She walked to the back of the bus, to the bathroom, and Richardson resisted the urge to turn around and watch her can wiggle under that short skirt.

Michael got up, took down Christy's pink suitcase from the overhead bin, and shot Richardson a dirty look before he took it back to her.

The bathroom was only six seats back, and Richardson could hear them talking.

Michael said, "Christy, why do you always gotta treat me like that?"

"Treat you like what?"

"Like I'm dumb."

"Oh for God's sake, Michael. Just give me my damn bag."

A pause.

"Christy?"

"What?"

"You ain't really sweet on that old dude, are you?"

Richardson didn't get to hear the answer. He felt the bus slow and then lurch as it came to a stop.

An excited flurry of voices rose from the front.

Richardson craned his neck to see. From the looks of it, zombies were blocking the road. Hundreds of them. A moment later, they were pounding on the sides of the bus with their palms, their moans sounding like water moving through old pipes.

The bus started to rock, and Richardson could see flashes of fear on the faces around him.

He got up and started toward the front.

Dr. Carnes was already there, leaning over the driver's shoulder.

Richardson heard her say, "Drive forward. Slowly now. Not fast enough to hurt them. Just push them out of the way."

The bus, which had been fitted with a sort of cattle guard, lurched forward in low gear. Richardson caught himself from falling over by grabbing the tops of the seats on either side of him. He watched in rapt fascination as the bus parted the crowd.

Carnes turned around and faced the rest of the group. "It's okay, everybody. We're through. Everybody take your seats please. We'll be there in ten minutes."

* * *

While they drove the last few miles into downtown, Richardson thought about how he'd write the back story, how San Antonio got to this point, zombies everywhere.

There was the obvious approach. Start with the hurricanes, five of them slamming into the Texas Gulf Coast in the span of three weeks, the city of Houston under twenty feet of water, the necrosis virus growing out of the nasty conditions there and spreading over the Gulf Coast.

He didn't like that though. It'd been done to death already, the news showing it every damn night. What he needed, he decided, was to focus on the quarantine, the military blockade around San Antonio and the other affected areas. That was where the real story was, the reason Carnes and her troop of college-campus liberals took a bus ride into this abandoned ruin that had once been the nation's seventh largest city, almost two million people.

He wondered again about Carnes, and decided the one unassailable fact about her was the strength of her convictions. She honestly believed that the zombies shambling along outside the bus deserved better than to be barricaded inside a shell of a city and forgotten. Richardson hadn't made up his mind on that. It was true they were alive, not like the reanimated corpses of a Romero movie, but their minds had been chewed to a honeycomb by the necrosis filovirus and their physical features distorted by rot. The only thing left intact was their ferocious capacity for aggression. They wouldn't hesitate to cannibalize an uninfected person, and they wouldn't ever show mercy or pity. But was that really a reason to kill 'em all, as Christy's boyfriend had suggested? Science might one day find a cure for them.

Richardson suspected that the judge who signed the court order allowing Carnes and her group to cross the barricade line must have felt equally conflicted.

The bus pulled in front of the Alamo, next to a big L-shaped memorial engraved with the names of the people who died inside fighting the Mexican army of General Santa Anna, and Richardson put his questions on the back burner. He looked around, getting his bearings. They'd stopped on North Alamo Street, a once-beautiful section of downtown that had been lavishly restored, paved with gray cobbled stone and trimmed with red brick, but was now crowded with the blackened skeletons of burned-out cars and thick with dust and garbage, weeds growing through cracks in the pavement. There was a broad, grassy, rectangular plaza between them and the famous façade of the old Spanish mission, and tall stone walls the same color as the street zigzagging off at odd angles on either side. Vegetation was everywhere, oak and mulberry and palm and bougainvillea and a spray of pink crepe myrtle blossoms, all growing wild, curling over the walls like green waves.

Beyond the Alamo was the Crockett Hotel. Next to that was the Menger Hotel, where Teddy Roosevelt recruited his Rough Riders. Before the outbreak, it was said to be the most haunted hotel in the United States. Opposite the Alamo, on Richardson's left, was the Gibbs Building, a six-story Gothic-looking structure that had evidently been gutted by fire during the outbreak.

There were no birds, no squirrels, no cats or stray dogs. The only thing moving was a single zombie, a fat, dark-skinned Hispanic man missing part of his left arm and part of the left side of his face. He walked with a limp, cutting a crooked line across the grassy plaza, not really coming at the bus, but headed in that general direction.

Christy and Michael returned to their seats, Christy now in tight, faded jeans and a little green half shirt over her camisole, tied in the front, the knot between her tits, the whole thing drawing Richardson's eye to the deep curve between her breasts.

Michael dropped into his seat, still sullen. Christy caught

Richardson looking at her chest and gave him a look that was both girlishly innocent and at the same time openly seductive.

Richardson looked away, his mouth dry.

At the front of the bus, Carnes took up the PA and started organizing the group. She'd told Richardson what to expect, and she didn't waste any time putting her plan into action.

The door opened and several students followed her out. They removed a few folding picnic tables from the cargo bins on the outside of the bus and carried them over to the cobbled walkway in front of the Alamo. They set up tables, returned to the bus, got baskets of food, and laid everything out, buffet-style. It looked to Richardson like spiral-sliced ham, dinner rolls, apples, pears, and processed American cheese in huge, orange, one-pound loaves.

Richardson watched the zombie as it moved through the plaza, anxious to see what would happen.

Nothing did.

The zombie seemed unaware of their presence, even as the students, under the watchful eyes of Dr. Carnes, stood not twenty feet from him.

The zombie continued on, crossed Alamo Street, then disappeared between two buildings and down a narrow alley.

When Carnes got back on the bus, she said, "Okay, everybody, this is the moment of truth. What we do here will go a long way toward getting these people the help they need. I want each of you to keep your eyes open. Make sure you wear your surgical gloves at all times. I don't want you to be afraid, but I do want you to be extremely careful. And remember to get plenty of pictures."

With that, Carnes told the bus driver to lay on the horn. He gave it five long blasts, stopped, paused for about thirty seconds, then gave it another five long blasts. Everybody on the bus was quiet, waiting, watching the streets that led into the plaza.

Christy reached across the aisle and touched the back of Richardson's hand. "This is so exciting, don't you think?"

Her smile reminded him of sunshine.

Somebody gasped. "Here they come. Over there."

Everyone moved to see. At first there were only a few stragglers, a few human train wrecks that limped painfully and blindly toward the unfamiliar sound.

"Moment of truth is right," Richardson murmured.

Christy swept a curtain of brown hair off her shoulder with a casual turn of her head. She smiled at him again.

Then, gradually, the plaza filled with zombies.

"Uh, Christy?" Michael looked from the window to his girlfriend. "Sweetie, are you sure you wanna do this?"

"Shush."

A few zombies approached the table, handled the food, and like babies, experimented with it by putting it in their mouths. The first ones to taste the food dove on the tables, knocking them over and spreading the food on the ground, and the resulting racket attracted the others. They swarmed the table like a football team on a loose fumble.

Richardson heard Michael echo his own thoughts. "Uh, Christy, I think this is a really stupid idea."

"Be quiet," she snapped.

"Christy, come on. Look at them."

"I mean it, Michael. Be quiet."

Michael watched the zombies eat, a snarl of disgust at the corner of his mouth. "Christy, please—"

"Don't," she said pointing a finger in his face. "Don't. You don't wanna come, don't come."

Michael looked at her, then past her, to Richardson, his thoughts playing out on his face. If I don't go with her, the old dude will. It seemed enough of a threat to calm his nerves.

They began off-loading the bus, Carnes on the PA, reminding them not to make any sudden moves or loud noises. "Stay calm, stay alert, stay safe," she said.

Richardson went outside and looked around, nose wrinkling from the smell of rotted flesh. Up close he found it hard to believe that these people were alive. He moved away from the bus, slowly, already thinking that this would be the opening scene of his article, the teaser. Lead off with the trembling sensation he felt all the way down to his toes. He stayed on the sharp edge of fear for several minutes, but by degrees relaxed. Looking around, he saw the others experiencing the same growing confidence he felt. They smiled at one another as they mingled with the zombies.

Carnes, her voice a forceful whisper, said, "Cameras out, everybody. Lots of pictures."

Richardson had brought his own camera, and he began snapping pictures. It was a weird, subdued scene, the low moaning of the zombies punctuated by the rapid clicking of twenty cameras. He positioned himself with his back to the bus, the Alamo's façade about a hundred feet away, the zombies feeding near the toppled picnic tables in the space between.

Christy appeared in front of him.

"Will you take my picture, Mr. Richardson?" she said, the look in her eye reminding him of Marilyn Monroe saying "Happy birthday, Mr. President."

She cocked one hip and folded her arms under her tits, pushing them up without making it obvious that's what she was doing.

He couldn't quite keep the smile from his face, and he was just about to take her picture when he heard one of the college kids, a thin, mop-haired boy with a scraggly goatee and KILL YOUR TELEVISION printed on his black T-shirt, scream.

A heavyset zombie female, maybe Hispanic, maybe black, though Richardson wasn't quite sure because the necrosis filovirus had blackened her skin to the color of charcoal, was clawing at the boy clumsily, and the boy was panicking.

"No," said Carnes, her voice still that same forceful whisper. "Zach, no. Use your hands. Push her to the tables with the others."

Zach was obviously terrified, but he did like he was told. He pushed the zombie's hands to one side, got behind her, and gently, but firmly, pushed her to the table.

"That's it," Carnes said. "Good, Zach."

To Richardson's amazement, the zombie didn't turn and try to fight. Once at the table, it fell in with the others, Zach forgotten.

"Okay, Zach," said Carnes, "step back. Let her go."

Zach did, and a giddy relief spread through the group.

To himself, Richardson said, "Huh, look at that."

* * *

Christy was in front of him again. She asked if he knew yet what he was going to write and then didn't give him a chance to answer.

"It looks like it's working, don't you think?"

"Well, nobody's been eaten yet," said Richardson. "I suppose that's something."

"You're not impressed by this? I mean, look at 'em. They're eating the food Dr. Carnes put out for 'em. They're not attacking anybody."

"That's true."

Christy swept a wave of brown hair off her face, her expression troubled.

"So why don't you think it's working?"

"I think it's too early to tell."

"What, exactly, do you need to see before you'll be convinced?" said Dr. Carnes, who'd been standing behind Richardson but was walking right at him now.

The woman was smug, high on her success, but her eyes were glinting.

"I don't know what I need to see," Richardson said.

"Well, what about this?" said Carnes, gesturing at the zombies around the toppled picnic tables.

"You're feeding them."

"Exactly."

"So what does that prove? Every single person who survived the original outbreak could have told you they were hungry."

"That's not the point and you know it."

"No, Dr. Carnes, I don't know it. What you've got here is a bunch of hungry zombies. That's all."

"What I've got here is proof that uninfected people can move through crowds of the infected without being attacked."

"I sincerely hope you're right, Dr. Carnes. Let's hope you're not merely chumming the waters."

"Chumming the waters?" Carnes shook her head in obvious disgust. "Look around you."

Richardson did, and saw the college kids taking pictures. One of them was even handing an apple to a zombie.

"This is working, Mr. Richardson. Can't you see that?"

"What happens when the food runs out?"

"Then we pack up and return. Tell the world that it's safe to come inside the quarantine line and start looking for a way to cure these people."

"That sounds reckless to me, Dr. Carnes."

"Reckless?" Carnes said, sounding righteously indignant. "It sounds like basic human decency to me. I hope you'll try to keep that in mind when you write your article."

She stormed off.

Richardson thought, *That is one crazy, mixed-up bitch.*

Michael spoke up. "Uh, Christy, there's a lot more of 'em comin' now. Why don't we go back to the bus, okay?"

"Hush," Christy said. "I told you, you don't wanna come, don't come."

"But Christy—"

"Go back if you want, Michael, but I'm staying here."

When she turned to Richardson again, the pouting smile was back on her face.

"You really don't think Dr. Carnes is on to something here?"

"No, Christy, I don't."

"Why not?"

"It's been eight months since the outbreak. Six months since the quarantine. None of these zombies have seen an uninfected person since then. I'm wondering how long it will take for their aggression to return."

Almost on cue, the zombies began to stand up from the overturned picnic tables.

Richardson watched them and felt the mood in the plaza sour. The zombies—*Jesus, more of them every time he turned around*—were moving toward the college kids.

Several students had put their cameras aside and were using their hands to push the zombies away the way Zach had done earlier.

A few students were beginning to call to Carnes, fear in their voices.

Carnes moved through the crowd, directing the students back to the bus.

Good, Richardson thought. *That's smart.*

"Christy," he said, "you and Michael... Oh shit!"

About twenty feet behind them, a girl was knocked off her feet by two male zombies. They fell on her, and in the time it took Richardson to register what was going on, the zombies were ripping the girl apart with their teeth and fingernails.

The girl screamed, and it was like throwing on a light switch, the zombies remembering now their cannibalistic impulses.

Chaos followed. Students ran, screaming, falling here and there as the zombies massed on them. About thirty feet to Richardson's left, Carnes was yelling, trying to keep order but seeing it fall apart all around her.

He saw Zach, the mop-haired boy with the KILL YOUR TELEVISION T-shirt, trying to push his way through the crowd. Zach turned one zombie around and pushed him into two others, but when he tried to run, one of them got a hand on the back of his baggy blue jeans and held him tight. Zach slapped at the zombie's arm but couldn't break free in time. Another zombie fell on him from behind, bit deep into his shoulder, and the last Richardson saw of the boy was a pair of arms clawing at the air like a drowning sailor sinking below the waves.

That was it for Richardson. A zombie stepped in front of him and he kicked it in the knee, knocking the zombie's legs from under him.

Christy was twenty feet away, her eyes flickering over the scene, mouth shaped for a scream that wouldn't come. Richardson ran to her and grabbed her wrist.

"Time to go," he said, and yanked on her arm.

He turned to the bus and froze in his tracks. A zombie was on top of the bus driver, tearing into his neck with his teeth.

Three more zombies huddled in and began to eat the man, his legs hanging off the bottom step of the bus.

"Michael," Christy said.

Richardson turned and realized he still had Christy's wrist in his hand. He saw her looking at Michael and Michael holding a pistol in one hand, the business end of the gun—a blued Colt Army 1911 from the looks of it—pointed at a zombie limping drunkenly toward him.

"Michael?"

Richardson said, "Where'd you get that?" The court order had specifically stated no weapons.

Michael didn't speak. He was terrified, the weapon shaking in his hand, the zombie still coming on like the gun wasn't there.

"Shoot him," Richardson said.

Michael glanced at Richardson, and Richardson knew that the boy was too scared to shoot.

A zombie crossed the grass behind Michael, stumbling his way.

Christy screamed.

Richardson said, "Michael, behind you."

Michael moved slowly, turning first to Richardson, then swinging his arm around the other way, practically putting it in the zombie's mouth.

The zombie grabbed Michael and bit down on his bicep, ripping out a big wad of meat. Michael's knees buckled, but he held onto the gun. The zombie tripped over him, landing across his legs, pinning Michael to the ground.

Richardson never let go of Christy's arm. He pulled her to where Michael was wrestling with the zombie and kicked it in the neck. The blow lifted the zombie off Michael. It rolled onto its shoulder, where it coughed and gagged. Richardson grabbed Michael by the shirt and pulled him to his feet, the boy not screaming, strangely docile and lethargic.

Shock, Richardson thought.

Richardson guided them through a gap in the crowd, the screams of students and the moans of zombies all around them, toward the stone wall to the right of the Alamo. There were porticos in the stone wall big enough to drive a car through, but they were blocked by black wrought-iron bars. The courtyard on the other side of the wall, overgrown with vegetation, looked promising, but they had to reach it first.

"We need to get him to cover," Richardson said.

A few zombies were following them, slow-moving, ugly bastards with their faces rotted away and their hands stained with blood.

Richardson watched them come, looking around for somewhere to run.

"Can't we get inside?" Christy asked. The confidence she'd shown while flirting with him was gone, like she'd reverted to a little girl again, no sexuality left. When Richardson looked down into her eyes he saw a frightened child, nothing more.

"This way," he said and pulled her toward the front door.

It was locked, but he'd expected that. The door looked old-fashioned, pine wood painted the green of old bronze, but when he yanked on it, it didn't give.

"Michael," he said, "let me have the gun."

Michael shook his head. "No way."

"Give me the gun!"

"No."

The zombies were getting closer now. Dead college students lay everywhere.

"Michael, please."

"Fuck you. I ain't giving you my gun."

I could take it, Richardson thought. *Punch him in the nose and end up wrestling for it, maybe winning, maybe getting his infected blood all over me. Meanwhile, those zombies keep coming.*

It wasn't worth it.

"Put the gun here," Richardson said, pointing at the doorknob. "Right here."

Michael, still thinking he was being asked to give up the gun, shook his head.

"You hold it, Michael. Put it right here and fire."

Maybe some of it got through, Richardson wasn't sure.

One zombie got out in front of the others and crossed the lawn leading to the door. Richardson stared at him and thought: *Jesus, his eyes. A fucking blank slate.*

"Come on, Michael. Shoot out the fucking lock. Put the gun right here and pull the damn trigger."

Michael did. The spent cartridge flew up and landed on the cobbled walkway before clattering into the grass.

Richardson kicked the door. Nothing. He kicked it again and it gave, but only a little. He let Christy go and forced the door open with his shoulder. It was painfully solid, hurting more than he thought it would after seeing it done so many times in the movies.

"Go," he said to Christy, and held the door while she helped Michael inside.

He saw a flash of green, moving fast.

Carnes.

She yelled something that sounded like "Wait, wait!" and Richardson stepped to one side as she ran through the door.

When she was in, Richardson pushed the door closed just as the weight of the zombies fell against the other side. He dug his feet into the floor, his back against the door, and pushed back with everything he had.

* * *

The door shook against his back. In front of him was a rectangular room about twenty feet deep and sixty feet wide. The walls were rough-hewn stone, the vaulted ceiling crisscrossed by bare cedar planks. There were a few antique tables and chairs behind fading velvet ropes, a few pictures of famous early Texans on the walls.

Christy had leaned Michael against the back wall, the girl hovering over him, trying to help.

Carnes was standing in the middle of the room, her face strangely warped, her lips moving but no sound coming out.

He could feel the weight of the zombies against the other side of the door, and he knew he couldn't hold them off for long. Looking around, he tried to find something to barricade the door. It had brackets on either side that had been bolted into the stone so a board could be used to barricade it, but there was no board. It was only a prop.

"Bring that table to me," he said to Carnes, pointing at a dust-covered table loaded with brochures.

No response.

"Carnes!"

No response. The woman was locked up inside herself, paralyzed by confusion.

"Christy."

Christy, from the back wall, said, "He's hurt real bad, Mr. Richardson."

"Christy, hurry. Bring me that table."

The girl, her face stained where her tears had made her makeup run, dragged the table over to him.

"Break one of the legs off," he said.

She tried. Couldn't do it.

"Stand here. Back against the door."

She did, and when she had it, Richardson stood and kicked one of the legs off the table. He jammed it into the bracket and pulled Christy away from the door.

Working quickly, he kicked the other legs off and used the table top as a wedge between the door's center bar and the floor.

Hold 'em for a few minutes, he thought.

When he turned back to the room, Christy was pleading with Dr. Carnes.

"He's real sick, Dr. Carnes. Please help him. I don't know what to do."

Carnes didn't even see her. She was off in her own little hell of collapsing reality.

"Mr. Richardson?"

Michael was sitting against the wall, the gun still in his lap, looking like he was about to go under. He was sweating, his face pale and pasty, his breathing uneven and shallow, head lolling on his shoulders like it wasn't attached.

Richardson turned to Christy, the girl all eyes, waiting for him to make it better.

"I'm sorry," he said.

Christy blinked.

"He'll change soon," Richardson said. "There's nothing we can do to stop it."

Christy didn't answer, but he could tell she was hearing him, that she understood, at least on some level.

"I need to get that gun from him."

Christy nodded.

He patted her shoulder because he didn't know what else to say and walked toward Michael, who watched him come.

"Michael, I need that gun."

"Go to hell."

Richardson thought, *If he says I'll have to pry it from his cold dead hands I'll kick his teeth in.*

"You can't use it. You can barely stand."

"Go to hell."

From behind him, Christy said, "Mr. Richardson, come quick."

Christy was at one of the barred windows, looking out at the plaza. Richardson crossed the room, past Carnes, who was still babbling nonsense, and stood next to Christy.

The scene was heartbreaking. The students were either being eaten or had changed and were doing some eating of their own. Twenty or so zombies crowded around the window, trying to punch through the glass to get them.

"Christy, we need Michael's gun."

"There's no way to help him?"

"He's gonna change soon, Christy. There's nothing we can do. But if we get that gun, we stand a chance of getting to the bus."

"Will we take him with us?"

"Christy...."

She nodded, but wouldn't look him in the eye.

Richardson thought, *Man, the poor girl.* And then, out loud, said, "Oh, no."

Michael had fallen on his side but was pushing himself up, climbing drunkenly to his feet.

Christy said, "Michael?"

"Stay back, Christy."

"But..."

"Stay back."

Richardson had read every single statement he could find by survivors of the original outbreak while he was preparing for this assignment, and he knew about fast-movers, zombies who had been in exceptional physical condition before they were infected and whose injuries were such that they could still move around easily after the infection set in. They could sprint, climb, jump, fight, just like an uninfected person, only they could do it longer and harder because their diseased minds couldn't recognize exhaustion or pain.

As soon as Michael stood up, Richardson knew he was going to be a fast-mover.

He ran at Richardson, a full sprint.

At the same time, the table leg snapped in the bracket and there was a slap as the table top fell to the floor. The door flew open, a mass of arms and legs and teeth trying to rush through the opening all at once.

Richardson jumped behind the door and pushed it closed again, holding it shut with his back and his legs as Michael narrowed the gap between them.

Richardson braced for the impact.

Michael was almost on him when Christy stepped out of nowhere with a rickety old pioneer chair over her head. She got in front of Michael and swung it down into his knees.

The chair broke apart, but it tripped him and he went sprawling headfirst into the wall to Richardson's left. The gun ended up somewhere in the shadows. Richardson heard it fall but didn't see where it landed.

Zombie Michael was stunned but not out for the count. He got up, his nose and lips bleeding, and turned around to go after Richardson again. But Richardson was still getting hit hard from behind, the door nearly jumping off the hinges, his legs buckling under the strain.

"Get the gun!"

Christy took a step, and the movement caught Michael's eye. He forgot about Richardson and thrust his bleeding hands out to grab Christy.

"Michael, please..."

"Push him out of the way. Like Zach did."

"Michael."

Her pleas were lost on Michael. All she was to him was something to be killed and eaten, and he limped toward her.

"Michael. Stop, please."

When the shot came, the orange burst of the muzzle flash lit the room like a strobe light.

Michael stopped. His hands fell to his sides, his shoulders hunched, and he fell face-down on the stone floor.

Carnes stood behind him, holding the smoking gun in both hands.

Christy looked down at her ex-boyfriend's body like it was somebody she didn't know.

"Dr. Carnes," said Richardson.

The English professor looked up at him, the gun still raised in both hands, looking like a cannon in the woman's delicate grip.

"Dr. Carnes, give me the gun, okay?"

She didn't move.

A hard shove at the door behind him nearly made Richardson's knees crumple. He couldn't last much longer.

"You did what you had to do," he said, his voice as calm as he could make it. "You know you did. Now please, give me the gun."

She lowered the weapon and handed it to him without looking him in the eyes.

His legs felt weak, and his back was being pounded by the door, but he took the gun with exaggerated calm.

They had to get out. The wall opposite him was solid stone, but to his left, on the short side-wall, was a window, about two feet by three feet.

"Christy, check that window. See if there's more of them out there."

"But..."

There was a hard shove on the door from the other side, and Richardson sank onto his butt. The door stayed open, arms and faces pushing farther and farther into the crack.

"Hurry!"

Christy ran to the window and looked into the overgrown fecundity of the courtyard.

"I don't see anyone."

"Bust it out."

"How?"

"With a chair. Anything."

She did.

"Dr. Carnes," he said, "you and Christy get outside. When you're through, I'll go."

Carnes stared at him.

"Can you move?"

"Yes," she said, weakly.

"Then go. Hurry. Please."

When the two women were through the window, Richardson pushed himself to his feet, stepped away from the door, and ran for the window. He was already climbing through it when the first zombies broke through.

* * *

They moved quietly through the overgrown courtyard, stopping at the south wall so Richardson could peek over it to see if it was clear.

He saw four zombies, all of them with their backs to him. They moved stiffly down a cobbled street toward the Alamo's façade.

He waited for them to round the corner onto the Alamo Street side of the building, then said, "We're going over."

"How are we gonna get out of here?" Christy said.

"The street is clear. I think most of them went inside where we were."

"But what if they didn't? What if they're all over the place, waiting for us?"

"Then we'll figure something else out." Richardson glanced at Carnes. "Are you ready to go?"

Carnes nodded.

"Okay, let's go."

He climbed to the top of the wall, straddled it, and helped them both over, first Christy, then Carnes.

They crept along the Alamo's south wall to the corner. Standing on the stone walkway that led around the Alamo, they could see the grassy plaza littered with the dead and dying, a few zombies still walking around, and beyond that the bus, the dead driver still on his back on the steps, his body holding the folding doors open.

Richardson could hear the low moaning of a few zombies in the courtyard on the other side of the wall, and the sound of many more inside the main visitor's center where they had been, where Michael had died.

"We can make it," he said. "But we need to hurry."

The two women nodded, and then they were running for the bus.

Richardson shot two zombies that got in their way, and they were at the bus, Richardson pulling the driver's body out while waving Christy and Carnes on board.

Richardson got behind the wheel, put it in gear, and they were off, mowing down zombies as they headed back for the quarantine line.

In his rearview mirror Richardson saw the two women, their ages right to be mother and daughter, sitting on opposite sides of the aisle, each looking out a different window, each in their own little world.

* * *

Six weeks later, Richardson was sitting at his kitchen table, reading Christy Carter's front page exposé in the Dallas *Morning News*.

Next to his chair was a suitcase. Richardson was leaving for Houston that afternoon, most of that city still under water almost two years after the hurricanes that had brought on the necrosis virus, patrolled now by gun boats that both enforced the quarantine and protected all the wealth of Houston's banks and jewelry stores and museums sunken beneath the new shape of Galveston Bay.

Christy's article was excellent, and he was stunned by the clarity and intelligence of her written voice.

He had chosen a more philosophical approach for his own article, concentrating on the politics of the quarantine and the legal issues surrounding the continuing effort on the part of People for an Ethical Solution to encourage medical research on a cure.

Christy had also written on the fundamental issue of right to life, but had gone about it in a radically different way. Her article put a human face on the problem—but not Michael's face, as Richardson had expected. She chose a much more surprising face.

"The best government statistics put the death toll for the outbreak at 4.3 million," Christy wrote. "Add to that another three million still infected, still wandering the streets of San Antonio, Houston, Corpus Christi, New Orleans, and at least a hundred other smaller towns across the Gulf Coast, and the loss of life is nothing short of a holocaust.

"The recent expedition to San Antonio has added twenty-six more lives to that holocaust.

"But there are also losses that can't be added neatly to any one column.

"Dr. Sylvia Carnes of The University of Texas at Austin is one such invisible casualty. Whatever judgment she may face in the courts, where the wrongful death suits of the students who accompanied her are still to be decided, and whatever judgment she receives from the conscience of the community, she will remain an emotional cripple. The very fabric of her belief structure has been stripped from her and torn to pieces, and in that sense, she is a microcosm of those of us left behind in the wake of so many tragedies."

After reading through that section again, Richardson sipped his coffee and looked out across his lawn where the morning sunlight stirred a lazy haze through the air. Focusing on Carnes was brilliant journalism. Her fractured belief system had given her a sort of brutal half-life, and in that sense she was a perfect parallel to the half-life existence of the zombies she had tried so hard to help.

Richardson made up his mind to call her and offer his congratulations. Journalism, he had told her, was about opinions, because that's where the story is, and oh man did that girl ever have a story.

Swallowed

The snake, a twenty-foot female Burmese python, slowly uncoiled as the man walked past. The snake's tongue flicked the air and tasted a miasma of death swirling around the man, though her reptilian brain made no connection between the man and the familiar, rotting taste. The snake saw only a man, stumbling, picking his way uncertainly through the tangled weeds. She saw an easy kill, nothing more.

The man tripped over an exposed root, and in that moment, the snake struck.

She lunged forward, biting the man high on the back of his thigh, her momentum knocking him to the ground, twisting him onto his side.

The kill was not difficult. Beyond a few weak attempts to bite back, the man fought little. His legs twitched. His hands groped ineffectually at her flanks. She ignored his hands and coiled around him, around his waist, his neck, and began to squeeze.

Her jaws unhinged, and the man and the snake became intimate as the slow ballet of predator and prey played out to its inevitable conclusion.

* * *

The snake was born in the Everglades. Her ancestors were pets released into the wild by owners who could no longer care for the giant reptiles. Those first generations squeezed out the wetland's top predators, creating an ecological nightmare. For a time, the authorities hunted the giant snake and her many cousins, but that stopped when humanity's dead rose from their graves and overwhelmed the living.

The snake knew nothing of that, of course. She knew only that she had eaten alligators and grown huge in this world without game wardens. And at two-hundred pounds, the man who tasted like death was a long meal, but went down soon enough, one gulp at a time.

* * *

A night passed, and when the sun came up it found the snake warming herself on a narrow strip of bald earth next to a scummy pond. The snake had spent the night in great pain. Her flanks were swollen, distended, her muscles twitching. Spasms of pain caused her head to bob. She opened her mouth and tried to vomit out the pain inside her.

But she couldn't.

And for a blinding moment, the pain became so intense her primitive reptilian mind couldn't recognize it as pain. All she knew was relief as her side burst open and the man who smelled like death spilled out in a streaming gooey mass, like a mockery of birth.

She was still reeling with pain that was infinitely more than pain when the meal, in its turn, began to feed upon her body.

* * *

Time is gone, but the man doesn't know it.

He knows only that life is gone. The heat that drove him here is gone. He must find more heat. He must find life.

He must feed.

He stands, strands of snake offal stretching like melted cheese from his body, and he walks, without a memory, without a rudder.

Sabbatical in the Ohio Methlands

Not *really* zombies.

Not like in the movies, anyway. To begin with, they're alive. And they don't eat their victims. They'll rape you, rob you, murder you, sure, but not eat you.

The rest of it's the same, though.

They lurch around looking dead. They smell dead. Boils, abscesses, old infected injuries—all do their part in approximating putrefaction. Sometimes, a murmuring haze of flies surrounds their eyes and mouths. They look like skeletons in leather sheets. Their knee joints have a bigger circumference than their thighs. Starvation and malnutrition are the norm. But their crippled movements and disoriented moaning can be deceptive. Step into the street with your head elsewhere, and they'll swarm you.

Afterward, your corpse will look like it's been eaten.

But they don't eat you. Just... tear you up.

I've seen it happen too many times. Some family in a station wagon, just passing through, gets lost, doesn't see the roadblocks. College kids looking for a gag. Survivalists, testing their mettle, and failing. I even watched them get an Ohio state trooper once. But usually those guys know better.

This is the sixth year I've been coming to what used to be Gatling, Ohio. Like most of the small towns in America's midsection, Gatling was abandoned after the Meth Rebellion of

2017, given over to the meth zombies who now wander its streets and sleep in the doorways of its uninspired, post-WWII architecture. The buildings are falling apart. Few windows remain unbroken. Insulation hangs from ceilings. Scrolls of wallpaper curl off walls. The only life is that which feeds off meth and wanders the streets, moaning like something out of a Romero film, looking for the high that will take them through the coming night.

Luckily, the little second-floor dentist office I've taken over as my observation point has escaped the depredations. During the day, when the meth zombies are most active, I can sit at the window and get film footage or dictate notes, whatever I feel like doing. At night, I sit in the old patient's chair and read Jack Finney novels and drink gin. It's diligent field work—don't get me wrong—but I enjoy my summers here in Gatling just the same.

Gene Northrop, a chemistry professor from Texas A&M, has a similar setup across town in the old New Life Baptist church. I've seen him around. He's working on a paper on aboriginal techniques for methamphetamine production in the post-industrial ruins of abandoned America. Sometimes, late at night, I'll hear a building explode at the edge of town, and I think to myself, *Ah, one of Gene's grad students just scored himself a paper.* Some night soon I'm going to visit him. Maybe we can compare notes.

In the meantime, I've been working on a paper on the mating habits of the female meth—

Okay, I need to change gears for a second.

There was a noise outside the door just a bit ago, and I had to make sure it wasn't a wrecking party. The males can be dangerous when they're scavenging for a high. I had to shoot a few of them earlier this month. I hated doing it, but I have to preserve this observation post.

Luckily, it was only Susan.

She started coming to my office two years ago. She's a white female, early 30s, which means she was in her teens when the Rebellion happened. The meth has charred most of her mind to cinders, but her survival instincts are still strong.

She caught me off guard the first time. It was late at night. I had gone through a lot of gin. I got up from my dentist's chair to jot some notes on something I'd seen that day, forgetting that the front door was still unlocked. I heard a floorboard creak and turned around. She was squatting in the middle of the floor, dressed in rags, her long, brown hair a frizzled, shaggy mass around her dirty face, nicks and cuts over her hands and arms.

Have you ever been watched by a squirrel? Same nervous, unblinking look I got from her.

I tried to speak, but she scrambled toward the door. She didn't make it, though. She was hungry, dehydrated, her body weak.

I gave her some clean water and let her sleep on my couch. When she woke the next morning, she was going through withdrawal. She looked at the clean clothes I'd dressed her in, touched her face that I'd scrubbed clean, and panicked. *Residual feelings of violation?* I wondered. I watched her from my desk. I put a military MRE on the floor. She snatched it up and backed toward the open door. I didn't make a move to stop her, just went on smiling.

I was delighted when she came back the next night.

We developed a routine. I'd leave the door cracked at night, a little food and water on the chair next to my bed. Though she never talked, she could still communicate, with her eyes and her body language.

She seemed grateful. I know I was.

I started calling her Susan, after this girl I used to dream of dating back in my grad-school days. I don't think my meth girl minded. It seemed to comfort to her, just as she became a comfort to me, a bulwark against the loneliness that used to overwhelm me here at night in the Methlands.

I've been back in Gatling for three days now. That first night, when I was still getting settled, she came to me. She had something to show me, a memento of our night together last August.

Now I'm sitting here at my desk, watching her rub her belly.

I wonder if her baby will be born without a soul, or if it will lose it along the way.

Like its father.

Two-and-a-Half Graves

If they'd come a few minutes earlier, the zombies would have surprised him in the bedroom, kneeling next to the bed, muttering his good-byes to his dead wife. They'd have found a middle-aged man in shabby clothes, dirty gray hair hanging in curtains over his face, his expression ashen with grief. They'd have found a broken man, turning the hog-tied woman onto her side, flinching as she began to struggle against the ropes. They'd have found him armed with only a kitchen knife, and that buried midway up the blade in the narrow gap between the base of her skull and the top of her spine. They could have torn him to pieces in that moment. He'd have been helpless, unable to rise to his own defense. But they came too late, and when they broke from the tree line and into his weed patch backyard, Mark Vogler was already on his feet and heading for the kitchen, where he had moved most of his tools.

At first there were only two of them, both rotting, slow-moving hulks, but there were almost certainly more in the dense cedar thicket that lined the yard. These two were part of the horde that had been trying to get at him for the last week, clawing holes in the boards he had nailed over his windows and doors, moaning all night long, melting like ghosts into the cedar thicket when he got drunk enough to stagger onto the back deck and take pot shots at them with his pistol.

Now, numb with grief—but not as numb as he thought he'd be—he leaned his forehead against a gap in the boards and watched the zombies shambling toward the house. He wasn't afraid, and he found that funny. He tried to tell himself that he should be afraid, that this time the zombies would sense how exhausted he was and claw at the windows and doors until they got inside, but instead, all he could think about was how long it had been since he'd slept last. What was it, two nights? Three?

He coughed. *Yeah,* he thought, *it's the flu. Probably be on my ass the next week at least.*

"You need to do it if you're gonna do it," he muttered to himself.

He grabbed an old Ruger pistol he kept on the counter and ran his finger over the trigger. The gun was a .357 with a blued barrel and walnut grips. Nothing fancy, but solid and reliable.

Probably the last solid and reliable thing left in this world.

His eyes snapped to a loose corner of the plywood board he'd nailed over the back door. A woman, her face streaked with blood, one eye clouded to a pale milky pink, was forcing her head and shoulders inside.

"Aren't you the smart one?" Vogler said. "I didn't see you."

Ropes of saliva and flecks of foam flew from the woman's bloody mouth. A stuttering growl rose in her throat, and her one remaining eye rolled in its socket with a feral intensity that only hunger could create.

He put the business end of the Ruger against the side of the woman's head. "You'll get nothing from me, you bitch," he said through clenched teeth, "trying to break into my home..."

He fired, and then everything the woman's brain had ever known and experienced sprayed across the rainwater-sodden floor.

He stood there, looking at the woman's mostly headless corpse, and thought about what it meant for a zombie to die. They had no thoughts, no feelings, no humanity. But the person they had once been had had all those things. Were they in there still? Even imperfectly recorded, like an echo? This woman, beneath all the rot and filth, looked to be about thirty. She would have gone to college, dealt with finding a job. She might have even had children, been a mother. She was old enough to have experienced love, and heartache, and joy, and beauty, too. All the things that made humanity great could very well have lived in that mind. Now, all those wonderful possibilities were but a smear on his kitchen wall.

The vulgarity of it made him ill.

The dull pad and drag of bare feet on the terracotta tiles of his back patio pulled his attention away. Both of the zombies he had seen earlier were there, their stiff, clumsy bodies bumping like blind men in a strange room against the rusted remains of his lawn furniture.

Vogler moved fast. He kicked the boards off the back door. With the dead woman's weight to pull them down, they tumbled away easily. The next moment he was through the door, his weapon trained on the lead zombie. Vogler fired, turned, then fired again at the second one. The first collapsed instantly from a solid head shot. The second fell back with a groan and tripped over a toppled chair. Flat on its back, twisting miserably like a bug trying to right itself, it let a horrible gurgling sound as a black, tar-like smear of old coagulated blood formed at its throat.

He kept the weapon trained on the second zombie, waiting for it get back up, but it didn't. It stared up at him, hacking like it was choking.

Vogler was looking at the zombie, but he was thinking of Margaret, his dead wife. His grief was real, that much he knew, but he felt like he was too shallow to grieve her the way she deserved to be grieved. She had loved him honestly, despite all his years of self-absorption and putting his career before her, despite his ability to convince himself that providing for her was the same thing as loving her, and that made him wonder if his grief was for her passing, or for himself having to live without her.

He thought, *Oh Jesus, am I that shallow? I am, aren't I?*

Vogler looked up at the tree line. The rest of the zombie horde had emerged. They stood inside what had once been his yard, staring at him with a vacuous menace. None blinked. The dead didn't do that.

"Get out of here!"

They didn't move. They didn't even flinch.

"Get!"

He ran down the steps and into the yard, screaming and waving his arms in the air like some mad prophet coming down from the hills to announce the end of days.

All but one of the zombies stumbled back into the woods. For some reason he had never figured out, they could be startled and turned away if you made enough noise.

All but a few. Some, almost as though they realized their advantage, stood their ground and stared.

"You better run, you son of a bitch."

But the zombie just stared. Vogler raised the pistol and closed one eye and put the front sight square on the zombie's head and pulled the trigger.

The gun blast echoed through the surrounding hills, and when the noise was gone, Vogler wondered at how quiet it was here at the end of the world. Like a graveyard on a Sunday morning.

* * *

He couldn't catch his breath as he remounted the stairs and went inside. In the darkened kitchen, he stood with one hand over his heart, trying to will himself to breathe.

And then he coughed.

He coughed hard, again and again, and each hack felt like something was inside him, trying to claw its way out. When the coughing finally subsided, he steadied himself against a granite counter top that had been the finest money could buy not so many years ago, before the necrosis filovirus and the military quarantine and all the useless madness that had come with those times.

He stared at the light fixture above the empty floor where their dining room table had once stood. The room seemed to swell and contract, swell and contract, like he was standing inside a giant lung, and he thought he was going to vomit. He wasn't turning into one of those things, he told himself. He hadn't been infected. This was just the flu.

Vogler had been a surgeon in the early days of the outbreak, and he'd heard patients describe what it felt like to undergo the change. They experienced nausea-inducing hallucinations, shortness of breath, a sense of drifting, inability to control their thoughts.

That wasn't what this was.

The worst things he would have to deal with would be fever, muscle weakness, chills, maybe a few headaches.

And then he remembered the pistol in his hand. Vogler looked down at it then and was surprised to see it was still there.

"Just make sure you save yourself a bullet." He was mildly amused at how easy it was to decide to use the gun on himself.

He wondered what it was going to taste like, the soot-stained metal.

Vogler stepped outside again to see if the horde had returned, but the yard was empty. He leaned against the porch railing and let his mind drift. Behind him stood an eight-thousand-square-foot monstrosity, a moldering Mediterranean-style villa that had been his dream home ten years ago when he built it for Margaret. It stood on top of a low, domed hill, commanding a view of other hills, other mansions. They were all wrecks now—all that remained of what had once been the Dominion, San Antonio's wealthiest neighborhood. Looking to the south, he saw the city skyline and the yellowish, hazy dust that rose from it. Those streets were crowded now with the ambulatory corpses of the victims of the necrosis filovirus.

He turned away.

There was an obligation waiting for him inside. Margaret, in the dying moment of clarity that had penetrated her fading, had asked him to bury her next to their son in the soft dirt beneath the old oak in the front lawn.

He had promised her he would.

"Promise me you will," she'd said, trying to sit up, trying to grab his arm, but unable to do either. "Tell me you will. Promise me."

At first he thought she repeated herself because of the infection waging war in her bloodstream. She wasn't thinking clearly. But then he saw the look on her face and he knew differently. He knew that her mind was as sharp as ever, at least for that moment.

Twenty-five years earlier, right after completing his residency, his head swollen with pride at his accomplishment, there had been a nurse, a sexy brunette with brown eyes and small breasts and graceful hips. A short, white-hot affair had followed. He ended it when Margaret found them out. And then, as she made him promise to bury her body next to their son's, he had seen an echo of the doubt and mistrust that had plagued their marriage during the decade after that affair. He felt its sudden return now like a knife in his gut.

He went to the bedroom, and with a great deal of difficulty, for the coughing had returned, he shouldered her shrouded corpse and a shovel and headed for the old oak tree in the front yard to do his widower's duty.

* * *

He dug for two hours, listening by turns to the slice and crunch of the shovel cutting into the earth and the moans of the zombie horde circling, just out of view.

He touched the pistol in his waistband and felt reassured by it. When he was done, he was going to lie down on the other side of his son's grave and eat the gun.

"It'll be like it used to be," he said to the simple cedar post marker at the head of his son's grave. The boy had been twenty years old when he died, but at that moment, Vogler thought of him as he had been many years earlier, a four-year-old child coming downstairs in the middle of the night to climb in bed between his parents.

Vogler wiped the sweat out of his eyes and went back to digging. Despite the coughing, despite the knowledge that there wouldn't be anybody to throw earth on top of him when he was done, he had a sense that the labor was a good thing, that he was making good on the most important promise he had ever made. It felt good to sweat. The stiffness in his lower back felt good. The pain was honest, and Margaret deserved that. After all the years and all the troubles, she deserved something honest from him.

* * *

Later, when the hole was finished and the body was inside and he had said all he could say in words to a woman who had shared his life with him and given so much of herself to him, he began to shovel the dirt in.

So absorbed was he with his work, so overheated by the unaccustomed exertion, that he failed to hear the big male zombie padding through the grass toward him.

He didn't so much as hear the zombie as feel the weight of its stare on his back. And when he did finally feel that weight, he spun around and let out a startled cry at the charging mass of tooth and nail bearing down upon him.

The zombie clawed at his face, knocking him down, tearing into him. Vogler put his hands up to keep the zombie's teeth away from his throat, and they fought, not as man and dead man, but as two wild things whose only weapons were the muscles and the fists and the teeth they were born with.

Vogler managed to get one hand into the zombie's mouth and grabbed onto its lower jaw. The zombie's teeth shredded the palm of his hand, but Vogler wouldn't let go. He twisted the jaw, and the dead man went down. But even then, even with the zombie on the ground, groaning, snarling, Vogler refused to let go. He pushed the zombie's head up and away, exposing the throat. He was infected already; there was no point in fear now. Vogler threw punch after punch into the soft flesh of the zombie's throat.

"You go to hell, you son of a bitch!" he roared, screaming the words with the rage of one who has seen the world around him die and has been unable to do a damned thing about it, even for all the wealth and power that had once been his to command.

The zombie convulsed under the blows, raking at Vogler's belly with his fingernails. But there was no stopping Vogler's attack. As a civilized man, he had a long way to fall to reach that savage state where only survival mattered, and when he did finally fall, when the protective veneer of reason and humanity peeled away and there was nothing left but the bright burning spark of primal rage inside him, he proved to be the stronger. He sank his teeth into the zombie's throat and tasted the corrupted flesh and then the polluted blood as the zombie gradually weakened.

The thing clawed his stomach once, twice, before it died its second death, and with that last swipe of its hand snagged the trigger guard of the Ruger and pulled it from Vogler's waistband. Vogler was bent over forward so that he couldn't feel the gun leave its seat. But he did hear it go off, and he did feel the bullet punch into his belly and tear through his organs like a boy with a stick ramming the pointed end into a fire-ant mound and stirring it until nothing but an angry mess remains. That was what his belly felt like. That was what the pain of being shot in the gut felt like.

Vogler coughed in disbelief, then pitched face-down in the soft, black dirt beneath the oak. He lay there, trying to catch his failing breath, his eyes growing darker by the second and his skin crawling with a sudden chill until it seemed he was the only being left alive on the barren, bald tip of the world, the blackness of space around him. The thought passed through his mind that in the time before the world died, he had been a surgeon, the head of a hospital... a wealthy man... a married man... a father. And now, he was a dying man, and none of it counted anymore because now he was none of those things. Now, he was merely a tree falling in the woods, unseen. Unheard.

Until he rose again, an empty husk of rotting meat.

The zombies closed in on him. He could hear them, he could hear their excited panting and their slobbering jowls slopping together, and he knew what was coming. Though he couldn't see, he could still feel, and he could sense rotted breath and wet teeth on his fingertips, the teeth pulling at the skin, almost gingerly but for their sharpness, taking a hesitant first taste of his flesh.

Starvation Army

From the window of his abominably small, second-story room, Jonathan Nettle could see the alley where he'd found the body earlier that morning. He'd accidentally stumbled onto the corpse while he was wandering the huge, unending slum of London's East End, looking for the homeless shelter on the Mile End Road where he was to take up his new post as assistant minister. He'd smelled the noisome stench moments before he came across the homeless man's body, and he'd spun on his heel and vomited all over the sidewalk when he saw the iridescent black flies swarming around the mouth and eyes. After that, he'd stumbled from the alley and grabbed the first policeman he saw. He babbled and pointed and grunted until, at last, he made himself understood enough for the policeman to follow him.

The policeman looked at the body, at the bruise-like splotches on the skin that weren't bruises, but lividity, at the emaciated, rail-skinny arms and legs, and merely nodded.

"Yer an American, ain't ye, sir?"

"Huh?" Nettle said, the back of his hand against his lips. "Uh, yes."

"What are ye doin' here in the East End?"

Nettle told him he was looking for the homeless shelter, and the policeman merely nodded. "The peg house yer lookin' for is over there," he said, and pointed over Nettle's shoulder.

Nettle could barely take his eyes off the body, but he did long enough to see the tumbledown, soot-stained building the policeman pointed out for him. He looked back at the policeman—at the bobby, he reminded himself—and said, "What... happened to him?"

"This bloke? Prob'ly starved to death'd be my guess, sir."

"Starved?"

"Aye," the bobby said.

Nettle had said nothing to that, only nodded as he tried to take in the wonder that a grown man could starve to death in the middle of the largest city on Earth, in the heart of the most powerful empire the world had ever known. He tried, but couldn't wrap his mind around it.

His stay was supposed to be brief, only long enough for him to get some experience with the great things William Booth and his "salvation army" were doing for the poor here in London, so he could take those practices back to his Methodist ministries in New York and Boston. But he could already tell that the "problem of the poor," which such great orators as the Reverend Merle Cary of New York had spoken of so eloquently to audiences up and down the New England seaboard all that preceding summer of 1875, was far worse than he had been led to believe.

Just then, as if on cue, several men began lugging bags of garbage out of the hospital across the street and dumping them on the sidewalk below Nettle's window. The bags split open and soon an almost liquid pile of corruption was festering in the open air. Nettle watched the pile grow into a shapeless mass of rotten vegetables, scraps of meat, orange peels, and bloody surgical rags and blankets. The street was a miasma of squabbling and obscene yelling and fighting, and yet no one said a word about the garbage. Indeed, after it had been sitting there for a few minutes, children converged on it, burying their arms in it up to their shoulders, digging for any kind of food they could find and devouring it on the spot.

One boy, a stunted little runt of perhaps six years old, came up with something black that might have once been a potato, and tried to steal away with it. Several older boys surrounded him, punched him until he fell, then kicked him until he gave up the nasty potato thing he clutched near his groin.

For Nettle, it was too much. His sister Anna had snuck a dozen oranges into his luggage as a treat for him. Fully aware that indiscriminate charity is cruel, he made up his mind to be cruel. He collected the oranges in a paper sack and went down to the street.

"How old are you, son?" he asked the boy.

"Twelve, sir."

Nettle blinked in shock. Twelve! And he had envisioned the boy a runt of six. *How this place must beat them down*, he thought.

He handed the boy the oranges, and the boy's eyes went wide, like he'd just been given all the jewels in Africa.

"Go on," Nettle said. "Enjoy."

The boy was gone faster than the sun from a November day, and Nettle, feeling a little better, went back up to his room to write a letter to his sister in New York.

* * *

The porter's name was Bill Lowell. He was a weathered, bent-back old man whose job it was to watch the door to the shelter and tell the poor wretches who came there when there was no more space available. Most nights, there was room for between twenty and fifty people, depending on the shelter's food stores and what work needed to be done—for the cost of a bed indoors and a hot meal was a day of hard, hard labor.

"We open the doors at six," Bill said to Nettle, who'd been told he'd work at each job in the shelter so he could better learn its overall operational strategy, "but the line'll start formin' 'fore noon. By four the blokes'll be lined up 'round the corner."

"Even when there's only room for a few of them?"

Bill shrugged. "We'll need to search 'em as they come inside," he said. "Sometimes, they try an' sneak tobacco inside in their brogues, and they ain't allowed that."

Nettle glanced through a window next to the door, and sure enough, a long line had already formed and was snaking its way down the sidewalk and around the corner. Word had gone out earlier that there was only room for twenty-five, and yet no one in the line seemed to want to leave his spot.

The faces he saw all looked hollow, the eyes vacuous. It wasn't until several days later that Nettle learned why everyone he saw shared the same corpselike expression. London law didn't allow the homeless to sleep outside at night. The idea was that if the homeless weren't allowed to sleep outside at night, they would find somewhere indoors to sleep. To those who only saw the problem from the stratospheric heights of wealth and power, it was a clear example of give a man a fish and he eats for a day, teach him to fish and he eats for a lifetime. The reality, though, was a homeless population that was constantly driven from one doorway to the next by the police, forced to stay awake by the toe of a boot or the bite of a baton, resulting in an expression of slack-jawed exhaustion that stared back at Nettle from every pair of eyes he met.

Bill himself had nearly shared that fate, he told Nettle. He had had a family once—a wife, three daughters, and a son—but had outlived them all. His wife and daughters he'd lost to scarlet fever, all within a month of each other, but the son survived and had helped Bill in his work as a carpenter in days past.

One day, Bill had been carrying a load of nails that was too much for him. "Something in me back just broke," Bill said. His load of nails had spilled, and he'd ended up flat on his back, unable to get up. He was taken to a hospital, but they refused to admit him, telling him, essentially, to "walk it off."

This he had tried to do, but two hours later was on his back again. He was taken to a different hospital, and this time spent three weeks in bed. He emerged a broken man, unable to do the hard labor that was, unfortunately, the only kind of work that he and most of the men like him were qualified to do, only to learn his son had fallen from a rooftop and died the week before his release. The boy was buried in a pauper's grave, unmarked, along with a dozen others.

He lived on the streets after that—carrying the banner, as the expression went—chased from one doorway to the next by the police, until, as luck would have it, he ended up in the Mile End Road shelter on the day they had an opening for a porter who could also do a little light carpentry. His nine-pounds-a-year salary made him a veritable Croesus among the East End's poor.

Nettle thought idly that such a man as Bill, who had narrowly escaped a cruel death by exposure and malnutrition, would be more charitable toward his fellow men, but such was not the case.

Much to Nettle's unease, Bill seemed to heartily enjoy his position of relative power over the poor and stared down his soot-blackened nose at all who entered, demanding from each their name, age, condition of destitution, and what kind of work they were good for, before searching them all with a rough, hard hand.

In one of his searches he found a ragged pouch of tobacco inside a man's sock. Bill beat the man with a stick, evidently left by the door for just such a purpose, and probably would have gone on beating him indefinitely, Nettle figured, had he not intervened.

When Nettle berated him for his violence, Bill only scoffed. "Why 'e's nothin' but a worthless beggar, 'e is," he said, and, with all the sour disposition of a man who kicks the cat because he's afraid to kick his wife, went to the door, where a wrecked shell of a man stood on the threshold waiting for admittance, and said, "Be gone, you. Full up!"

"Please, sir," the human wreck said. "Please, I ain't 'ad food in me belly for five days."

"Full up!" Bill said.

Nettle's heart broke to see the pain in the man's eyes, and before Bill could close the door, he was at Bill's shoulder and said, "We can take this man in, I think."

"But, sir," Bill said, "there's only room for twenty-five tonight. We're full up."

"And that man," Nettle said, pointing at the bleeding bag of bones Bill had beaten for the insolence of smoking cheap tobacco, "was to be number twenty-five. Now, I believe, this man is twenty-five."

Bill said nothing, but his eyes did.

"Thank 'e, sir," said the wreck, and walked inside.

*　*　*

Bill's other job at the shelter, after the doors were locked and the homeless shuffled inside, was to monitor the bathing room.

Making the homeless take a bath seemed like a good idea to Nettle—that is, until he saw the process in motion. The overnighters were all lined up, and one by one let down into a dark room with a single tub of warm water and a single threadbare towel hanging from a hook on the wall. Each man used the same water and towel as the man before him, and by the time the man Nettle had forced Bill to let in got his turn, the water in that tub was a frightful stew.

But the human wreck didn't notice. He stripped off his rags and his appearance made Nettle gasp. His body had no meat on it. He was all ribs and distended belly, his back a mass of dried and fresh new blood where he'd been attacked by vermin.

He cleaned off several layers of dirt and blood and changed into a shirt and pants from the shelter's wardrobe. Then he followed the others to the dining hall for a meal of stale bread and skilly—a sort of oatmeal mixed with tepid water so unclean Nettle doubted a dog would drink it—and he would have received that meal had he not had the misfortune to pass Bill on his way inside.

"You!" Bill said, his eyes turning hard as flints with surprised anger, his tone like that of a man who's just found the boy who made his daughter pregnant and then made a run for it.

The man stopped in his tracks.

"Look who we 'ave 'ere," Bill said loudly, looking around at the crowd.

Slowly, every head in the place turned to look.

The man kept his eyes on the floor.

"I'll be damned if it ain't Barlow the Butcher. Look 'ere, we got

Barlow the Butcher!"

This meant nothing to Nettle, but it clearly did to the peg-house crowd, for in short order, they became a riotous mob. They fell on Barlow and began to beat on him with a savagery that would have made a tribe of cannibals blush.

Nettle waded in and pulled Barlow from the flurry of fists. Barlow, though, didn't wait around to thank him. As soon as he was clear of the mob, he made for the door and ran into the night.

Nettle was left with a decision. He was ringed by angry faces, some bleeding where they'd been hit by others trying to land blows on Barlow, and he had a feeling he knew what would happen if he stayed there, now that they had the taste of blood. He wisely went for the door himself, stepping out into the street in time to see Barlow, or rather, a crowd of homeless at the end of the street, separating for Barlow, as he rounded the corner onto Stepney Green.

Nettle ran after him, and managed to follow him for a good ways before he lost him in the maze of the East End's soot-stained back alleys. He became lost in short order, every cross street and alley meeting him with endless vistas of tumbledown misery and bricks.

Trying to find something familiar, he eventually stumbled onto the Brown Hay Road, where he stopped in front of an enormous abandoned warehouse. It was a blackened, eyeless hulk, not a single window down its entire length, and it made him feel strangely uneasy. There were, Nettle had seen already, very few empty buildings in London's East End. Real estate, *any* real estate, was at a premium, as landlords could pack as many as eight families into a home no bigger than the small, one-story apartment he had shared in New York with his mother and his sister, Anna. One was more likely, he'd been told, to see a giraffe swimming down the Thames than to find an unoccupied building in the East End.

But the moldy warehouse in front of him was most certainly abandoned, and something about it made the skin crawl down his spine. And then someone was there, staggering toward him from the other side of the street. A patchwork of shadows played across the man's face, but the little Nettle could see was ghastly. The man's joints had swollen, and his body had withered away to almost nothing. His skin was black in places, almost mummified, like it had begun to rot, and it wasn't until he got halfway across the street that Nettle could tell part of the man's leg had been torn up as if by some sort of animal.

The man raised his hands and flexed his fingers in a weak grab at Nettle, moaning as he stumbled closer. At first, Nettle thought it was just a moan, meaning nothing beyond the pain it obviously conveyed, then he recognized the word inside the pain.

"Fooooood," the man moaned.

Nettle turned on his heel, thinking robbery, and started to walk the other way.

"Fooooood," the man groaned again.

"See here," Nettle said, "I don't have anything for you."

He was very close to running and had already stepped up his pace, when a hansom cab lurched around the corner at a full sprint and mowed the man down. The driver of the hansom never slowed and, a moment later, he was gone.

Nettle was frozen with shock. What was left of the man after he'd been trampled by the horses and his body sliced open and dragged by the hansom's wheels was in two gory pieces connected by a clotted smear of liquefied meat.

The man's legs were still in the street, but his torso was near the curb. Nettle staggered that way, hands over his mouth, and knelt down next to the mess that the hansom had made of the man.

He started to pray... and the man opened his eyes.

Nettle fell backward onto the wet cobblestones. The man's eyes were horrible, like staring into the void.

"Fooooood," he groaned, and tried to claw his way toward Nettle, his fingers digging so hard into the edges of the cobblestones that the fingernails shattered and tore.

Nettle got up and ran and ran and ran. He ran till he broke down, and then he cried. He was still crying when, by chance, he stumbled back onto the Mile End Road.

* * *

The next morning, still badly shaken by his encounter, Nettle packed his bags and knelt by his bed to pray. He had fully expected to leave that afternoon, but his prayers had taken him in another direction, and when he rose to his feet he had decided to stay, half-convinced that what he seen the night before couldn't have happened. He was upset, nothing more.

Nettle's faith had never led him astray, and the next few days, and a chance encounter with the man the mob had chased out of the peg house on his horrible first night there, reinforced the wisdom of the decision he had made during prayer.

Nettle took to wandering up and down the Mile End Road, watching the people as they struggled for existence, and he noticed a curious little thing. The homeless always seemed to keep one eye on the spittle-flecked sidewalks, and when they'd see a morsel, they'd snatch it up and eat it on the fly. Most, it seemed, could pluck an orange peel or an apple core from the cobblestones without ever losing a step.

Late one afternoon, Nettle had been watching people pass, and Barlow had been coming the other way on the same sidewalk. Barlow had stooped to pick up something nasty, and when he rose, his nose collided with Nettle's chest, for Nettle was a good six inches the taller.

"Oh, hello," Nettle said, and had a devil of a time over the next few moments trying to assure the man that he had no intention of braining him to death.

They talked in the eaves of a coffee shop, and gradually the look of a rabbit trying to find an opening through a pack of hounds faded from Barlow's eyes. Then a strange thing happened. Nettle, whose over-stimulated humanitarian urges were in danger of melting down if he didn't find some specific point, some single human face to put on all this misery he had been witnessing, bought a pint of beer for Barlow, who was desperately in need of some kind person to buy him a pint of beer. It was the first pint of beer Nettle had ever bought, and it was the first full pint of beer Barlow had had in a long time. Nettle bought a second round, and by that afternoon, as the windows of the coffee shop sizzled with rain, he had come to a conclusion. He was not going to be the salvation for *all* the world's poor—indeed, there was no way he could be, and it was vain to think so—but he could be the door to *this* man's salvation. Nettle had a project now, something he could manage.

So they sat there in the coffee shop, the rich, well-meaning American, and the homeless, nearly starved Londoner, and the American talked about God and goodness and reward, and the Londoner drank his beer and nodded.

* * *

Over the next week, they met in the afternoons at the same coffee shop, and gradually Nettle realized that it wasn't the man's grotesque, almost troglodyte appearance that had sparked his philanthropy, but rather his cynicism. The man cared little for his own life and not at all for anyone else's, and Nettle found it hard to believe that a creature who so hated life could actually go on living.

"Beer," Barlow said. "Beer's what makes a man feel like a man. You can take all the rest of it away, but you take away a man's beer, and there ain't no reason left for 'im to go on bein'."

Nettle squinted at his own almost untouched beer and thought about that as a philosophy of life, and it seemed tragic, empty.

"What about a family?" he asked. "A home? A wife and kids?"

Barlow snorted with laughter. "I saw enough of that growin' up," he said. "I saw what me ma did for me old man. That was enough. Made 'im mis'rable, she did, always a-bangin' me brothers and sisters about, makin' 'is 'ome a noisy racket. 'E no sooner walk through the door and she'd be a-yellin' at 'im, barkin' at 'im like a dog. Take me word for it, mate, and don't waste yer time on a wife 'n kids. Do nothin' but take yer 'ard-earned money and keep you from drinkin' a beer when it suits you."

Nettle was stunned, bewildered. Such a wasted life! His mind raced for a response, for something worthwhile to say, and at last, he found it. "William," he said, "I want you to pray with me. Will you do that?"

"Pray?"

"Yes, William. There's a power in prayer that has sustained me through my hard times. I think it can do the same for you."

Barlow wrinkled his brow, then a huge smile crossed his face. "Let's pray for another beer, mate. You want me to pray? I'll pray for that."

* * *

But Barlow wasn't Nettle's only project. He was still expected to learn the ropes at the shelter, spending time in each of the numerous jobs necessary to keep the operation going day to day, and a few nights later, he was back with Bill, the porter, passing out blankets in the sleeping quarters. The overnighters would come in, take a blanket from Nettle, and head to a long, narrow room with two large oaken beams traversing its length. Rough pieces of canvas were stretched between the beams, and the men slept on the canvas. When he first heard about the arrangement, and before he had seen it, Nettle thought of seamen in hammocks, rocking to sleep with the rhythms of the open sea, but the reality was nothing like that, and the actual arrangement lacked any of the adventurous dignity a landsman could envision for the life of a sailor at sea. The men were packed in shoulder to shoulder, and the room was dreadfully noisy with snores and coughs and breaking wind, and in the right light, the whole room shimmered with a living cloud of fleas.

He was watching this sad display with a heavy heart when Bill appeared at his shoulder.

"What are you about, sir, talkin' with Barlow the Butcher?"

"Excuse me?" he said, alarmed by the man's tone, even though he was a good six inches taller, and maybe forty pounds heavier.

"You become 'is reg'lar drinkin' mate's what I 'ear."

"I have not," Nettle protested. He stammered, trying to rise to his own defense, and finally managed to tell Bill his plan, how his goal was the man's salvation.

Bill just laughed.

"What's wrong with going after a lost sheep?" Nettle said.

"'E ain't no sheep," Bill said. "A devil, aye, but 'e ain't no sheep."

"What do you mean?"

"There's an em'ty warehouse down on the Brown Hay Road. D'you know it? A big, ugly brute of a buildin'?"

"I've seen it," Nettle said, cringing inwardly at the memory of the beggar and the hansom cab.

"Your mate used to be the union man there. 'Bout two years ago."

Nettle eyed him warily.

"Did 'e tell you 'bout the people 'e killed there?"

"Killed? What are you talking about?"

Bill sneered at Nettle. "Aye, I thought not."

"Tell me what you mean, sir. You cannot accuse a man of such a crime and not state your proof."

Bill only shook his head. "Nothin' was ever proved 'gainst 'im. Didn't 'ave no blood on 'is 'ands. None that the courts could see, anyway. But 'e killed 'em all right. Just as pretty as you please."

Nettle searched the man's face for some indication that this was a joke. It had to be. He searched the creases in the old man's face, the cracked red map of lines that colored the whites of his eyes, but found nothing to indicate that this was a joke.

"When you say killed, do you mean...?"

"I mean 'e murdered 'em. Sure as the Pope eats fish on Fridays. Murdered more'n an 'undred people. Men, wimmen, and children, just as pretty as you please."

Nettle felt his legs go to gelatin. He fell against the wall and said, "A hundred people?"

"Aye."

"But, how?"

"Why, 'e starved 'em. Locked 'em in that warehouse for full on twelve days. When they finally opened 'er up, every one of 'em, men, wimmen, and children, was dead as dead can be." Then he leaned close and said, "I 'eard tell some of them bodies was eaten on."

"That's impossible," Nettle countered. "How could he do such a thing?"

"I already tol' you, sir. 'E was the union man, and those people went on strike. The comp'ny tol' 'im to fix the problem, and 'e did."

"A man can't starve to death in twelve days," Nettle said.

"You've seen these men," Bill said. "Not a one's more than a week away from death's door."

"But somebody would have done something to stop him," Nettle said. "You can't just kill a hundred people and expect to get away with it. Somebody would have said something."

But Nettle didn't need see the blank expression on Bill's face to know that wasn't true. Not here in the East End.

Feeling angry and confused and betrayed, Nettle ran from the peg house for the coffee house where he and Barlow had been meeting. He knew no other place to look for the man, but as it turned out, it wasn't necessary to look anywhere else. He found Barlow in the back alley behind the shop, rifling through a paper bag of trash he'd found on the curb, pulling out little bits of orange peels and tearing what remained of the pulp from the pith with his blackened front teeth.

"Mr. Barlow," Nettle called out from across the street.

Barlow looked up and smiled. But then his smile fell. Perhaps he saw the savage expression in Nettle's eyes, or heard something sinister in his tone, but whatever it was, his expression instantly changed, and he ran into the night.

Nettle didn't bother to chase him. It was enough, for the moment, to see him run. That was all the proof he needed that Mr. Barlow, also known as Barlow the Butcher, was a devil of the highest magnitude.

* * *

Some men snap by degrees. Like green wood, they bend a long ways before the tension takes its inevitable course. But other men break like porcelain. They cleave with sudden fury, shattering into thousands of irredeemable pieces, their edges left razor sharp.

Nettle was of the later sort, and when his mind snapped, it came with the illusion of sudden clarity. It seemed he was thinking clearly now for the first time, as if somebody had turned on a light switch in his mind, and the path before him seemed clearer now than it had ever been before. He suddenly saw in Barlow, not an individual's face to put on all of humanity's troubles, but a cause of its misery, and there was only one thing to do with such causes. The fact that he had befriended such a beast, that he had bought such evil a drink, for God's sake, didn't terrify him so much as instill in him a sense of personal responsibility. His proximity had given him ownership over the ending to Barlow's sordid little history, and he set out to bring that history to a close.

He carried the banner that night, walking the streets of the East End without stopping for rest or sleep—indeed, without even feeling the need for rest or sleep—ferreting out the hiding places of the homeless, but with his mind on only one man.

He caught up with Barlow in a doorway, the man sitting on the top step, his knees bunched up to his chest and his head bent down between them, trying to sleep.

Nettle kicked his foot. "Wake up," he said. "I want a word with you."

Barlow thought him a policeman at first, and had already half pulled himself to his feet when the haze of sleep left him entirely, and he realized who was standing in front of him.

"You owe me an answer, Mr. Barlow."

But Barlow didn't stand still to give it. He turned and ran with all the energy a scared, weather-beaten, and prematurely old man could muster.

Nettle followed him at a jog, yelling "I want an answer!" over and over at Barlow's back, and as they slipped deeper and deeper into the warren of slimy streets that were the bowels of the East End, a cold, light rain began to fall.

Nettle closed on him in a back alley off the Brown Hay Road, the streets deserted now and splashy beneath their feet. Barlow had curled up under a flight of stairs, trying to hide his face with his arms.

"You have some explaining to do," Nettle said. The rain rolled off his face unnoticed.

Barlow stared at him with abject fear.

"What did you do? Answer me!"

"For the love of all that's 'oly, sir, please don't yell. You'll—"

"I'll what? Wake the dead? Go on, you villain, say it! Say it! Are you afraid they'll hear us?"

Barlow looked seasick. His eyes pleaded for silence but got none.

"Spill it!" Nettle roared. "Tell me what you did."

Nettle waited, and for a moment, there was no sound but the pattering of a gentle rain on cobblestones, but then it came, as both Nettle and Barlow knew that it most assuredly would, the sound of slow, plodding feet dragging on the cobblestones behind them.

Nettle looked over his shoulder and saw a small crowd of

shamblers in the mist. There were men, women, even children. Their faces were dark with disease and their cheeks empty from extreme hunger. Their eyes were carrion eyes, and a smell that could only be death's smell preceded them, filling the street with its sad, inexorable power.

A man in front raised his arms, and it looked like one of his hands had been partially eaten. He groaned "Fooooood" and Barlow jumped to his feet and tried to run.

"Where are you going?" Nettle yelled after him. "Don't you know you can't run from this?"

Barlow didn't make it very far, only to the middle of the Brown Hay Road. There, he stopped, wheeling around in panic, surrounded by the dead on every side. They stepped out of every doorway, out of every alley, from behind every staircase, taking shape in the shadows. He fell to his knees in front of Nettle and started to cry.

"Please," he begged.

"Tell what you've done," Nettle said.

Barlow looked at the groaning, starving dead, and he shook his head no. NO, NO, NO, NO, NO!

"Say it," Nettle said. "While there's still time."

But there wasn't any time. Barlow could no more belly up to the magnitude of what he'd done than he could force himself to stop breathing, and as the rotting dead shouldered their way past Nettle and closed on Barlow, all he could do was close his eyes.

The dead tore at Barlow with their hands and their teeth, ripping his flesh like fabric. Nettle stumbled away, into the dark, and as he walked, he heard Barlow's screams carry on and on and on. They seemed to go on far longer than it was possible for any one man to suffer, but go on they did, and they echoed in Nettle's mind even after the shrillness disappeared from his ears.

After that, Nettle wandered, his mind unhinged, until he began to see people. He tried to tell them what he had seen, but they flinched away from him, alarmed at the intensity in his eyes and the urgency in his voice and the complete lack of sense in his speech.

As day broke, a russet stain behind plum-colored smoke clouds, Nettle collapsed less than fifty feet from the doors of Stepney Green Hospital. He lay there, lips moving soundlessly, eyes still as glass beads, until an orderly from the hospital knelt beside him and said, "Hey, mate, are you hurt? What is it? Are you 'ungry?"

If the horror wasn't on Nettle's face, it was nonetheless there, in his mind. *Eat*, he thought, and sensed his body in complete revolt at the idea. *God no, I'll never eat again.*

State of the Union

I know when I'm being lied to. It's not hard to figure out, even when you're a stranger in a country halfway around the world and you don't speak the language. Bullshit smells the same, no matter how it sounds. And that's what our Chinese hosts were trying to shovel down our throats.

Bullshit.

Pure, unadulterated bullshit.

Our group went down for dinner at eight p.m. We stepped off the elevator but barely made it into the hotel lobby before a couple of blue-shirted cops started yelling at us to go back upstairs.

"What's this all about?" asked Brad Owens. He was our leader, a Young Democrat from Columbia University. Tall, slender, and dignified, Brad stood an easy six inches taller than the cops, but it didn't seem to impress them at all.

"You go back upstairs," one of the cops said. "Go now."

"But I want to know what's going on," Brad insisted. He pointed to the reception hall. "They're supposed to be throwing us a party."

"No party for you. Party over. You go now. Go upstairs."

While Brad was busy arguing with the Chinese cops, I was looking through the glass doors of our hotel. Outside, Beijing was in the middle of a riot. I heard screams overlapping screams. I saw people running for their lives, others throwing rocks. Right outside the front doors, a small crowd knocked down an injured man and swarmed over him, like they were trying to pull him apart.

"But why do we have to go upstairs?" Brad asked.

The concierge came over. He looked utterly frazzled, and more than a little distracted, but he kept his tone level and his smile bright when he talked to us.

"Please," he said with a slight bow. His accent was good, even if the syntax was off. "Please, you and your friends to go upstairs please. We have the flu outside."

"The flu?" Brad said.

I looked out across the Beijing skyline and saw buildings on fire in the distance.

"People don't riot because of the flu," said Jim Bowman, our Young Republican representative.

The concierge's smile wavered for a moment. "You to go upstairs to your rooms now," he said and then muttered something to the cops in Chinese.

The next moment we were being hustled upstairs and forced into our rooms.

I tried the door, but it was locked from the outside.

I beat on it with my fists and got no reply.

I looked out the peephole and saw the cops pacing the hallway. They looked scared and anxious, and I didn't like it. One of them kept swallowing, his Adam's apple pumping up and down in his throat, looking to his partner for some clue what they were supposed to do.

I gave up on the door and sat down on the foot of the bed and tried to get online. Nothing worked. Email, Livejournal, Twitter, Facebook, even Google was down. I lowered my iPad and tried my iPhone. Same thing. I had been sending emails all day. I had even sent my latest article to my editor at *The Crimson* right before I took my shower and got dressed for dinner. But now, nothing. Just a "network connection error" message.

That's when it really hit me. Not only was I a stranger in a strange land, but the Chinese government had somehow managed to shut down the Internet. My one umbilical cord to the real world had just been cut.

It hadn't seemed real, standing in the lobby and watching Beijing tear itself apart, but once I found out the Internet was down... well, that was the clincher.

We were being lied to.

And like the old Bob Dylan song goes, "You don't need a weatherman to know which way the wind blows."

* * *

Okay, so what do you need to know?

Introductions first, I guess.

My name is Mark Wellerman—though I suppose you already know that, my name being what it is. These days, I run a small farm in Georgia. It's not much, but I grow all my own food, raise my own livestock, make my own bullets. I can take care of myself. That's a far cry from the plans I had growing up, but don't think for a minute that I'm a failure. Like I said, this farm makes all the food a man could ever need, and there is no fortune greater than that.

Believe me. I know that better than anyone.

I'm twenty-four now, but I was twenty-two when this story I'm telling you happened. I was a senior at Harvard, majoring in Journalism. I had the world at my feet, every door ahead standing wide open. And that's how I landed in Beijing that summer. I was one of two-dozen college students from across the United States selected to take part in an exchange program to China called "Our Best, Your Best."

Our group was called the "Young Americans." We were supposed to represent the best and brightest of America's up-and-coming generation. We were a cross-section of this once great country, our own mini melting pot. We had Brad Owens, our Young Democrat from Columbia; Jim Bowman, a Young Republican from the University of Texas at Austin; and Sandra Palmer, a junior Tea Party Patriot from the University of Nebraska—all three of them intent on becoming president one day. But we had a lot more than politics going for us. We had a cop from a junior college in Texas, a West Point cadet, a teacher's assistant working on her master's degree at Florida State, a UAW assembly lineman from Michigan doing an online graduate degree in Pension Fund Management, computer programmers, rich kids, poor kids... We had it all. Hell, we even had a guy who was attending UC Berkley illegally but got to go with us anyway because of the DREAM Act. Between the twenty-four us, we were America.

For better or for worse.

Most of the trip up to that last night in the hotel was mindless arguing, everybody talking and nobody listening. I had plenty to write about, but it still wore me down. I remember feeling irritable every time Brad or Jim or Sandra opened their mouths. The bickering just seemed pointless.

But all that changed that night. I hadn't taken off my clothes. I was standing at my window, looking across downtown Beijing twenty stories below, every now and then catching the wail of a siren or the muffled cry of a nearby scream, when the Chinese cops burst through the door. One of them went for me, the other for my luggage. As I watched, the cop tossed my iPhone, my iPad, even my headphones into the trash. Then he crammed some clothes into my backpack and threw it at me.

"But, my phone...," I said.

He said something in Chinese and pointed to his partner, who pushed me outside.

Everyone else was already standing there, trying to get somebody to tell them what was going on. Jim Bowman was yelling, and it wasn't hard to see why. The cops had pulled him and Sandra out of bed without even giving Sandra a chance to put on her pants. She was standing behind him, tugging her jeans over her hips and looking embarrassed as hell.

Those of us who could speak a little Chinese tried to get answers out of the cops, but they weren't talking. They hustled us downstairs and out the back door.

As soon as the doors to the parking lot opened, we could hear the sound of screams and gunshots and sirens. I saw what looked like military helicopters sprinting overhead. I watched them race over the heart of the city, and when I looked down to street level, I saw a group of burned and bleeding people limping toward us. One of them was so badly burned I couldn't tell if it was a man or a woman. The poor devil was black as charcoal, still trailing wisps of smoke. The others behind were less burned, but each was terribly wounded, clothes dark with coagulated blood.

One of the girls in our group screamed, and the cops hurried her onto the bus. Then, while the rest of us watched in horror, one of the cops went to the crowd and, with deliberate headshots, shot the wounded one by one. I couldn't believe it. The cop never even gave them a chance to run. He just shot them. And weirder still, not a single one of that crowd flinched, even with a rifle pointed at their faces. It was like they didn't know what was happening.

The next moment, we were on the bus. Our driver, a thin, terrified-looking man in shabby clothes, turned the bus toward the street with a lurch and built up speed. The shooting we'd just witnessed had left us stunned and silent. Cowed, I guess you'd say. We sat in our seats, staring out the windows at the destruction and the insane crowds banging on the sides of the bus, and I don't think any of us even thought to ask where we were being taken.

Just like I don't think any of us thought to use the word *zombie*.

At least at that point.

* * *

From our hotel they drove us to the Beijing West Railway Station. Let me say this, first and foremost, on the behalf of the Chinese.

They took care of us.

They never once forgot that we were their guests. They could have left us in that hotel to die along with everyone else. I'm pretty sure, had we been in the U.S., that's what would have happened. But the Chinese had a sense of obligation so strong, so ingrained, that even in the face of a zombie apocalypse, they took real pains to get us out of harm's way. They had no idea the hell they were condemning us to, and I cannot fault them for what came afterward.

They tried to be good hosts.

They really did.

* * *

The railway station was a mad, screaming hive of humanity. Hundreds of thousands of people were surging toward the platforms, trying to board trains. In that mad scramble to the trains, we lost Virginia Wilder, our teacher from Florida; and Wade Mallum, our UAW representative. I don't know how it happened, but I saw Jim and Sandra running from where Virginia and Wade went down.

"Those crazy yellow bastards are eating each other," Sandra said.

"What?" I said. I had only known Sandra for a few weeks, but I was already aware of her ability to say things that defied the logic used by sane people.

"They got Virginia and Wade," Jim said. "We couldn't save them."

"What do you mean?"

"They were dead weight slowing us down." He was winded, but he managed to turn to Sandra and smile. "We're okay."

I just stared at him, dumbfounded. Amid the deafening roar of hundreds of thousands of a panicking people, after watching two of our group get trampled and possibly eaten, he had the audacity to call them "dead weight."

But I didn't get the chance to call him on his words, for at that moment, our escorts managed to zipper open a path through the crowd and get us into a fairly new, fairly clean commuter car. No frills, no special compartments. Just three rows of seats on either side of a center aisle, like a small jet airliner.

We had the car to ourselves.

I dropped into a window seat and looked across the crowded platform. I found it hard to believe we'd ended up the only ones in our car. As we pulled away from the platform, I saw people screaming for a chance to get on. Mothers held up their babies, begging us to take them. Hundreds jumped onto the outside of the train and held on as long as they could. It was a sorry, sad sight, and as Jim and Sandra and Brad began to scream at each other about whose fault all this was, I slipped farther down into my seat and pressed my hands over my ears and tried to block out the screams of all those poor people falling away behind us.

* * *

We didn't make it very far.

As soon as we cleared the gates, people surged against the sides of the train. I heard their bodies thudding against metal and felt the train lurch as they collapsed onto tracks and were run over.

I looked to one side and saw our entire group with their faces pressed against the windows, none of them speaking, but all of them wearing stunned, horrified expressions upon their faces.

"My God," I heard someone say. "Look at all of them. There's so many."

And there were, too.

Hundreds of thousands of them.

I looked out the window, and all I could see were faces closing in around us. They pressed against the train, swarmed over top of it.

Suddenly the train lurched and came to a violent, shuddering halt. All of us were thrown from our seats. For a moment, I felt like I was getting pushed forward, like I was on the crest of a wave. And then, just as suddenly, I hit the deck and banged my head against the bottom of a seat.

I blacked out for a second.

When I came to, I was groggy, disoriented. I stood up and looked around. My hair felt wet. I touched it and came away with blood on my fingers. Sandra Palmer had her hand over her forehead, a runner of blood oozing between her fingers. Her mouth was twisted, like she was about to scream, or cry, but couldn't decide which. Brad Owens had landed in a heap against the forward door. Jim Bowman was right next to him. His arm looked broken.

"They've knocked us off the rails," somebody said.

"Impossible," someone else said.

"Take a look if you don't believe me."

Several of us went to the window, and I could tell at a glance he was right. From where I stood, I could see the half-dozen cars ahead of us, the lead car was jackknifed across the tracks.

"How is that possible?" the girl next to me asked.

I shook my head. But I knew. I think we all knew. We'd run over so many bodies the wheels had just skipped the tracks.

And now an army hundreds of thousands strong was surging against our train car, banging on the side panels. The combined roar of their moans and screams and their fists pounding on the sides of the train was deafening. The girl next to me, a Culinary Arts major from SMU, was in tears.

For a moment I wanted to take her in my arms and hold her. But before I got the chance, Jake Arguello, our Texas cop, started hollering from the rear of the car.

"They're breaking in the door back!"

Billy Gantz, our West Point cadet, rushed that way. "I'll help you."

I watched the two of them punch and kick a Chinese woman

who had managed to squeeze through the busted door. She fell back into the writhing mass of hands and faces, and they slammed what was left of the door against the surging crowd.

Jake put his back against the door to brace it.

"I've got it!" he yelled. "Get something to help me hold it."

A metal handrail had snapped and fallen to the ground. Billy scooped it up and jammed it into well of the doorway on the opposite side. Once it was in place it looked like a curtain rod between the two doors. It was an elegantly simple solution. The harder the crowd pressed from one side, the more pressure it put against the doors on the opposite side, where the crowd was also pushing inward.

Billy rushed into the door well and pulled Jake back into the car. We gathered around to look at him, then recoiled. His back had been shredded by fingernails. He was bleeding badly and screaming in pain.

"Those fuckin' yellow bastards," Sandra said. "We gotta stop 'em."

"No!" Brad said. "They're cold. They're hungry. They're tired and poor. We should let them in."

"What?" said Jim. "Are you fucking insane?"

Brad raised his chin. "No, I'm not. We will be judged on how we handle ourselves here. Those people are scared. I think we have a moral obligation to share our resources."

"I'm not sharing anything with them."

Brad was standing at the opposite end of the car, still nursing his bruised shoulder. He scanned the rest of us to see who had spoken, and saw Tynice Jackson staring back at him. She'd been Brad's biggest cheerleader throughout the first part of our trip, defending him every time Jim and Sandra railed against his leadership, but now she stood defiant, arms akimbo.

Brad steepled his fingers together in front of his belt. "Tynice," he said patiently, "we're going through a rough patch right now. We need to approach this logically."

"Logically?" said Jim. "Dude, they tried to kill our cop. How much more logical do you need to be than that?"

"This isn't a job for law enforcement," Brad said.

"Well, it's pretty much become a job for law enforcement," Tynice shot back, "because you won't do anything about it. Get over here and help. As long as you're standing way over there out of harm's way, you got no business to talk."

I was frantically writing it all down, thankful I had stayed awake during my shorthand class, when Jake started to convulse.

"Something's happening!" said Billy. "He's foaming at the mouth."

He was. I watched Jake shaking on the floor. He was bleeding from the corners of his eyes and from his nose. He was trembling like we'd just pulled him from a frozen pond.

"What's happening to him?" Sandra said. "Those yellow bastards did something to him, didn't they?"

Nobody answered her.

Wayne Scott, a second-year med student at Johns Hopkins, rushed over to Jake's side and looked into his eyes. The foam at Jake's mouth was turning pink from blood.

"His pupils are dilating," Wayne said. "He's going into cardiac arrest."

"Help him," somebody said.

"I can't. I'd need a...."

Wayne trailed off mid-sentence. Jake's convulsions suddenly stopped, and now he looked like a tire rapidly going flat. A faint, rattling gasp rose from Jake's throat, and then he went still, his bloodshot eyes staring toward the ceiling, the only movement a runner of blood leaking down his cheek from one nostril.

"Is he...?" Jim said.

Wayne looked up at him and nodded. "It happened so fast," he muttered. "I couldn't do anything."

None of us spoke for a long moment. We all stood there, looking at our dead friend. I saw the same dawning terror on all their faces. What were we going to do? Who was going to bail us out?

I honestly had no idea, and I'm pretty sure none of the others did either.

Outside, the roar of the crowd continued. Their moaning was awful. I tried not to listen to it, to block it out, but it was impossible. The sound made my skin crawl, and all I wanted to do was go to the corner and throw up.

"Something's happening," Wayne said.

I stood on my tiptoes to get a look at what he was doing. He was still kneeling at Jake's side, but his expression had changed to disgust, and he was rocking back on his haunches away from Jake.

Jake's dead gaze had been turned toward the ceiling, looking at nothing, but now it was locked on Wayne.

"I thought you said he was dead," Jim said.

Before Wayne could answer, Jake sat up. He looked at the circle of horrified faces staring down at him, and lunged for Wayne. Wayne tried to push him away, but Jake was already on top of him, clawing at his face and biting at Wayne's fingers as Wayne tried to turn Jake's chin away.

None of us moved. I think we were all too shocked. One of Wayne's fingers strayed too close to Jake's mouth, and Jake bit it off. Blood gushed from the wound. Wayne opened his mouth to scream, but at that instant, Jake locked his teeth onto Wayne's throat and silenced him.

Only then did the rest of us react.

Billy, our West Point cadet, rushed in and pulled Jake off of Wayne. He threw Jake to one side, and was about to check on Wayne, when Jake got back to his feet. He reached for Billy and started moaning.

"Get the fuck back, man," Billy said.

Jake kept coming.

"I'm serious, dude, take a step back."

Jake swiped at him with bloody fingernails. Billy sidestepped easily and swept Jake's legs out from under him, dropping him to the ground.

Before Jake could get up again, Billy grabbed another piece of handrail that had fallen from the ceiling. Gripping it like a police baton, he took up a position between Jake and the rest of us.

"Come on, man, don't come any closer."

Jake's eyes were dead and vacant. If he heard a word Billy said, there was no recognition of it in his expression.

His hands came up again, clutching at Billy.

"Shit," Billy said, and swung the piece of handrail at Jake, hitting him across the flat of his jaw.

Metal hit bone with a sickening crunch, and Jake collapsed onto the back of a chair. Anybody else would have stayed that way, or maybe even slid to the floor, unconscious. But Jake showed no sign of pain. He straightened up immediately, his face a smashed and bleeding mess, and staggered toward Billy a second time.

Billy took a step back, shaking his head in disbelief.

"Do something," Brad said. His cool, calm veneer was gone. The look on his face was positively frantic.

I saw movement from the floor, behind Brad. It was Wayne. He had been convulsing, the same as Jake had done, but now he was rising to his feet. When he turned to face the rest of us, I saw a large flap of skin hanging from his throat like a bloody napkin.

One of the others pulled Brad out of the way, and the next instant, Billy was standing between Wayne and Jake, the two of them closing in on him from either side.

But Billy kept his cool. Holding the handrail like a spear, he jammed it into Jake's chest, impaling him with it.

A raspy gargle escaped Jake's lips, but the enormous shaft of metal sticking through his chest didn't slow him down at all.

"What the hell?" Billy said.

"They're zombies," said the girl from SMU. "Oh my God."

The word was like a peel of thunder in our midst. Jake's imperviousness to pain; Wayne's injuries; the moaning crowd outside; the burned people we'd seen the police shooting back at the hotel: they all made sense now. All through school, most of us had listened to those idiots who talked so gleefully about the coming zombie apocalypse and laughed at them.

But none of us were laughing now.

And Billy wasn't wasting any time, either. He kicked at one of the wall speakers until it broke loose from its mounts. Then he scooped it up, lifted it two-handed over his head, and brought it down on top of Jake's head.

That dropped him.

Jake collapsed in a heap and didn't move anymore.

By that point Wayne was almost on top of Billy, but Billy was able to step to one side at the last instant, kick the back of Wayne's knees, and drop him to the floor so that he could finish him with another two-handed blow to the back of the head.

When it was done, Billy stood over the bodies of our two friends, his chest heaving like a bellows, and looked at Brad, Jim and Sandra.

"Well," he said, "what now?"

* * *

Over the next three days, Billy, our representative from West Point, emerged as our greatest resource. He worked tirelessly. I don't think I saw him stop once.

Our first problem was what to do with the bodies of Jake and Wayne. We couldn't leave them inside, we all knew that, but it didn't seem like there was any other way to get rid of them.

It was Billy who proposed pushing them out the half-windows up near the overhead luggage racks. They were high enough up on the side of the train that the zombies outside couldn't force their way in. The only trouble was, no one wanted to touch the bodies. Finally, Brad ordered Billy to do it, and the rest of us watched as he dragged the bodies of Jake and Wayne up to the window and shoved them out.

The zombies grabbed the bodies before they'd even cleared the window and began to rip them to pieces.

But none of us had the stomach to watch that.

We all turned away and pretended it wasn't happening.

Later that afternoon, it became obvious we were going to have to do something about going to the bathroom. Pissing was no trouble for the guys. They could just go over to the door well and piss down the short flight of stairs. But the girls, and the guys who had to take a dump, couldn't do that. Putting your back to the door where all those zombies were trying to break in was like taunting them. They pressed even harder to get in.

Plus, there was the issue of privacy.

Brad put Billy to work removing the seats from the floor. He used a dime to unscrew them, and once he had them loose, he hoisted them to the head of the car and arranged them like a horseshoe, like cubicle walls, so that people could do their business behind a sort of screen. The smell was bad, but it was best we could do under the circumstances.

As night came on and we started to tire, Billy worked at prying loose the seat cushions on the few remaining chairs so that we could have pillows for our heads. I used mine as a writing desk, where I continued to scribble notes about what was said and done.

Later still, it started to rain.

Billy got excited, though at first none of us knew why. Then he pulled down the plastic covers from the overhead lights and slid one of them out of a luggage rack window, forming a sort of gutter to catch the rain. It trickled down inside the car, where Billy caught it in an empty water bottle.

"We're gonna need water," he said to Brad. "You guys help me."

"Good idea," Brad said, and though I could tell it plagued Jim and Sandra to admit it, they thought so, too.

Brad, Jim, and Sandra ordered the rest of us to partner up and do as Billy was doing, and within a few minutes, we'd filled every container we could find.

When we were done, Brad said, "Do you think that's enough?"

"For a few days, maybe," said Billy. "Who knows? We'll have to start conserving and rationing. And if anyone's got any food, that's gonna be an issue as well."

Once again, it was as if a peal of thunder had gone through our group. I don't know if any of the others had already considered the food issue, but I certainly hadn't. I looked around the car and saw a few others pulling their backpacks close to their chests.

Outside, the zombies went on moaning, and inside, Billy kept on working.

Sometime during the early morning, the zombies knocked down part of the door. The sudden rise in volume woke everyone, except for Billy, who had evidently never gone to sleep.

In the dark it was hard to see what was happening, but after my eyes adjusted, I saw Billy hacking at the hands reaching through the door.

"Bring me that chair," Billy said to Sandra and Jim. With his chin he was gesturing at the cushionless frame of a chair at their feet. "Hurry! I need to brace this door."

Jim grabbed the guy next to him and pushed him toward the door. "Take it to him!"

"Why me?" the guy said.

"Hurry!"

Jim could be commanding when he yelled, and the guy obeyed almost reflexively. He picked the chair up and took it to Billy. He stopped well short of the doorway, though, and held it out to Billy like he was trying to feed a rope to someone clinging to the side of a cliff. Billy managed to get a hold of it and jam it into the door well, and between the chair and the handrail he and Jake had installed the day before, the doors were secure again.

"That'll hold them for now," he said. "But we're going to need something else to make sure it holds."

Brad nodded.

"Okay," he said. "You do that. Get somebody to help you."

Billy looked around for a volunteer, but nobody would look him in the eyes.

In disgust, he shook his head and went off to do it himself.

* * *

Around noon the next day, Tynice went into a diabetic seizure.

"Somebody needs to get her a candy bar or something," Brad said. "Who's got a candy bar?"

He looked around the room, his gaze finally settling on Russell Bailey, a computer programmer from UT Austin.

"Russell, I saw a Hershey bar in your bag."

Russell pulled backpack tight against his chest. "I'm not giving her my food."

"Russell, you have to. She needs it."

"Well, I need it to. We're gonna run out of food soon, and what am I gonna do then?"

"Russell," Brad said, "this is for the good of the group. You have a lot and she doesn't have any. You need to give her some of yours."

"Bullshit," he said. "It's not my fault she didn't bring what she needed. I have food in my bag because I had the foresight to put it there. If she didn't do the same, why is that my problem?"

"Because it's the right thing to do."

"Give her some of yours, then."

"Russell, that's not helpful."

Then Brad motioned to Billy. "Get his food. Distribute it around."

"Don't," Russell said, pleading with Billy. "Please don't."

"Give me the bag, Russell," Billy said.

Russell shook his head, and Billy, wearing a look of grim determination, moved in to take it from him.

* * *

Over the next four days, we lost six people. Tynice and Gustavo both went into diabetic shock and died. The other four, weakened by a lack of food and no water, gradually shut down, and when we woke to the sunrise on the morning of the fifth day, they were dead. Once again Billy crushed their heads to keep them from coming back and pushed the bodies out the window. Again we all looked away as the ever-growing crowd of zombies outside ate their corpses.

It rained later that day, and we were able to get more water, but the food shortage was becoming critical. We were down to a dozen people, all of whom were starving, and one small package of beef jerky.

"We need to divide this up," said Jim. "Here, I'll do it."

"No you won't," said Brad. "We decide together."

"Oh that's great," said the girl from SMU. "And while the two of you argue about it, the rest of us starve. Just hand a piece to everybody."

Brad and Jim and Sandra went off to a corner of the car and talked about it. When they came back, they each had a big piece of jerky. They handed some of the smaller pieces around and told us to divide it up.

"But there's not enough here for any of us," said Billy.

"Times are hard," Brad said. "I know. I understand. But we'll just have to tighten our belts."

I got a piece and went to one side to eat it. I hadn't had anything in more than a day and tore into it eagerly.

A moment later, Brad and Jim and Sandra went to Billy and whispered to him. He looked upset, but he didn't yell. He just took his piece of jerky and tore it into three parts and gave each of them a piece. Then he went to the far side of the car and sat down. He looked utterly exhausted and used up, but he didn't protest.

Then they came to me. Brad asked me to give up what I had left for them.

He said as the leaders they needed to stay sharp.

They couldn't afford to go hungry.

"Can't do it," I said. "I'm the Press. I'm an observer. You can't do anything that keeps me from that role."

They reluctantly agreed and went off to get what was left of the jerky from the others.

* * *

The next morning, Billy was dead.

None of us had the energy to move. We were all starving, most of us were sick. And—always—there was the constant roar of the moaning crowd just outside, reminding us that we were not long for this world.

"What are we gonna do?" asked the girl from SMU.

"I think it's plain what we have to do," said Brad. He looked at Jim and Sandra, and though they didn't want to agree with a Democrat just out of principle, they still nodded their heads in assent.

"I don't understand," the girl said. "What? What are we gonna do?"

"We have to eat," Brad said.

The girl looked at him, dumbfounded, not understanding.

"Eat what?"

Brad, with his mouth set in a harsh, grimacing frown, pointed at the body of the soldier who had done so much for all of us.

* * *

Two weeks later, there were only four of us left—Brad, Jim, Sandra, and myself.

Sandra was not doing well.

Actually, none of us were doing well, but she was feeling really bad. We hadn't been able to cook any of the friends we'd eaten, and the shock of consuming all that raw, human flesh was doing terrible things to our system.

Sandra was doubled over on her side, holding her gut with both hands and moaning like one of the zombies outside.

Jim was sitting next to her, stroking her hair.

"I'm dying," she said.

"You're not going to die," Jim said. "You're just sick. This'll pass."

She looked up at him, and there was pain and fear in her eyes, but also acceptance. That acceptance was hardest thing for me to see, for I had seen it before, on the others that we'd already eaten. And when people started to get that look in their eyes, it was a self-fulfilling prophecy.

It was only a matter of time.

"I'm dying, Jim. I know it."

He didn't say anything, for I think he knew it too.

"Promise me," she said. Her voice was weak, raspy.

"Anything," he said, still stroking her hair.

For a moment, as she strained to look toward Brad Owens, who was sitting against the opposite wall, the acceptance and fear in her eyes changed to hatred.

"Don't let he him eat me. I don't want some liberal bastard eating me. I can't die knowing some liberal sack of shit lived another day because of me."

She wanted to say more, but another wave of pain shot through her gut and she let out a choked scream.

"She's delirious," Jim said to me.

But when he put his hand back on her face and pushed the hair out of her face, she was dead.

"Sandra?" Brad said. "Sandra, no, baby, no!"

He lifted her head and cradled it in his lap, rocking her corpse gently, like a child he was trying to put to sleep.

* * *

An hour or so later, Brad came over to him with the piece of metal from one of the seats that we'd been using to carve meat off of our friends.

"It's time," he said.

"Fuck off," Jim said. "You're not touching her."

"Jim," Brad said. "Please don't do this. We have to survive."

"She didn't want a sorry sack of shit like you touching her. No worthless Democrat is going to touch her."

"I've as much right to her corpse as you do."

"Like hell."

I knew what was going to happen even before they lunged at each other. Jim knocked the blade from Brad's hand and the next instant they were rolling around on the ground, their hands at each other's throats.

I took complete notes of what happened during the fight, but I guess that really doesn't matter now. The end result was that they strangled each other. Democrat and Republican, neither would quit until they'd snuffed the life out of the other, and now they're both dead.

So I sat there, the only member of the Young Americans left alive.

And a short while later, I picked up the blade and started eating.

* * *

I was rescued by the Chinese Army a week later.

They hadn't planned on finding me there. They hadn't planned on finding anyone alive, I don't think. Someone told me they were looking for the train, that they had spotted it from the air and went in to retrieve it because they needed it to deliver troops across the country. The zombie apocalypse, they told me, had been contained. For the most part. A few pockets of zombies remained, but those were being taken care of. I was lucky to be alive, they told me, but I could tell they didn't think much of me for it. The first soldiers to board the train had taken one look at me, and at the pile of bones surrounding me, and had turned their heads to vomit.

News of what had happened went ahead of me.

The Chinese Army put me on a cargo ship and sent me back to the States. The ship's crew seemed to already know everything about me, and that made meal times rough. As soon as I would enter the mess hall, the others would get up to leave. No one, it seemed, could stomach watching me eat.

No one, it seemed, even back in the States, could watch me eat.

Live with that long enough, and it hardens you.

That's why I live here, on this farm in Georgia, where I grow my own food and raise my own livestock.

I live alone, and I like it just fine.

That way, there's nobody to turn up their nose if I like to eat the occasional steak raw. Besides, it's nobody business but mine.

This is still the goddamned U.S. of A., for Christ's sake.

Author's Notes

Resurrecting Mindy

Faking it is nothing new in zombie stories. The idea that you can evade a horde of zombies by pretending to be one of them is compelling in that it makes possible a great deal of metaphoric frontloading. It's also a great way to capture the mood of your piece. For example, it was done with great humor in *Shaun of the Dead*, and with equal parts horror in *The Walking Dead*. My favorite example of faking it is in Adam-Troy Castro's story "Dead Like Me," in which conformity is treated as the ultimate act of self-loathing. "Resurrecting Mindy" was written for an anthology of Christmas-themed horror stories. When I sat down to write the story, I knew I wanted to riff on O. Henry's "The Gift of the Magi," arguably one of the most famous Christmas stories outside of the Gospel of Luke. I knew I also wanted to write my own faker story. So I did both with "Resurrecting Mindy."

Dating in Dead World

Most of the stories in this collection were written for a particular magazine or anthology. "Dating in Dead World" was written just because I felt like it. I had this idea for a guy who made his living delivering messages between compounds in a world long-since overrun by zombies, and the story just took off from there. I sat down to write it early one morning in September, 2005, and when I quit for the day later that afternoon, I had finished it. I think I went through it a couple of times after that, just to polish it, but the story pretty much came out fully formed. I love it when they do that.

Bug Out or Hunker Down

Attitudes are changing toward zombies. More and more, otherwise "normal" people are surprising themselves with a newfound appreciation for the undead *du jour*. Friends of my parents, for example, will approach me in hushed tones (because they know I write this stuff) and say, "Have you seen that show, *The Walking Dead*? That's pretty good, isn't it?" I smile and nod. *The Walking Dead*, both the graphic novel and the television show, has done wonders for the zombie's public image. But there are the literary snobs out there who refuse to see beyond the vast droves of poorly written zombie stuff currently floating around out there. They read something crappy and assume the rest of the genre must be like that too. Inevitably, one of these literary snobs will level the accusation that most of this stuff is just a sick fascination with survival. While I don't condemn zombie fiction for that fascination, I kind of see their point. In fact, I've come up with a name for that trend in the genre. I call it Survival Porn because, in many of these stories, the contents of one's bug-out bag, or the weapons one carries, are described with an almost pornographic thrill. I don't do much in that vein, but this piece certainly qualifies. Also, I've had a number of requests to turn this into a novel. Who knows? I might do that one day. I just need to come up with some pornographic-style title. Maybe I'll call it *Jugs and Big Guns*.

Bury My Heart at Marvin Gardens

This one was never supposed to be published, at least not publicly. In 2011, I lost a very good friend named Jon Michael Freiger. Jon was one of the kindest human beings I've ever known.

We loved playing Monopoly, and our conversations always worked their way around to horror, another mutual love of ours. When Jon died unexpectedly, leaving a wife and a young baby, his widow asked me to write a zombie story for him that would go into the program they'd pass out at the funeral. Well, I wrote the story, this story, but after much discussion we decided not to put it into the program. Jon's friends would get it, and some of his family probably would too, but we decided most of those in attendance would simply find it weird and out of place. So, I put it in a drawer and left it there. For a long time it was too private to do anything with. But some time has gone by since his death, and while I still feel his absence keenly, I decided to put his story into this collection because it really does capture the great times I had with him. And remembering those good times is probably the best way to honor those who matter most. Miss you every day, my friend.

Zombies and Their Haunts

This little bit of non-fiction was written for Tor.com as part the publicity tour for John Joseph Adams' *The Living Dead 2*. I got a lot of great feedback from it, so I decided to put the piece into this collection. Hopefully, you'll never look at an abandoned building the same way again.

The Day the Music Died

Back in the early days of my police career, I would, from time to time, work overtime jobs as security at concerts and stuff like that. For the most part, the money was good, and I got to watch some free shows to boot. But then, for one show, my assignment was back stage, escorting a certain rock star (who I shall not name because he's one of my mom's favorites) from the stage to the limo. My job was, I thought, pretty straightforward. Keep the weirdoes from mobbing Mr. So and So. Easy enough. But then this guy's manager or whatever he was pulls me aside and tells me there are some special conditions I have to follow. No one, he said, including me, was to speak with Mr. So and So unless spoken to. And no one, he said, including me, was to look Mr. So and So in the eyes. "You can't be serious," I said, unable to keep from laughing. "That's the stupidest thing I've ever heard." He didn't laugh, though. He told me he was completely serious, and that if I couldn't follow those instructions, they would find somebody who would. I told them good luck and farewell and went on with life. Years later, I was asked to do a zombie story for an anthology arranged around holidays, and for some reason, that rock star's manager popped into my head. What sort of things, I wondered, must a manager like that do for his client? This story grew out of that question.

Survivors

"Survivors" was written for an anthology I edited with Michelle McCrary called *Dead Set*. The idea for the story came from something I saw while driving my police car through the plaza in front of the Alamo—a location, by the way, that figures prominently in another story in this collection. Anyway, I'm driving my police car through downtown, when a sudden gust of wind kicked up a wall of dust that rolled down the street like a big, brown wave. As the dust began to settle, I saw people stumbling across the street, half choked and nearly blind from the dust. After seeing that, this story practically wrote itself.

Suburbia of the Dead

One of my favorite horror stories of all time is Joe R. Lansdale's "The Shaggy House." I love the idea that a house can kill a neighborhood by polluting it like a cancer. Well, last year, I happened to be driving through one of the desolate neighborhoods east of downtown San Antonio. Many decades ago, that area was the retreat of San Antonio's über-wealthy. On every hill there is a mansion—they are decrepit wrecks now, but most are still there. Looking at those ruined mansions, I got to thinking how a neighborhood dies. Joe R. Lansdale's story came back to me at that point, and so, one morning, just after breakfast, I sat down at the kitchen table to write my version of "The Shaggy House."

Paradise of the Living Dead

One of the greatest stories ever told is Cabeza de Vaca's *Adventures in the Unknown Interior of America*. This guy was shipwrecked during a hurricane off the coast of Galveston, waded ashore, and spent the next four years wandering Texas and parts of the modern-day American Southwest. During that time, he fought both for and against the many Indian tribes there, was taken hostage several times, held and traded as a slave, threatened with execution dozens of times, was spared for his knowledge of medicine and astronomy, and was eventually revered as a god before finally making his way back to Spain. Seriously, Daniel Defoe couldn't have come up with a better tale of survival. The origin of "Paradise of the Living Dead" is a chapter in Cabeza de Vaca's memoirs in which he describes coming ashore after the shipwreck. It seems there were these clams in the water, and their shells were so sharp they cut up the survivors, even though most were wearing armor. All I did was add a nasty little defense mechanism to those clams.

Jimmy Finder

One of the most common gripes I hear about my book *Dead City* is that characters keep stepping into seemingly empty streets, only to find it crawling with zombies the next instant. Now I usually don't pay attention to criticisms, but that one really aggravated me because, as a cop, I've seen empty streets suddenly flood with people. Hell, it even happens in the middle of the night. Someone will get shot, or a car will get wrapped around a tree, and the next thing you know, that quiet little street is standing-room only. When I wrote the zombie scenes in *Dead City*, I was coming at it from that angle. But I get that some people need a more concrete explanation, so, when I got an invitation to write a zombie novella for IDW's ongoing series,

Zombies vs. Robots, I thought I would give the people what they want and explain once and for all why zombies do what they do.

Bugging Out

I was on a zombie panel a few years ago when this guy in the audience stands up and says, "Mr. McKinney, you've got to see the compound I've built. Man, I've got everything me and my family needs to survive the zombie apocalypse. We're ready!" This actually happens pretty regularly at conventions, I'm told, and it got me thinking about how easy it would be to fall in love with the idea of surviving the zombie apocalypse. Then I happened to catch an episode of *Hoarders*, and this story was born.

Ethical Solution

After *Dead City* had been on the shelves for a few months, I started getting emails from people who loved Ken Stoler. And just as many from people who hated him. No one, it seemed, was on the fence about him, which is exactly how I hoped he would come across. Ken Stoler generated so much attention, in fact, that I decided to put his ideas to the test.

But, as in "Survivors," which would come along two years later, I sensed that Ken Stoler wasn't the right person to take that test. At the end of *Dead City*, Ken Stoler has gone on speaking tours and manages to make quite a few friends, and just as many enemies ...much as his character did with *Dead City*'s readers. The way I looked at it, I had created a wide world outside the confines of *Dead City*'s covers: Why not bring in a fresh batch of characters, nearly all of whom are caught up in Ken Stoler's cause? Sending them back into San Antonio would give me a chance to color a little doubt into Eddie Hudson's version of events, and it would also give me a chance to show how the rest of the country had been affected by the Outbreak.

And it would give me a chance to introduce a man destined to become one of the most important characters in the whole Dead World series.

Ben Richardson is single, mid-thirties, smart, but not pompously so. He's a staff writer for *The Atlantic*. He was born and raised in Port Arthur, Texas, just like Janis Joplin, and when the first reports of cannibalism started coming out of Houston right after Hurricane Mardell, Ben went into action. He decided right then to write the definitive history of the Outbreak, covering every aspect of the zombie plague, from the lofty but ultimately empty, speeches on the White House lawn to the plight of the lowliest individual hiding out in the back alleys of a ruined town.

Just before the events in "Ethical Solution," which takes place about eight months after Eddie's ending to *Dead City*, Ben Richardson gets wind of an English professor from the University of Texas at Austin named Dr. Sylvia Carnes. Dr. Carnes has bought Ken Stoler's cause hook, line and sinker, and now she plans to take a chartered bus through the military quarantine that surrounds San Antonio. She has about forty students with her, each one a member of the local chapter of People for an Ethical Solution, and a court order authorizing her to enter the quarantine zone. The idea, she tells Ben, is to show the rest of the country that the infected—she refuses to call them zombies—can be handled in a humane way by normal people. This, she hopes, will open the door to meaningful research into a cure.

Ben Richardson is naturally skeptical. He and Sylvia Carnes fall on opposite sides of the issue, but he nonetheless maintains an open mind and convinces her that he should come along on her expedition into San Antonio.

One of the complaints I got from San Antonio locals who read *Dead City* was that I didn't mention many of the city's wonderful landmarks, such as the Alamo. Well, okay, I said. You want the Alamo, I'll give you the Alamo. So the basic plot of "Ethical Solutions," if you know anything about the Battle of the Alamo, wasn't hard to imagine. The more important part of that story was the way the debate between Sylvia Carnes and Ben Richardson develops. They cover quite a bit of ground during "Ethical Solutions," but even still, neither character is any closer to winning over the other by the end.

Real agreement, in fact, wouldn't happen for another eight years—and three books—later, when the two of them met again in the crumbling ruins of St. Louis.

But that's a different story.

Swallowed

Snakes creep me out. Plain and simple, they make my skin crawl. So when I read the reports coming out of the Florida Everglades that people had been releasing boa constrictors into the wild, and that those snakes were eating deer and alligators and growing to enormous sizes, I knew what I had to do... sic a zombie on them!

Sabbatical in the Ohio Methlands

Just about everybody, I think, has seen those websites that show the way people deteriorate under a meth addiction. Well, back in my patrol-officer days, I had to deal with meth heads all the time, and I'm here to tell you, those websites aren't exaggerating. There were times, when dealing with a dozen or so meth heads at once, that I felt like I was in the middle of a real-life zombie apocalypse. I channeled that when Bruce Boston and Marge Simon asked me to write a flash fiction piece for their stint as guest editors over at *The Pedestal Magazine*. The only trouble was that I was on a camping trip at Enchanted Rock when the invitation came in, and I ended up having to write this story on my cell phone. That was the first time I ever wrote a story on my phone, and here's hoping that it will be the last!

Two and a Half Graves

I had a dream one night that zombies were eating my fingers. Seriously. One of the craziest dreams I've ever had. Anyway, when I woke up, I was a little freaked out and I started writing down some ideas on what it would feel like to have zombies eating your fingers. Those notes turned into this story.

Starvation Army

Stories take on a life of their own after they're published, and that was certainly the case with "Starvation Army." Written for Kim Paffenroth's anthology of historical zombie fiction, *History is Dead*, "Starvation Army" was not well-received by readers. In fact, quite a few seem to have genuinely hated it. Most of the reviews criticized it for being more of a ghost story than a zombie story. And yet, for all the negative feedback, the professional critics gave it a warm reception. It was listed as an Honorable Mention in one of Ellen Datlow's *Year's Best Fantasy and Horror*, and it got great write ups from half-a-dozen major magazines. I don't know what any of that says about the story, but I do know that I'm proud of it.

State of the Union

There's no quick answer to that question: "Where do you get your ideas?" Ideas come from everywhere. Even the most insignificant moments can give way to ideas. "State of the Union" came from a conversation I had with my wife one night while watching TV. It was during the height of the Occupy Wall Street movement, and the news show we were watching had collected six experts for a roundtable discussion. Well, it didn't take long before these six experts were talking over each other, getting angry, and generally acting like children. My wife turned to me and said, "My God, this country is eating itself alive." Boom, a story was born. To make it work, though, I needed a frame, and for that, I turned to Mark Twain's masterpiece of social satire, "Cannibalism in the Cars," which is why this story is dedicated to him.

A Reader's Guide to Dead World
by
Joe McKinney

Featuring everything you ever wanted to know about Dead City,
Apocalypse of the Dead, Flesh Eaters, Mutated *and the other stories
making up the Dead World Series.*

I didn't set out to become a writer.

Growing up, I used to write the occasional spooky tale, drafting
it out longhand with a cheap ball-point pen on a yellow legal pad.
Once the story was finished, I'd tear out the pages, staple them
together, and leave them on the corner of my desk for a week or so
before throwing them away. I never placed any significance on what
I was doing. I never had any intention of doing anything with my
stories. Writing wasn't something I saw myself doing one day. It was
just something I did.

And then, in the winter of 2003, I became a father. I remember
leaning my head against the glass, looking in on the nursery,
watching my baby sleep. Proud as I was, I felt this overpowering
need to preserve the essence of the man looking in on that nursery,
because I knew that one day, the little girl sleeping in there would
want to know something about her father that growing up with him
and living under his rule would never teach her.

Sometimes a thought like that is merely an impulse, a
momentary thing that slips away like a dream upon waking.

That wasn't the case with me. Over the next few months, the thought gained traction, until I couldn't keep it in any longer. I took up my pen and my legal pad and got to writing. Eventually, I did about eighty pages of an SF novel called *The Edge of the Map*. It was high space-opera in the classic 1950s vein. And it was pure crap. Every time I started writing, I wondered what in the hell I was doing. I wondered why I bothered. Not a word of it felt genuine.

And even worse, I wasn't doing a thing to answer the original impulse that made me want to start writing in the first place.

Briefly, I considered taking up painting.

But then I realized that if I was going to do this thing right, I needed to be true to what I loved. Love, after all, was what this was all about.

I grew up on a steady diet of monster movies and horror fiction. My first literary infatuation was with horror, and it occurred to me that if I had any chance of doing this thing the way it ought to be done, I needed to write what I loved. *Dead City*, my first published novel, sprang from that decision.

I was lucky *Dead City* landed when it did. It put me on the crest of the zombie revival that began around 2005 with Brian Keene's *The Rising*, and because *Dead City* came out through a large publishing house, I got some good exposure. The book sold well, which in turn led to a career in writing.

Dead City has grown into the Dead World series, which to date includes four novels and half a dozen stories. The novels are easy to come by, the stories less so. At least for the time being. But even if you haven't read the stories, or in case you missed one of the novels, there's no need to worry. I wrote each and every entry in the series in such a way that a reader can come to any novel, any story, in any order, and still feel like they're caught up with the overall storyline. This makes it easy on the reader coming to the Dead World for the first time, but has also caused more than a few readers to ask what I think the overall series' preferred chronology is. So, just because I like doing things like this, I've put together a little reader's guide to walk you, the reader, through the Dead World I've created. I've tried to avoid spoilers, while at the same time providing useful information. If you have specific questions, please feel free to add them to the comments section below. I'll answer those questions in full, without regard to spoilers.

Enjoy your tour.

DEAD CITY

Dead City (Pinnacle; November, 2006). Reprinted with a new cover and the first five chapters of Apocalypse of the Dead *(Pinnacle; November, 2010).*

Why zombies?

To answer that, I have to turn back to the summer of 1983. I was fourteen. That summer gave me two landmarks in my education. The first was George Romero's *Night of the Living Dead*, a movie that scared the ever-loving crap out of me. I watched it one night on cable and slept cradling a baseball bat for the next month. I dreamt of the living dead circling my house in the night, rattling the walls with their endless moans, forcing their way inside. No movie had ever done that to me before. Very few have done it since.

And then, just when I thought I had learned what real scary was, Hurricane Alicia made landfall. I grew up in Clear Lake City, a little suburb south of Houston. We were just across the lake from the mouth of the Houston Ship Channel and the numerous shrimp camps down in Kemah, and we were square in the bull's-eye of the storm.

I spent all night in a closet, listening to the storm trying its hardest to rip my house from its foundation and send it sailing off like a kite. The next morning, I went to the front door and looked out over a sea of caramel-colored water. Every roof was missing shingles. Trees were toppled. Cars and trucks were submerged to their roofs. I saw a water moccasin glide through the swing set in my neighbor's back yard. And at the entrance to my subdivision was a shrimp boat that had been carried seven miles inland by the storm surge. The destruction was staggering, and for a boy of fourteen, it felt a bit like the world had been turned upside down.

Of course, my fear didn't last long. Later that day my best friend came by in a canoe, and we paddled all around the neighborhood, acting like river explorers heading up the Amazon in search of The Creature from the Black Lagoon. It was a blast.

But even as the fear of those two landmark events subsided, my fascination with them grew. So when I sat down to write a story about how terrifyingly complex the world had become for me as a brand-new father, I found myself turning back to the two most frightening encounters of my youth.

The Rise of the Zombies

A basic principle of disaster mitigation theory is to plan for the disasters you're most likely to face. It does little good for a police department in North Dakota, for example, to plan for a hurricane. But here in San Antonio, we are only 170 miles from the Gulf of Mexico. That makes us far enough away from the coast to avoid all but a few gusty rain storms, yet close enough to act as the evacuation point for every coastal city from Brownsville to New Orleans. So when the San Antonio Police Department trains for hurricanes, they train for the near-total evacuation and relocation of multiple coastal cities, including some, such as Houston, that are nearly three times San Antonio's size.

The mission is enormous, requiring all the logistical planning of a military invasion—only in reverse—and the analogy was not lost upon me when I started thinking of a cause for my zombie outbreak.

Before the action in *Dead City*, Houston has been hit by four major hurricanes. The first of these storms was a Category 3 storm named Gabrielle, that fizzled to a tropical storm just before making landfall. Most of the population in the Houston-Galveston area, which totals about five million, did as they were asked and evacuated in anticipation of a huge storm. But when Gabrielle turned into a lot of nothing, most of those who evacuated felt cheated and stupid for wasting their time. And then, a week and a half later, a second mandatory evacuation order was issued, this one in preparation for Hurricane Hector. With Gabrielle still fresh in everyone's mind, the majority of the Houston-Galveston area refused to evacuate.

Hector knocked Houston back on its heels. The storm did enormous damage, managing to flood most of the sea-level communities between Galveston and South Houston, where the majority of the nation's oil and gas and chemical plants are located. Millions of people were trapped as the flood waters carried spilled oil and chemicals into the flooded suburbs. All electrical power was knocked out. Fresh water was unavailable. The city's sewage lines back-spilled into the flood waters. That sewage mingled with the oil and the chemicals from the refineries and the drowned bodies rotting in the scorching Texas heat.

The federal government has a long tradition (one going back at least as far as the Johnson Administration) of getting caught with its pants down when it comes to disasters in the Gulf of Mexico, and then compounding that negligence with painfully slow, inadequate follow up. It's just the way things go, and in the Dead World, Hurricane Hector was no exception. For a critical span of eight days, local authorities received only token aid from Washington. And when the federal government finally did decide to act in a meaningful way, it was too late, for Hurricane Kyle was waiting just offshore, and it was bigger and badder than Hector ever thought of being.

Kyle tipped the scales. The storm surge was immense and flooded the entire city. So severe was the flooding that most experts believed Kyle permanently altered the shape of the coastline. What was once the nation's third largest population center became the bottom of a shallow sea.

In the midst of the destruction and suffering, the military begins evacuating refugees by the hundreds of thousands to San Antonio's Lackland Air Force Base. But what nobody realizes at this early point is that some of these refugees are infected with the necrosis filovirus, a hemorrhagic fever akin to Ebola, Marburg, and the Crimean-Congo viruses. The necrosis filovirus is a level 4 biosafety hazard, but unlike its more well-documented cousins, the necrosis filovirus is incredibly fast-acting. Whereas a person contracting Ebola or Marburg exhibits headache, backache, and other flu-like symptoms within five to ten days, a person infected with the necrosis filovirus shows symptoms within a few hours. Complete depersonalization and aggression and a near invulnerability to pain rapidly manifest, turning the infected person essentially into a zombie. The illusion is all the more complete when observers see the clouded pupils and encounter the smell of rotting flesh. The only difference between the zombies in the Dead World and the zombies developed in the Romero mythos is that the Dead World zombies are still alive.

It doesn't take long for the infected to be transported to San Antonio's hospitals, where the infection spreads. As *Dead City* opens, the infected have already overloaded the hospitals and spread among the general population. The Outbreak, as the first wave of the zombie apocalypse in the Dead World universe is called, is underway.

Eddie Hudson

The narrator of *Dead City* is Eddie Hudson, a young patrolman, husband, and father stationed on the west side of San Antonio. Eddie's nothing special. He's not a very good shot. He has no special knowledge or skills. And he's certainly not the brightest bulb in the box. I've read several reader responses on Amazon and other book forums that see this as some kind of deficiency, but I think those readers miss the point. This is not a book, after all, about kicking tons of zombie ass. Sure, a lot of zombie ass gets kicked, but that is incidental to the main point of the book, which is both to show the fragility of our modern world and to suggest a possible remedy for that fragility.

I've read several other zombie novels that feature main characters that are unmitigated bad asses—Jonathan Maberry's *Patient Zero* and J.L. Bourne's *Day by Day Armaggedon* come immediately to mind—but I didn't want that for *Dead City*. I wanted someone who could stand in for the reader, someone with whom they could identify rather than hero worship.

There is a medieval play called *Everyman*. Most people who took a freshman English Lit class are probably familiar with it. The play opens with Death informing Everyman his time is up, it's time to go. Everyman pleads to stay. Death tells him no, he has to die, but if he can get somebody to come with him, he's welcome to bring a companion. One by one, the allegorical figures of wealth, friends, family, and all the others turn their back on Everyman, saying they'd gladly go with him on a journey of life, but not of death. Eventually, only Good Deeds agrees to go with Everyman into the grave, and through a combination of Good Deeds and contrition Everyman eventually ascends to heaven. Nearly everybody gets that the play is an allegory meant to show the importance of confession and penance in the Christian's journey to salvation. But *Everyman* is also, in many ways, the basis for Eddie Hudson's journey through the first night of the zombie apocalypse.

Eddie's journey takes place over three acts. In the first act, most of the San Antonio Police Department, and in fact much of the City's ability to respond to any sort of crisis, is completely destroyed. Eddie Hudson is used to being part of a large army of sorts, with the full might of the Department ready to come to his aid at the touch of a button. That is gone at the end of the first act.

The second act opens with Eddie emotionally adrift. With all of his former advantages gone, he doesn't quite know what to do. And then, while wandering through the ruins of a gas station in his old patrol district, he finds his best friend and former partner, Marcus Acosta. Eddie and Marcus are basically a variant of the Odd Couple. Eddie is a family man, with all the attachments and obligations that implies. But for Marcus, the end of the world means nothing more than the end of alimony payments. Still, they are best friends, committed to each other's welfare.

But friendship can only take Eddie so far, and like Everyman before him, eventually he has to go on without Marcus at his side, and at the beginning of the third act, we find Eddie standing alone once again, surrounded, facing certain death. Of course he manages to escape (he is narrating the story, after all, so you know he has to live through it), and his experiences here prepare him not only for his reunion with his wife and child, but also for his ultimate redemption. And now that he has achieved control over part of his world, the real challenge of rebuilding that world begins.

The parallels to Everyman are pretty obvious. Both characters get their friends and resources stripped from them by events outside their control. Gradually they are left with nothing but themselves, their ultimate salvation dependent upon their actions.

But despite the parallels, *Dead City* is by no means a religious allegory. It's purely secular. My intention in *Dead City* was to show how thin the veneer of our society really is. And you don't need a zombie apocalypse to prove that. Even a localized disaster can show that our control over our lives is tenuous at best. But unlike a flood or a forest fire or a train wreck, only a zombie apocalypse can turn one's friends and family into insensible agents of destruction, and that's why Eddie Hudson has to fight a city full of zombies.

A Note on the Geography of *Dead City*

Before I leave Eddie's part of the story I need answer one of the most common questions I get about *Dead City*. If you were ever in the Air Force, chances are you've been to San Antonio. And nearly everyone, even the non-Air Force types, has heard of the Alamo. In fact, tens of millions of Americans have visited it since the late 1960s. In other words, San Antonio is well known to a great many Americans, and even a great many foreign travelers.

Quite a few have contacted me and remarked that, while they know San Antonio well, they don't recognize most of the street names I reference in the book.

They're quite right.

In fact, though the locations I describe are well known, and in most cases easy to recognize, I've given them different names.

I did this for two reasons.

The first reason is that I was completely ignorant of professional publishing and its rules when I wrote *Dead City*. I didn't know the rules about using real places fictitiously, and so I figured that if I didn't know if it was okay to say a particular incident occurred at the corner of Zarzamora and Culebra, I probably shouldn't do it. My reasoning was that I was writing about a big city. What was the harm in making up a few street names?

The second reason is a little more complex. The San Antonio Police Department has very specific rules about its officers writing for publication. Not only do they take a suspicious view of officers giving away police tactics and procedures, but they also want to preserve their valuable relationship with the public they serve. I had nightmares of some community activist throwing my book at the feet of City Council and saying, "So, this is what the San Antonio Police Department thinks of my neighborhood!"

I did not want to explain that scene to Internal Affairs.

So, I made up some street names. The places are real, but they're called by different names. The first line of the book is a good example. The empty parking lot near the corner of Seafarer and Rood is actually the empty parking lot near the intersection of Roanoke Street and Culebra. I think there's an Auto Zone there now, but at the time I wrote *Dead City*, it was a vacant lot.

So, where did the names come from?

Well, at the time I wrote the book, I was finishing up my

master's degree in English from the University of Texas at San Antonio. I was reading a lot of poetry, preparing for my comps. If you want to find your way around *Dead City*, don't bother with a map. You'll have better luck with the table of contents of *The Norton Anthology of English Literature.*

Survivors

"Survivors," originally published in Dead Set: A Zombie Anthology, *edited by Joe McKinney and Michelle McCrary (23 House Publishing; February, 2010).*

I didn't write *Dead City* with the intention of turning it into a series, mainly because I find most series annoying. Sure, *The Lord of the Rings* was cool. I also liked the Dave Robicheaux books by James Lee Burke. But with nearly everything else, the magic that worked in the first book tends to become tedious and annoying about midway through the second book.

Even so, I get why authors love to do them. First and foremost, they make money. A lot of readers, I guess, enjoy the comfort of covering familiar ground. I don't begrudge them that. Hell, I followed *Buffy* through all seven seasons. I even kept on with *Angel* after that. So I'm not saying there's anything wrong with covering familiar ground. It is what it is. Sometimes it works. Publishers know this, and so they encourage their authors to turn good ideas into lucrative franchises.

I have nothing against making money. In fact, I rather enjoy making money. But there has to be more to it than that. If money was all there was, storytelling would be down there on the very bottom of the career ladder. It may be that Stephen King makes so much cash he needs to build a warehouse out back just to store it all, but we can't all be Stephen King. Most writers, in fact, make a shockingly low wage. The figures get even more embarrassing when you start figuring the actual money earned per time spent writing. It's a wonder really, that anybody does this job at all.

But we do it. And every year, hundreds of thousands of authors submit their manuscripts to publishers in the hopes that they will be able to do it, too.

I can't speak for anyone else, but for me, the physical process of creating stories is hugely rewarding. There are innumerable hours spent in frustration and self-doubt, but there are also those wonderful moments when all the cylinders are firing and the story is pouring out of you and you feel like you've lost yourself in your imagination. Those moments keep writers coming back for more of this abuse we call writing for a living.

Writing a novel, even when it comes with white-hot moments of excitement like I've just described, is mentally exhausting. When I was done with *Dead City*, I developed a sort of separation anxiety. Though I didn't have any real desire to revisit Eddie Hudson, at least not right away, I did want to go back to the world I had created. Houston, after all, was still underwater, and though San Antonio was mostly cleared of the infected by the end of *Dead City*, other parts of the Gulf Coast were not so lucky. There were other parts of Dead World that needed exploring, and for that reason, I began to think of the possibility of doing a series of books, each one following a different set of characters through some other part of Dead World. That way, I could assuage my separation anxiety without doing the very thing that so frustrated me as a reader. I could have my cake and eat it too.

Meanwhile, I was writing other stories and publishing them here and there. One of the stories I published after *Dead City* was a vampire tale called "Down in the Cellar" in *Nights of Blood 2: More Legends of the Vampire,* edited by Bob Nailor and Elyse Salpeter, and released by 23 House Publishing. I was impressed by the way 23 House did business, and I wrote Mitchel Whitington, the managing editor, to let him know. As it turns out, Mitchel enjoyed my story a great deal and had tracked down a copy of *Dead City* as well. He told me he was getting a zombie-themed anthology together and asked if I'd be interested in co-editing it with a fabulous lady named Michelle McCrary, organizer of the Shreveport Zombie Walk. I agreed right away.

As I was thinking of the short story I would write for the book, I kept coming back to one of the major criticisms I received of *Dead City*. Eddie Hudson's story was one of redemption, and to tell that story I needed to compress time. One night was just about perfect for my purposes. (Remember Scrooge's surprise in "A Christmas Carol":

"And the spirits have done it all in just one night!") I could have ended the book after Chapter 33, but I felt like I wanted to show the change in Eddie after the one night of hell described in the rest of the book, which is why I included Chapter 34.

That told the story the way I thought it should be told. But, as I mentioned earlier, quite a few readers thought differently. They wanted details of the six weeks that pass between Chapter 33 and 34. I felt for them, because I wanted to write about that part of the overall story, but my instincts told me that Eddie Hudson was not the right person to tell of that confusing time. That part of the story would have to wait.

And then *Dead Set* came along, and I saw my chance to tell the story of those missing six weeks.

Hence we have "Survivors," my contribution to the anthology.

The main character is James Canavan, a Marine corporal from Houston on assignment in San Antonio. Canavan and his platoon have been tasked with a very simple mission. Their lieutenant is pinned down with a few survivors. Canavan is to take his men into downtown, rescue the lieutenant and any uninfected survivors, and get them to safety.

But of course nothing is ever as easy as it sounds, especially when there are hundreds of thousands of zombies flooding into the area. Despite deploying prodigious firepower, Canavan's squad is son torn apart, Canavan himself the sole survivor. While trying to fight his way out of the compromised area, he encounters a dying woman in a bombed-out bank. Amid the swirling dust and the moaning hordes of zombies, the two share a tense and bitter moment that changes Canavan forever.

When I wrote "Survivors," I knew the main thematic drive had to be survivor guilt. The missing six weeks from *Dead City* were a time of rebuilding, or at least an attempt at rebuilding, and survivor guilt is an unfortunate symptom of that process. After all, there can't be a need to rebuild without an equally strong sense that something has been lost that is worth rebuilding. Those who live through traumatic moments of loss know this. They know there is a drive to throw oneself headlong into any kind of mind-numbing labor and that that labor is at once an urge to destroy oneself while building up the memory of those who have died.

What was needed, I decided, was an outsider, someone who

could bring in a firsthand account of what happened in Houston, while also commenting on the deep sense of loss through the rebuilding process.

That meant telling a very dark story, which certainly describes James Canavan's adventures in San Antonio.

Ethical Solution

"Ethical Solution," originally published as "People for the Ethical Treatment of Zombies," in The Harrow, *Volume 10, Number 5 (2007).*

There is an elementary school teacher in *Dead City* named Ken Stoler, and if Eddie Hudson were here with us today, he would tell you that God never made a sorrier sack of shit than Ken Stoler.

Stoler and Eddie spend the middle third of the book arguing about the philosophical and moral implications of a world populated by zombies. Eddie, being who he is, finds the conversation pointless. But Stoler won't let it go. He has discovered that the zombies aren't really dead, as Eddie believes. They are very much alive but infected with a disease that eats away their minds until they are completely depersonalized. They feel no pain, only aggression, so they continue to attack even when mortally wounded.

Eddie never sees Stoler's point. For him, it is a matter of kill or be killed. The zombies don't allow another option, so he intends to be the one doing the killing.

Stoler, on the other hand, refuses to heap violence on the zombies. "You wouldn't kill someone just because they have the flu, would you?" he argues.

"I would if they were trying to eat me," Eddie counters, rather petulantly, and rather ineffectively. He lacks the mental horsepower necessary to debate Ken Stoler, and they both know it. Stoler hopes to use this to his advantage and convert Eddie. He wants to quarantine the entire Gulf Coast and pressure the government to research the disease that turns the infected into zombies. Every infected person, he argues, deserves to be rehabilitated. We can no more hold them criminally liable for their acts of murder and cannibalism than we can hold an insane person responsible for murdering.

That, of course, is not an effective argument to use on a cop, and though Eddie tries to respond intelligently, all he does is trip over his tongue. When Ken Stoler leaves the book, it is none too soon for Eddie Hudson.

Ben Richardson

After *Dead City* had been on the shelves for a few months, I started getting emails from people who loved Ken Stoler. And just as many from people who hated him. No one, it seemed, was on the fence about him, which is exactly how I hoped he would come across. Ken Stoler generated so much attention, in fact, that I decided to put his ideas to the test.

But, as in "Survivors," which would come along two years later, I sensed that Ken Stoler wasn't the right person. At the end of *Dead City*, Stoler has gone on speaking tours and makes quite a few friends, and just as many enemies...much as his character did with *Dead City*'s readers. The way I looked at it, I had created a wide world outside the confines of *Dead City*'s covers: Why not bring in a fresh batch of characters, nearly all caught up in Ken Stoler's cause? Sending them into San Antonio would give me a chance to color a little doubt into Eddie Hudson's version of events, and it would also give me a chance to show how the rest of the country had been affected by the Outbreak.

And I could introduce a man destined to become one of the most important characters in the whole Dead World series.

Ben Richardson.

Ben is single, mid-thirties, smart, but not pompously so. He's a staff writer for *The Atlantic*. He was born and raised in Port Arthur, Texas, like Janis Joplin, and when the first reports of cannibalism emerged from Houston after Hurricane Mardell, Ben went into action. He decided to write the definitive history of the Outbreak, covering every aspect of the zombie plague, from the lofty, but ultimately empty, speeches on the White House lawn to the plight of the lowliest individual hiding in the back alleys of a ruined town.

Just before the events in "Ethical Solution," which takes place about eight months after Eddie's ending to *Dead City*, Ben Richardson gets wind of an English professor from the University of Texas at Austin named Dr. Sylvia Carnes. Dr. Carnes has bought Ken Stoler's cause, hook, line and sinker, and now she plans to take a chartered bus through the military quarantine that surrounds San Antonio. She has about forty students with her, each a member of the local chapter of People for an Ethical Solution, and a court order authorizing her to enter the quarantine zone. The idea, she tells Ben, is to show the rest of the country that the infected—she refuses to call them zombies—can be handled in a humane way by normal people. This, she hopes, will open the door to meaningful research into a cure.

Richardson is naturally skeptical. He and Carnes fall on opposite sides of the issue, but he maintains an open mind and convinces her that he should accompany her expedition into San Antonio.

One of the complaints I got from San Antonio locals who read *Dead City* was that I didn't mention many of the city's wonderful landmarks, such as the Alamo. Well, okay, I said. You want the Alamo, I'll give you the Alamo. So the basic plot of "Ethical Solutions," if you know anything about the Battle of the Alamo, wasn't hard to imagine. The more important part of that story was the way the debate between Sylvia Carnes and Ben Richardson develops. They cover quite a bit of ground during "Ethical Solutions," but even still, neither character is any closer to winning over the other by the end.

Real agreement, in fact, wouldn't happen for another eight years—and three books—later, when the two of them met again in the crumbling ruins of St. Louis.

But that's a different story.

APOCALYPSE OF THE DEAD

Apocalypse of the Dead *(Pinnacle; November, 2010).*

Dead City meant to show a private view of the apocalypse. Hence the first-person narrative… the constant focus on family… the mounting sense of claustrophobia… the book's events spanning a single night. All were a deliberate part of the overall point of view.

When I sat down to write the next book in the series, I felt I had to go the other way. I needed to cut a wide path. I needed to show the zombie apocalypse going global. I envisioned multiple groups of characters fleeing the advancing zombie hordes, seeking shelter in the frozen expanse of the North Dakota Grasslands. In my mind I saw a huge novel, both in scope and in size, an homage to the giant Stephen King horror novels of the 1970s.

Turns out, my publisher was thinking along the same lines. The folks at Kensington called me and said, "What do you think about writing an epic?"

"An epic?" I said.

"Yeah, you know, a huge book. Really do it up. Blow the whole world up, that kind of thing. A really epic book."

Now, I have a confession to make: flagrant misuse of the word *epic* is a pet peeve of mine. Aloud I told my publisher of my idea and shared in his enthusiasm that we were going to be in business again; but inside, I was groaning, for I knew then that people would erroneously pin the tag of epic on the book that was to become *Apocalypse of the Dead*.

Why does that bother me so much?

I'm glad you asked.

The Nature of the Epic

Homer's *The Iliad* and *The Odyssey*—those were epic poems. Virgil's *Aenied*, Dante's *The Divine Comedy*, Milton's *Paradise Lost*—all epics.

Stephen King's *The Stand*—not an epic.

Joe McKinney's *Apocalypse of the Dead*—also not an epic.

Why?

You see, we've gotten sloppy with our genres these days. And I don't mean genre as in horror, or science fiction, or romance. I mean genre in the more traditional sense. Genre as it pertains to specific literary forms, such as comedy, or tragedy, or even in slightly narrower poetic terms, such as the elegy, or the ode.

I was trained to read literature as an academic. Dealing in the finer points of literary terms was my stock in trade for a good long while. And when you talk about literary terms with the familiarity that some people reserve for sports statistics, you can't help but flinch inwardly when somebody misappropriates a significant term.

Hence my consternation with the inappropriate use of *epic*.

For too long we've called books epic because they're huge. Somebody puts out a 700-page novel and the next you know it's being called the next big epic fantasy, or SF novel, or whatever.

But epic should—and does—mean more than simply big.

In traditional academic terms, an epic is a long, narrative poem defining the significant heroes and historical context of a nation. That is why Homer's epics focus on the exploits of Greek heroes such as Odysseus and Achilles and Agamemnon. That is why Virgil's *Aeneid* tells the story of Aeneas, who escaped the fall of Troy in *The Iliad* to become one of the founding mythological figures of Rome. That is why Dante's *The Divine Comedy* populates the afterlife with real people from Italy's warring city states. That is why Milton's *Paradise Lost* can be read as a commentary on England's brief flirtation with a purely legislative government under Cromwell.

Epics define the culture and the values of a nation. And, as you will no doubt remember from your freshman Intro to British Literature, they have a number of other distinct conventions meant to telegraph the work's genre to its reader.

For example, they begin in *medias res*, or, in English, "in the midst of things." This is why *Star Wars* started with episode four... and you can pause here to pat yourself on the back if you clicked on this before you finished the sentence.

True epics can also be read as maps of a given culture's cosmology. Reading an epic, you not only learn the limits of a culture's physical world but of their spiritual world as well. That is why Dante's *The Divine Comedy* takes us first through hell, then purgatory, and finally to heaven. Milton's *Paradise Lost* is also a clear example of this.

Also, epics use things such as heroic epithets and catalogs and godly intervention and long digressive passages. And their authors generally telegraph their intentions to write epics early in their career by first earning their writing chops with pastoral poetry.

That does not apply to *Apocalypse of the Dead*. I didn't do any of the things outlined above. Neither did Stephen King in *The Stand*. Neither did Robert Jordan in The Wheel of Time series. Neither did any of the other modern scribblers you can think of. In fact, about as close as any American author has ever come to writing a true epic is Melville with *Moby Dick*.

(You in the back. Sit down and stop waving your hands in protest: Lucas never finished the Star Wars series, and if it ain't finished, it ain't an epic. I'm not budging for Edmund Spenser, so I'm sure as hell not gonna do it for George Lucas. You can't move me on that point.)

And here's why *Moby Dick* is as close as an American author has ever come to the epic. Epics encapsulate the sum total of a nation's experience, and the way they do that is by being encyclopedic. In other words, they absorb all other poetic forms current in their day and age and therefore make them subservient to their narrative.

Melville does this with drama, with biblical exegesis, with shipping news, with science, with action, with comedy, and on and on.

I was aware of all this when I wrote the outline for *Apocalypse of the Dead*. I knew the book would—undeservedly—be called an epic. And for that reason, I threw in a couple of nods to those who, like me, cringe at the misuse of the word.

The most conspicuous of these nods comes on pages 320 and 321 of the first Kensington edition, when Ben Richardson quotes some of the bad poetry he's seen pinned to the shirts of zombies they've encountered.

Students of English epitaphs will notice several vaguely familiar poems, the most obvious of which are for William Bunn and the dentist John Hannity. Both of these poems, and several of the other zombie-themed epitaphs quoted in this section, are loose adaptations of famous folk rhymes from the British Isles. I expect my English and Irish cousins will recognize the rhymes before most American readers, simply because the poems are a part of their culture and not the American one, but just in case some American reader figures it out first... Bravo to you! You got the joke.

The Quarantine Authority

I've already mentioned that Ben Richardson is one of the most important characters in the entire Dead World series, and here's why.

Aside from being an active participant in the book's events, Ben is also my stand in. Ben Richardson began the post-apocalyptic phase of his life as a journalist, determined to describe every aspect of the zombie apocalypse in what he intended to be the definitive history. When *Apocalypse of the Dead* begins, Ben is already compiling his book. Not only does he narrow in on the human cost of the tragedy, but he also writes authoritatively on the political machinations behind it. Through him, and specifically, through his journals, we learn the shape of this world that is devolving into anarchy.

In the early days of the Outbreak, the only thing that divides the

American people from complete destruction is The Gulf Region Quarantine Authority. These men—and yes, they are a not-so-thinly veiled commentary on the U.S. government's pathetically inept approach to illegal immigration—are basically the modern equivalent of the Little Dutch Boy with his finger in the dyke. They are a Band-Aid for the patient who is rapidly bleeding to death.

Here's what Ben Richardson has to say about them:

From the notebooks of Ben Richardson. Houston, Texas: July 5th 5:40 am

We've got about twenty minutes until takeoff, and I wanted to jot down a few notes about the quarantine zone. Sometimes I find it hard to wrap my mind around how big it is. The logistical scope of the project is simply staggering.

Back in its heyday, the U.S. Customs and Border Protection Agency patrolled the 2,000 miles of border land between the United States and Mexico. Of the Agency's 11,000 agents, more than 9,500 of them worked along that 2,000 mile stretch of desert. They hunted drug dealers and illegal aliens with a huge array of tools, everything from satellite imagery and publicly-accessible webcams to helicopters, horses, and plain old-fashioned shoe leather. Even so, the border had more holes in it than a fishing net.

In comparison, the Gulf Region Quarantine Authority only has to patrol 1,100 miles of wall reaching from Gulfport, Mississippi to Brownsville, Texas, paralleling the freeway system wherever possible to aid in supply and reinforcement of problem areas. The GRQA keeps this stretch of metal fencing and sentry towers and barbed wire secure with just over 10,000 agents, most of them former CBP and National Guardsmen and cops. They are aided at sea by the U.S. Coast Guard and in Mexico by federal troops.

Yet despite their numerical advantage over the old U.S. Customs and Border Protection Agency, their job is infinitely harder. Nobody in the old CBP thought too much of it that a steady stream of illegals got through the border every day. They just shrugged and went on with life. But the GRQA can't afford to let even a single zombie through. That would spell disaster. The pressure is high, the price of failure is apocalyptic.

Their job terrifies me. These guys are frequently posted outside of major metropolitan areas where the zombie populations are thickest. Day and night they have to listen to that constant moaning. They have to stand by and listen to the plaintive cries for help from the Unincorporated Civilian Casualties, the Gulf Region Quarantine Authority's official designation for the people who were unable to make it out of the zone before the walls went up and who were sealed inside. Hearing that for just a few weeks is demoralizing. I can't imagine what it would be like to hear it every single day for months and years at a time.

Even worse, I can't imagine what it would be like to grow used to hearing it.

It is little wonder that so many of the GRQA go AWOL at least once or twice a year. Or that they are never punished for it when they do. Most don't even get their pay docked.

And it's no wonder that the leading cause of death among GRQA agents is suicide.

Actually, I'm surprised it doesn't happen more often than it does....

The Chosen One

Playing opposite Ben Richardson is the Dead World's second most important character, Nate Royal.

Nate is an unlikely hero. When we first meet Nate, he's a small fish in a small pond. He's sitting on a park bench, watching the world go by, feeling impotent and angry at the deal he's been given, when suddenly he sees the sexy young wife of the town's leading attorney. Nate, who's dealt with this woman before, zeroes in on her as the cause of all his problems, and he sets out to abduct her.

This is our introduction to Nate Royal, and from the start, we find him difficult to like. But then something happens. Nate gets attacked by a zombie. He's wounded, and because he's heard on the TV about what happens to people who get infected by a zombie, he slinks off to die in a neighbor's tool shed.

Only Nate doesn't turn. He is immune to the necrosis filovirus.

When the military doctors in the area discover his unusual condition, they pack him off to Minot Air Force Base in North Dakota. Once there, Nate meets a military doctor named Mark Kellogg, and while the two of them never really become friends, they develop a unique relationship.

Kellogg is an intellectual. He's a military officer, true, but he doesn't think of himself that way. In his mind, he's a doctor who just so happens to wear a uniform to work. Kellogg ends up taking Nate under his wing, and as the two men get to know each other, the novel's key theme of rejecting nihilism comes to the forefront. Because Nate is most certainly not an intellectual, he lacks the specialized language to discuss nihilism like a philosopher. He only knows what he feels.

This presents Dr. Kellogg with an obvious problem. Nate Royal, because of his immunity, represents humanity's greatest hope. And yet Nate, who so despises the universe's seeming lack of concern for his fate that he seeks comfort in suicide, is unwilling to play the hero. Their relationship is as much a statement on how an older generation attempts to hand the baton of responsibility to the next as it is a rejection of the classical hero archetype. Nate is definitely not a hero, yet is called upon to play one. If *Apocalypse of the Dead* had been a World War II story, he might have reluctantly lived up to the challenge. But I don't think modern American culture quite believes in heroes. Comic books are more popular today than ever before. So too are songs and movies about superheroes. And yet, time after time, those same modern offerings on the hero give us flawed characters who don't live up to what's expected of them. The phenomenon even extends into politics, where Barrack Obama failed to live up to the media image of hope and change that propelled him into office. I've been watching this trend over the last decade or so, and perhaps that explains why I selected a hero who not only rejects the role of hero, but can't even be convinced to take on the challenge reluctantly. Time and again, Dr. Kellogg has to lift Nate and push him in the right direction. And can one truly be called a hero if there is no free will in the actions that would traditionally qualify one for hero status?

The Persistence of Jonestown

The original title of *Apocalypse of the Dead* was *Resistance*. I changed the title after a lengthy and at times heated discussion with my editor and agent. Though I've come to like *Apocalypse of the Dead* as a title, I still, in many ways, prefer the original title. *Resistance* is not quite so in your face, and it conveys the book's central theme of rejecting nihilism. Each of the book's character sets—Michael Barnes and Ben Richardson; Dr. Mark Kellogg and Nate Royal; Ed Moore and Billy Kline; Jasper and Aaron; Colin and Kyra—to some degree play out this theme. When I was plotting out the book, I knew I wanted to end with a microcosm of the apocalypse. I also wanted that ending to speak directly to nihilism. And, as has become my *modus operandi* when I need to craft major plot elements, I turned to my youth for inspiration. What I found there was Jonestown.

I was ten years old when the news broke about the mass suicides in Jonestown. I remember watching the seemingly endless footage of dead, rotting bodies stacked on top of each in the ditches surrounding Jonestown—my parents on the couch behind me too horrified to snap to the fact that their ten-year-old probably shouldn't be watching such things on TV—and feeling completely repulsed. How, I asked, could so many people just give up on life? How could one man convince so many people to do something so ridiculous?

Those questions stayed with me, even as I made jokes with my friends about drinking the Kool-Aid. Over the years, the legacy of Jonestown continued to bother me. I read a great deal about Jim Jones and his followers and the final days there in the jungles of Guyana, and I've never made any secret that I drew a great deal of the conclusion of *Apocalypse of the Dead* from that research, but in all my studies I never found an answer to my original question. I found lots of wild-ass guesses concealed as educated theories, but nothing that really, solidly, answered the question.

I think we have a deep-seated need to belong somewhere. We're social animals, and in many ways, successfully fitting into our given society is emotionally healthy. But beyond fitting in, we also want to know that our lives have value, even if we never grow rich or get famous or add to the collective knowledge of mankind. Cults, of course, provide for this by a creating the illusion of family, a sense of inclusion. Gangs do the same thing. So does high school football, and turning out in droves to support a pro-sports team, or blogging, or belonging to professional organizations and gardening clubs. The point is we seek out ways to be included. That's a healthy instinct, up to a point. The problem with cults like the People's Temple or Heaven's Gate or political institutions like the Nazi Party is that our desire for inclusion gets easily perverted into a rabid fervor that grows beyond our individual ability to control. And when that happens, all hell breaks loose.

At one point in *Apocalypse of the Dead*, Dr. Mark Kellogg tells Nate Royal,

> We are put into this hostile, alien world as isolated individuals. We can learn to like other people, even love them, but we can't ever truly know them, and so we remain isolated. We're not allowed to know why life has meaning, not for sure anyway, and yet we feel compelled to create some sort of answer. It's an absurd downward spiral of impossible things, and yet it's our lives.

And Nate, with dawning comprehension, asks, "So what does that mean? Are you saying that a world based on bad reasons is enough?" The two eventually decide that this is so. A world based on bad reasons is enough. Their answer makes sense within the context of their relationship but falls short of satisfactory in light of Jonestown and the fictional counterpart of those events in the novel.

Apocalypse of the Dead doesn't provide any real answers. Indeed, I don't know if there are any. But each character wrestles with what happens at the Grasslands in their own way, and maybe readers will find a branching-off point that helps them to answer the real life mystery of why good people can abruptly lose their minds, as happened in Jonestown.

We shall see.

But for now, the mystery of Jonestown persists.

FLESH EATERS

Flesh Eaters *(Pinnacle; April, 2011)*

For about a year after *Dead City* sold to Kensington, I did nothing but write short stories. I was cranking them out at a fevered pace, sometimes as many as three a week, and selling most of them. It became almost like a drug for me.

"Ethical Solutions" was a product of that addiction.

And then, at the end of that year, my agent came calling for another book. "A sequel to *Dead City*, maybe?"

As I said, I never had any intention of becoming a writer. I just wanted to write. I hadn't given any thought whatsoever to another book. I told him my thoughts on sequels, and he seemed disappointed, but asked what else I had.

I didn't have anything written, but I did have an idea for a police procedural set against the backdrop of a pandemic flu outbreak. "I could expand that story idea into a novel," I said.

He liked the idea, and I got to work on *Quarantined*. The book sold and went on to garner a Stoker® nomination from the Horror Writers Association for Superior Achievement in a Novel.

But the thrill of selling a second novel, coupled with my agent's interest in another zombie novel, got me curious about the rest of the world I had created in *Dead City*. Specifically, I turned my attention to Houston. I had left most of the city under water, and because the city had been evacuated so poorly, and then shut off behind quarantine walls shortly afterwards, all the treasures of the nation's third largest city lay ripe for plundering. All those banks with their vaults full of cash… all those museums with their walls covered in priceless art… all those jewelry stores with their diamonds on display… they got me thinking. Imagine someone desperate enough, someone skilled enough, someone brave enough… they could run the Coast Guard blockade out in the Gulf, scuba dive into the flooded ruins, and take anything they wanted. All they had to do was avoid the soldiers guarding the walls and the nearly two million zombies still wandering inside the city.

From that, the third book in the Dead World series, *Flesh Eaters*, was born.

Disaster Mitigation

I knew I wanted a heist story to act as the plot's spine. Originally, I planned to have a team of four men and women scuba dive into the flooded city, grab the cash, dodge a few zombies, and maybe make it out alive. Along the way, they would do battle with the Quarantine Authority and a wild bunch of gangsters. It was going to be great fun.

And then, after I started writing my plot synopsis and story outline, I realized I was making the same mistake I'd made with *The Edge of the Map*, my failed SF book from several years earlier. The heist story I'd envisioned didn't have anything authentic to it. Sometimes a writer's best ally is that little voice inside his head that yells "Bullshit!" and luckily mine was working that day.

Luckier still, I listened.

Once again I turned to my personal experiences. Living through a hurricane was one of the most frightening events of my life, while the weeks I spent working in the shelters after Katrina and Rita were some of the most exhausting I've ever spent. It occurred to me that if I was going to write an effective storyline, it would have to involve those two elements. I decided I would tell the story of how the first zombies appeared and spread to the rest of the Gulf Coast. I would tell the story of the hurricanes that sunk Houston and created the Dead World. I would tell, in other words, a prequel to *Dead City*.

Oh, and there would be a heist in there as well.

The Crucible of Duty

The main character of *Flesh Eaters* is Eleanor Norton, a sergeant with the Houston Police Department's Emergency Operations Command. She is also a wife and a mother. As the storms roll in and the City of Houston falls apart, Eleanor is caught between her job and her family, unable to devote her complete attention to either. Aware that she is spreading herself too thinly, Eleanor confronts head-on the novel's main theme: What is duty?

As the novel begins, Eleanor thinks she has a handle on this question. She has done her homework and has thoroughly prepared her family to shelter in place during a hurricane. Her husband and daughter have more than enough food, water, and medical supplies to get them through a few weeks without power and running water. Eleanor, in fact, has made preparation a near obsession. But, as she finds out, mere preparation is insufficient. There is a greater danger than raw sewage and flood waters, and its name is boredom. While she's at work, her family is stuck at home, literally unable to leave their front door, and while they have plenty to eat and drink, the perpetual boredom leaves them angry and restless.

Meanwhile, at work, Eleanor is being pulled in a hundred directions at once. Because of its unique placement near the nexus of Houston's freeway system, the University of Houston's campus is turned into a refugee center. As the nearly 2.5 million people living between Galveston and the City of Houston proper flee northwards, the sick and the old and ill-prepared stop at the campus for protection. The shelters quickly swell to unmanageable numbers, which leads to many more problems, such as dysentery, cholera, starvation, and a host of sanitation problems and medical shortages generally found only in third-world nations. Between salvaging boats to evacuate the refugees and struggling to maintain order, Eleanor spends long hours, and sometimes days on end, at the campus. When she returns home, which is surrounded by flood waters, she finds her husband and daughter have been fighting their own battle with boredom and that their resentment of her apparent freedom has reached a boil. Being home soon becomes as much work as being at her job.

But Eleanor isn't the only one dealing with the seemingly mutually exclusive demands of first-responder work and family life. Her boss, Captain Mark Shaw, has been passed over for promotion to Deputy Chief and feels that his assignment at the Emergency Operations Command is basically the department's way of putting him out to pasture. But when the hurricanes hit, and his command post at the University of Houston campus becomes the only legitimate police authority in the area, Captain Mark Shaw finds himself the man on top, the place where the buck stops. He is confronted not only with the demands of organizing shelters and evacuating those shelters, but also of being the father. Shaw's two sons are both Houston Police Officers, and he knows that there isn't going to be much of a future for them. The city they've known as home all their lives is, after all, under water. Once the disaster is managed, his two sons will almost certainly be out of work, everything they own washed out to sea. As Captain Shaw sees it, he has two duties: evacuate the citizens who have entrusted him with their safety and see to it that his sons are provided for after the disaster has passed.

It seems like an impossible task, but Shaw has a plan. Through his connections as head of the EOC, he has learned of a local bank with seven-million dollars in cash abandoned in its vault. The bank is flooded and the property and the money declared a total loss by the insurance companies. He and his sons recover the money. Now, the only task is getting out of Houston alive.

Of course, the zombies make that difficult. When Eleanor Norton learns of the heist, the Shaws find themselves stuck between survival, doing their duty to the refugees, and looking out for their own futures. In a lesser man, this wouldn't be a dilemma at all. Self-interest would take over and the problem would work itself out. But Captain Mark Shaw is not a lesser man. Some men have religion, Captain Mark Shaw has duty. He is deeply conflicted by his role in the bank heist, and this proves to be his crisis of faith, for he sees the money as his greatest sin and at the same time the key to providing for his family.

It is an issue that only becomes murkier as he and Eleanor Norton battle it out in the flooded ruins of Houston, but their debate on duty places *Flesh Eaters* squarely into the overall themes of family and community that run through every work in the Dead World series.

MUTATED

Mutated *(Pinnacle; September, 2012).*

The first three books in the Dead World series are generally lumped as post-apocalyptic literature, and I'm okay with that. It doesn't bother me in the same way that calling *Apocalypse of the Dead* an epic does. But even so, I feel compelled to point out that none of the first three books are truly post-apocalyptic. They are, more properly, disaster stories. Apocalyptic stories. The "post" part of the post-apocalyptic tag is missing.

Until *Mutated* I hadn't played much with the world after the zombie outbreak. My short story "Dating in Dead World" covered some of that ground, but there's only so much you can do in the limited space of a novella. I wanted to show, in detail, where the scenarios I had put in place would lead. So, in *Mutated*, we have the Dead World approximately eight years after the events in *Apocalypse of the Dead*. It is now a world of abandoned cities and crumbling roads and a population so decimated that a traveler can walk for days without seeing another human being. And it is the Dead

World's final word on post-apocalyptic events.

Post-Apocalyptic Landscapes

For as long as I can remember, I've thrilled at the sight of abandoned buildings. Something about those dark, empty windows, the vacant doorways, the sepulchral quiet of an empty train station or hotel lobby, spoke of discontinuity and of trauma. There was a vacancy in those wrecks that evoked loss and heartache and the memory of dreams that have fallen by the wayside. They were a sort of negative space in the landscape, symbols of our world's mortality.

And then zombies came along, and I fell in love with them for many of the same reasons.

But here's the thing.

It took me a while—as a writer, I mean—to figure out that abandoned buildings, and even abandoned cities, don't just appear because a horde of zombies happen to show up. Sure, most everybody gets eaten, so you end up with a lot of buildings and few people, but it goes a little deeper than that. Zombies and abandoned buildings, it seems to me, are actually two sides of the same coin. Aside from the obvious similarity—that they are both miserable wrecks somehow still on their feet—both are symbols of a world that is at odds with itself and looking for new direction. And in that way, zombies merge symbolically with the abandoned buildings they haunt in ways that other monsters never really achieve with the settings of their stories.

But just because the zombie and the abandoned building are intimately related symbols doesn't mean that they function in exactly the same way.

Consider the abandoned building first.

When a building dies, it becomes an empty hull, and yet it does not fall. At least not right away. Its hollow rooms become as silent as the grave; but, when you enter it, its desolate inner spaces somehow still hum with the collected sediment of the life that once thrived there.

When we look at graffiti scrawled across fine Italian marble tiles, or a filthy doll face-up in a crumbling warehouse parking lot, or weeds growing up between the desks in a ruined schoolhouse, we're not just seeing destruction. We're also seeing what once was and what could be again. In other words, we're seeing past, present, and future all at the same time.

The operative force at work here is memory. Within the mind, memory links past, present, and future. But in our post-apocalyptic landscapes, our minds need a mnemonic aid... and that aid is the abandoned building. The moldering wreck before us forces us to consciously engage in the process of temporal continuity, rather than blindly stumble through it.

Put another way, we become like Wordsworth daydreaming over the ruins of Tintern Abbey. Like Wordsworth, we're witnessing destruction, but pondering renovation, because we are by nature a creative species that needs to reshape the world in order to live in it. That is our biological imperative.

And so, in the end, the abandoned building becomes a symbol of creative courage.

But consider the abandoned building's corollary, the zombie.

Zombies are, really, single-serving versions of the apocalypse. Apocalyptic stories deal with the end of the world. Generally, they give us a glimpse of the world before catastrophe, which becomes an imperfect Eden of sorts. They then spin off into terrifying scenarios for the end of the world. And finally, we see the survivors living on, existing solely on the strength of their own wills. There are variations within the formula, of course, but those are the nuts and bolts of it.

When we look at the zombie, we get the same thing—but in microcosm. We see the living person prior to death, and this equates to the world before the apocalypse (or the ghost of what the abandoned building used to be). We see the living person's death, and this equates to the cataclysmic event that precipitates the apocalypse (or the moldering wreck of an abandoned building). And finally, we see the shambling corpse wandering the wasteland in search of prey, and this equates to the post-apocalyptic world feeding off its own death.

In this final note, the symbolic functions of the abandoned building and the zombie diverge. As I've mentioned, the abandoned building, so long as it stands, calls to our creative instincts to rebuild. But the zombie, so long as it stands, speaks only to our ultimate mortality.

And so, the ruined hotel or office park becomes our mind's cathedral, the spiritual and creative sanctuary of our memory, while

Joe McKinney

the zombie becomes the devil that drives us into it.

I see a satisfying sense of symmetry there.

Old Friends

Writing *Mutated* gave me the chance to tie up loose ends from previous books. For example, the last time we heard of Ken Stoler, he was leading a national campaign to protect the rights of the infected. Dr. Sylvia Carnes, the University of Texas English professor and acolyte of Ken Stoler, was last seen driving off in a chartered bus after losing all her students in an ill-fated trip into San Antonio. And when we said good-bye to Ben Richardson and the rest of the escapees from the Grasslands cult at the end of *Apocalypse of the Dead*, they were walking into a military convoy. So not only is *Mutated* unique in that it is the only truly post-apocalyptic book in the series, but it is also the only novel in the bunch that can truly be called a traditional sequel.

The book begins with Ben Richardson, who never quit working on his history of the zombie outbreak. Since escaping the Grasslands at the end of *Apocalypse of the Dead*, he has crisscrossed the United States, searching out survivors and gathering their stories and writing about his observations. Excerpts from his book are peppered throughout *Mutated*, and from those excerpts, it becomes clear that Richardson knows that his work will never be finished. The idea of writing the book has become his crutch, the one thing that enables him to get up every morning and go on living in a world that has otherwise lost its meaning for him.

And then, while hiding from a roving band of zombies in the ruins of a St. Louis Pizza Hut, he runs into Dr. Sylvia Carnes, in the company of two young women and two bodyguards. Unbeknownst to Richardson, Carnes and her group have fled a compound run by Stoler to meet a doctor who may have developed a cure for the necrosis filovirus.

But the world Carnes and the others have escaped into is not so simple. Stoler's community is at war with a man known as the Zombie King. This man, whose skin has turned a dark red from rosacea, has built an army of zombies and uninfected human soldiers. The Red Man also wants to capture Carnes and her people. Thrown together in the ruins and dodging common foes, Richardson and Carnes join forces, and together they go on a quest down the Mississippi River to find the man who might be able to save the human race from itself.

A Note on the Dead World's Geography

The Mississippi River was a deliberate choice for Richardson and Carnes' quest. Not only is it an iconic American landmark, and not only is it the roadmap for Huckleberry Finn's far more famous quest, but it also happens to be dead in the middle of the continental United States.

Go back through all the stories in the Dead World and you'll see that they all converge on middle America. While no one part of the United States is more or less American than any other part, the Heartland is just that... the heart of America. Taking the story to the Heartland is a metaphor, really, for the series' overall theme that our survival is based on our ability to form a strong, healthy community.

Walking With Zombies: A Natural History of the Undead

Let's talk about zombies for a bit more. In the Dead World, the necrosis filovirus spreads through exposure to the bodily fluids of an infected zombie, and the usual vector is a bite. The virus causes the complete depersonalization of the infected person, essentially turning them into a zombie.

It does not kill them, however. Living, infected people exist as mindless husks, intent solely on aggression. They can't care for themselves in any meaningful way, and they have no sense of danger or the ability to avoid it. And in most cases, they are so badly injured by the contact that caused their initial infection that secondary infections are rampant. What this means in practical terms is that most of the infected die off soon after getting infected, either from their initial injuries, from injuries incurred while hunting food, or from the food itself. Imagine a zombie feeding on something that's been dead in the middle of the road for a few days, and you can see what I mean.

In *Apocalypse of the Dead*, Ben Richardson and Michael Barnes get trapped on a rooftop. Richardson realizes that the zombies below are using strategy to flush out prey. The shock is nearly too much for him. He had been so certain that the infected needed to be exterminated outright after his trip to San Antonio with Dr. Carnes in "Ethical Solutions" that he had ceased thinking of them as humans. But now, watching them use strategy, all his certainty disappears.

But what he doesn't realize, at least right away, is that the longer they live, the zombies change. To be sure, the change is gradual. But it is happening.

The zombies Eddie Hudson and Eleanor Norton face are Stage 1, freshly infected and almost completely depersonalized. They are incapable of reason and have no capacity to anticipate the actions of others. In some cases, they are so far gone that they can't even recognize other zombies. Most of the time, these zombies are the traditional slow movers of the Romero movies. There are a few, however, who can move with great speed. Eddie Hudson calls these "fast movers," infected persons who were in excellent physical condition at the time they were turned and who were infected by injuries so minor that their ability to move was not impaired. Luckily, they are few and far between.

Assuming a zombie survives his or her first eight months or so of undead life, they begin to change into Stage 2 zombies. These are the zombies that Ben Richardson and Michael Barnes face in the flooded ruins of Houston. They are capable of using simple strategies, such as cooperative hunting, to corner prey. In most cases, Stage 2 zombies are still slow moving.

It is extremely rare for a zombie to advance beyond Stage 2, but a few live long enough to manage it. Stage 3 zombies have regained a much of their fine motor skills and are even capable can even approximate language through grunts and primitive gestures. Dr. Mark Kellogg experiments with a few Stage 3 zombies in *Apocalypse of the Dead*. It is rather like trying to keep chimpanzees as pets, he realizes. Left alone for too long, they can, and will, break locks, feign injuries or sleep, and in some cases respond to their names and other verbal cues. They are, however, still aggressive to a fault, and unable to contain their impulses.

Before the Red Man, no one envisioned a Stage 4 zombie. The idea of someone completely, or even mostly, regaining their sense of self after being infected seemed too implausible to be considered a threat. But that is exactly what the Red Man is, a Stage 4 zombie. The Red Man has regained nearly all of his memories and his sense of self, but the necrosis filovirus has left him hopelessly insane. It has also given him the ability to communicate through normal speech with his army, and through grunts, smells, and moaning, with the zombies. He is the next step in evolution in this world made up of two different species of humanity.

The Red Man's only natural enemy is the man who doesn't play by the rules that have made him *Mutated*.

Nate Royal Returns

Nate Royal, for all his many faults, is immune to the necrosis filovirus. This puts him in direct opposition to the Red Man: the man who becomes the ultimate zombie versus the man who can never become a zombie. A meeting between the two is inevitable.

While hiding in an abandoned farmhouse from an army of zombies, Ben Richardson and Sylvia Carnes witness Nate Royal's first confrontation with the Red Man. What they see is impossible, at least according to the rules by which they've come to live. It also opens up new realms of possibilities. A man immune to the zombie virus could redefine the struggle they have spent their lives fighting for.

The only trouble is Nate himself.

Nate has never had things very easy. Dr. Mark Kellogg was able to help Nate along, but only after many hours of shared suffering and individual attention. Now that Kellogg is gone, Nate is like a compass needle spinning aimlessly around the dial, trying to find his true north.

But Nate remains vital, for even after all these years, he still carries the flash drive that Dr. Mark Kellogg put around his neck just before he died. Contained in that flash drive is the answer that humanity has been waiting for, the cure to the necrosis filovirus. The trouble is that Nate has run out of gas, spiritually speaking. Kellogg's guidance has brought him only so far. And now, eight years after Kellogg's death, Nate finds himself once again ready to give up and die.

Then he finds Ben Richardson. While the two of them float down the Mississippi, Nate rediscovers the true north he has been missing. He takes from Ben Richardson the guidance he needs to confront the Red Man.

Whether, ultimately, he is successful, depends on your point of view. What kind of future do you want?

Dating in Dead World

"Dating in Dead World," originally published in THE LIVING DEAD 2, *edited by John Joseph Adams (Nightshade Books; September, 2010).*

"Dating in Dead World" is the last entry, chronologically speaking, in the Dead World series. The main character is Andrew Hudson, the baby Eddie Hudson spent a night of hell trying to rescue in Dead City.

It's been almost twenty years since Hurricane Mardell swept through Houston, flooding the city and giving birth to a virus that turns the living into the walking dead. The world has been overrun by zombies and left in ruin. But there are still groups of people alive, and they are carving out an existence in the wasteland.

Some of the survivors have moved into protective compounds, but Andrew Hudson wasn't lucky enough to grow up in one of those. He was raised as a street urchin in the ruins of San Antonio, where he makes a living as a special courier between the strongholds of the Dead World's warlords. During one of those runs he had the good fortune to meet the daughter of the area's most powerful warlord, and he won her heart.

Now, they're going on their first date. How hard could that be, right? Kids have been dating forever. Well, when taking your date out involves high-speed pursuits through zombie-infested ruins and being used as pawns in an underhanded power grab, nothing is as easy as it seems.

"Dating in Dead World" was written about the time that Kensington Publishing asked me to do another zombie book. I had made a few readers mad with the ending to *Dead City*, and I wanted to address the criticism before I went on with the rest of the series.

And that meant writing about Eddie Hudson again. The thing to remember about Eddie Hudson is that he is not a reliable reporter. Most people get that wrong about him. He's deeply fractured by the events he recounts in the novel, and the optimism he expresses at the end of the story is... well, let's just say he's not telling you everything. He's telling you about the world he wants to believe in, not the world as it really is. "Dating in Dead World" came from that issue. And because "Dating in Dead World" was written to refute Eddie Hudson's optimism, the logical lead for the story was Eddie's son, Andrew Hudson. So this story really becomes as much a conversation between father and son as it does a commentary on the Dead World series itself.

John Joseph Adams, editor of *The Living Dead 2*, asked me where "Dating in Dead World" came from—not just the idea for the story, but the personal background of the story. I think the answer hinges on personal accountability. I find it impossible to respect people who can't accept responsibility for their actions. That's something I learned from my dad, and something I'll always be thankful for. Case in point. He gave me some important advice on personal responsibility. Right before I left for my first date, he gave me the only bit of parental sex education I ever received. "Remember this," he said. "You will be held personally accountable for everything that happens to that girl from the moment she leaves her front door to the moment she walks back in it. Conduct yourself accordingly." It wasn't until after I'd written "Dating in Dead World" that I realized I was channeling that advice. I guess it took.

Read Andrew Hudson's take on his first date and see if you don't agree.

Toward a Preferred Chronology

People keep asking me if they need to read the Dead World in a certain order. With the exception of *Mutated*, I'd so no. You can read any piece in the series in any order and still come away with a perfectly clear understanding of what's going on. And come to think of it, you could even read *Mutated* first and still have that understanding.

So the simple answer is no, there is no preferred chronology. Read on. Enjoy yourself.

Okay, that was for all those folks who are completely new to the series. The rest of you, those who have read at least one of the books and are looking for some insight into the rest of the series, what follows is for you. If you want to read the Dead World series the way the author would like the series read, this is it:

Flesh Eaters
Dead City
"Survivors"
"Ethical Solutions"
"The Crossing"
Apocalypse of the Dead
Mutated
"Dating in Dead World"

Joe McKinney has been a patrol officer for the San Antonio Police Department, a homicide detective, a disaster mitigation specialist, a patrol commander, and a successful novelist. His books include the four-part Dead World series, *Quarantined*, *Inheritance*, *Lost Girl of the Lake*, *The Savage Dead*, *Crooked House* and *Dodging Bullets*. His short fiction has been collected in *The Red Empire and Other Stories* and *Dating in Dead World*. In 2011, McKinney received the Horror Writers Association's Bram Stoker Award® for Best Novel. For more information go to http://joemckinney.wordpress.com.

JONATHAN MABERRY,
JOE R. LANSDALE, GARY BRAUNBECK,
HARRY SHANNON and JOE McKINNEY

LIMBUS
INC.

BOOK II

EDITED BY BRETT J. TALLEY

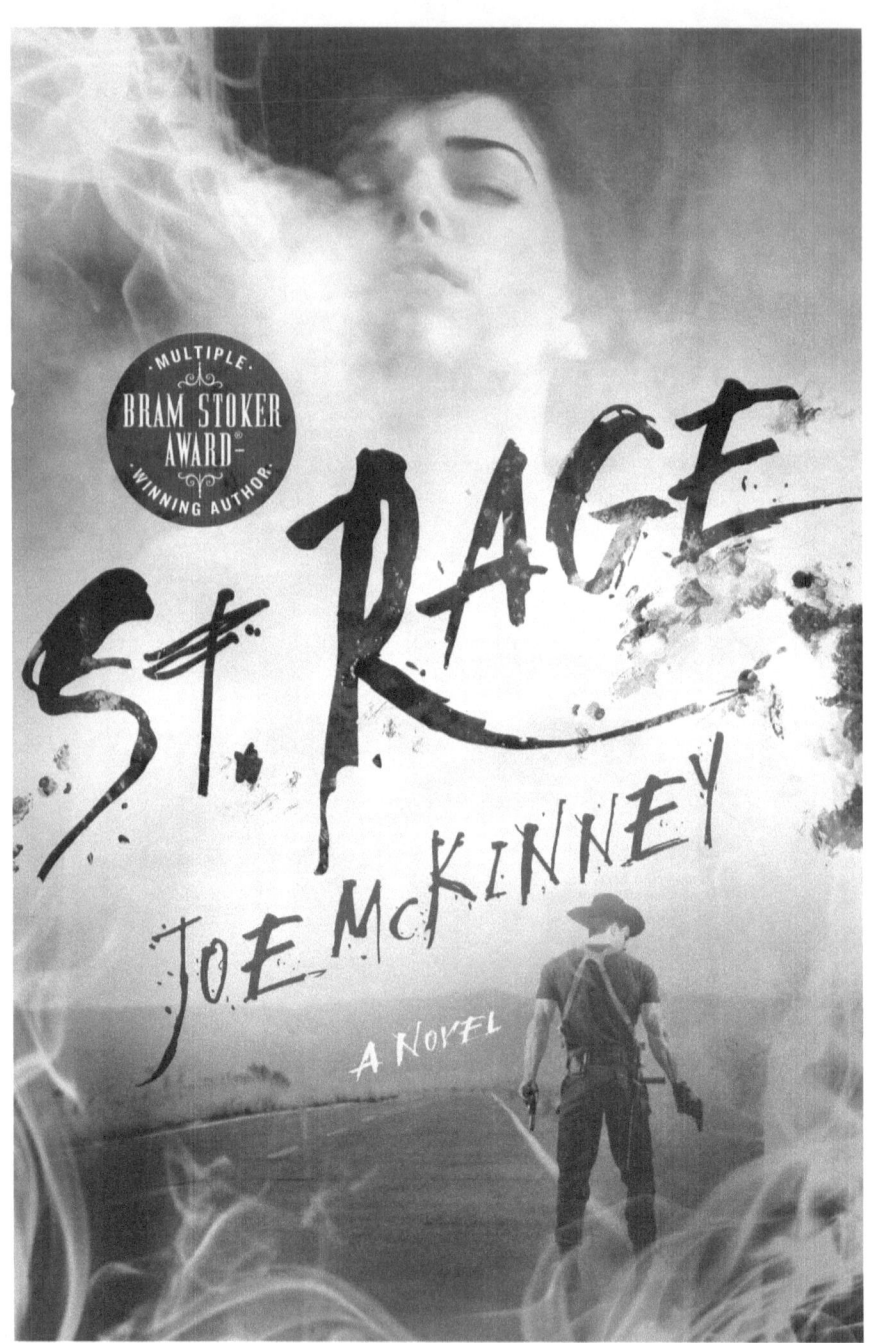

St. Rage

JOE McKINNEY

A NOVEL

MULTIPLE BRAM STOKER AWARD-WINNING AUTHOR

www.ingramcontent.com/pod-product-compliance
Lightning Source LLC
Chambersburg PA
CBHW032237010726
47494CB00002B/532